THE SAINT

THE ACES SERIES, BOOK #7

New York Times Bestselling Author

CRISTIN HARBER

ISBN: 978-1-951085-25-4

www.cristinharber.com

DEDICATION

To everyone going through the dark and battling challenges;
may happily ever after, whatever that looks like, find you.

CHAPTER ONE

ARLINGTON, VIRGINIA

RUSHING FOOTSTEPS AND panicked voices pulled Amelia Stone awake. In the upstairs guest bedroom of her sister's house, she pinched her eyes shut as though she could force herself back to sleep. Rain pattered on the windows like fall-inspired white noise. Just as she pulled the thick comforter up to her chin, drifting back to sleep, the sounds from the first floor wafted into her room again. *Worried voices? Fast-moving feet?*

She propped herself on her elbows and squinted through the dark room. It was barely illuminated by an overcast night and a crack of dim light that poured through the ajar door. She'd watched a cheesy horror movie with her sister and brother-in-law before bed, and maybe that was why she heard—or thought she heard—voices from downstairs. Any scary movie worth its salt started with pandemonium at home.

Amelia sat up in bed. The sleep-soaked cobwebs in her mind slowly faded. Hailey and Jonathan's voices were clearer. Though she couldn't make out the words, the muffled sentiments rang out as urgent and problematic.

She crept out of bed, pulled a sweatshirt over her shorts-and-shirt pajama set, and opened the door an inch. Even at their noisiest, Hailey and Jonathan Dumont were reserved and quiet.

"Hails?" Amelia stepped into the hallway and padded barefoot to the top of the staircase. *Are they fighting?* She couldn't fathom that. "Guys, is everything okay?"

No answer came. A shiver ran down Amelia's spine and up her bare legs.

The house was a small colonial in a nice neighborhood. They'd converted the first floor from a traditional layout to an open concept. Their shared office space was the only closed-off area. That Amelia suddenly couldn't hear them was as worrying as their voices had been a moment before.

Amelia perched at the top of the stairs and couldn't understand why the lights were out if Hailey and Jonathan were up and active. "Hailey?"

The house was quiet again. Amelia couldn't see either of them from her vantage point at the top of the stairs and didn't want to butt in if they were arguing. But they never argued, and something about their tone was unnerving. They weren't angry or frustrated. Were they anxious? Frightened?

She heard them again. Amelia crept down a few stairs and pinpointed them in their office, but she couldn't make out the conversation—and she shouldn't eavesdrop. But she couldn't help it and tiptoed farther down.

"…they know…"

"…in danger… assets…"

"…missing… help…"

Jonathan's rushed steps approached from the home office. "They know, Hailey. And if they do, we're in trouble."

Amelia scurried up to the middle of the staircase. She bit her lip then faced the unavoidable. "Is everything okay?"

Jonathan stopped short at the base of the stairs. He was almost panting and ran a hand over his face as though trying to get his act together. It didn't help. "You're awake." He cast a furtive glance out the slender glass panes framing the double doors of their home entrance.

She sank onto her bottom and held onto the banister. "What's wrong?"

If not for her sister and brother-in-law whisper-panicking in the middle of the night, Amelia would've thought they were debating the plot points of the night's movie. She'd never seen Jonathan anything but composed. Affable and smart, her brother-in-law was the poster child for calm, cool, and collected—just like Hailey.

"Jonathan, *what's wrong?*"

He pinched the bridge of his nose and closed his eyes as though answers to the unexplained problem were painted on the insides of his lids.

The weight of the world rested on his shoulders. For every second he didn't answer, a cavernous, concrete-lined pit at the bottom of Amelia's stomach grew heavier.

Finally, Jonathan clipped, "We've got to get her out of here."

"Me?"

Hailey walked across the beautiful living room decorated with paintings and sculptures they'd brought home from work trips abroad. She moved to her husband's side. Unfamiliar worry lines creased her forehead, and she bit her bottom lip much like Amelia was doing. Their mannerisms were quite similar, though not their personalities. Hailey was just as unflappable as Jonathan. If she'd had an anxious moment in her life, her sister had known how to channel that emotion into a productive one—not Amelia. When nerves and anxiety hit, Amelia felt it then buried it. She wore it heavy across her chest like a secret cloak. She might get the job done, but it wasn't pretty.

"It could be a false alarm." Hailey checked the slender window on the front door just as her husband had. The tense lines that had creased across Hailey's forehead deepened, belying that hope.

Jonathan's lips pulled down. "How did they let this happen? We've been so careful."

"Powerful people with infinite resources," Hailey mumbled. "It's always been a risk."

Amelia tried to understand the cryptic conversation. Jonathan and Hailey were two of the quietest people Amelia had ever known. Hailey was a professor of art history. Jonathan was a researcher for high-end auction houses. They were smart, reserved, and not prone to hyperbole.

Maybe one of Jonathan's high-end buyers was unhappy with a purchase. Amelia had heard them discuss multimillion-dollar transactions. She could appreciate buyer's remorse after dropping as much as the annual budget of a small town on a single piece of artwork. "You two are freaking me out."

A long, dark look passed between Hailey and Jonathan, conveying a silent, terrifying message that Amelia didn't understand. Hailey's gaze flitted from her husband toward the front door as though she could see through the heavy double doors and into the shadowy night. "If we're right, we don't have long—we need help."

Jonathan nodded. "We're right. Amelia needs to get someplace safe—"

Amelia's eyes peeled wide open. "It's not *safe* here?"

"Not anymore," Hailey whispered. The fear in her face transformed into something Amelia couldn't describe. It was almost guilt—or sadness. "I'm sorry we dragged you into this."

"Into *what*?" Exasperation had an iron grip on Amelia's chest and continued to crank up the tension.

They ignored her. Hailey hurried from the foyer and disappeared into the unlit living room.

"This will sound crazy," Jonathan said, "but you have to do what she tells you to do."

Sound crazy? Amelia was watching craziness unfold in front of her. She replayed his words in her head but didn't ask him to explain. They wouldn't. That much was clear.

Hailey returned with a permanent marker, adding another layer of what made little sense. She rushed up the stairs and grabbed Amelia's hand. When her sister touched her, Amelia realized she'd been clinging to the railing. Hailey pulled her down the stairs. "Go out the back door. Get to your car—"

"Not her car," Jonathan called from the shadowy office. "And we can't use her phone either."

"You're right." Hailey paused but didn't let go of her as she searched the dark foyer for answers. "We have keys to the Callaghans'."

"Yeah, yeah. Good idea." Jonathan returned with a book tucked under his arm and what looked like a bank deposit bag the size of a pencil case. He unlocked the zipper with a short, fat key and pulled out two cell phones.

"We check on their cat and water their plants sometimes," Hailey explained as though any of her words could make sense. "When they visit their grandkids out of state. And they're always day-tripping."

"You want me to wake your neighbors up in the middle of the night? And say what?" Amelia's pulse punched in her neck. She pulled her hand from Hailey, but her sister wouldn't let go.

"No. Don't wake them. Just go in and use their phone." Hailey finally released Amelia's hand. "They have a landline. Check in the kitchen or living room."

"Chances are," Jonathan added as he walked out of view, "they won't even be home."

Hailey uncapped the marker with her teeth and scrawled a phone number on the inside of Amelia's forearm. "Go out the back door. Stay low. Go to the house across the street. The one with ferns on their front porch. Use their back door. Don't turn on any lights."

The ink dried on her arm, cool and chemically scented. Her nose wrinkled as she stared at the numbers clearly written on her skin.

Jonathan returned with the book and a key chain. "Leave this on any bookshelf, and use this key to get in their back door." He indicated a single house key capped with purple plastic. "Jiggle it if it sticks."

"I'm not going anywhere." Amelia shrank from the key. Everything would change if she followed their directions, if it hadn't already.

"Call this number." Hailey capped the marker. "And say—you need to listen, Amelia. You have to repeat these exact words."

Amelia tore her gaze from the key chain dangling in Jonathan's hand to Hailey. The desperation painted on her face made Amelia's stomach turn.

She shook her head. "Not until you tell me what's going on."

"We don't have time."

"Why?" *This has to be a nightmare. If only I could wake up.* "If someone's coming here, we should all leave. Or call the cops."

Hailey didn't acknowledge the reasonable options. "Banana. Light bulb. Chicken. Heart."

"*What?*"

"I can't explain. You have to remember this."

"No, I don't—"

"*Amelia.* Listen." Gone was Amelia's unflappable sister. Hailey's sharp expression was unfamiliar and dangerous. "Say it. Repeat it. You need to remember this if you're going to get us help. Banana. Light bulb. Chicken. Heart."

Banana. Light bulb. Chicken. Heart?

"Say it!" Hailey smacked her hand on the railing. "Banana. Light bulb. Chicken. Heart." Her sister had *never* raised her voice.

Panic closed Amelia's throat. "Banana. Light bulb. Chicken. Heart," she managed.

"Good." Hailey guided Amelia off the stairs. "Remember those words in that order. Say it again."

"Banana. Light bulb. Chicken. Heart."

Hailey moved next to her husband. "Call the number. Say those words. Tell them we need help. They'll handle everything else."

"Until they do," Jonathan added. "Stay inside, and stay put. Head down and away from the windows. No lights. No nothing. Wait until they say you're okay."

"They who?"

"Whoever answers the phone." He stared at Amelia as though he wanted to push her out the door. "Go. Now."

Hailey stepped closer. Her pinched lips rolled together as though too much had to be left unsaid. "Banana. Light bulb. Chicken. Heart."

"Banana. Light bulb. Chicken. Heart," Amelia repeated, defeated. "Why can't you come with me?"

"We have a duty to—" Hailey caught herself with a nearly imperceptible shake of her head. "We just can't leave. Not yet."

Duty to what? Serve? Honor? Protect? They worked on antiques, on insured possessions owned by people who managed their own security and protection. Hailey and Jonathan didn't slink around in dark houses, whispering about danger and demanding Amelia break into someone's house with a string of random words.

"You're scaring me."

"I'm sorry, but you have to do this. I'll explain as much as I can later—and, Amelia, I love you."

A strange noise caught their attention. They froze for a nanosecond. Jonathan moved first. He grabbed Amelia and dragged her toward the back door. "Don't turn around. Don't look back. Get to the Callaghans'. Leave the book. Keep the lights off. Lock the door. Call the number. Tell them we need help."

CHAPTER TWO

JONATHAN PULLED AMELIA through the living room. The scent of popcorn still hung in the air from their night watching movies on the big screen, when life was predictable and normal. Hailey and Jonathan were her closest friends, her role models. They were everything Amelia had ever hoped for: stability, comfort, love.

The plush carpet under her feet was a sudden reminder that she didn't have shoes on. "I need my shoes."

He grimaced as though they didn't have time for such frivolity but didn't stop. "Hailey keeps some by the back door."

A pair of old running shoes that Hailey used in the garden waited innocently. Amelia shoved her feet into the too large, long-ago-double-knotted sneakers that were nearing their last wears.

He grabbed her shoulder. "This is as serious as it gets. Stay out of sight, and get into the Callaghans'."

"This is absurd." Tears sprang into Amelia's eyes. She couldn't think straight and didn't know what to say.

"Do it for your sister." He opened the door and released her shoulder with a small shove. "Go."

Amelia tucked the book under her arm and gripped the key chain so tightly that the key's teeth bit into her palm. The back door shut behind her. She was alone in the cool night.

Moisture hung heavily in the air. The October rain had tapered off, but the haziness of shadows swirled and cloaked the backyard. With a phone number written on her arm and nonsense to remember, she ran from the back of their house and ducked through a neighbor's yard as though she was a child playing hide-and-seek. The rain-soaked grass coated her shoes. Water sprinkled and sprayed over her arms and legs as she darted too close to shrubbery.

After a quick search for trouble, Amelia sprinted across the street. She was suddenly reminded of years before, when she and Hailey had snuck out of their aunt's house as teenagers. The sleeping world had been theirs to explore. They'd been through hell when their parents died in a car crash, and their distant aunt, twice removed and somehow related to them, hadn't been thrilled to take them in. Their parents' life insurance was the only reason she'd accepted the duty. Life at their new home had been sad and lonely, but when they slipped out of the basement window, they were free to frolic in the night. Tonight was nothing like that.

Amelia saw the house with the ferns on the front porch and hurried across the damp grass, footsteps squishing until she reached the Callaghans' driveway. Her breaths thundered. She was in shape, a runner by nature, but could barely catch her breath as she skirted around the car parked in front of the garage. Amelia ducked by a headlight, hid, and searched for danger. Nothing was out of place. The dreary night was almost peaceful except for the roar of her blood in her ears. She swallowed and tried to regain her composure. The night's mundanity was enough to question everyone's sanity.

She stared across the street toward Hailey's house. Nothing looked amiss. It certainly didn't show the frenzy of alarm happening inside. Their house matched the others in their neighborhood. The front porch lights blazed, haloed in the light fog. Nice cars sat in the driveways of well-manicured suburbia. A few parked cars lined the street. Humid condensation and beaded rainwater glazed over their windows—except for one car.

Her pulse stuttered. Amelia ducked lower and studied the vehicle. The water on the windows didn't match any other car, and—her heart froze. *Is someone behind the wheel?* She squinted. *Maybe? Or maybe not?* Her paranoia was causing her eyes to play tricks on her, but no matter the logic Amelia attempted to apply, she couldn't shake how out of place the car seemed.

Jonathan's voice echoed in her head. *Don't look back.* She needed to do what they'd said, to help Hailey. Amelia ducked behind the neighbors' car.

She had her marching orders but was certain she should commit the outlier car to memory. Though she didn't know types or brands or makes or models, she did her best to memorize the car then rushed behind the Callaghans' house.

The fence gate creaked but otherwise opened uneventfully. She checked over her shoulder and ran into the backyard. The back door was illuminated by a dim light. Her heartbeat galloped. Amelia's shaking hands fumbled with the key, but it slid easily into the back door. She turned it—it stuck.

"Shit."

Jonathan had predicted that. Her hands vibrated like she might over-dose on adrenaline. Amelia drew her hands away and watched them tremble. She inhaled and let it out slowly, dropped her hands to her sides, and pressed them to her thighs as though she could force the shakes to abate. *Pull it together.* Amelia tried the key again, that time with a careful jiggle.

Nothing.

It didn't budge.

Sweat broke out on her back. Panicked tears pricked the back of her throat. "Shit, shit, shit."

She slammed her palm next to the back door's window frame and jiggled the key harder—it turned as though her shaking hand had been given the touch of Harry Houdini.

Relief flooded her. The doorknob twisted easily. Warm air escaped from inside the cozy house as the cold realization of her actions was clear. With or without a key, she was breaking and entering.

That could land her in jail. *Why didn't they call for help from Hailey's house? Or use their cell phones?* Amelia's stomach plummeted. *Did Jonathan say the Callaghans were home or not? That they traveled? Are they traveling now?* It didn't matter at that point. She was already in the thick of it.

Amelia slipped farther into the cozy house, and her heart hammered loudly enough to wake everyone within a fifty-mile radius. Her hands still shook as she locked the door from the inside and found herself in a kitchen.

Frozen like a statue, Amelia swept her gaze through the room, barely lit by the decorative fixture over the sink. She inched farther inside. Her wet oversized shoes squeaked, and Amelia stepped out of them. The house smelled as though someone had baked thousands of sugar cookies and blueberry muffins in its oven over the years. Cookbooks lined the wall. A crocheted doily topped with figurine salt-and-pepper shakers held court in the center of a prominent kitchen table.

A cat meowed. Amelia jumped and silenced her half scream by clamping a hand over her mouth to drown the sound and keep her heart from escaping. A dull thump of it jumping sounded nearby.

"It's a cat," she scolded herself. One she didn't see. "Kitty?"

Now looking for a phone and a stealthy cat, Amelia crept toward the built-in desk on the opposite side of the kitchen. The desk was half buried by books and clutter. Cooking and gardening magazines were piled in front of a row of mismatched nature field guides at the back of the desk. Worn hardcover novels were interspersed with the field guides. An untidy pile of mail and a cordless phone sat next to a child's handmade ceramic pen holder.

Amelia shoved Jonathan's book in with the field guides and rushed for the handset. The cat jumped onto the desk. Amelia screamed again and threw herself back against the refrigerator. The cold metal felt good against her back. The cat jumped onto the floor and rubbed itself against her ankle, calming her thundering pulse.

"Good kitty. Nice kitty." She dipped to pet the cat, and a wall calendar caught her eye. She approached it cautiously. The Callaghans were very busy people, and if the date was correct, they were gone for the night for a quick trip to New York City.

She was alone—except for the cat. The fact that she wouldn't be arrested for breaking and entering offered slight reassurance. At least, she wouldn't be arrested immediately. She was on a mission. She could get in and out and be done with this mess. Amelia grabbed the cordless phone and moved into the living room. *Banana. Light bulb. Chicken. Heart.* Four little words were supposed to make everything better.

This is insane. She pulled the drapes back and checked the car across the street that had caught her eye. She wasn't sure if its windows looked different than the others. She stared at it—its driver's door opened. Her stomach catapulted. Fear sliced down her neck. A tall man stood and stared back at her as though he wasn't sure if *she* was real. He shut the car door and strode her way.

"Shit." She jerked away from the window. Was he really coming toward the house?

She peeked out again. The front passenger and back seat doors had opened. Three others got out. They moved toward Hailey's house, but the driver was jogging toward Amelia.

"Fuck."

This was real. It was serious. She needed help. Hailey and Jonathan needed help. What had she been waiting for?

Her fingers vibrated again like she'd mainlined espresso. She read the permanent marker on her arm and dialed the phone number, moving toward the stairs at the center of the house. Every horror movie ever made showed the ditzy girl running deeper into the house before her murder, but running out the front door didn't seem like the right move either.

A noise thumped against the solid double front doors. The beep of a disconnected phone line bleated in her ear. She'd messed up the number Hailey had written. Calling 911 would've been better. But Hailey and Jonathan were specific. Amelia had to use their special phone number and silly list of words.

Amelia checked the numbers written on her forearm again and redialed. The door thumping stopped, but she couldn't move. The phone line rang that time, but the call seemed very far away, and it rang and rang and rang.

CHAPTER THREE

A PINT-SIZED GROWL reverberated from under the war room table. Camden Brooks half-heartedly hid his smile as a dog bone the size of an armored vehicle pressed against his boot.

Jared "Boss Man" Westin leveled Camden with a look that could have bowled over a brick wall. "Something I said amusing?"

Camden tamped down his grin. "Nope."

"Because I'm telling you about an assignment that could leave you in a body bag if you don't listen."

"Understood, Boss Man."

Another growl came from under the table. Most of the men on Camden's team tried not to laugh as Thelma, Jared's bulldog, attacked the rawhide. The puppy had doubled in size since the summer, but Thelma didn't know it and still thought she was a little dog with oversized toys as she attacked her treasure underneath Titan Group's conference table.

Camden nudged the dinosaur femur away from his boot. Thelma returned the toy to where it had been after leveraging the side of his foot to get the best hold. She barked at the bone and did her best to wrestle it into submission. Boss Man glowered.

Across from Camden, Chance and Sawyer threatened to laugh. If they broke, Camden would fall apart. Their boss wouldn't give anyone else grief if they did. Camden was the sole focus of Jared's growing irritation. He ran a hand over his face and cupped his mouth, catching a glance at Liam, their team leader. Liam was going to laugh but not before he silently warned Camden to keep his act together.

Jared's phone vibrated on the table. His glare narrowed on Camden as he swiped the phone and stood. "Your ass has been saved by the bell."

Thelma nabbed her bone and fought through boots and chair legs to trot after Jared. Tough-guy Boss Man waited until his dog had walked through the door with the dinosaur leg before pulling it shut behind himself.

Hagan let out a long whistle. "You are going to get him on your bad side before nine in the morning." He snickered. "That takes a special talent, you know that, Cam?"

Camden crossed his arms and leaned back into his chair. "Jared loves me."

"Like a hole in the head," Liam muttered.

Liam had tried to mentor Camden over the years. It had worked, more or less. Camden's arrival in Abu Dhabi had been coupled with Titan's very nice paycheck and benefit package. He'd been a little wild. Jared hadn't been all that amused even if Camden thought his boss was a wild man too. Liam had pushed Camden to have fun but focus on their assignments so that he didn't die on the job. That wouldn't happen. He listened when it mattered.

The heavy door swung open again. Jared's scowl had deepened. After a sweeping glance at the team, his storming eyes landed on Camden again.

Shit.

"Everyone out." Boss Man didn't have to say "except for you"—every man in the room read that loud and clear.

Sawyer and Chance gave Camden a pitying glance.

Liam slapped him on the shoulder. "Nice knowing you, buddy."

"Shut the hell up, and go do something productive." Jared stalked to the head of the war-room table. His dark brows furrowed as the door shut soundly. As though he didn't know where to start, Jared glared and scrubbed a hand over his face. "Look, Camden…"

But nothing else came. Jared wasn't one to mince words. He sure as shit wasn't one to be without them.

"Yeah?"

Boss Man said nothing.

Well, hell. What had Camden done to get canned? His stomach sank.

The last straw had apparently been laughing at his damn dog. That didn't sound like Jared Westin, but part of his maverick nature was doing the unexpected.

"If you're going to fire me, then fire me. You don't need to sugarcoat it."

Boss Man hadn't sugarcoated a thing in his life. Camden wasn't sure why he was starting then.

The corners of Jared's mouth twitched. "Why am I firing you?"

Camden lifted his shoulders. "No idea."

"You know, everyone thinks you're happy-go-lucky, have a good time, party a little too hard, laugh a little too much. But I see through that bullshit, you know that?"

He raised his shoulders again.

"No, I'm not firing you, dipshit."

Camden didn't relax. "Then what are you doing?"

He cracked his knuckles. "Your attitude is one of the reasons I like you. You come off as a liability, but I think that makes you good at your job. You ask the right questions even when no one wants those questions asked. You force the situation when it needs to be forced."

Had Jared instituted a new policy for employee performance reviews? "Thanks?"

Jared ignored the sarcasm. "The CIA has a massive clusterfuck on their hands and is asking for a favor." He tapped his teeth together as though making a decision that he wasn't sure about. "A personnel database was breached. They don't know how deep or who has access."

"Shit," Camden muttered, not thinking about himself anymore.

"Yeah. Exactly." Jared paced the narrow end of the war room.

They had a global staff and a number of ghost teams whom Camden knew nothing about. Were they in danger?

Finally, Jared returned to the head of the table with a grim expression. "As of right now, this is what we know: Covert assignments and real names have been paired up and put into the wrong hands."

Information like that would easily pair spies with their cover stories and covert assignments for what they were. "Fuck."

He offered a tight nod of agreement. "But they don't know who has the intel or how it's been exploited."

Camden pulled in a heavy breath. "Christ. That's a problem."

"Now for the favor. They don't have enough resources to monitor every asset and their handlers. So they've given out contact information and passcodes to function like a 911 call center for spooks. We are amongst the contractors that will help facilitate this global communication network."

Camden nodded but wondered why he was the only person having this conversation with Jared. Their team leader seemed more suited to the briefing.

"You need to work with Amanda and Shah," Jared continued. "Their tech know-how will ensure a smooth setup, but your understanding of operational requirements will expedite any required assistance."

What the hell did that mean?

"This is really important to understand: We're not the help."

"We're not?"

They were always the help. That was one reason the job was so much fun. They could swoop in and save the day and swoop right out without any long-term responsibility. Here today, gone tomorrow. That could've been his personal motto.

"We're not. At least not right now. There's no telling where in the world a mayday call could come from. Paris or Paraguay." He shrugged. "So, you're good to oversee this?"

Am I? It was more of a job for Liam—anyone else, really. He wasn't the manager type.

Jared eyed him as though an actual choice had been offered. "Cat got your tongue, or what?"

Jared wanted an answer. Liam wanted Camden to step up and take on more responsibility. He wasn't sure that was what his team leader had been talking about. Tied to an office, waiting for a phone call that might not come—that sounded a lot like hell.

"Camden, there isn't a single day that you've been on my payroll that I haven't thought, 'Why don't you know when to shut the hell up?' Now you're sitting there, staring at me like you don't know what to say."

"This is like desk duty? Doesn't the US headquarters handle this type of job?"

A crease furrowed at Jared's brow, but then he shrugged. "Fair question. Semi-related to this shit storm, no one in that office is available to handle incoming calls that may or may not come."

This was desk duty. "I'm the guy you throw out of planes and into fires."

Jared nodded. "You still are. But this time, the fire's at the CIA, and it's burning hot in a way no one understands yet."

Potentially interesting. But hadn't Jared just threatened him with a body bag fifteen minutes ago?

"Look, man," Jared said. "You're right. I can see your hesitation. This might be a big ol' nothing burger."

Exactly... So a shit job for Jared's least favorite employee. Got it.

"But this is the thing. It takes a certain kind of pain in the ass to deal with the CIA. If this nothing burger turns into a phone call, and if that phone call turns into something, I want you dealing with the Agency. You have the right personality for it."

Was that a compliment? Camden wasn't sure.

Jared shrugged. "But it'll probably be nothing. You hang out in the operation center and shoot the shit with Amanda and Shah. Easy workday. What do you think? You game?"

"Probably boring with the potential for more complicated?" He pursed his lips. "I don't know if I'm your best guy on the job."

"Brother, I dig more complicated. It's how I pass my days." Boss Man crossed his arms. "And I think you do too."

Boss Man wasn't wrong. Most of their jobs were sit and wait anyway. Wait for ignition. Wait for the target. Wait for the go. He could collect a paycheck and sit on his ass in the comfort of the operations center.

How bad could it be? "All right. I'm in."

THE OPERATIONAL NERVE center of Titan's Abu Dhabi headquarters hummed with electronics. Cool air pumped into the room. Screens covered the walls. Workstations sat empty without any jobs monitored at the moment.

Camden sat in a rolling chair and pushed back as a football sailed toward him. He easily snapped the ball to his chest. An electronic beep announced someone entering. The outer door whooshed open, and Amanda Carter walked in.

Her eyes locked onto Cam, arm cocked and ready to throw the football, then onto Shah. "You two are going to break something expensive."

"*Everything's* expensive in here," Shah pointed out.

Camden dropped his arm and instead tossed the ball to himself. "Oh, come on. Don't sound like Liam."

"I sound like someone who knows the cost of this equipment and the hours spent setting it up."

"We're being careful." He patted the football and nodded to Shah before lofting it his way.

Shah caught it. "We have to do something. I'm bored out of my mind."

The special phone line that apparently required the three of them to rotate in shifts was silent. At least they'd adopted a buddy system. Otherwise, this assignment, which had initially piqued his interest, would be unbearable.

Its highlight had been the bare-bones CIA briefing that elaborated vaguely on what Jared had previously explained: Hackers discovered the identities of covert agents. No one seemed to know which agents, if they were current or former, or even which continents they were on.

Still, Boss Man had the three of them focus their attention on a phone line that never rang. Camden caught the ball and gave it a smack.

"Well, you're off duty now." Amanda shooed Camden toward the door. "Go before you break something."

"We just ordered food." Shah caught the ball. "And we're on a streak. We can't leave until one of us fumbles."

The phone rang. Camden's head snapped toward the desk. It wasn't a call made to Titan's phone system. The screen on the desk console lit up with the caller's location: Arlington, Virginia, thousands of miles away. Excitement—or at least boredom-killing interest—jumped in his chest, and he answered.

CHAPTER FOUR

A MAN ANSWERED Amelia's call, but with the blood rushing in her ears, he sounded terribly far away. Glass shattered in the kitchen. A locked door hadn't stopped her pursuer, and her reptile brain had panicked. She couldn't speak on the phone or run from danger. She had options: freeze, fight, or flee. In the grand evolutionary sense, she was dead meat.

The cat brushed against her leg. Its softness shocked her system. She gasped as though she hadn't remembered to breathe in hours. The cat walked its little toe beans over her bare feet. The sensation kickstarted her nervous system into gear and gave her two options: fight or flee. The man's scary face came into her mind, and she vaulted up the stairs.

The cat wove and ran between her feet. Her sweaty palm gripped the phone as though the person who answered might be able to pull her through the phone line to safety. "Hello?"

Nothing.

Her pulse screamed in her ears. "Hello?" She pressed the phone to her ear.

No one was there. They'd hung up.

Amelia paused at the top of the stairs and listened. The man was probably listening for her too. She needed to hide. The main bedroom would be the first place anyone would check. She couldn't hide in there.

Closets? Too easy. Bathrooms? Where did someone go to hide from the unknown? She didn't have time to discover the best hiding spot and dove into a bedroom. Swimming awards and dated posters hung on the walls. It was a time capsule of a teenager's bedroom before they'd left home for college a decade before.

She hit Redial again and tried the closet. *Nope.* The stench of mothballs hit. It was too packed with clothes and boxes for her to fit in anyway.

"Hello?" a man said in her ear.

Amelia jumped. In the half second since she redialed, she'd forgotten she even held a phone. "Don't hang up," she begged, slipping to the far side of a full-size bed and shoving herself underneath. Dust bunnies and storage boxes claimed most of the space.

"Do you have your passcode?" he asked.

Amelia heard footsteps. They moved in the opposite direction of the room she was in. "I need help," she finally whispered.

"Passcode, or I have to disconnect."

This wasn't happening. This was a nightmare. No one was chasing her. Her sister and brother-in-law were safe. Amelia hadn't broken into a house and wasn't hiding under a stranger's bed.

The cat slipped under the bed skirt and nuzzled her shoulder, once again grounding her in the midst of insanity. The passcode had to be the strange list of words that Hailey demanded Amelia memorize. "Banana. Light bulb. Chicken. Heart."

"And you are?"

"Amelia. Can you help us?"

The pause hung for eons before his voice mixed indecipherably with voices in the background. "I don't have an Amelia."

"What about Hailey and Jonathan? The Dumonts?" she pleaded. "Because they said you would help. I need help. *Help me.*" Tears caught in her throat. "Help us."

"Give me a second," he said and muffled his voice as he spoke to someone else. "Help's coming. I called in your location after you first called and hung up."

"When will they be here?" She pinched her eyes. "My sister and brother-in-law are across the street. But there's a man here too. He followed me." Should she say that Hailey and Jonathan had Amelia sneak into a neighbor's home? The guy hadn't even asked what was wrong. She needed to call 911.

After too long of a beat, he asked, "Who are you?"

"Amelia Stone."

"And…?"

"And what?" she cried.

"I have to know something more than that, lady."

"Hailey said not to call the cops. She said to call you. That you would help, and I need help!" Her heart and lungs pummeled her chest. Amelia tried to compose herself, but the only thing she managed was to keep from crying. "We need help. I don't know what's going on, but I trust my sister, and she trusts you." She squeezed her eyes shut, wishing for the millionth time that she was having a bad dream she would wake up from. "There's a man here, and I'm hiding under a fuckin' bed. *Help me.*"

"Okay, okay. I'm listening. I'm helping," he said then to someone else said, "I don't care what protocol says." He cleared his throat. "Amelia? You there?"

"Uh-huh."

"Tell me who your sister and brother-in-law are?"

"Hailey and Jonath—" The footsteps creaked in the hall. She wanted to sob but swallowed her terror. Tears leaked down her cheeks.

"Amelia?"

She whimpered. Of all the ways she could have imagined dying, this wasn't something she could have conjured up. She didn't even like to watch horror movies. Why had they watched a scary movie earlier? Everyone died. End of story—and what a predictable one at that. Amelia much preferred the predictability of rom-coms: movies filled with lots of love, the main characters didn't die, she usually laughed, and there was a guaranteed happily ever after. God, were those going to be her last thoughts? She never should have run upstairs.

"The man who followed you, you hear him?"

"Uh-huh." She also heard the cat as it followed her under the bed and ignored her jabs to push it away.

Not only should Amelia not have run upstairs, she shouldn't have let the cat in the room. It would give her location away. Slipping between the boxes, the cat crawled from under the bed and back out again. She batted it away with her free hand.

"If you can tell me without him hearing: Where is he?"

"Hallway," she managed as the cat massaged its front paws on her thighs. Amelia pushed it away. "Right outside where I am."

"Shit," the man muttered. "Do you have any training?"

"What kind?"

"Tactical? Self-defense?"

"I'm an event planner." The only things she was trained in were buffet menus and color-coded motifs.

"Shit," the man said again but this time with far more conviction. "Tell me everything you know about the situation."

Amelia squeezed her eyes closed and listened to make sure the footsteps weren't coming closer. "One person came toward me. Three toward Hailey and Jonathan—"

"Focus on your situation."

"A man came inside. Broke in." *Like me*, but she didn't see any benefit to sharing that detail.

The cat stopped trying to cuddle and positioned its body facing the door. He could hear the intruder better than she could. "He's in the hall bathroom."

"Good. That's great. Take a breath. In through your nose. Out through your mouth. Nice and easy."

She tried. His voice was more calming than his orders. He wouldn't cut it as a yogi unless they offered yoga at boot camp, but he sounded like he could talk his way out of a shitstorm. The cat slipped from under the bed.

"Where are you?" he asked.

"Under a bed."

"A *fuckin'* bed. I remember. Only tell me new intel. Main bedroom? Guest bedroom?"

She almost smiled. "A teenager's room."

"What's around you?"

"A bed skirt. An abandoned water bottle and T-shirt. I'm half hidden on one side by shoeboxes. Lots of crap."

"Do you have any weapons?"

"Are you kidding? I'm not even wearing shoes."

"That's fine. You don't need shoes," he said in a way that was oddly relaxed. "Amelia, right?"

"Mm-hmm. He's close."

After another eternally long moment, he said, "I'm going to stay on the phone with you. I've enhanced the response coming—"

"Does that mean more cops?"

"Something like that. Where is he now?"

She tried to recall the layout. "Another bedroom—no, the hall again. Coming closer—"

The door creaked open. Her lungs hurtled into her throat, but she caught her scream before the whole neighborhood heard. Amelia tried the technique suggested by her boot camp yogi. She breathed in through her nose, out through her mouth—in and out, in and out, just as the man on the phone, a military yoga zen drill sergeant who coached her breathing as though he were yelling, *"Right foot! Left foot!"* had demanded she do. *In through my nose. Out through my mouth.*

Her heartbeat slowed from its runaway pace. *In and out. One breath in. Another breath out.* Amelia tried to disappear as the bedroom door opened wider.

Cautious footsteps entered. She held her breath as the man walked by and kicked the bed skirt in search of her hiding spot. The closet door opened. Clothes clattered, torn off their hangers. Amelia replayed the voice of the man on the phone. She didn't even have to have her shoes on. Just take it nice and easy.

"Is he in there now?" the man whispered on the phone, and taking her silence as an answer, continued, "If he finds you, fight back. Don't freeze. Don't try to reason. Don't waste your energy screaming. Bite. Use your elbow. Use your fingernails. Knee him in the nuts. Fight dirty. Do you hear me?"

The other man seemed to pause his search and said, "Yeah? Hello?" as though taking a phone call. He sat on the bed. "What do you want?"

The bedsprings squeaked and sank down. Amelia flattened herself against the floor, terrified he could feel her through the mattress.

"Not yet," the man on the bed said as the bed springs groaned. "Don't know. Call back if you find out first."

He grumbled and didn't get off the bed. Even her shallowest breaths seemed to roar and reverberate. Her hands were sweating, but her grip on the phone felt like she was clinging to a life raft. Amelia tried to imagine the man on the phone pressed to her ear. He was calm to her helplessness, lethally trained to her unskilled incapability. Why hadn't she taken self-defense classes?

"Amelia?" he whispered.

His voice was like honey. Trustworthy. The way he spoke, the way he sounded was as though he had the ability to protect her no matter the threat. She wanted to cry, and more than that, she wanted him to reassure her that all would somehow work out.

"Rub your finger over the mouthpiece if you want me to keep talking. Do nothing if you need me to shut up."

He seemed to have read her mind. Eons passed as she cautiously repositioned her hand and fluttered her fingers over the bottom of the phone.

"Okay, I read you loud and clear," he said quietly. "I'm here. You're doing great."

She almost snorted. Tears leaked out of her eyes.

"I can hear your breathing. Try to quiet that for me. Can you do that, Amelia?"

Absolutely not. But she tried. Amelia swallowed and listened to the even cadence of his voice, his breathing, the way he remained in control and calm.

"Easy breath in, easy breath out," he whispered. "Good girl. Just like that."

Her panic didn't subside, but the hammering explosions in her chest slowed as he spoke.

"In... and out..."

The intruder pushed off the bed, walked across the bedroom, and jostled the window blinds. "This fucking night."

Yeah, she could say the same thing, buddy.

He moved to the foot of the bed and re-kicked the bed skirt. He nudged a box against her foot. Amelia didn't move a muscle. He kicked it again as though testing the resistance—the cat hissed. It thumped across the floor, hissing again.

Heavy footsteps jerked back. "Christ."

The cat jumped on and off the bed.

The intruder let out a low rumble of laughter. "Stupid fucking cat." His footsteps nudged the bed skirt again, but he stopped short. "Yeah, what?" he said, answering another phone call. "Not yet, man. It's been thirty fucking seconds." He crossed the bedroom and stopped near the window, standing closer to Amelia than he had when moving the shoeboxes under the foot of the bed. "Now? What about—yeah, I hear you. Fine."

And just like that, he left the room. The footsteps were swift. He didn't try to hide the sounds he made when rushing down the stairs.

"He's gone," she let out, choking on relief. "He took a call and left."

"That's good. Stay put until I say so. Okay?"

She wasn't claustrophobic, but being trapped under the bed and ordered to stay put when the intruder could come back made her skin crawl. Hot panic curled in her chest. She wanted to push her arms out and move her legs. Amelia needed to push the mattress off of herself as though it were lying across her chest, pushing the oxygen from her lungs. Her pulse quickened and thundered loudly in her ears. "I need to get up. I have to get up."

"Stay put, Amelia. Another two minutes."

She counted the seconds. *One, two, three, four*— "I can't. I have to—"

The cat returned. It nuzzled her shoulder. Tears slipped from her eyes. The silky soft fur brushed her damp cheek. It almost made the tears fall faster. A rough tongue scratched her chin. The cat purred. Its toe beans pressed against her arm. Amelia's breaths slowed. She focused on the cat and gripped the phone.

Amelia's claustrophobia slowly dissipated as she stared at the bottom of the box spring. The cat was petting her as though it knew she was teetering on the edge of a full-scale mental breakdown. "Who are you?"

His rough laughter was laid back. "Just a guy doing my job."

Ha. At times, she'd sworn event planning in Washington, DC, was as stressful as it could get. People with their VIP personalities were her bread and butter. Those people hired her company because she was unaffected by status, job title, or bank account size. Amelia had absolutely nothing on this guy. His composed nature reminded her of Hailey and Jonathan.

"What's your name?" she asked.

"We don't usually trade in personal details."

"I don't know who *we* is, but I need to know. Please." She laughed quietly, voice shaking and in every way the opposite of his collected demeanor. "Don't make me beg while I'm hiding under a bed."

"A *fuckin'* bed," he joked.

Her lips quirked. "Tell me who you are."

"Camden."

No last name, which was to be expected—if it was even his real name. Still, she believed everything else he'd said. *Why not something so trivial?* It didn't *feel* trivial to her. This man was legendary. He'd saved her life by simply being on the phone.

"Thanks, Camden."

He waited for an extra beat. "The agents are there. You're going to hear them come in. Okay?"

"What about my sister—"

"They're arriving simultaneously. They'll find you and your sister soon."

Voices called her name from the first floor. She could hear law enforcement clearing the rooms as they fanned throughout the house. "I can hear them."

"All right. They'll take care of the situation—I hope everything works out for you."

She swallowed hard. "Things don't work out well when they have to call you, do they?"

He laughed soberly as though she'd hit the nail on the head. "You did great tonight. Whatever happens, know that few people could have kept it together the way you did."

CHAPTER FIVE

T HE GRAY SEDAN was gone, replaced by the spinning blue, white, and red lights of law enforcement vehicles. Amelia wasn't sure how so many police cruisers and unmarked cars had fit into the neighborhood. The sheer number of people standing on sidewalks and in the Dumonts' and Callaghans' driveways was enough to fill a high school gymnasium.

Despite all that, Amelia didn't know anything and had been all but trapped, ordered to stay put until Hailey and Jonathan were brought out. She shivered under the jacket someone had draped over her. Official-looking people with badges milled about the damp, foggy night. The rookie cop in charge of babysitting her looked as thrilled as she felt to wait, uninformed and ignored.

His radio crackled. He jumped at the chance to be involved. "Yeah, go ahead."

Amelia didn't catch the garbled order. The police academy must teach cadets how to decipher mumbles from static. Exhaustion flamed her irritability. If Amelia couldn't find her sister and head to bed soon, she would scream. Standing around and shivering wasn't making her mood any more congenial.

The rookie cop scanned the street then beckoned her. "Come with me."

They weaved between unmarked cars through the labyrinth of uniformed people with badges and guns. Amelia miscalculated the curb while wearing Hailey's wet, oversized shoes and stumbled. The rookie cop didn't notice that she nearly face-planted.

Amelia caught up and found him with two suit-clad men. Neither wore ties. Both flipped their badges at her with such speed and finesse that she didn't get a good look at them. Her brain garbled their names as though her hearing was filtered through cotton balls. She didn't introduce herself. Everyone seemed to already know who she was.

The rookie cop was more animated than he'd been in the last hour, as if he wanted to impress the two men they were standing before. When the two suits shooed him away, disappointment dragged his features into an exhausted frown. She wanted to snap that at least he could go home to his family and his nice warm bed, not worrying that everything he understood about his world had been turned upside down.

Amelia crossed her arms over her chest. "Where's my sister and broth-er-in-law? Can I talk to them now?" Their scrutiny made her unsteady. Apprehension tightened in her chest. Something was wrong with the only family Amelia had. "What?"

"I'm sorry. Jonathan didn't make it."

"Wait. What? No." Her equilibrium tilted. Amelia's legs went weak. *Didn't make it* sounded like he died, like the nightmare was only getting worse. "What do you mean 'didn't make it'?"

One man's frown dipped. The other's brow furrowed. "Single shot to the back of the head. Found in the kitchen."

Bile rose into her strangled throat. A tornado of words echoed and slammed in her pounding head. Their unemotional faces focused on her like she was a specimen in a lab. *Jonathan didn't make it?* "No. That's not possible."

As if on cue, a gurney with a covered body was brought out the front door.

Her hands covered her face. "No." Her knees turned to noodles. "*No.*"

One of the men grasped her by the elbow, half holding her up, half turning her away from Jonathan. "Take a deep breath, Ms. Stone."

His hold on her arm pinched too tightly. The pain refocused her from Jonathan to the here and now. Maybe he did that on purpose. Maybe he was trying to help. Her noodle knees regained their sea legs, and after a minute, he let go of her arm. Tears streamed down her cheeks. "Wait—" Her chin snapped up. "What about Hailey?"

Both stared at Amelia as though she was supposed to tell them.

The man who had held her up asked, "Was she with you?"

"No." Suddenly, the cold night air was hot and sour. Dread curled deep in her gut. She couldn't take a deep breath. Her stomach revolted and threatened to be sick. A retching hiccup convulsed in her belly. "She was with Jonathan."

One of the men shook his head. The other's lips pinched.

"*Yes*. She was with him." Panic threaded her dread. Glass shards tumbled in her lungs as she tried to breathe. "They stayed inside. Together. They told me to leave. To call the number. To get help." Amelia turned back toward their house. *It was good that Hailey wasn't inside, wasn't it?* "She escaped?"

"Fleeing the scene is a possibility," the quieter of the two said.

Both held her gaze with an air of suspicion. "Possibility" was said as though the chance of it was beyond what she could hope for.

"What else could it be? She was taken?" *By Jonathan's murderer? God...* If Amelia had only run faster, if she hadn't searched the street for trouble but had rushed into the Callaghans' house, help would have arrived sooner. She'd been frozen in a neighbor's driveway and then kitchen while someone took Hailey and killed Jonathan. Suffocating guilt pummeled her.

The man raised his shoulder. "We're processing the scene. There's only one thing we're certain about: There's no sign of your sister."

CAMDEN KNEW THE phone wouldn't ring again, and even if it did, the odds of the caller being related to the previous night's call would be slim to none. The chance that he even intercepted one of the CIA's calls was so slight that it would probably never happen again. He had no idea how many other phone centers could have picked up Amelia's call, and while there was a problem with agents in danger, they would only call when they were up shit creek and grasping at their last shreds of hope. Still, he watched the phone intently as if he could will Amelia to call again.

"Cam, you don't have to be here." Amanda placed a coffee cup in front of him.

"It's fine." After Amelia called, he'd camped in the operation center in case she called again. He wanted to know what had happened and if everyone was safe. He wondered if Amelia had been reunited with her family.

His normal assignments didn't attach an emotional component. If people were scared, that was fine, because Titan was there. They would swoop in and save the day. If they were in danger, again, all would be okay. His team would eliminate threats—job done. He could kick back with a beer and not think about the details of the assignment ever again.

This was different. It was a situation completely out of his control. Camden wanted to know more. He wanted details on the fallout. Amelia was safe. Help had arrived. That was important. But he wondered if the CIA agents had been able to help Jonathan and Hailey Dumont.

Camden had used Titan's resources, not exactly with permission, and searched what was available in their databases—nothing. He turned to Google and learned she was a professor. He was a researcher. Neither looked particularly like a spy, but not everyone could be James Bond or Jason Bourne.

Camden sent a request for more information to Parker Black, the man who oversaw Titan Group's global technology operations, but the request was unanswered. Either Parker was on assignment, or he was ignoring Camden. Either way, he shouldn't have asked Parker.

Camden ran a hand over his face. He and bureaucracy weren't great partners. Would Parker say something to their boss? Jared wasn't in the business of wild goose chases and didn't want anyone on his team playing the role of unnecessary hero. Maybe that was what Camden was doing. He certainly wasn't supposed to stay on the phone and talk Amelia through the situation. Their orders were clear: Call for assistance if threats were deemed real.

The phone rang. He jerked back. Amanda and Shah paused their conversation. Another call for the second day in a row was an anomaly, if the last week had been any indication. He answered.

"Camden?"

Amelia's voice washed over him. Hearing from her was confirmation that she was safe—but he'd already known that. There was more to the feeling, and he had no idea what it was—maybe concern or worry. He didn't know why.

"Passcode?"

"We talked last night."

Of course, he knew that. Still, he had rules. Not to mention, Shah and Amanda were watching. As much as he wanted to hear from her, as many questions as he had, she couldn't just call. "Passcode, or I have to disconnect."

"No, no, no. Wait," she pleaded. "Please wait."

Why was she calling? He drew a deep breath. It *could* be a test. But the means of tripping him up felt off. He wondered if Jared would screw with him like that. He checked his watch. It was almost the same time as she had called the day before. If only he'd checked to see if her local news had turned up any report in her neighborhood, then at least he could rule out if this was some kind of employment test. "Passcode, or—"

"Do you know how many times I've called this number until I was finally routed to you?" she asked.

He didn't mean to smile. He turned his chair so that he didn't face Amanda and Shah. "I have to hang up."

"Four stupid words will keep you on the phone with me?"

"Well… yeah."

"*Camden.* I know it's you from last night."

He scrubbed a hand over his face. He should disconnect the call, yet curiosity didn't let him.

She let out a bone-crushingly exhausted breath. "Banana. Light bulb. Chicken. Heart. Does that make you happy?"

The corners of his lips quirked. He chuckled. "Not sure about happy, but my bases are covered."

"So, it's Camden, right?"

"Yeah, Amelia. That's me."

"You remember my name?"

Amanda and Shah inched closer. Camden wanted to shoo them away. "Yeah, I remember your name. I don't usually sit and answer calls, and even if I did, yours will probably be one of the most interesting I'd ever get. So, yeah, I remember your name." He probably always would. Her story would stick with him.

"I've been redialing this number over and over," she admitted. "But it wasn't you."

His index finger tapped against the handset. "I have no idea how many other places take these calls. But it's probably a few."

"Everyone hangs up on me."

He laughed and wondered how many times she'd called. Had she given the passcode each time? Or asked for him by name? The CIA could be tracking her calls. Jared could.

"You're not supposed to call this number if there isn't an emergency."

"Don't hang up," she pleaded. "Please."

His index finger tapped again. This was a test—one he was certain he was already failing. *Goodbye, Titan career. Hello... motel security?* That would be all that he would get if Boss Man deemed he'd screwed up with a CIA asset—or an asset's family member. But he still hadn't hung up. "Why are you looking for me?"

"No one will tell me anything."

He almost laughed. "I can't tell you. Even if I knew. Which I don't."

"You knew enough to listen to 'Banana. Light bulb. Chicken. Heart.' Or whatever. That's more than anyone else."

He ran a hand over his face like he could scrub away his hesitation. Camden wasn't one to overthink. Amanda and Shah were watching him in a way that made the room feel small. "You shouldn't..." *What? Say that? What did it matter?* "I should go—"

"My sister is missing. My brother-in-law is dead," she whispered. "I talked to investigators, and they act as though I'm hiding Hailey in my back pocket. And there are these people... They say they worked with my sister. It doesn't make sense. I don't have any answers, and the things that I have been told are... They just don't make sense."

He rubbed the back of his neck. "I can't help you."

"Where are you?" After a moment, she let out a defeated breath. "Of course, you can't tell me that. No one can tell me anything."

"I need to keep this line open—"

She scoffed. "Right. Because whoever you are, wherever you work, you want me to believe that you don't have call waiting? Even if I didn't call a hundred times before I found you and talk to a hundred different people, do you expect me to believe that your super-secret call center doesn't have more than one phone line for your super-secret bullshit? Got it."

His lips quirked. Camden dropped his head back and stared at the lights in the ceiling. He pinched the bridge of his nose and shook his head. No one would tell her anything other than an approved cover story, and no matter what they told Amelia, a well-thought-out cover story wouldn't matter if there wasn't a body to bury. Missing people were almost harder to process than murdered ones. The lack of a body meant hope. Hope wasn't helpful. It wasn't kind. It was a torment that loved ones fought against, praying that one day, life would return to normal. Most times, it never did.

"I'm going to find my sister." She paused as though expecting him to shoo her away from the plan. But he didn't, and Amelia grumbled. "Lord knows no one else is doing anything to help Hailey—"

"You don't know that." The CIA tracked its assets. If one went off the grid, they would dedicate resources to resolving the situation and, if need be and circumstances allowed, the recovery of remains.

"I thought you could help me."

"Me? I can't." He couldn't say that he was Titan or not CIA. He couldn't say squat.

"You don't even know what helping would entail. How can you say no without knowing what I want from you?"

His mouth pinched. "All right, Amelia, forget the fact that my boss would fire my ass on the spot for even having this phone call. Call me curious. What do you want from me?"

Amanda and Shah crept closer. Camden waved them back.

"Are they listening? Your boss, I mean?"

He glanced around the operations center with its surveillance equipment and technology that could probably track a fart on the International Space Station. He didn't know and wouldn't lie to her, so he punted the question with a half answer. "This is a secure line."

"A secure line," she repeated with a dry laugh. "My sister didn't teach art history, did she?"

Is anyone just an art history teacher? If they lived in the Washington, DC, metro area, the answer was probably a fifty-fifty chance they were an art-aficionado-slash-CIA-operative. "You know she did. Everything you know about her and her husband was real."

"But there was more. Another layer I didn't know about. Right?"

Camden wouldn't answer her, but he didn't have to. Amelia already knew. Cops had probably talked to her then swiftly deposited her into the capable hands of men with obscure badges and dubious backgrounds. Their conversations would have had far more substance but somehow without any information to decipher.

"What does a secure line mean?" she asked. "Like in the movies? Untappable. Untraceable."

He shrugged. "Just as it sounds. No one can access the line. It's safe."

"For people like my sister to call into if they're in trouble."

He repositioned and leaned back in the office chair. "Look, Amelia. It's late for you. The middle of the night, right? You should get some sleep and forget this phone number. All right?"

"Even if I wanted to, I can't get the permanent marker off the inside of my forearm. I woke up and thought the whole thing had been a nightmare. But then I looked down and saw my sister's chicken scratch in black Sharpie on my skin. I think I'm going to see your phone number in my head for the rest of my life."

Fuck. That wasn't going to help her move forward from whatever she'd stumbled upon.

Camden didn't have any advice. "You should talk to someone—"

"*I am.* You."

He rolled his eyes toward the ceiling. Her stubbornness was a pain in the ass. But he sort of appreciated her tenacity. "Someone who knows what to say. Because..." He sucked in his cheeks and tried to play out a few responses. She deserved the genuine truth, and he didn't have that. "I don't feel like I'm doing right by you or this conversation."

The phone line was quiet. He wished she would hang up and forget everything. At least, part of him wished that. Another growing part of him was curious. He wished Amanda and Shah weren't listening.

She broke the silence. "You know…"

Hanging up was the right thing to do. Reporting the conversation was another right thing to do. But according to his track record, doing the right thing wasn't his usual modus operandi, at least according to Boss Man. Camden never thought he was doing wrong, necessarily. He just wasn't falling in line.

"Camden, you're the only person who talks to me for more than two seconds. Even if you're trying to get me to hang up first."

He laughed quietly but kept listening.

"And you're the only person who isn't actively trying to make me forget what I think I saw."

"Yes, I am." But that was interesting. He wondered what the spooks in badges were trying to convince her had happened. He bit his tongue to keep from asking. She was giving him all the more proof that he needed to hang up the phone. "Take care of yourself. Okay, Amelia?"

She didn't answer. Camden needed a second to realize she'd hung up on him. Well, she probably threw her phone across the room. He didn't blame her.

"That was interesting." Amanda perched on the edge of the table in the center of the operations center. "First, you stay on the phone long past when you should."

"Second," Shah continued, "you talk to her…" He gestured as if there were more to the story. "Because, why?"

"She needed someone to talk to." Camden scanned the room for the football and found it nestled in a chair on the far side.

"Not to mention"—Amanda crossed her arms—"how many times did she have to call to get routed here?"

"No telling." Camden retrieved the football and tossed it to himself, not very high but enough that he had something to do with his hands. "She's having a hard time finding information."

"Of which you have any?"

"No," he confirmed. "But her brother-in-law is dead, and her sister is missing. She's looking for answers." Camden tossed and caught the football. "You can't tell me that you wouldn't walk through hell to find information about your family." He already knew Amanda had lived through a wild ride of her own more than once and had done a few things that some might see as illogical. But she'd had her reasons. Camden wasn't sure about Shah but would bet he would do the same. He dropped into a swivel chair. "I don't blame her."

The three of them sat with their thoughts. The only sound that broke the silence was the hum of the technology that surrounded them and the repetitive clap of Camden toying with the football.

"She had no idea?" Shah asked.

"Of her family's involvement in the CIA?" He scoffed. "Didn't sound like it."

"That's one hell of a way to find out."

Camden clapped the football between his hands. "I want to know more about what happened in Arlington."

Amanda moved to a computer terminal adjacent to Shah. "We could poke around and see what there is to see."

"I already tried," Camden admitted.

Both Shah and Amanda grinned like his effort was adorable but Camden shouldn't question the experts at work. "I don't want to get you guys in trouble."

"It's just research," Amanda said.

"And here I thought I was the impulsive one."

"This isn't your impulsivity." Amanda's fingers flew across the keyboard. "It's scratching a professional itch."

Shah scooted to his computer. "I'm curious too. Let's see what there is to see."

Camden's curiosity was multiplying to a level beyond what he would admit. He rolled his chair behind Shah.

The man looked back over his shoulder and said, "Give me room to work."

Amanda leaned back from her keyboard. "There's something about the Dumonts' handler that's been redacted. There's another point of contact, but I'm not sure how long they've been connected."

"Do you recognize the name?" Shah asked.

"No." She clicked her mouse a few times and typed again. "Nothing but a profile of an up-and-coming socialite who—" Amanda scrolled. "Get this. Beth Tourne seems to love ritzy, glitzy parties and expensive things." She turned toward them. "Like art."

Camden's eyebrows inched up. "*Seems* like that would be a good connection for an art history professor and her auction-house husband to know."

"Seems like," Amanda agreed.

As the door opened, Jared Westin strode in, trailed by his bulldog. Their boss didn't look pleased. Then again, he never did. "Thelma, sit." Thelma plopped at his boots. "What are you three getting into?"

"We got a call yesterday—"

"Yeah. I know. What are you getting into now?"

There was a good chance that Boss Man already knew exactly what they were doing, not because he listened in on their conversations or spied on their devices but because he had a scarily uncanny ability to know everything all the time. It never worked out in Camden's favor.

"Snooping around," Shah explained with a casualness that Camden wished would disappear.

At the very least, Shah could have made their snooping sound like research.

Boss Man snorted.

"Do you know Beth Tourne?" Amanda asked.

His molars ground. Camden wished both she and Shah would shut their traps.

"Why?"

She clucked. "That wasn't an answer, Boss Man."

Jared's scowl softened the slightest degree. He wasn't that much older than they were, but he managed to have an old-soul air about him. He also managed to look pissed off most of the time, which made it hard to decipher when he was really irritated. As far as Camden could guess, Jared was actually that irritated all the time. But he didn't like to be around to find out.

"Beth Tourne?" Jared's square jaw ticked. "CIA?"

Amanda nodded.

"What do you know?" Jared asked. "Why are you asking?"

Camden noted that he hadn't given an answer as to whether he knew Beth Tourne. Anyone could have guessed they were speaking of someone on the CIA's payroll.

"She hasn't been with them long," Amanda shared. "Likely establishing a cover."

"A cover as what?"

"Something froufrou with DC movers and shakers."

Jared grimaced. "Yeah, no. We haven't crossed paths." He turned his attention to Camden, who readied himself for a lecture in which the moral of the story would tell him to focus on work and ignore anything else shouting for his attention. Instead, Jared narrowed his eyes. "If the lady calls again, don't hang up on her on my account."

With that, Jared left.

The group waited a minute after the door shut behind him before anyone spoke.

"He knows more than he's letting on," Shah said.

"Always does," Amanda agreed.

Maybe that was true, but that wasn't what was making energy gather in Camden's chest. She might call again. His phone buzzed with a notification from Parker Black. Camden swiped the message open and read. His jaw fell open.

"What?" Shah inched closer. "Your face says about a hundred things, and I'm too nosy to wait for you to share."

He lifted his screen. "Parker sent Amelia Stone's contact information."

CHAPTER SIX

"COMING. COMING." AMELIA crawled out of bed and pulled on a sweatshirt. She wasn't in the mood to deal with whoever was ringing the doorbell of her first-floor condo. She'd had her fill of nosy neighbors for the past few days. The news reports had spun Jonathan's murder and Hailey's disappearance as a possible domestic dispute. They'd named Amelia as a witness who had mistakenly thought someone had broken in when she heard an unexpected disturbance. Left out of the story were pretty much all the facts about what had actually happened.

For whatever reason, friends and acquaintances thought they should stop by to share condolences when she hadn't answered their phone calls and text messages. The only calls she'd taken were from Jonathan's parents, who lived in France. They weren't exactly her family, but she supposed they were the only things she had left.

The doorbell rang again as she wiped the sleep from her tired eyes. It was so early. Why would anyone stop by at this hour? "Coming!"

She threw open the front door and pulled back abruptly. It wasn't the nosy neighbor patrol but rather the two men who had notified her of Jonathan's passing and asked where Hailey was. Amelia caught herself, semi-embarrassed that she had been dangerously close to yelling, "What do you want?" out her front door.

"Ms. Stone." The man who had caught her elbow when her legs threatened to give out greeted her with a practiced smile. She saw it was meant to make her feel more at ease. Nerves skipped down her spine, and her hackles rose.

"Agent Frank Fitzgerald," he continued, reintroducing himself. "And this is Agent Michael Bennett."

They both flipped open their badges and flipped them shut again, giving Amelia just enough time to see how official they were yet not nearly enough time to read what they said. She kept a hand on the front door and had never wished more for a storm door or recording doorbell. Both might be purchases in the near future. "Do you have news about my sister?"

"Could we come in?" Agent Fitzgerald asked.

Tension made her lungs tighten as if the oxygen had been pulled from the fall air. Why didn't they answer? Her fingers clutched the door. "Did you find her? Is she—" She feared they were notifying her of Hailey's death. Blood rushed in her ears. Amelia had turned her cell phone ringer off. Maybe they'd called. Maybe—

"Ms. Stone," Agent Fitzgerald said, interrupting her tragic spiral. "Take a deep breath. It's okay."

Liar. Nothing would ever be okay again.

"Can we come in?" He offered an understanding nod that she didn't trust.

Warning bells rang. She wished someone else were home with her. Why had she ignored her friends? What about the man on the phone? Did Camden know these men? Did they work for the same agency? Even if they did, she would feel more comfortable if Camden the Mystery Man had vouched for them or, better yet, had accompanied them.

"Ms. Stone, can we come in?" Agent Fitzgerald asked again.

Amelia bit her lip. "Do you know—" A fierce, instinctive wave of distrust cut her off before she said Camden's name aloud. "Please tell me if you found Hailey."

"We have not." Agent Bennett shifted his stance and leveled a hard, cold stare at her as though he and Agent Fitzgerald were trying to force their way into her condo without touching her. "We'd like to ask you a few more questions about the man who followed you into the Callaghans' home."

Agent Bennett was the bad cop to Agent Fitzgerald's good cop. They were playing roles. Amelia tried to appreciate that, but no matter who played what role, they didn't bear news on Hailey. Her shoulders slumped. She reminded herself that no news was partially good news. Hailey wasn't dead—at least, not that they knew of. Tears burned the back of her throat. "Sure." She stepped back and turned so they wouldn't see her wipe her eyes. "Come in."

She led them into her small condo. The lemon-yellow walls and bright white trim had always made her happy. Right then, they were too much to stand.

"Would you like something to drink?" She switched the electric kettle on. "Tea?"

"We're fine."

Amelia gestured to her living room and took a seat across from the men. Their dark suits were like a uniform: generic yet uncommon, as though they would stand out in a crowd but be impossible to describe.

"Who do you work for?"

"The federal government," Agent Fitzgerald answered. "An interagency task force."

If she'd had the energy, her eyes would have rolled hard enough to knock her over. "Well… yeah. But specifically?"

"What do you know about Hailey and Jonathan's employer?"

Why couldn't she get a straight answer from these two? "Their employer? As in they worked for the same place?" She stared at the agents. They wanted to know what secrets she knew. Truthfully, she didn't know any, but she was starting to have guesses that didn't make much sense. "My sister worked for a college in DC, and Jonathan?" She shrugged. "He worked for himself and contracted with auction houses."

They waited with practiced silence for her to continue.

"But I've guessed recently that I didn't really know who my sister was." She bit her lip, which was already chewed and chapped. "I didn't. Did I?"

They were unreadable. She'd always touted her talent for decoding emotion. After all, as an event planner of corporate schmoozefests and decadent weddings, she had to be able to foresee emotions a mile away. If the mother of the bride was getting ready to happy-sob like a rhinoceros with allergies in the middle of the ceremony, Amelia could see it coming and head off a scene-stealing nose-blowing sob session. If the groom was having cold feet the night of the rehearsal dinner, Amelia sensed it before the groomsmen did. If players in a hostile corporate takeover were trying to work over an overworked assistant and milk information, she could tactfully move the corporate henchmen along and save someone their job without so much as breaking a sweat.

But right then, Amelia was scoring zero out of two on Agents Fitzgerald and Bennett. Neither man gave her anything to work with. "Are you going to tell me anything, or do I stay in the dark and keep guessing?"

"We're not authorized to share information on their employment."

That was as much of a confirmation as she would get out of those two, but a nonanswer was something. "Gotcha." Though the kettle signaled the water was hot enough for tea, she didn't bother to make herself a cup. "Can you tell me why news reporters are dragging Hailey's name through the mud?"

Bennett shrugged as though he hadn't a clue.

Fitzgerald added, "It'd help to stay focused on this conversation."

Her molars ground. "What do you want to know about the man who tried to find me?"

"We'd just like you to tell us everything again. In case something slipped your mind—"

"Nothing slipped my mind. Every minute detail has been permanently carved into my brain."

They offered understanding nods. "Let's go through the exercise anyway," Bennett suggested.

A lilt in Bennett's voice sent an eerie feeling up her spine, as if they weren't looking for more information but rather testing her story.

"Starting with the description of the man that came into the Callaghans' house. Short? Tall? Black? White?"

"White. Tall." She'd already given them that information.

"If you met with a sketch artist, could you describe the man enough to get a visual representation?"

"I don't know." The details were clear. She remembered the close-cut hair, the sharp shoulders, and a long stride, but she didn't know how to explain that to an artist. Amelia chewed her lip again. They didn't like her answer, and she couldn't shake the feeling that the conversation was a test, one she didn't understand and couldn't have prepared for. "Maybe. Probably."

"That's not what I expected you to say." Bennett's deep disappointment permeated his expression. He glanced at Fitzgerald. "Did you?"

"It wasn't as if I saw his eye color. I was hiding from him."

"All right." Fitzgerald nodded at her reasoning and leaned back, relaxing against her couch like he and Bennett might be there a while. "Have you heard from your sister? Seen her?"

Her head cocked to one side. "What? No."

"Are you sure?" Bennett pressed.

"*Am I sure?*" She drew back. "Of course I'm sure."

"Did Hailey or Jonathan tell you anything and ask you to keep it quiet? Maybe they shared information but said not to share?"

"Other than the phone number and code words, they wouldn't tell me anything at all."

"*Nothing else?*"

She tried to piece together the night, but everything was very foggy. Her memories weren't even in order, like she could see the trauma in unorganized snapshots. "I just wanted to call 911, but they said no."

Bennett pursed his mouth. "Anything else you want to share with us before we head back to the office and keep digging?"

Shouldn't they *go somewhere* and *look* for Hailey?

"Anything at all," Fitzgerald prompted.

They were putting too much pressure on her. Amelia revisited her two conversations with Camden. That didn't feel relevant, and besides, they had to know about their first phone call. The second one, she hoped they didn't. She'd redialed like a manic stalker until she reconnected with him. That was embarrassing, but she had to speak with the only person who'd actually helped in this whole mess. Camden was separate from what Fitzgerald and Bennett needed and sort of weirdly personal, even if he'd hadn't given her any information.

"All right, then," Bennett said, as though he didn't entirely believe her. "Thank you for your time."

God. That really pissed her off. She leaned forward. "Don't you think I would have mentioned if I'd seen Hailey?"

"Perhaps."

Perhaps? "I've been *trying* to get information out of anyone I could have *for days*. If Hailey had stopped by. If she'd called, if she magically stopped by, I would have said something."

"We're just doing our job," Fitzgerald offered.

"*I* asked *you* if you'd found her. Why would I ask that if I'd talked to her?"

They stood and promised to follow up, as if they hadn't heard Amelia snap at them.

Their perfunctory farewells made her want to scream as she let them out of the house. She closed the door with more gusto than was necessary and watched out the window to ensure they drove away. Only once she was sure they were gone did she return to the couch.

Her incredulity doubled as she replayed the conversation. They seemed to think she knew where Hailey was. Did she look like a woman who knew anything right now? She didn't need a mirror to see her rat's nest of hair that had been tied in a bun or her perpetually tear-swollen eyes.

Pain blossomed in her chest. Amelia missed Hailey so much that she couldn't breathe. Her gaze dropped to her arm, and she pulled the sweatshirt cuff up until she could see the faint numbers still legible on there. Her sister's handwriting was fading. It reminded her of the worst night of her life. Yet it was the last thing she had from Hailey.

CHAPTER SEVEN

THE LONG DAY had turned into a longer night. Sunlight disappeared earlier and earlier. The beautiful bright fall leaves had turned from their vivid yellows and reds to dreary, drab browns, as if the universe was in mourning. The sun hid. The leaves started to drop. Everywhere Amelia looked, life was moving on with a painful heaviness.

She'd spoken with Jonathan's parents. The plans for the funeral had been delayed—his body hadn't been released from the medical examiner, and the Dumonts would be traveling from out of the country, but they had asked if she wanted to include a ceremony for Hailey during his funeral. Amelia hadn't been able to say anything except that missing didn't mean dead.

They were kind and quiet, much like Jonathan. His parents clearly loved Hailey too. They all agreed the investigators were wrong about a domestic-dispute-turned-homicide. *Small miracles.* She wouldn't have been able to bear their judgement.

Still, she was depleted, mentally exhausted. But for whatever reason, sleep was elusive.

She'd never had problems sleeping. Now, every noise made her jump. Her mind raced from question to question. Memories replayed. Decisions were doubted.

Amelia glanced at the medicine bottles lined on her nightstand like little soldiers who promised sweet dreams: melatonin, allergy medicine, over-the-counter sleep aids. It was a smorgasbord of medication that had raised the eyebrows of the clerk at the pharmacy's checkout counter. She hadn't been able to decide which would be the best option to send her to dreamland and had bought everything.

"Sometimes, a nightcap works best," the clerk had offered.

"I'll put it on my list of things to try."

He finished scanning her purchases with pity in his eyes. The man had no idea how bad it really was.

She checked the time on her phone again. A half hour should have gone by, but only three minutes had passed. She still hadn't decided which pills to take, so she took none and stared at the bottles in the dark.

"Eeny, meenie, miney, moe..." Sleeping pills scared her. What if she took one and didn't wake up when she needed to? What if she'd taken one that night at Hailey and Jonathan's? Maybe she would be dead like her brother-in-law or missing like her sister. Or maybe nothing would have happened because she'd have been in the house and scared away whoever attacked her family.

That was the least likely situation, but it wasn't a zero percent chance. Guilt squeezed her chest. A sleeping pill might knock her out, or, since they weren't exactly potent pills, she'd be groggy and awake, wanting to sleep and worrying about when the sun would rise.

Instead of choosing which to take, Amelia grabbed her phone and redialed the number that would eventually reach Camden. He answered on the first ring.

"Do you ever take a night off?" she asked.

The rich roll of his laughter sent an unexpected wave of warmth through her chest. "How'd you get this number?" he asked.

She rolled onto her side and fluffed the pillow under her cheek. "What do you mean? I called the banana-light-bulb-chicken-heart number, and here you are."

"You got me the first time?"

"Yeah."

He laughed. "You were routed to my cell phone."

"What?" She sat up. "What... How?"

"I don't know. Do you have a pen handy?"

"Why?"

"Well, you might as well call me direct next time."

The tension in her chest relaxed as she sank back onto her pillow. A small, shy grin pulled at her cheeks. "Text it to me."

He confirmed that the number on his screen was hers and shot her a message. "There."

"You think I'm crazy for calling you, don't you?" she asked.

"I think," he said, his tone playful, "you've got a knack for keeping things interesting."

The tips of her ears warmed. "That's a polite way of saying yes."

"Do you think I'd give my number out to a crazy lady?"

Smiling, she hesitated. "Maybe? You're one of those sneaky agents that does secret things. So I don't think giving your number to a crazy lady ranks high on your risk list."

His easygoing laughter poured through the phone again. "I'm not whoever you think I am."

"You don't wear nondescript suits and dark sunglasses, flashing your badge like some guy playing the part in a movie?"

"Not a chance, sweetheart, and if you want the truth, I don't even have a badge."

"You're telling me I've been calling a *pretend* secret agent?" She laughed for the first time since the day everything went down. It was so foreign to Amelia that it felt like she'd broken an unwritten rule.

"I've said nothing that would make you think I'm a secret agent."

"You didn't have to. The code words and special phone number gave you away. Not to mention the fact that you were totally chill while someone was hunting me down. And I've seen your coworkers. So—"

"Whoever you've met, they aren't my teammates. That's one thing you can take to the bank."

"Teammates. That's an interesting choice of words."

"Maybe so…" He remained quiet, as though he'd wished he'd kept his mouth shut.

She hated that he might hang up. "Now that you've said too much, do you have to go?"

"I didn't, and I don't."

"All right…" She didn't believe him. Amelia shut her eyes. She liked his voice: honey smooth and warmly rough, unwavering. Even when the quiet hung between them, Camden didn't act as though the silence was as unnerving as she found it to be. "How many calls like mine do you get? There can't be super-top-secret problems that often."

"Honestly? You're my first."

"Huh… How come? Nothing ever goes wrong?"

"Not when I'm on duty," he teased.

"Have you ever heard that correlation is not connected to causation?" She smiled at his quiet laughter.

"We—the company I work for—were helping a federal agency with a problem."

"How did you manage to say all those words without saying a damn thing?"

"Just talented."

She stared at the ceiling of her bedroom and wondered how the stars had aligned to connect them. "I think Hailey and Jonathan worked for the government."

Camden didn't respond.

He didn't ask why she thought that, and he didn't dispel her of the notion.

Amelia cleared her throat and wished she could turn off her mind. "The stuff on the news about them is made up. I can't fathom how any reporter has been able to say things that never happened. They do so with such confidence, as if they were told lies from a reputable source."

Camden hummed noncommittally.

For the first time, she was telling someone her perspective. Thus far, every other conversation had been filled with condolences and mourning. None were about the craziness of the situation. She'd told no one what happened that night except for Camden, Bennett, and Fitzgerald, and she wasn't sure why. They hadn't told her to keep her story to herself. Maybe they didn't have to because it sounded impossible. "The agents who have stayed in contact with me are not normal."

"What's normal anyway?"

"You know what I mean. They talk in circles. They're not regular cops. I think it's something related to national security or spying."

Camden hummed again.

She couldn't believe she was saying her guesses out loud. Even more crazily, she couldn't believe he wasn't calling her absurd. "You're not saying anything."

"I think we both know that I can't confirm or deny a damn thing. Even if I knew."

"Which you don't..." She didn't entirely believe him, but he wasn't hanging up or laughing at her guesses. That was a kind of acknowledgment. "Are you in a top-secret lair somewhere? A nuclear fallout shelter? A secret room in the basement of the US Capitol?"

"I could tell you, but then I'd have to kill you."

"See, that's not fair." She chuckled. "You probably know how to without leaving a trace."

"All kidding aside, you doing okay, Amelia?"

A warm feeling swelled in her chest. It was almost enough to help her forget why she couldn't fall asleep. "You remember my name?"

"Well... yeah. Why would I give my number to someone if I didn't know their name?"

"Is Camden your real name?"

"Yeah. Cam. Camden. Whichever works."

She tried to imagine what he might look like: tall, broad, strong. At least his confidence made him sound that way. "That first night, you weren't supposed to tell me your name, were you?"

"Not really. No."

"Why did you?" she wondered aloud.

"You sounded scared."

What did he imagine her to be like? Feeble and afraid. Unable to help herself and begging someone on the phone to save her. It wasn't a great mental image. Amelia bit her bottom lip. "You weren't wrong."

Silence hung between them. It wasn't awkward—more like it was waiting for something else, but she didn't know what.

"Why did you call me tonight?" he asked.

Maybe she'd been scared, but not in the same way as that night. She was scared of the unknown, scared of the illogical. "I couldn't sleep. I can't get my mind to stop racing. So much doesn't make sense. Like the agents. The ones you don't work with, I guess. The same ones I spoke with the first night. They came by." Amelia rolled onto her back. "They asked if I'd seen my sister."

"If you'd *seen* your sister?"

"Yeah…"

"Huh. Seems like that's something you would've mentioned to someone."

"Exactly."

"What else?" he asked.

"They stopped by unannounced. Their questions made me uneasy, as if they thought I wasn't telling them a piece of important information. Then they just left. They didn't get the answer they wanted, so poof, they walked out."

He waited for a beat. "That's how it can be. They're searching for your sister and don't have time for pleasantries. I wouldn't hold it against them."

"Do you trust the people you work with?—I know, I know. You're not one of the suits with dark glasses. But you're in the same orbit, aren't you? Do you trust them?"

He paused again long enough that she noticed her heartbeat thump with each passing moment. "Of course."

She didn't believe him. "Eh, the jury's out on whether or not you're telling me the truth."

He laughed. "Ouch."

"So, you didn't say. Do you work in a secret basement office in the Capitol?"

He kept laughing. "No, why?"

"What about at the CIA? Or the FBI headquarters?" Those were in the DC area, weren't they? It seemed like he would be based nearby.

"You're just going to throw out all the mysterious federal agencies you can think of, aren't you?"

She snorted, but that might have been her plan. "Has anyone ever told you that you're an evasive answerer?"

"All part of my training," he joked. "Why don't you get some sleep? If the agents stop by again, answer their questions, and try not to read too much into what they say or don't."

"Is that what you would do?" she asked.

"Probably. Yeah."

"I don't believe you."

"Get some sleep, and take care of yourself, Amelia."

She didn't have a reason to keep him on the phone but didn't want the call to end. His voice was soothing and made her feel safe, as though this man with all the answers and some of the excuses could erase the nightmare she'd been trying to manage.

The line disconnected. She checked her text messages and saw his number. She opened the message.

Camden Brooks

Just his name. To the point and without bullshit—just like him. She saved him in her phone. His name and number were comforting, but they didn't make her any sleepier.

Amelia rolled onto her back again and stared at the ceiling. She decided against taking sleeping medicine and futilely tried a couple of tricks. She counted sheep, but that became a game of how fast she could think of the numbers. Then Amelia tried to count backward from a thousand. The task proved boring but not in a way that made her drowsy.

Sleep. Go to sleep. Demanding that she fall asleep only made her more frustrated and wider awake.

Her phone screen illuminated on the nightstand with a silent incoming phone call, and she smiled when she saw his name. She answered, "Hey."

"Amelia. Hey."

Her heart hammered a hundred miles an hour. The way he said her name made her insides flip.

"I'm glad it's you," she said.

"How many people call you in the middle of the night?"

Her stomach fluttered. She grinned into her pillow. "Only you."

"Good to hear."

She curled her knees to her belly and held the phone close. "Did you decide to tell me about your super-secret office?"

The quiet rumble of his amusement skimmed over her senses. "No. Sorry to disappoint."

He wouldn't disappoint her. "You would not believe the secret lair I've conjured up in my head."

"Trust me. The place I work is more than you can imagine."

"I have a very creative, very vivid imagination." She caught herself, wondering if that sounded like something other than how she meant it. A blush warmed her cheeks, and she quickly added, "Did you ever watch that movie *Men in Black*? The one with Will Smith and the aliens? That's about where my head's at."

He laughed. "Pretty close. Sans the aliens."

"Ah, man. Too bad."

"I don't mean to keep you up. I know it's the middle of the night where you are—"

"But not you?"

"Not exactly—that's for another day, okay?"

She liked that their conversation would continue. Amelia snuggled against her pillow. "Okay."

"I had a quick thought, and I'm probably off base and out of line, but what the hell."

"I'm all ears."

"If you see those agents again and your gut tells you something's off... I want you to listen to your gut."

She rolled her lips together. Gone were the warm and fuzzy feelings that had enveloped her like a safe cocoon. He knew better than she, and his words sounded a lot like a warning. She trusted him. As random and unknown as he was, he was the only person on her side.

"Do you know who they are?" she asked.

"No. I swear, but... you never know in my line of work."

"The super-secret phone-answering profession."

He chortled. "Yeah. Exactly. Those are my people, even if they're not. We're all in the same orbit, like you said. We all have our motivations and marching orders. Sometimes it gets a bit murky."

"Murky?"

"You should watch out for yourself."

Concern needled the bottom of her stomach. He was validating what she sensed.

"Do you know more than you're telling me?"

"I swear I don't. But I know the system, and that's enough to listen to your instincts. Promise me?"

Her instincts said Camden was where she should put her trust. If she didn't know which way was up, she would ask him. Her sister had trusted him—even if it hadn't been Camden specifically. That was what Amelia would lean into.

"I promise."

CHAPTER EIGHT

C AMDEN SAT AT the bar on the far barstool in one of the restaurants that his teammates weren't likely to frequent. He wasn't sure where the avoidance came from. He rolled a glass half-filled with Coke between his palms and studied the upscale space.

Titan Group's Abu Dhabi headquarters was as far away as Amelia Stone likely imagined. Camden tried to conjure up what she might think of his workplace, but no matter what she came up with, it probably wasn't going to be a two-tower gilded skyscraper hotel.

The building served as an exclusive hotel that catered to princes and billionaires, at least on the surface. In reality, it was an elaborate cover that brought in money and provided a safe place in the somewhat inhospitable, unpredictable Middle East region.

Jared started Titan Group out of sheer willpower, strong connections, and an unflappable sense of right and wrong. But Titan also played in the gray. They took jobs that weren't necessarily paid for, and that hotel helped to foot the bill.

Titan's Abu Dhabi headquarters was hard for Camden to absorb. Growing up in New Jersey, he hadn't known anything like that existed. He'd joined the army after a recruiter promised he would see the world. Naively, he'd believed the man.

Yeah, he'd seen the world, but where he was currently was a better fit: more flexibility, more adventure, more excitement. He was an everyday guy living in the land of more, more, more, where Maseratis were a dime a dozen.

Most people were probably like him and couldn't fathom the place. *Could Amelia?* She'd mentioned a creative, vivid imagination. Her words lingered in his mind and tightened the muscles in his chest. He couldn't explain why. He didn't know anything about her and purposefully hadn't searched the internet for her picture.

That hadn't stopped Shah and Amanda, though. Shah reported on Amelia's lack of social media with the exception of an event-planning company she owned. Amanda had needed only a fraction of a second to find Amelia's picture. Still, Camden had refused to look.

He could explain his indifference to social media. People posted only what they wanted the world to see, and it was rarely the truth. Amelia Stone didn't want anyone to see much. What did that say? He was curious.

Amanda had also found pages of internet hits on Amelia's company, Events and Occasions. Many corporate and philanthropic organizations appeared to have utilized her services. Events and Occasions was also often mentioned on society pages that showed off weddings and parties of the who's who in Washington, DC.

Camden had scrolled through a few of the company's online hits. Without dropping Amelia's name, they managed to share that she was an excellent event planner. She liked to be behind the scenes. She was successful and well regarded. He could see that in the woman he'd spoken to on the phone. He also sensed from her success and their brief conversations that she was someone that wouldn't be told a cover story without pressing for the truth.

Out of the corner of his eye, Camden saw Liam walk up to the bar. He sighed, not in the mood to talk. It wasn't because he'd been assigned to desk duty for what felt like a hellacious amount of time, it was that desk duty had given him a puzzle he couldn't stop thinking about. Maybe Camden shouldn't have taken a break in that restaurant. If he'd really wanted to be alone, he could've gone to his apartment.

Liam pulled himself onto a barstool and ordered a Coke.

Camden raised his chin when the bartender asked if he wanted his soda topped off as well. "What's going on, man?"

Liam thanked the bartender for his drink and turned to Camden. "What the hell are you doing in here? Didn't think this place was your scene."

He shrugged in agreement. "I didn't think this place was anyone's scene unless the ladies wanted a celebration or a party." He was astounded by how their team had morphed from a gathering of single men to family guys. He didn't begrudge anyone their happiness but did find it perplexing.

"Yet here you are," Liam pointed out.

He nodded. "What's up, man?"

"I don't know. Boss Man wanted me to feel something out, and here I find you hiding."

He shot Liam a glance. "I'm not hiding."

"If you say so." Liam took a long drink and set the glass down. "You feel like going back to the US for bit?"

Camden's eyebrow arched. His heart kickstarted. "What for?"

"To have a sit-down with Beth Tourne."

"From the CIA?"

"Do you know another Beth Tourne?"

"I don't know *any* Beth Tournes. There's probably a better person to meet with one of their people." If not Liam, then Chance, Hagan, or Sawyer would be a more responsible Titan representative. They were dependable, trusted. They were the ones assigned to complicated jobs that required more gravitas than he had ever been interested in giving to a project.

Liam narrowed his gaze and scrutinized Camden. "Huh."

"What?"

"What the hell is going on with you?"

"Nothing."

"Then since when are you not raring to go on assignment?" Liam pressed.

Camden raised his shoulders with feigned indifference. He couldn't shake his fascination with Amelia Stone, and that was enough that he wanted to avoid Beth Tourne.

Liam sipped his soda. "I'm not one to question Boss Man. He usually has a plan and a dozen backup plans."

That, Camden knew all too well, which made him even more uncomfortable, especially since he wanted to learn more about Amelia with each passing moment. "Jared could find someone who's on the same continent as her."

"Obviously, Cam, but he said you."

Camden pursed his lips. A hundred thoughts ran through his head. He drummed his fingers against the sweating soda glass. "Any update as to why the CIA had to farm out its call center?"

Liam shook his head. "Ask Beth." He gave him a hard look. "Any reason in particular you don't want to take a cushy job?"

He batted the drink between his palms and wished it were a football instead. At least that would help him think. "You know the girl? Amelia Stone? She was thrown into all this without any information. No one's debriefed her. She sees the bullshit cover story, yet no one is telling her a damn thing."

"Maybe they want *you* to do their dirty work."

"Maybe." *Would that be such a bad thing? Yeah, it would.* He didn't realize it until right then, but he'd put Amelia Stone on one hell of a pedestal. "It'd be a no-brainer if you wanted me to haul ass into a building with some terrorist trying to blow my brains out. But the CIA? I don't know if I have the stomach for their particular blend of bullshit."

"Do you think *Amelia* has what it takes to stomach it?"

Camden half laughed. "I think that woman can handle anything thrown at her." He lifted his shoulders again. "Whether she should have to or not? I don't know. That's a different story."

TITAN'S PRIVATE JET touched down at Dulles Airport outside Washington, DC. Camden scrubbed a hand over his face and into his dark tousled hair. The time change wouldn't bother him. Neither would the solitude of a solo gig. But he wasn't sure about an assignment that was more talk than action. His work preference could be summarized as: get in, get the job done, get out. Talking to spooks wasn't the least bit interesting.

The jet came to a stop at a private terminal. He glanced out the oval window. A standard black Suburban with government plates was waiting for him to deplane. His mind skipped through his upcoming day. The Suburban would take him to meet Beth. Parker had briefed Camden on her but hadn't had much to say. Beth was new to the CIA. She had a redacted personal history that had led her to a job in which she could reinvent her life and live it up as a party girl. Beth was doing her damnedest to be photographed at exclusive parties on the arms of DC's diplomatic and political crowd. Camden wondered if any those parties had been handled by Events and Occasions. All in all, Beth and Camden wouldn't have much in common.

A US customs inspector boarded the jet. He had a quick conversation with the flight staff then Camden. Their paperwork and passports were processed, and he was free to deplane.

Camden thanked the flight crew and retrieved his duffel bag. The crisp fall air was refreshing, even if tinged with diesel fuel and burnt brake rubber. The bright morning sunlight reflected off the runway. A man wearing a suit and dark sunglasses jumped out of the driver's seat and opened the back passenger door.

Camden cleared his throat. "Hey. Morning."

"Mr. Brooks." The driver scanned their surroundings as he waited for Camden to get in. "I hope you had a nice flight."

"Slept through most of it." He reached for the door, but it was closed for him. Camden shifted uncomfortably on the leather seat. "You know," he said when the driver sat behind the steering wheel, "I'm normally the guy who scans the perimeter for threat assessments."

The driver nodded as if he understood Camden's background and eased the vehicle toward the private terminal exit. "Just doing my job. You work for Titan Group?"

Camden nodded. "Yeah. Ever work with us?"

"Absolutely. Chauffeur duty isn't my usual. There's a Titan team based nearby. They're rowdy but a good bunch." He glanced in the rearview mirror. "Where are you based out of?"

"Abu Dhabi." They passed through a security checkpoint. "Very different from where I used to call home."

"Where was that?"

"New Jersey."

He laughed. "How'd you end up out there?"

Camden shook his head. "Sometimes, I don't look before I leap. But it's worked out pretty good."

They rolled out of the airport and onto the express lanes toward Washington, DC. The CIA had offered an upscale apartment near Beth's, but when given the choice between a swanky place in DC or a more private small house in Virginia, he'd chosen the suburbs. Small and private trumped swank every day of the week. But before he could check out the housing arrangements, Camden had to deal with Beth.

He wore dark pants and a shirt that could transition from a twelve-hour flight to a boardroom meeting without much headache. Almost an hour later, they pulled up to the Hay-Adams Hotel. Camden had known what to expect of the fancy hotel and the people that would go in and out of its sophisticated space. He had only guesses about the CIA's goals in meeting him.

"You can leave your belongings here." The driver slowed near some construction barriers and pulled into a handsome horseshoe driveway.

"Pretty good-looking place." Camden eyed the strategic cover of the column-flanked portico that protectively guarded the hotel's entrance, then he studied his surroundings.

Meticulously tended landscaping painted a beautiful barrier between the hotel and the taxi-lined street. Considering the gilded hotel where he lived and worked, Camden wasn't sure why he felt so out of place.

"Definitely nothing to sneeze at."

The driver laughed. "That's one of the best ways I've heard this place described."

They parked in front of an arching door flanked by gaslit candles. Camden jumped out before the man behind the wheel could try to get his door. "Thanks for the lift."

The lobby reminded Camden of his hotel home in Abu Dhabi. The two hotels didn't look alike—the Abu Dhabi hotel lobby was gilded and gleaming in a way that couldn't touch the Hay-Adams's old money sophistication. Both hotels held an air of expectation. Those who crossed their thresholds were people who did things in the world—some for the better, some for themselves. But they were both places where access and privilege were both expected and guarded.

Beth waited in the lobby for him. Even without Parker's briefing and her headshot, Camden would have known her the moment his gaze landed on her. Though understated, she stood out in a way that demanded notice. She had a great smile, and her presence probably made anyone whose hand she shook believe every word that slipped out of her mouth. Camden didn't trust her.

She walked toward him with the confidence of a woman without a worry in the world, hand outstretched, eyes sighting him like a cruise missile locking onto a target. "How was your flight?" Her grip was strong.

The corners of his lips rose. "Uneventful."

"Those are the best kinds of flights." She led them through the posh lobby to a restaurant where she bypassed the staff and brought Camden to a private room set with a small table for four. Beth closed the glass-paned French doors behind herself and gestured for him to take a seat.

"Are we expecting others to join us?" *Amelia?* Anticipation percolated in his chest. Of course she wouldn't join them. There would be no reason. But that didn't quell the odd hope that she would appear.

"I just like room to spread out." Beth tilted her head. "And, if I'm being honest…"

Camden doubted whatever she'd say next would be true.

"This room makes me feel like a princess."

All right. No Amelia. That was good. Also, maybe Beth *had* told the truth. Who wouldn't feel like royalty with the starched white linens and crystal glasses? The window treatments could've been hung in Buckingham Palace. The table setting was fit for dinner with a king.

Camden chose a seat that faced the French doors and gave him a good angle on the windows. If someone had to have their back to the world, it would be Beth.

She didn't seem to notice and easily took the spot across from him, asking, "Have you eaten here before?"

"Nope."

Beth picked up the menu placard placed artfully on their plates. "I hope you're hungry. I really love the kitchen here. The—"

"You've been in the kitchen?" He hated the pretentious way she was buttering him up and wished she'd cut to the chase.

Her eyebrow crooked, and a smile curved. "I love their menu. If you're a mushroom guy, their mushroom omelet will make your eyes roll to the back of your head. But if you don't mind the wait, the oatmeal soufflé is so good."

"I'm more of a bacon-and-potatoes-breakfast kinda guy."

"You could do both. Uncle Sam's treat."

He tried to gauge her behavior and sense what she wanted, though she wasn't easy to read. "So, whom am I talking to right now? The CIA or the socialite?"

"Can't it be both?" Beth followed his gaze and turned as their waitress arrived with a friendly greeting and an offer of still or sparkling water. He went with still. Beth asked for sparkling—no big surprise there. They both ordered the oatmeal soufflé. He also asked for side orders of bacon, ham, and potatoes. Beth requested espresso. Camden asked for coffee without bells and whistles. Their predictability was nearly comical.

"All right." He crossed his arms. "Consider me adequately wined and dined."

Beth scowled. "Our order hasn't even been called into the kitchen yet."

"Why did I fly halfway around the world to meet with you?"

"You're not even going to pretend to have a good time first?"

He forced a smile so large and fake he could've been on a toothpaste commercial. "Loving every moment." His face returned to normal.

The waitress returned with coffee service with as many bells and whis-tles as were possible. Fresh fruit plates arrived.

"We didn't order that," Camden pointed out.

Beth rolled her eyes but speared her melon with her fork. "Back to the business at hand." She nibbled. "I'm mostly here to answer your questions and let the powers that be know if you're too nosy."

His eyebrows arched. He found her honesty disarming, which only made him more suspicious. "Is that right?"

"More or less." She shrugged dismissively. "We've had quite the clusterfuck on our hands, and I don't know when it will wrap up. The fallout's been scattershot and *bad*."

"Do you know if Hailey Dumont is still alive?"

Beth chewed thoughtfully. "I don't." Her next shrug was far less unencumbered. A heaviness pulled her shoulders down even as she tried to hide her reaction. "I hope she is. I wasn't their handler, but I spent a lot of time playing intermediary between them and…" She gestured blankly with her fork as if the Dumonts' social network was hard to explain.

"They were your friends?"

Her eyebrows arched as her eyes went down and searched for the best piece of fruit. She used her fork to scoot each piece around. "Yes." She swallowed hard and stabbed a grape, which she ate quickly. Beth sipped her sparkling water. "We circulated in many of the same social circles. Though they worked on assignments that I didn't go anywhere near other than to meet the movers and shakers. Hailey and Jonathan were hands-on in a way that didn't work for my cover."

What kind of work could art people get into that a socialite wouldn't want to associate with? "You going to leave me hanging like that, or what?"

Her lips curled as if she had a secret that amused her to no end. "I'm going to introduce you to someone who worked with them. It'll be easier than reading you in from a redacted report. She can explain things in a way that I quite honestly don't know how to."

"Why isn't she here too?"

Beth grinned. "Lots of reasons. But the biggest one is that seeing her office makes her job… easier to appreciate and less scary."

He laughed. "I don't scare easily, Beth Tourne."

"Ohhh, big surprise, Camden Brooks. But you'll have to trust me."

Agitation fueled his foot, which tapped under the table. He wasn't the person who needed to meet anyone. He wasn't the one searching for answers. "Why aren't you talking to Amelia Stone about this?" He didn't want to ask why she wasn't there, since she had no reason to be at their breakfast meeting—except she was the one with all the questions for the CIA. "You have two agents breathing down her neck. They're unhelpful and making her problems worse."

Beth took a deep breath and let it out slowly. She set her fork down, pursed her lips, and looked out the window. "I really wish Amelia hadn't been there."

"Well, she was." Camden took a bite of melon. "I bet she wished nothing happened to her family to start with."

Beth nodded.

"You guys need to rein in your bulldogs. The ones who have been knocking on her door, asking her asinine questions. She's a civilian."

Beth demurred, fanning his aggravation.

He tried to recalibrate his attitude. Camden lifted his coffee cup, which was delicate enough that he might crack it if he didn't pay attention when setting it down. "What's going on? What actually happened?"

Beth laser focused her attention on the lone strawberry left on her plate. She moved it around with her fork and eventually ate it, at which she point she chewed methodically and bought time to formulate her answer. "You're aware that we are dealing with an ongoing breach in our network?"

"Yeah. That's how I was pulled into this whole mess."

"Many covers were blown. Everyone was on a heightened alert. One of the Dumonts' targets likely realized they were under surveillance and..." Beth frowned. "They turned the situation around and eliminated the Dumonts."

"That doesn't make any sense. Why take Hailey if they killed Jonathan?"

"How do you know it's a they and not a singular person?" Beth volleyed.

God. He disliked the way the CIA did business. Everything was fun and games.

Camden smirked. "Other than what Amelia saw, I meant the royal, all-encompassing they. Because I don't know jack shit."

Beth studied him. "If Amelia's story is to be believed—"

"*If it's to be believed?* I was on the phone with her."

"You heard what she wanted you to believe."

"Oh, give me a break."

"I'm simply pointing out that you don't know who she is and only believed her because she added tears to her voice and panic to her words. She could've played you—"

"Are you out of your—" He caught himself and bit the inside of his cheeks. "*They* went after her and the Dumonts simultaneously. *They* probably see her as a potential witness. Their worst-case scenario was probably Amelia reaching out for help, which she did. I don't know why you don't have her in protective custody."

Beth ignored his jab.

Camden shook his head. He wasn't going to get anything from Beth. He ran a hand over his face. "Other than your harebrained idea about Amelia, you don't know who they are?"

Beth shook her head. "Not the slightest clue. But remember, I'm not a handler. I wouldn't be privy to that information."

He lifted his palms, frustrated. "Why isn't their handler here?"

The corners of Beth's eyes tightened. Her expression faltered almost imperceptibly before she neutralized it. "She's dead."

"Well… shit."

That caught him off guard. The Dumonts weren't the only victims.

"I'm guessing natural causes have been ruled out."

"They have."

"Are your powers that be assuming the same person who went after the Dumonts went after the handler?"

"That's so far above my pay grade that I haven't asked."

Camden sipped his coffee and thought over the situation. "Their handler's dead. Jonathan's dead. Hailey is missing. They took her because…?"

Beth shrugged as if his wildest guesses could be valid.

Camden continued, "They'll interrogate her until she breaks. And if she doesn't, it'll be the same fate as if she had."

Beth nodded. "Survival is unlikely."

"And you have no idea what they want to know?"

"Not a clue. No one read me into the information they were passing along."

How did this all circle back to Amelia? Why had investigators asked if she was aware of her sister's location? "What's going to happen with Amelia?"

"The public-facing investigation will turn up as many salacious possibilities as possible. Names will be muddied, and motives will be tossed around like confetti."

"Anything to murk up the investigation," he concluded. "Bet their families will love that."

"That's the ugly truth of things." Beth swept her hair off her face. "Collateral damage will be small and manageable. It's really just Amelia."

"No parents or other siblings?"

"Hailey and Amelia have a distant aunt who begrudgingly fostered them when they were teenagers. From all reports, it wasn't a happy home, and there hasn't been contact in years."

Amelia didn't have any family other than Hailey.

He shook his head. "What about his family?"

"His parents have lived in France for years."

Beth wasn't telling him something.

Camden scrutinized her. "And?"

"I assume they're devastated about their son. I haven't spoken with them."

Camden waited for whatever Beth was dragging out.

Beth relented. "They're familiar with the possibilities that might unfold during this process."

He gave Beth a sidelong glance. "They're spooks too?"

Her facial expression confirmed his assumption. "You know I couldn't tell you that even if I knew."

"Which, of course, you don't," he muttered.

"Of course."

The waitress arrived and served their main course. If decadence was a dish, it was oatmeal soufflé with fresh fruit compote. He wouldn't have guessed oatmeal could look as regal as the room in which they were dining, but it did. Camden tried the piping hot, light-as-air soufflé and had to give Beth credit for all but demanding he order the dish. This thing was treat enough for him to ignore the bacon and potato side dishes he'd ordered.

They finished their soufflés before talking shop again, as though the rough-and-ugly world they lived in shouldn't touch their meal. Finally, Camden picked at his bacon and potatoes while Beth sipped her espresso. "I think Amelia needs to be read in as much as she can be."

Beth laughed. "What purpose would that serve?"

"She knows a lot more than—"

"And she'll forget it."

"Oh, come on. That's bullshit. She knows what she knows, whether you confirm anything or not."

"I have no influence whatsoever when it comes to the spin."

"Your spin masters have agents asking questions like if she's seen her sister. What kind of crap is that?"

"Like I said. It's going to get ugly before it gets better."

He'd learned all he could from meeting Beth. "Why the hell am I here? We could have had this conversation over a secure line."

Beth studied him and lowered her gaze to her espresso, forehead pinched as though trying to work through calculus.

"What is it, Beth?" He laid his napkin on the table. "Because I'm done. Thanks for the great meal and all, but you're holding back, and I've wasted my time."

"If we tell her about her sister, it will change everything about their relationship."

"Do you think Amelia cares?" He scoffed. "Hell, since when does the CIA care about emotional fallout?"

"I don't know her, but for whatever reason, you seem to know what she thinks about. Care to explain that?"

Her accusation stopped him cold. He should push back and demand Beth stay in her lane. He could tell her to worry about the relatives of their agent, but that wouldn't help Amelia. She wanted answers, and he wanted them for her. "She deserves to know."

"If she learns about Hailey, Amelia will open herself up to a world she didn't know about. To dangers she's otherwise inoculated to."

"I think she wants to find her sister and doesn't care if you pull back the curtain on whatever seedy, sketchy situation you're so worried will sully her worldview. Give the woman an opportunity to handle the information instead of gaslighting her with a bullshit cover story?"

Beth gave a small shrug. "Again, none of this is my call, but I will pass along your thoughts."

He smiled flatly.

"Are you going to see her while you're out here?" Beth asked.

"No."

His answer surprised them both. Beth eyed him expectantly and cupped her hands around the espresso. "Stick around for a couple days. We may need Titan's help closing up loose ends with the Dumont investigation."

"Aye, aye, captain." But Camden didn't take marching orders from the CIA. He would follow whatever directives Boss Man handed out.

CHAPTER NINE

AMELIA LAID HER cell phone on the coffee table and curled into a ball on her couch. She had punted her work responsibilities to her assistant–turned–business partner Veronica, just as Amelia had every day for the last week. *Or has it been a week and a half?* She hadn't done a good job of keeping track. Events and Occasions was a small but successful operation. Veronica would keep the trains running.

The last item on Amelia's to-do list was a conversation with Jonathan's parents. They were distraught. No parent should ever bury a child. But they worried over *her*, as though they could handle their grief better than Amelia. That only made her feel worse. She wasn't sure how much worse she could feel at the moment and decided to call them later.

The doorbell rang. *Seriously?* She couldn't escape from the world. Mental exhaustion pulled her eyelids shut. Why hadn't she hung a No Soliciting sign on the front door? Or she could have taped a piece of cardboard with "No" written in giant letters over the doorbell to warn away visitors. Either would have been loud and clear: Stay away. But she hadn't—too tired, too devastated, too everything.

The doorbell rang again.

"Go away."

Then her cell phone rang. Would this nightmare of a day ever end?

A loud, thumping knock banged on her door.

Good God. Come on. Couldn't the world leave her to mope in peace? "Fine. Coming!"

Amelia wrapped the fluffy blanket around her shoulders and, clad in her pajamas in the middle of the afternoon, dragged herself toward the door. She glanced out the peephole, and her heart stopped, frozen with dread that cemented in her veins with a sick, nauseating despair. Police cruiser lights twirled behind Agents Fitzgerald and Bennet. Hailey had been found.

Amelia opened the door, dizzy with a wave of grief. But the churning in her stomach worsened when she saw behind the two men. Half a dozen police vehicles lined her condominium parking lot.

"Wh-What's going on?"

Fitzgerald's and Bennett's jaws were locked in the same no-nonsense position. Their hard stares locked on her as though she were a criminal. "This is a warrant to search the premises, your vehicle, and all electronic devices."

That didn't make sense. "What? Mine?"

"You can come outside." Fitzgerald gave her bare feet and pajamas a once-over. "Or we can assign an officer to stand with you inside."

"Inside... my condo?" They wanted to look in her house? "Why?"

Fitzgerald beckoned to a female officer who was about Amelia's age and barked, "Stay with her."

"Ma'am," the other woman greeted Amelia professionally as she stepped inside.

Amelia stumbled back. Bennett held up the search warrant. She couldn't focus, much less read the document. She backed up until she hit the wall. Law enforcement streamed into her house.

"This is about... my sister?" Of course it was. *Do I need a lawyer?* But she was the victim—*one* of the victims. "Why would I know anything about Hailey and Jonathan?"

The agents entering her condo wore matching uniforms of khaki pants and white polo shirts. They never looked Amelia in the eye as they tromped into her small space with their bags and containers as though they were going to find evidence.

Amelia found Bennet and Fitzgerald in her kitchen. She focused her wobbly attention on the nicer of the two. "I don't understand."

"Read the warrant," Bennett answered for Fitzgerald.

"Or get an attorney to read it," Fitzgerald suggested.

An attorney. God. She knew hundreds of attorneys. Some days, everyone in the DC metro area seemed to be one, but she didn't know what kinds of lawyers they were. Her business had a CPA who was also an attorney. Her neighbor two doors down might have been one also. A solid percentage of her clients were attorneys. Instinctively, she thought of calling Hailey. Hailey always knew what to do. It had been that way since they were kids. But a punch slammed Amelia in the gut. She couldn't call Hailey.

The group of agents moved through her space with practiced efficiency, as if they knew where her makeshift home office was situated and where her bedroom was. Someone snagged her laptop. Another bagged her cell phone.

"Um, can I make a phone call first?"

The officer assigned as the babysitter shook her head. "I can take you to get dressed and call you an Uber."

"They're taking my car?"

"It will take a while to search it. They won't impound it unless they need a more thorough review, but they'll take your phone—"

This was too much. They were treating her like a criminal, like Jonathan's murderer. Her despair boiled into fury.

Amelia stormed into her kitchen, tears falling down her cheeks. She didn't understand. "Why is this happening?"

Was she in trouble? They thought she was hiding Hailey? Or had killed Jonathan? That didn't make sense. Before that day, the closest Amelia had been to getting in trouble was looking the other way when a client crammed more people than had RSVPed into an event hall. Amelia's level of trouble was upsetting the fire marshal. This was not the fire marshal. This was far beyond code violations. This was needing a criminal attorney.

Bennett approached her with an expression that turned her stomach.

"What?" she asked.

They couldn't have found anything. There was nothing to find. She had nothing to do with this.

"What's wrong?"

"Amelia Stone, you're under arrest for the murder of Jonathan and

Hailey Dumont—"

"*Hailey?*" Her knees buckled.

The female officer caught her before Amelia's limp noodle legs let her hit the floor.

"You found my sister—" Bile churned into her throat. "She's dead?"

"Anything you say can and will be used against you…"

The officer holding Amelia on her feet managed to turn her around. The cold snap of a handcuff bit her wrist.

They were arresting her. She didn't know what reason they had to be in her condo or what they had found. She'd told them everything—more than that, she knew she hadn't done anything to hurt her family. Questions tornadoed through her mind. The second handcuff secured her other wrist.

Tears poured down her cheeks. "You found Hailey?"

"Do you understand these rights?"

Amelia understood nothing, neither the words they were saying nor their line of questioning throughout the investigation. They hadn't specified that Hailey had been found. No one said Hailey wasn't alive. But they'd said *murder*.

Agent Fitzgerald took a pair of shoes from the pile of abandoned footwear by her front door and dropped them at her feet. "Slip these on."

Amelia obeyed and awkwardly shoved her feet into them like sandals.

Then Fitzgerald nodded to the officer at Amelia's side. "Grab her a coat."

After a moment, one was draped over her shoulders. They tugged her along. She was like a zombie. Amelia moved as though she weren't in control of her body, as if she were watching herself in a movie. They shuffled her toward an oversized unmarked Suburban in a parking lot filled with spectators and flashing lights. Her stomach sloshed with every step. Bile teased the back of her throat as though she would retch.

"Watch your head," the officer said, all but lifting Amelia into the back of the blacked-out vehicle that swallowed her whole.

The back seat of her idling prison was warm and new-car scented. Heat wrapped around her as she lost control, sobbing as the officer buckled her into place, hands caught behind her back.

She needed to ask for a lawyer. She needed to make a phone call. But the words wouldn't come out of her mouth. She wanted to talk to Camden. Did anyone here know him? Could she call him? He wasn't a lawyer. All she needed to do was demand a lawyer—they would sort out this nightmare—but when she opened her mouth, the only thing that came out was, "Is Hailey really dead?"

CHAPTER TEN

AFTER THE HAY-ADAMS brunch meeting with Beth, Camden spent the afternoon debriefing with Parker, though he didn't think there was all that much to discuss. Afterward, Camden met up with a few of the guys he knew on Titan's US team. They went out for beers, but Amelia never left his mind. The next day, she was still there as he stepped off the metro at Union Station.

They didn't have a reason to meet. For all intents and purposes, he was finished with this job. Camden's only responsibility was to wait for Jared and the CIA to decide nothing was left to discuss—though Beth had thought he should meet one of the Dumonts' points of contact. Still, that didn't have anything to do with Amelia—and Amelia was the person he wanted to meet with.

But that would be strange. He couldn't just ask a random person he'd spoken to on a phone call to meet up. However, it wasn't just one phone call, and she wasn't a random person, at least not anymore.

After overthinking the situation, Camden decided the only meeting he needed to have was with his family. New Jersey was a short couple of hours away if he jumped on Amtrak. Surprising his brothers would be exactly what he needed to clear his mind. That was the plan.

With a train ticket purchased and half an hour to kill, Camden mixed in with the morning commuter crowd and searched for a coffee shop. He found a deli that served breakfast and no-fuss coffee. The smell of cheesy, melty breakfast sandwiches made his mouth water.

He got in line and took his phone out. He could text Amelia. Or he could delete her number and never talk to her again. Camden scrubbed a hand over his face. This wasn't like him. He never doubted himself, especially when it came to women.

Was this a woman thing? She'd certainly piqued his interest.

The problem was they'd never met. He didn't even know what she looked like. That had been a purposeful decision. It was like a built-in barrier to avoid a complication. Somehow, someway, he liked Amelia a lot—insomuch as a person could like another *a lot* after a few short although somewhat life-changing conversations.

The line hadn't moved. A dull grumble of complaints surrounded Camden as he cleared his mind of Amelia.

"We don't have fifty everything bagels," the cashier told the man in front of Camden. By the sound of it, that wasn't the first time it had been said. "I have about a dozen left. That's it. Take it or leave it."

Camden had totally zoned out and now glanced at the time. He still had plenty of room to spare before his train departed, but a big order from the guy in front of him might screw up his schedule.

"Look, I don't think you understand." The man in front of Camden leaned onto the counter. "The bagels are for *very important* people, and if I don't show up on the Hill with them, *very important* people are going to be upset. So, can you find them or defrost them or whatever you have to do so I can pay and be on my way?"

The exasperated cashier blinked slowly. "We. Don't. Have. Them."

"I heard what you said." The guy pulled out his wallet and extracted a wad of cash. "But there's a really solid tip—"

"I'm going on break," the cashier announced.

The line of waiting customers groaned.

"Come on, asshole," someone said from behind Camden. "Get a fuck-ing grip. They don't have what you want."

The man in front of Camden turned to face off against the line. "If I don't have the bagels when I walk into my office, I'm gonna get fired. So, fuck you, and give me a minute while I get this straightened out."

"Fuckin' hell," Camden muttered under his breath. He pinched the bridge of his nose, remembering why he hated Washington, DC, and most everyone inside its city limits. The majority of the area's residents were fine. But that special breed of jackass drawn to politics and power grated on his senses.

Another cashier, looking forewarned and fully capable of handling customers who caused headaches, took the place of the first. Her gaze skipped straight to Camden. "Can I help whoever's next?"

He sidestepped the jackass holding up the line. "I'll take a number two."

"You can't cut in front of me, asshole."

"A number two," Camden repeated. "*On an everything bagel.*"

"Oh, give me a fuckin' break. That's my everything bagel."

The corners of his lips quirked. He normally would've ordered an Asiago bagel. *Not today.* "Don't think it is."

"Anything else?" the cashier asked.

"Large coffee. Black."

Camden casually tapped his credit card on the reader and gave the cashier a nice tip and a commiserating grimace when she returned with the steaming hot cup.

"Next?" the cashier called, still ignoring the man huffing about his VIP order of everything bagels.

He stepped around the man and moved to the far counter to wait for his order. A muted television showed the local news. The meteorologist pointed at a map of falling temperatures as fall turned into winter. DC was pretty that time of year. That was about the only thing the place had going for it.

He checked the time and glanced at the line again, where the man was still ranting about the very important people on the Hill. The line of customers progressed without him. Camden might have been wrong, but he was pretty sure he'd started a trend. The next several orders included at least one everything bagel.

In record time, his order was called. The waxy paper bag crinkled in his hand. He grabbed a handful of napkins and caught sight of the television screen again. The mugshot of a woman about his age was above a chyron that read Arlington Double Murder Suspect Arrested. A prickle of unease slid down his spine. "Hey." Camden gestured toward the television. "Would you mind turning that up?"

The woman bagging orders glanced over her shoulder. Another person shrugged and unmuted the local broadcast.

"Thanks."

But the news anchor had pivoted to another story. The screen flashed to a brightly smiling reporter who stood in front of a building with its front door wrapped in a brilliant red bow. The closed-captioning scrolled across the bottom of the screen, announcing the ribbon cutting for a recently completed renovation of a community center.

"You can mute it again. Thanks." Camden took a seat, pulled out his phone, and searched the internet for an arrest in a double murder in Arlington, Virginia.

It didn't take long. Amelia Stone had been charged with two counts of murder. There weren't many details. Her mug shot landed like a gut punch thrown by a missile launcher. Amelia Stone's delicate features were distorted by red-rimmed, puffy eyes partially framed by a half moon of dark circles. Her raven hair hung limply behind her back. He couldn't stop staring at the woman he'd spoken to—at the woman he had helped and knew to be innocent—but he finally tore himself away from the mug shot and searched for additional information.

He didn't get much beyond the repetitive facts regurgitated by local news. But that was because the charges were bullshit. *Fuck.* Beth had said everything would get worse before it got better. Had she known this was about to happen? His heart hammered. Why were they setting up Amelia? They had to have a hundred and one ways to accomplish their goal without ruining the woman's life.

Beth owed him answers. He swiped the news coverage away and called her. Each passing ring fanned his irritation. Finally, she answered. He couldn't tell if she'd been waiting for his call.

"You better fix this," Camden barked, "and it better happen now."

"I don't take orders from you, buddy."

Camden grabbed his breakfast and coffee in one hand and stormed back toward the metro. He wasn't heading to New Jersey anymore. Where to would be determined. But for the moment, he was hellbent on retracing his steps to go somewhere else—to Titan or to Beth. He didn't fuckin' know, but he was on his way. "Call your boss. Call the agents. *Call someone*. Fix it now."

"Or what? You're going to yell at me some more? This isn't my call. She isn't my case. I told you the situation would get worse—"

"Before it got better. Got it. That's what you said. So make it better."

"I can't."

He stopped in the middle of foot traffic. Commuters streamed by, jostling him as he impeded their flow. He couldn't think. Sometimes, he didn't think things through, but right then, he simply *couldn't*. He couldn't see the play or the reasons why. He couldn't see the answers or how to fix the problem. The unknown was infuriating. But more than that, the helplessness that had a stranglehold on him was enough to drive him mad.

He considered his options. *His boss?* Looping in Jared would be complicated—mostly because Boss Man would want to know why. Why did Camden care? Why had he maintained contact with Amelia? Then again, what did it matter if Jared had twenty questions? Boss Man was the one who'd sent him halfway across the world to be there. "I'll call Jared Westin."

Beth's pause spoke volumes. "You're not going to call Mr. Westin over some small-potatoes problem."

Mr. Westin—that spoke even louder volumes. It wasn't lost on Camden that his boss was one of those VIPs, but he'd become powerful without the glad-handing and ass-kissing that seemed ingrained in so many VIP types circulating in DC. It also helped that Jared scared most people. He was something of a military maverick who had connections and money and didn't care about either as long as the job got done. "Watch me."

CHAPTER ELEVEN

AMELIA COULD BARELY eat. She hadn't slept much as she sat in solitary confinement. Days and nights blurred as she grieved until she wasn't sure how much time had passed since she'd been arrested. No one would tell her about Hailey, not even her attorney. Maybe Hailey wasn't dead. Maybe everything was a misunderstanding.

Amelia knew only one thing without a shred of doubt. This place wasn't a normal lockup facility. She hadn't spent time in jail before, but that couldn't be where police usually deposited criminals.

Then again, the police weren't the ones that had arrested her. The FBI or the CIA or some alphabet-soup agency that didn't have to name itself was responsible for that. Everyone she encountered acted as though she were a mix between a serial killer and a terrorist. No one looked at her. They didn't speak to her. She hadn't been housed with other inmates. Perhaps their treatment was standard operating procedure for introducing inmates to a new facility, but that didn't feel right. Then again, the only situations she had to compare to were what she'd seen on television or in the movies.

Her attorney hadn't said anything about her treatment. She didn't know the man, and the man didn't try to know her. He was simply a lawyer she'd connected with from a list of criminal law firms. Her attorney hadn't listened to her pleas of innocence. He was all business and only wanted to explain the next step: an arraignment. They would be able to learn what evidence existed. Until he had more time to look into such things, he really wanted nothing to do with a conversation. So much for that huge amount of money she'd had to agree to as a deposit for services—that didn't get her even a friendly smile.

The bolted lock on her door turned. The door swung open, and a female guard entered. She held a small package in her hands and eyed her warily.

"On your feet," the guard said.

Amelia stumbled up.

"Let's go," she ordered.

Without asking where or why, she exited her cell. Another woman officer hovered close, holding a brown paper bag. She gestured for Amelia to walk farther into the dank hallway. Amelia trudged forward and, flanked by both guards, traversed the gunmetal-gray labyrinth until they ended up in a large, empty hallway that smelled of mold and mildew.

She walked on rubber mats until they entered a space where showerheads lined the far wall. It wasn't the same bathroom as where she'd showered under a guard's supervision before. Maybe they were transferring her to a new area where she would interact with others. Talking or bunking with others held no appeal.

"Get cleaned up." The first guard offered the small package. "You're out."

"Out where?"

They didn't answer. Amelia blinked and took the package, which was more like a paper bag than a box. The contents included a thin, paperlike towel, a comb, a bar of soap, a travel-size deodorant, and flimsy sandals bound up like a roll of quarters.

The other woman set the larger paper bag on a metal bench. "You've got three minutes." She nodded to the bag. "Your clothes—time's ticking."

Amelia hadn't realized she was waiting for privacy. Of course they wouldn't give it to her. Each time she'd showered, it had been with an armed guard nearby. She tucked her chin to her chest and crossed the open space. Awkwardly, Amelia placed her toiletries next to the paper bag of her clothes and chose a shower to use. Humiliation curled through her as she stripped. The water was tepid at best.

"You don't have all day."

She ducked under the lukewarm spray and scrubbed the waxy soap from her hair to her toes. It didn't suds but slipped over her skin, leaving a soapy film that had to be rubbed off with her hands. Despite her best attempts, her greasy hair wasn't much cleaner than before she stepped under the water. She rubbed the bar of soap up from the nape of her neck and into the strands tucked behind her ears.

"One minute to be done and dressed."

Amelia propped the soap on the tile that jutted out of the wall. It slid off. She tried again. It slid again.

"Pick up your crap. This isn't a pigsty."

"Trying." She ducked out of the water and rushed to the bench. Shivers erupted over her skin as she placed the bar of soap on the bench. Amelia waited for a nanosecond to ensure it wouldn't slide onto the floor then returned to the shower. Her thin sandals thwacked the wet tile floor as she rushed into the just-above-room-temperature spray of water and furiously scrubbed her hair free of sudsless soap.

"Towel off. Let's move. We don't have all day."

"Trying." Amelia turned off the shower and, chin ducked again, hurried to dry off with the paperlike towel. She pulled out clothes—*her* clothes—and a slice of hope pierced her chest as she pulled out the jacket and pajamas she'd worn when arrested.

Amelia struggled to pull clothes over her still-wet skin. Finally, she slipped her feet into her shoes. "What should I do with my stuff?" She gestured at the dirty clothes, soap, and poor excuse for a towel.

"Pick it up," a guard said as though Amelia were an idiot. "Let's go."

Her cheeks flushed. Wet hair dripped down her back. They retraced their path to her solitary cell. Once alone again, Amelia used a cheap plastic comb to detangle her hair in front of the plastic mirror next to her cot and toilet. The comb didn't help. She used her fingers instead as a flood of questions floated to mind.

Had her attorney secured her bail?

Was this what she had to wear to her arraignment?

Why wouldn't anyone tell her anything?

She had neither detangled her hair nor come up with answers to her questions before a different guard opened her cell door.

"Put your hands out," the guard said.

The man handcuffed her and led her out of the cell. Just as before, a secondary guard awaited outside the door and walked with them as though Amelia were dangerous enough to need two armed officers escorting her through locked, empty halls.

That time, they walked in a different direction. She couldn't recall if she'd been that way before or if she was walking toward freedom. The journey brought her past more people. She saw several other inmates, all wearing orange jumpsuits. They had far greater freedom than she'd had and were grouped together in common areas or in cells that housed several beds.

After navigating a series of locked doors and pass-throughs, Amelia was led into a garage bay. An oversized black SUV waited, the driver's door open. A man the size of a mountain stepped out. He wasn't her attorney. He was no one she'd ever met before, but the fury on his face and the storm in his dark slate eyes told Amelia his name before he opened his mouth.

When he did, it was a guttural growl that left no question as to who he was. "Get those fucking cuffs off of her." Tension ticked in his chiseled jaw as she was unshackled. "Are you okay?"

She almost laughed. "I haven't been okay in weeks—Camden?"

He rolled his lips together as though he were fighting back a hundred things to say, but he nodded. "I'm sorry it took this long for me to get to you."

Tears blurred her eyes, and Amelia moved toward him. She wrapped her arms around his strong neck, stifling a sob, and let gratitude wash over her. She tried to say thank you. Genuinely, she tried to let go of him, but she felt like she was holding onto safety and sanity. He would keep her safe. He would protect her, just as he had the first time they'd spoken.

"It's okay." One hand cupped the back of her head as the other soothed the length of her spine as though they'd been friends for years. "I promise it's going to be okay."

CHAPTER TWELVE

THICK SHEETS OF rain poured down as Camden pulled out of the federal prison complex. The weather had only gotten uglier since he first arrived almost two hours before. The wait hadn't been good for his attitude. They had certainly known he was coming, but the CIA didn't care. They were there to screw around. He checked the mirrors and watched for tails.

He glanced over. Her arms were crossed over her chest. She rubbed the thin coat over her arms. He turned the heat up, but her rubbing her arms might have been a self-soothing technique as much as it was trying to warm herself.

"Where are we going?" Amelia asked.

He would take her anywhere she wanted, but he guessed the eventual destination would be her condo. "Wherever you want. Your home?"

She wouldn't look over. Amelia rolled her lips together and gnawed on the bottom one, as though that might ease her apprehension. "Yeah. Sure. That makes sense."

"We don't have to go there. Somewhere else?"

"No, you're right…"

He stole another glance. "Amelia, consider me your taxi. If there's someplace else, just say the word. If you need to call someone and let them know where you are, tell me."

Maybe she didn't trust him. He certainly wouldn't trust anyone if he'd lived through the bullshit she'd experienced.

"No." She still chewed on her lip. "I don't want to inconvenience you…"

Was she kidding?

"…but could we stop someplace for drive-through? I'm starving."

He had to laugh. He'd been worried she didn't feel safe, but she was hungry. He should've thought of that. The food in prison had probably been crap. "Of course."

"I'll pay you back."

"Don't worry about that." They were still about an hour from Arlington. He recalled an exit with several options not too far away. "Burgers? Tacos? Subs? What are you feeling?"

"All of the above?" she joked tentatively, as though testing out how much she could lean on him. "How about subs?"

"Sounds like a plan." He checked his side view mirrors then spent another moment studying the woman curled into a ball in the passenger seat.

Her lips were rolled together, pressed into a tight line as she stared out the window.

"Do you need to call someone?"

She shook her head. "I paid an enormous amount of money for a lawyer. He was supposed to pass along a message to my business partner." Barely raising her drooping shoulders, Amelia shrugged half-heartedly.

The woman was defeated. Even her attorney didn't have her trust. A small part of Camden itched to make things right in her world.

She continued, "It either got to Veronica, or all hell's broken loose, and my company is in a tailspin. Not much I can do either way right now. It will probably be in a tailspin anyway. Who wants their corporate meeting planned by an accused murderer? Forget weddings or bar mitzvahs."

Her bitterness was warranted. Again, the niggling itch to fix her world scratched just beneath the surface of his chest.

"Maybe a friend?" he asked.

The corners of her mouth dipped as her frown tugged down. She fidgeted with the sleeve of her jacket. "I don't want to explain to anyone that I didn't kill my sister and brother-in-law. Even people who know me would have to jump through serious cognitive hurdles to be okay with me. I mean, I was arrested. That doesn't happen unless there's a preponderance of evidence. At least, that's what I used to think."

Her flat affect worried Camden. He stole another glance. He couldn't stop. She was tired—beautiful but exhausted, with the spark he'd heard over the phone beaten out of her.

"Let's get some decent food in you, and if you change your mind, let me know."

A sign along the highway came into view and listed fast food and gas stops.

He changed lanes and exited. "Know what you want?"

"Turkey and cheese. As big as they'll let you order."

Well, she might've been quiet and staring out the window, but at least she still had her appetite. He parked in front of the brightly lit sign. "Anything else?"

"Bottle of iced tea if they have it. Lemonade if it's just fountain drinks."

"Be right back."

The shop had no line. Camden ordered, keeping a protective eye on their vehicle. Another car pulled in and blocked his direct line of sight. He rubbed the back of his neck and repositioned so that he could wait for their food and see her simultaneously. He didn't think the CIA would swoop her back into custody, but he never would've thought they'd arrest her for murder. Shit happened. He would be ready for it.

His phone buzzed with a text message. Beth's name made him double-check on Amelia before reading the message. She was staring blankly out the window. His jaw clenched. Camden drew in a deep, angry breath and swiped his phone.

Beth: How is she?

"How the fuck do you think she's doing?" he muttered. Instead of asking that, Camden tried to come up with a more professional response but couldn't. In the end, he typed out his initial thoughts, F-bombs and all, and hit Send.

Beth: I want to meet with her.

He snorted. There was an absolutely zero percent chance he would let Beth anywhere near Amelia.

Camden: *Are you out of your mind?*

He had no justification for putting his foot down, but he did it anyway. His boot would slam over and over until Beth understood she couldn't get her deceptive claws into Amelia. Besides, no way would Amelia go for a meeting with the people who facilitated her arrest. She was traumatized, downtrodden. Her fiery spark was so dim that Camden worried it would stay dark. Beth buzzed his phone again.

Beth: *I'm out of town for the next three days. I'll arrange a meeting when I get back.*

Camden: *What part of "you're out of your mind" said to you, "Hey, let's consider this idea a go"?*

Beth: *I'm not the bad guy.*

Camden: *I could argue all day long that you're wrong.*

His order was called. He pocketed his phone and picked up their food. As the rain beat down, he jogged to the driver's side, wondering when—or even if—he would find a good time to bring up Beth. "Here you go. Twelve-inch turkey, toasted with extra cheese." He handed over her bag and placed the drinks on the center console. "And a lemonade."

"Oh, you're a saint."

Camden snorted. "I've been called a lot of things, but that's a first." He unwrapped his Italian sub and folded the paper along the bottom half. The rain drilled over the roof and windshield. He gestured to the convenience store across the parking lot. "Anything else before we go?"

"No. Thanks." Her nervous gaze darted about the rainy night. "If we're not in a rush, you don't have to eat while you drive."

"I'm your chauffeur. We go wherever, whenever you want."

"A chauffeur, huh?" Amelia played with the cap of her lemonade bottle. "Who knew life's luxuries were earned with a little bit of prison time?"

"I think you've earned that and a lot more after the government's little stunt. You can probably put your attorney to work on damages and restitution."

Amelia cocked her head and, after a long moment, put the lemonade back in the cup holder as though doing so took all her mental energy. She stared into her lap then finally tilted her head toward him. "What do you mean? What stunt?"

He stopped chewing then swallowed hard. "What do you mean, what do I mean?"

"Why would the government owe me—I mean, *I* think they should. But why would anyone else?"

The sub paper crinkled in his hand. The rain smacked. Every little noise stood out as silence rolled between them. His mind jumped back to earlier. She'd hugged him—she'd been *surprised* by him. "Your lawyer didn't talk to you?"

"I haven't talked to my lawyer in days."

His mouth went dry. His mind drafted several new text messages to Beth that were infinitely less friendly. "You mean... no one talked to you about this?"

"The guards had me shower and change out of my jumpsuit, and then they walked me out to you. No one said a word." Her eyes widened. "I thought my attorney bailed me out or something. And you... I don't know... just magically appeared."

"God. No." Camden pinched the bridge of his nose. "Amelia. You're out of there. Done. As if it never happened."

"But..."

"I'm positive there's an army of CIA tech dudes scouring the internet to erase any trace that this ever happened."

Eyes wide, her jaw dropped. "Are you serious?"

"Yeah, sweetheart. Dead serious. This isn't even like a presidential pardon. This is erasing the past." He threaded a hand into his hair, completely unsure where to begin. He didn't have specifics, only his marching orders after unleashing Jared Westin on Beth's bosses. "I can't believe no one told you." Camden laid a hand on her shoulder and squeezed. "Everything's going to be okay."

He thought she might smile or celebrate, but Amelia collapsed as though she didn't have to hold up the weight of the world. She twisted her fingers together and watched the raindrops splatter onto the windshield and roll away. "I don't know what to say." She turned to him again, uncertain, and quietly offered, "Thanks."

"I didn't do it."

The corners of her eyes tightened. Her forehead tensed as she studied him. After a long moment of scrutiny, her lips quirked. "I think you'd say that even if you arranged the whole thing with the president."

"You're giving me too much credit."

"Doubtful."

She dropped her head back and drew in a deep breath as though catching her footing in life once again. But then she froze, and the relief drained from her expression. "Did they find my sister?"

He didn't want to deliver bad news. Part of him hated that she still held out hope. Part of him admired her tenacious, albeit semi-delusional, faith that Hailey was waiting for rescue. After all, a majority of his assignments involved rescuing people whose chances of survival were low to nonexistent. Without question, he would find Hailey for Amelia. He just wished he had some idea how to do that.

"Not that I know of."

She nodded and sank in on herself. The inside of the vehicle felt dark and lonely as she processed that. Finally, Amelia picked up her sub and took another bite. They polished off their subs without talking. The engine and heater lowly hummed. The rain blurred the outside world. He didn't know what else to say and broke the quiet by turning the windshield wipers back on.

"Do you care if I doze off while you drive?" she asked.

"Of course not." Camden balled up his trash and took a long drink of his Coke before pulling back onto the road. Two minutes later, Amelia was asleep, breathing softly as he cruised down the highway.

An hour later, they arrived at her condominium complex. He was happy to see they hadn't plastered her door with crime-scene tape. Camden parked in the spot closest to her place.

Amelia slowly woke up. "We're here?" She wiped her eyes and glanced out the window. "You're parked in my spot... Which means my car is...?" She checked the other windows. "Not here."

"Five bucks and another sub says it'll be here by morning."

She laughed quietly, rubbing sleep from her eyes. "You're optimistic." Her face fell. "I don't have my house keys."

"I'll get us in without hurting your door if they locked it."

"You don't think they did?"

He shrugged, not trusting anything that had happened to that point. "They probably secured it somehow." Camden pulled out his wallet. "Give me a minute."

"I don't think a credit card in the doorjamb will work on my deadbolt."

He winked. "Probably not."

A minute later, pocketing a key-picking set, he returned to the SUV. "Your palace awaits."

"Really?" She blinked. "Just like that?"

He nudged his head toward her door. "Go see for yourself."

She studied the front of her condo and pulled her lower lip into her mouth, nervously biting it. "Will you go inside with me? Unless you have someplace else to be."

That was the least he could do. "Sure. I'm all yours. Whatever will make you feel safe."

★　★　★

AMELIA WASN'T SURE what to expect. They walked in the rain toward the front door. Each step closer became heavier. Nothing seemed out of place. Even the front porch light was on. But uncertainty danced in her stomach. Rain slogged over her. When she could almost touch her front door, she stopped abruptly. Her heart raced. Grief roared in her chest. Panic paralyzed her legs. She couldn't move. She felt like walking inside would be a reminder of the domino fall of events that had ruined her life.

Camden rested his strong hands on her shoulders. Like a powerful, protective force of nature, he remained behind her, not pushing her on or promising life would return to normal when she walked inside. He simply stood there to support her. Rain dripped down her cheeks and plastered her hair to her head. He squeezed the tense muscles under his long fingers. "Do you want to leave?"

Embarrassment and anxiety curled together and wound up her spine. "This is so stupid."

"It's not. You've been through hell."

She turned and lifted her chin. His hands ran down her arms and fell away. Rain poured over them, soaking through her coat. "Why is this so hard?"

"I don't know." He shook his head like life wasn't fair. Like he didn't have an explanation. "Let's get out of here. I'll take you anywhere you want to go."

But she had nowhere and no one. She didn't want to see anyone and couldn't imagine where she might ask him to take her. Floundering in the middle of a rainstorm made her feel like a fool. She wiped the water off her cheeks and shook her head, determined to push through her reluctance. "No, I can do this."

Without giving herself a chance to overthink the situation, she opened the front door and let them in. "Oh God."

"Holy crap," he muttered.

She hadn't imagined they'd trashed her place, but all her belongings had been strewn everywhere. Amelia inched inside as though walking through a minefield. Her stomach turned. She held out a hand to block Camden from viewing the disaster zone that used to be her cute condo. "It did not look like this when they arrested me."

He let out a long whistle. "They absolutely wrecked your place. What the fuck?"

Tears sprang into her eyes, but she refused to let them fall. She didn't want him to think she was superficial enough to cry over tossed drawers and disheveled cushions.

"Let me look around before you go any farther." He sidestepped her position by the door. "I'll do a quick assessment."

What did it matter? She could see the damage that had been done. Amelia trailed her fingers along a wall. They'd taken her pictures down.

The frames were partially stacked on a side table. They'd opened her mail and left unorganized stacks next to the picture frames. On the floor, someone had piled the books from the shelves. "They really didn't have to do this," she told him as he returned from her bedroom.

"You have no idea," he muttered. "Prepare yourself. It's a mess."

Amelia walked into her bedroom. The mattress lay against the wall. The box frame lay over one of the two windows. The blinds were up, and the lights had been left on. Her neighbors would have plenty to gossip about. Her pillows had even been removed from their cases. She picked up a discarded pillow sham and held it out as if it might be contaminated. "What was I hiding in my pillows? National secrets?"

Camden's gaze swept through the room. "They were looking for something. That's for sure."

"I can't stay here."

"Yeah. I get that." He eyed her drawers hanging out of the dresser and the pile of clothes mounded on the floor. Some items had been scattered as though people had walked over her clothing and kicked away anything that had caught on their shoes. "Why don't you pack a bag?"

"Yeah. I'll stay at..." *At Hailey's* popped to mind first. Amelia cringed. When would her mind stop jumping to Hailey as though her sister were an option? She squeezed her eyes shut and turned to Camden. "When will I stop thinking my sister is a phone call away? That I can just drive over to her house and stay in her guest room like I have a hundred times before?"

He avoided stepping on her clothes and moved to her side. Again, he squeezed her shoulder. Her chin dropped. Her wet hair clung to her cheeks. She couldn't hide the tears anymore. They burned on her cheeks. She missed her sister, missed her life. "When will it stop hurting?"

His thick, muscled arms encircled her, and she folded into him. His hold was so safe. He was so warm. The steady beat of his heart was all the answer he offered. This guy wasn't the type to tell her to shake it off or to say the cliché bullshit that time would heal. For that, she was eternally grateful.

Finally, her tears stopped. But she wasn't ready to pull away from the safe cocoon of his protective hold. "Maybe I'll stay here and hide from the real world."

Laughter rumbled in his chest. Her smile curved against his sternum. She drew in a deep breath. He smelled peppery and masculine—which reminded her that she smelled like prison soap. Amelia jumped back, flustered and blushing. "Sorry. I need a shower in the worst way."

He cracked a handsome grin that made his eyes shine with amusement. "I didn't notice."

She looked toward her bathroom, longing for a hot shower but terrified that they'd done as much damage in there as they had throughout her condo.

He seemed to read her mind. "You want to jump in the shower before we do anything else? How much could they do to your bathroom?"

Probably a lot. "If they dumped my soaps, I'll lose it. That'll be the straw that breaks me."

"If they did, we'll handle it."

"You're one of those can-do people, aren't you?"

"Maybe I am." He sauntered over to the bathroom and flipped the light on. "It looks like the rest of the place."

A dejected groan caught in her throat. "Really? What the hell?" She tipped her head back, trying to channel his can-do attitude, but remembered she'd recently been talked into a new shampoo and conditioner set that was supposed to be otherworldly. It had come with a price tag to match. "What about my shampoos?"

He craned his neck but shrugged. "Can't see them. All right. This is the plan: You shower and pack a bag. They've put me up in a safe house not far from here. It has only one bedroom, but I'm sure the couch is a pullout, and even if it's not, the couch is huge. I've fallen asleep on it almost every night I've been here. And there's two bathrooms. You can have one all to yourself." He studied her face. "You can trust me. I give you my word."

He was about the only person on earth she trusted. But his offer was more generous than she had any right to hope for. He kept doing things for her—rescuing her from prison and then from her tossed condo. She wasn't a taker and didn't want to leech. "I can't."

"Why not?"

"It's an inconvenience for you."

"It's a safe house. It exists for the sole purpose of housing people when shit hits the fan." He gestured to her clothes, mattress, and box spring. "It's hit the fan, sweetheart." He walked over to the windows, pulled her mattress back, and fixed the blinds, but there was no space for him to set the mattress up. Her dresser drawers were in the way. "You can't stay here." He returned it to the window. "Look, if you don't want to stay where I am, I'll leave you there and get a hotel room. No big deal."

"That's ridiculous."

"It's not. You should be somewhere safe. *Like a safe house.*"

She shook her head. Her life didn't make sense anymore. "Why are you doing this?"

He almost laughed. "That's a hell of a great question."

"That's not an answer."

He pursed his lips and nodded thoughtfully. "It won't make sense."

"Ha. Nothing in my life makes sense. Try me."

Camden paced around her piles of clothes and back again. He didn't meet her eyes at first, as though trying to decide how much of what he wanted to say should be shared. "That first night that you called... I'd never heard someone so scared who still kept their composure."

"I wasn't composed."

"What you did—how you held it together..." The corners of his lips quirked, and he side-eyed her as though she were remarkable. "You made an impression."

Her jaw slackened. She blushed under his absurd gaze. He thought entirely too much of her. "I hid under a bed and tried not to cry."

"Tomato. To-mah-toe." He shrugged. "Not many people in your position would still be alive."

She didn't know what to say.

"So," he finally asked, breaking the silence that had swallowed her up. "The safe-house plan works for you?"

Amelia's skin tingled. "Really. I can't ask you to sleep on the couch."

"You're not asking, and it's where I've been sleeping anyway."

She chewed on her bottom lip. "You don't mind?"

He half laughed and shook his head. "Not even a little bit. Promise." He hooked his thumb over his shoulder. "I'm going to go put your sofa back together and have a seat. Take as long as you need."

"I can hurry—"

"*Amelia.*" He leveled her with a serious look. "Waiting on you isn't some great imposition. Take a shower. Chill out. Blow-dry your hair or whatever. I'm going to put furniture back together and kick back until you're ready."

"You don't have to."

"Shit, babe, are you listening to me? *I know.* But I'm going to anyway."

She crossed her arms. "'No' doesn't usually work on you, does it?"

"*No.*" Entertained, his dark eyes brightened. "I usually get my way."

A shiver ran down the back of her neck. "Noted."

She turned toward the bathroom and discovered the army of agents hadn't found it necessary to dump out her new shampoo or conditioner. They didn't even touch her bath gels or soaps.

Ten minutes later, Amelia had lathered her hair into a soapy mound and dropped her head back into the steamy shower to let the bubbles wash away. She scrubbed her skin until it was pink, and when she could find nothing else to do, she lingered under the hot spray and tried to forget everything—at least for a few minutes.

Everything except for Camden.

He was impossible to ignore. This wasn't the time to notice her savior had all the makings of an action-movie hero: dark tousled hair and smoldering eyes, muscles for days, and a jawline that could halt traffic. But that wasn't what she'd first registered when he arrived to rescue her. Amelia clocked him as unflappable safety personified. After all, he was the boot-camp yogi, who had told her how to breathe while someone was trying to kill her.

She was registering him now. She couldn't help it. He was a chauffeur-turned-real-estate-agent who was putting her couch back together after feeding her fast food. That was one hell of an original spin on the knight in shining armor, but that was what he was. But that made her the damsel in distress, and she wasn't sure that title sat well with her.

Amelia turned off the shower and wrapped herself in a thick towel. Blowing out her hair didn't take long, but then she took an extra few minutes to slather her arms and legs in lotion. He *had* said not to rush, and she wanted to luxuriate after her time in prison.

Packing her bag took longer than expected. She hadn't factored in the ground search required to locate everything she wanted. By the time she returned to the living room, Camden was relaxed on her couch, and her living room didn't look like a tornado disaster zone. Her eyes widened at the dramatic change. "Cam." She spun in a circle. "You didn't have to do all this."

"It's done." The chairs had been returned to the dining room. The cushions and throw blankets were back on the couch. Framed pictures had been returned to the hooks on the walls. All her kitchen cabinet doors had been shut. It almost looked normal. He'd even propped up a picture of her and Hailey from the stack on the table. "Ready to roll?"

Amelia's heart ricocheted. She picked up the photo. "Thank you."

"That's your sister?" he asked.

"Yeah. From my birthday party a couple months ago. We were at the beach." They had worn matching wraparound sun dresses. "We always threw each other fun birthday parties. It was sort of our thing." Amelia gave a watery smile and held the picture to her chest. Her eyes closed against the tears that burned them and clogged the back of her throat. "I'll never have a family party again."

But that might not be true. Hailey could be anywhere. They could have killed her like they did Jonathan—whoever *they* were—but they also might not have.

"What if she's not dead?" she asked. "What if she's out there waiting for help, and no one is looking for her?"

Camden inhaled and let it out slowly. "I don't know."

Her chin dropped.

"They go after their asset. They don't just leave them to drown if it can be helped."

Another *they*. There were so many unknowns. "Whoever they are, *they* have gone through a lot to make the world think Hailey is dead."

He didn't disagree.

Amelia realized that he likely not only knew who *they* were but might work for them. Camden had said they would stay in a safe house. He was driving a big black government-issue vehicle. *They* could all be the same people. But he'd promised her she was safe with him. Did she believe it?

Yes. She did.

CHAPTER THIRTEEN

THE OVERSIZED SUV maneuvered onto the narrow street in Del Ray Alexandria. Large trees, sparse with the remnants of brown leaves that hadn't fallen, watched protectively over the parked cars and cute houses that sat sleepily on the cold, rainy night. Amelia watched as Camden circled the block.

"For all the evasive maneuvering tactics I've been trained on," he said, "nothing helps when trying to park this beast in this neighborhood."

He turned again and found a postage-stamp–sized parking spot. She had her doubts as he threw the vehicle into reverse, but with two quick moves, Camden had parked at the curb.

They stepped out of the warmth and into the blustery night. She immediately missed the close proximity to Camden. She felt they'd been sheltered safely from the world and stepping outside would ruin it.

He grabbed her overstuffed carry-on bag and led the way through the quiet neighborhood patchworked with small bungalows and craftsman houses. Some were brimming with personality, with art in the yards and windows. Others were neat and tidy without personality. But none of the homes were the same, forming a mismatched masterpiece far different from her boring condo complex.

"I've held events in Del Ray a couple times," Amelia said as she kept pace with his ground-covering stride. "There are fun restaurants and bars to rent out for small weddings or corporate cocktail hours. Especially if the client is trying for a non-DC vibe."

"I've never been here before. I just asked not to be in a swanky DC hotel."

They walked up to one of the generic houses with the shades drawn tight on the windows. A No Soliciting sticker had been placed above the doorbell. He turned the key in the door and led the way into the dark. Camden locked the door behind them and hung his keys on a hook. He turned on a light switch as they went in and dropped her bag at the bottom of a staircase. "Make yourself at home."

Amelia did a quick inspection from the entryway. "As safe houses go, this seems to be what I'd expect." The furnishings were generic and decidedly bachelor-pad–esque: sprawling leather couch, big-screen television. A football sat on a coffee table. Maybe he was a sports guy. "Did that come with the house?"

He laughed, scooped up the ball, and tossed it to himself before he turned on another light in the living room that opened into a kitchen. "It flew here with me."

He flew here? Her debt to him was only growing. That was the moment she should thank him again profusely and excuse herself. He hadn't signed up to socialize. Just to be her rescuer. This saint of a man had gone above and beyond to help when she had no one in her corner. Yet she didn't walk away. She couldn't. She felt a pull to learn more about him. "Where are you from?"

"I grew up in New Jersey."

"Are you more of a Jersey Shore type or Hoboken?"

He tossed the football overhead and caught it. "What makes you think I'm either?"

Amelia shrugged and admitted, "Those are the only two places I know anything about. I took a shot."

Gently, he lofted the football her way. Somehow, she caught it and marveled at herself, surprise widening her eyes.

His grin hitched. "Good catch." Camden leaned against the counter and crossed his arms over a chest as wide as the northern seaboard. "I'm from a town north of Trenton—pretty industrial, where there's not much except for hardworking people working harder than they probably should."

He didn't say those were his people, but she thought they were: hardworking and with an ethic that didn't quit—the kind of moral code that would find her when she needed help. She ran her finger along the lacing of the football. "You and Hailey don't work for the same people, right?"

"No. We're… in the same orbit, but you couldn't even call it the same industry."

"You answered the phone number she told me to call."

"Sometimes our assignments cross, but we have different employers."

She didn't know what to make of that. She couldn't compare it to the way corporate event planning interacted with all industries. Or could she? She didn't know enough about him to hazard a guess.

Outside, the wind picked up, and a low gusting howl smacked against the windows. She turned toward them. The pulled blinds blocked the view, but Amelia could imagine the large, nearly bare trees waving their branches as the storm picked up. Sheets of rain pummeled the house. It made her feel very alone with this larger-than-life man. He'd earned her trust, but she didn't know if she'd made the right decision.

"You should tell me who you work for," she said.

He gave her a funny look and walked toward the refrigerator. "How come?"

Because she was staying in the house with a stranger and essentially knew nothing about him. By his facial expression, she guessed he wasn't allowed to share the name of the supersecret employer that had the ability to pluck her from prison. "How about this: What's your last name?"

"Brooks."

"Camden Brooks from New Jersey. Family?"

He laughed. "Yup. I've got one of those."

"I don't."

He faltered. "I didn't mean…"

Amelia set the football on the kitchen counter. "It's fine." She twisted her fingers together. "My parents died in a car accident."

He shoved his hands in his pockets. "I really didn't mean—"

"Honestly, it's fine."

She didn't like the pity in his face and looked beyond him. The kitchen was tidy. She didn't suspect he'd cooked while staying there. The counters were empty except for the football and a toaster. The hand towel looked as clean as the day it left the store. She took a seat on a barstool at the counter as he opened the fridge, pulled out two bottles of water, and took the other barstool.

Camden cleared his voice and said, "Hailey and Jonathan worked for an agency that was breached. No one knows still the extent of the problem, but at the time, their agency issued an all hands on deck. Anyone who could—"

"That's you. A different agency."

"We're probably considered contractors in this situation."

"Oh."

He set one of the water bottles in front of her and cracked open the other. After a long pull, he added, "My company was able to help when the request came in. I was assigned to pick up the phone if any calls were routed our way, and that's how we came to meet."

"Serendipity, I suppose."

"I suppose." He chuckled and rolled the water bottle between his hands. "What else do you want to know?"

Oh, about a million other things. If this is a safe house, where do you usually live? Do you normally travel, rescuing people out of prison? She couldn't imagine a day job like that, but she hadn't imagined extraordinary day jobs really existed.

His chiseled jawline shifted with a curious half grin. "Nothing?"

"I have questions… but I don't know where to start."

He nodded as though he understood. "Start with the basics."

"All right." She opened her water bottle and took a small sip. "So you're not with the government?"

"Correct."

"But your vehicle had government plates." She cocked her head. "How does that work?"

"The government contracts with my company. It's their show and, for the most part, their resources."

"Who do you work for?" she tried again.

That time, he offered without hesitation, "Titan Group."

Amelia raised her shoulders. "Doesn't ring any bells. Guess they don't plan galas or networking happy hours."

His lips quirked as though she'd asked if his company flew rockets to Mars or trained ballerinas. "Nope. Not unless your events need hostage negotiators or armed reconnaissance."

"Oh..."

Amelia suddenly saw where Camden fit in the world. It wasn't chauffeuring prison releasees through the suburbs or reassembling her tossed furniture. He was the type of person who jumped from helicopters or scaled enemy-covered mountains. He was the type of person who helped spies and spooks and civilians who were in far over their heads.

Her throat had gone dry at the revelation, and she sipped her water again. "It hadn't occurred to me to offer those services to my clients." Her mind reeled as more pieces of the puzzle clicked into place, but she tried to downplay the eye-opener. "Maybe that's a niche I should look into. *Clients in need of hostage negotiators.*"

He laughed, sounding casual and cool, like nothing he'd shared was a big deal. "You don't want the headaches that come when we have to show up."

That raised the question of where had he come from.

"Where did you fly in from?" she asked.

He rolled the water bottle between his hands then capped it. "The Middle East."

Her lips parted, and she blinked. He'd come all this way to help her out. What were Hailey and Jonathan involved in? "Really?"

He nodded.

She waited for him to elaborate. More than a dozen countries existed in the Middle East. "Is your location a secret?"

"Do you know what a ghost team is?"

Her lips pursed as she thought the phrase over. There was surely a joke to be had about the supernatural and zombies, but she didn't have the energy to find it. "Nope. That's what Titan Group is? A ghost team?"

Ghosts floated through walls. They weren't seen unless they wanted to be, and they yelled *boo*. Camden was handsome—sexy, if she was being honest—but that didn't mean he couldn't be scary. Shadows lay behind his dark eyes, not to mention his size. His presence projected the distinct possibility that he could morph into something scary.

"How to explain a ghost team." He ran a hand into his hair and mussed it as he thought. "There are a lot of moving parts to Titan."

Her eyebrow arched. "Well, that's not vague or anything."

He grinned. "It's a privately held special ops company that focuses on military and security issues. We have multiple teams. Some are considered ghosts. We're more off the books than other teams."

"Oh… so no happy-hour schmooze fests?"

"Yeah, no. We're not known for networking."

She laughed.

"There's a US-based team that is more the face of the company. They're not all that far from here."

"But they weren't the ones to help me out."

He shook his head and didn't offer an explanation.

Amelia peeled at her water bottle label. She couldn't find the edge of it and turned the bottle, lost in thought. She dragged her nail along the wrapper. "Can you tell me more about ghost teams? What do you do? Specifically."

"Sure. It's pretty simple. Just a group that works together on security projects."

"That doesn't sound very ghostlike."

He nodded, amused. "We get in and out. No connections. No loose ends. No assignments that can be tracked to anyone else."

Like Hailey and Jonathan. "That's very… interesting? Terrifying?"

He laughed. "Both? Guess it depends on who you ask."

"You and I live in *very* different worlds." Though she wasn't living in her own anymore. Amelia had passed all the responsibility to Veronica and hadn't had a moment's desire to check in. Veronica would understand that all Amelia's thoughts had been focused on her sister. Where was Hailey? Was she scared? Hurt? Was Hailey hoping that Amelia had called the phone number that would fix everything? "Do you know how to find Hailey?"

"There are people working on that."

That wasn't an answer. She glared. "You're certain about that, Cam?"

His expression faltered.

"Because they've done a lot to prove she's dead. Why?" She shook her head. "What on earth would be the reason to arrest me? To build a bullshit case." Amelia pressed her fingers to her temples. "My arrest wasn't based in reality. So why? Who are they trying to prove Hailey's death to?"

Camden raised his shoulders. "I have no idea. The details that were shared with me were... sanitized."

"*Sanitized?*" She snorted. "Everything is smoke and mirrors and lies and—" Her stomach turned. She'd had the same thought more than once, but maybe Camden would confirm it. "Did they work for the CIA?"

"It's not my place—"

"Camden. Come on. Tell me the truth. Or as much of the truth as you can tell me. Please?"

"The begging is killing me, sweetheart. Knowing a specific agency won't change—"

"You're the only one who has been truthful. You're the only one I trust right now. Tell me."

He held her gaze for an eternity. She didn't know if answering would break the law or if he didn't think she could handle the truth.

"They did." Camden's eyebrows rose as though to ask if that made any difference.

The CIA. Hailey and Jonathan worked for an intelligence agency. They lived their lives one way and secretly worked on projects they'd never uttered a breath about. "I knew that had to be the case. Nothing else made sense."

The wind howled around the house. The lights flickered. Amelia finally found the edge of the water bottle wrapper and tore it free from the glue. She unwound the wrapper and studied the naked bottle, tilting it to one side then the other, watching the water catch and fill the bottle's creases. "I really didn't know them as well as I thought I did."

His eye met hers and wouldn't let go. "They were the people you knew them as. I promise. The professor. The researcher. The sister and brother-in-law. They were very much those people you knew."

"I'm not—"

The lights went out. The slow hum of appliances quieted. She shivered. They sat in the dark. He made no move to find a candle or use the flashlight on his phone. Amelia appreciated the cloak of darkness. Right then, she wanted to stay hidden.

Camden eased off his barstool. "You okay?"

"I'm not scared of the dark, if that's what you're asking," she half joked.

"Stay put a second." He pulled out his cell phone, turned on the flashlight, and opened two kitchen drawers before extracting an elongated lighter from a drawer and a package of four short, fat candles. "A well-stocked safe house always makes life easier."

He lit two candles and left them on the breakfast bar between them then placed the remaining two on the coffee table. He lit them and returned to the kitchen. "Are you hungry?"

She shook her head. The turkey sub had filled her up, and since she hadn't had much of an appetite for prison food, her stomach wasn't in a rush to digest it.

Camden made a peanut butter sandwich and polished it off before he cleaned up his mess, putting the knife in the dishwasher and peanut butter in the cabinet.

"You're efficient," she pointed out.

"And you note things people do and then tell them."

She laughed to herself. "Guess I do. I never noticed that. Yet somehow I missed that my sister, the person I'm closest to, worked for a bunch of spies."

The wind picked up again. Camden leaned against the sink counter. Candlelight danced across his features. "It was their job to hide their work from you. They were trained to keep you in the dark."

"I guess."

"You sound like you don't like what they did."

She shrugged. "It's not that. It's the lying."

"You can't take offense to it. The people who do their kind of work are looking out for the greater good in the world. You know what I mean? They wouldn't sign up for that kind of trouble and make sacrifices that we'll have no idea about if they didn't want to leave the place better and safer than they found it."

When he put it like that… "Our parents died when we were young, and I think it killed Hailey that she wasn't old enough to charge out into the world and take care of us."

"How old were you?"

"I was nine. Almost ten. She was twelve."

"You said they were in a car accident. Want to tell me what happened?"

Amelia toyed with the water bottle. "Someone was trying to find a gas station and playing with the GPS on their phone while it was raining. Their choice changed the course of so many lives."

"Damn. I'm sorry."

That was a dark time, maybe almost as dark as right then. Amelia was hoping Hailey would be found. There wasn't even a scant hint of hope when their parents died. It had been complete and utter devastation.

"We lived with some family member that CPS found and we'd never heard of. I think she took us in for the stipend the state paid." She balled up the water bottle wrapper in her hands, making it crinkle. "It wasn't easy, coming from a life so ideal it could've been on a postcard to then living with someone who literally didn't care. But we did it. What choice did we have?"

"Not much, I guess." He opened the refrigerator and retrieved two beer bottles. Camden held them up. After she nodded, he uncapped and handed one over.

"Thanks."

They took long pulls of the cold beers. She couldn't have imagined how her day would turn out when she woke up that morning in solitary confinement. Safe and warm, drinking a beer during a power outage wasn't something she could have dreamt up. "What about your family?"

He smiled. "It's a big, loud family. Lots of brothers. A dad who's a good sport about it all and a mother who's impatiently waiting for grandchildren."

"None yet?"

"Nope. The woman raised a hell of a brood that would be hard to tie down."

Amelia laughed. *Tied down* sounded like an awful punishment, yet she knew exactly what he meant. She had orchestrated many weddings at which she didn't think the couple had a snowball's chance in hell of survival. Then Amelia thought about Hailey and Jonathan. They were perfectly matched. *Tied down? More like tied together.* "Maybe no one's tied down when it's the right match."

His index finger tapped against his beer bottle. Camden rolled his bottom lip into his mouth then took a long drink. "Maybe so."

CHAPTER FOURTEEN

THE POWER HADN'T returned, and their second round of beer bottles was empty. They had moved to the couch and talked for hours. He liked watching her, studying her. He liked the way her mind worked. One question had led to another and then another, and before he knew it, the meeting of two semi-strangers had become the formation of a bond. A tenuous friendship, perhaps.

Perhaps more. That was what Liam would call his impulsiveness. Camden saw a pretty girl and was jumping for more of her. But he swore this was different. The enigmatic pull he'd felt from the first phone call was all the more potent, and since he'd met her in person, since he'd seen the way her dark hair hung over her shoulders with a slight wave and how her eyes danced when she laughed or narrowed when she interrogated him, he couldn't force himself to go to bed and give them space.

It didn't really matter, though. Beyond the fact that she was essentially a client and a grieving woman who'd been fucked by the system, he could be called back to Abu Dhabi at any time.

Still, he wanted to sit there all night. He wanted more, if he wasn't lying to himself. He could reach out and touch her hair, her skin. He wanted to breathe her in—man, those beers were doing a number on him. He ran a hand over his face and into his hair with a long, reprobative sigh.

"Oh," she said. "I didn't realize what time it was."

His chest tightened. Regret needled under his skin. She'd taken his actions as exhaustion when they had been anything but. Camden checked the time: far past midnight. He would have guessed it was pushing eleven. They'd covered a lot of her questions, and he was sure she had more, but she was probably tired.

"You need to get some sleep," he said.

She glanced toward the dark stairs. "I wish the power would come back on."

He was glad it had gone out. It had pulled them together on the couch. He gathered their empty beers and deposited them in the recycling can. "I'll walk you upstairs and make sure you have everything you need."

Camden followed Amelia up the stairs to the only bedroom. She set a candle on the nightstand. It danced and bathed her in a buttery golden light. Fuck, why the hell was his mind registering her like that? He needed to get a move on instead of focusing on the woman in a way he very much needed to ignore.

"This place is all yours." He walked through the bedroom to the bathroom and gathered his toiletries. The space was small but clean. It wasn't stocked like her condo, but generic supplies were kept for anyone who needed them. "If you need anything, you know where I'll be."

"Honestly, Cam. I can sleep on the couch."

He considered all the shitty places he'd slept in over the years: bunked in the cold desert night, trapped in a tundra shack, sweating through his clothes in a jungle. The couch suited him more than the bed anyway. "I think I was raised better than that."

He didn't know why he said that. It was true, but he didn't usually trot out quips about how he was raised. Maybe he was trying to impress her. Either way, he sounded like an idiot.

Amelia hugged him. She simply wrapped her arms around his neck as though it were something they'd done a hundred times, and every part of him lit up like lightning streaking across the sky. His breath caught, and his fingers ached to flex into her softness. Camden tried to rationalize the connection. He tried to downplay their interaction and the sparks igniting from their physical touch. She *had* hugged him at the prison. So, they'd hugged twice—only twice. The unexpected familiarity of holding her would have been off-putting if it didn't feel so fucking good.

Her arms tightened around his neck. Her lips brushed just below his earlobe. "Thanks, Cam."

A shiver cascaded from the spot her lips grazed, and the hairs on the back of his neck shot to attention. Her soft cheek pressed against his. One forearm snaked around the small of her back and held her still against his torso. His heart drummed a heavy staccato. He should've pulled away, but he ignored all his responsibility and tightened his arms around her, hugging, holding.

The seconds ticked by. He breathed her in, trying to rationalize the way he held her in the flickering darkness, and he came up with absolutely nothing. Holding onto her was rash. Irresponsible. He needed to let go, but he didn't know how the hell that was going to happen when his body was memorizing the way hers pressed against his and stupid things like the sweet smell of her shampoo.

"I haven't felt this safe in days." Amelia leaned into him.

Well, fuck. That wasn't going to tamp down his interest. Arousal pounded in his blood. If he couldn't rationalize his reaction to her, he needed to understand her reaction to him. He swallowed hard and mentally fought for clarity. She was seeking reassurance. Safety. Something that was very different from his racing thoughts about her sweet mouth and pliable body. Right then, he needed to do everything by the book or, at the very least, not be a piece of shit and take advantage of their dynamic.

His chin dropped to the top of her head and brushed her silky hair. Camden didn't kiss her, but he damn well wanted to. "You should go to bed."

"Cam..."

He didn't trust himself and pretended not to hear the soft way she said his name, but he sure as hell didn't step back to give himself space.

Amelia tipped her chin up. *God, those eyes.* They were dark pools of wonder and—he clearly saw it—desire. His blood raced faster. His lips tingled. Candlelight danced over her features. He had wanted to touch her since their first phone call. Primally, he'd wanted to keep her safe and chase away the man who chased her. It had killed him that he was thousands of miles away, and then he was awestruck that she hadn't crumbled under pressure. She'd been so close to not making it through the night.

But she had, and after that first night, the more they talked, the more he needed to find out who the strong woman on the other line of the phone was. He'd been attracted to her without knowing what she looked like, and now holding her, Camden couldn't think straight.

They needed space. Daylight. A long night's rest. They needed many, many things that didn't exist in that bedroom. Camden brushed her hair behind her ear and forced himself to let go.

Cold air invaded the space between them. Her frown was almost enough for him to say, "Fuck it." They could use the two beers as an excuse for a bad decision.

He squeezed her biceps and trailed his palm to her elbow before finally pulling away. "Good night, Amelia."

CAMDEN AWOKE TO a sound. He sat up and blinked in the darkness. It was still the middle of the night. The wind and rain still battled outside. Without electricity, the house had cooled. He shivered and heard the sound again.

It had come from the bedroom. Amelia had left the door open, explaining that after spending nights in solitary confinement, she hadn't even wanted the appearance of being locked in.

"Amelia?" he called softly enough to not wake her but loud enough to get her attention if she was calling for him.

He got no answer.

He strained to filter the weather from what might be her calls when he heard it again.

Camden padded barefoot across the living room and up the stairs. He wasn't sure what was happening until he stood at the bedroom door and saw Amelia thrashing under the covers. Her words were frightened but unintelligible.

"Amelia? You're sleep talking."

Actually, it was more like a night terror. He stepped to the foot of the bed. Her legs had tangled in the comforter. The only word he was certain of was "no."

"Hey." He gripped her ankle and squeezed. "Easy." That didn't stop her nightmare. Camden moved to the top of the bed and perched on the edge. "Amelia. You're dreaming."

She snapped up with a gasp, one hand outstretched. Her wild eyes scanned the room until she saw him. "God..." Her outstretched hand folded to her chest. "That nightmare." She tried to catch her breath. "It keeps coming back." Her head dropped back, breath racing as though she'd finished a marathon. Finally, she leaned against him. "I don't even know what happens in it. But it's the same thing. I can't run. I can't hide. I don't know what from. I just"—she rolled her forehead against his arm—"know I'm going to die."

"You're safe," he promised. "Slow your breathing. It's okay."

She inhaled a long, shaky breath.

"There you go. Hold it for a second, and let it out."

Amelia followed his instructions.

"Just like that. Take another deep breath... Hold it... There you go. Let it out, nice and easy."

She half laughed and rested her cheek on his shoulder, looking up at him. "You're pretty good at knowing what I need to do."

Camden smoothed a hand over her hair. "Just had to catch your breath. That's all."

"You did that on the first night," she whispered. "Made me catch my breath. You probably kept me from freaking out and trying to run out of the house."

"That probably wouldn't have gone well."

She shook her head. "Not at all. You helped... and that cat."

He grinned. "What cat?"

Amelia slipped off his shoulder, lay down, and tugged him to lie beside her. The queen-size mattress had more than enough room for them to have their own space, but she scooted her pillow closer to his as though she didn't feel safe in a CIA safe house and he was what would keep her from the nightmares. He lay on his side and watched as she stared at the ceiling.

She kept her voice low and explained, "The one from the house I broke into." After a moment, she glanced at him and searched his expression for a reprimand. She wouldn't find it, but that didn't keep her from looking. "Did you know I broke into that house?"

"If you were trying to save your family, then I don't care either way."

She watched him like she didn't believe him, but her uncertainty slowly, curiously changed. Finally, her gaze returned to the ceiling. "The cat scared the crap out of me." She laughed quietly. "It restarted my heart. You know 'fight or freeze'? I had frozen when that man was coming for me. The cat snapped me out of it." She faced him again. "Do you believe in guardian angels or higher powers?"

"In the form of a cat?"

She elbowed him with a laugh and looked away. Maybe she couldn't share her story and look at him simultaneously. "I ran up the stairs. By then, I managed to speak when you answered. Everything was such a blur." She closed her eyes, perhaps replaying all that happened. "I crawled under a bed and wedged against the wall. It was such a small space. The bed frame came to right here." She held her hand a couple of inches above her nose. "The footsteps came closer. My heart crawled into my throat. The space felt like it was shrinking." She paused again and stared at nothing. "You made me breathe, and the cat grounded me. Your voice and its soft fur." She turned on her side and faced him again. "I wouldn't be alive if not for that." She laughed self-deprecatingly. "That part is never in my nightmare."

He gave her a playful elbow. "Maybe it wouldn't be so scary if we were there."

She laughed, which he took as a win. Then Amelia sobered and whispered, "I didn't mean to wake you up."

"Don't worry about it."

She shivered and pulled the comforter up. The house was much colder than when they'd gone to sleep. She eyed his bare chest. He'd been sleeping in sweatpants and hadn't bothered to find a shirt before coming upstairs. Body heat was the best way to keep warm. He bit his tongue to keep that to himself. Her covers were working overtime to keep him in check.

"Are you cold?" she asked.

Come on, Amelia. Don't tempt me. He propped up on his side. "I'll let you get back to sleep."

That was what was needed, what kept him from being a massive ass-hole. She was pouring her soul out to him about trauma that would haunt her for years, and he was thinking about body heat. What the hell was wrong with him?

"Sleep," she said, mulling the word over as though it were a pill she needed to take. "I've always been the one in charge. The provider. The boss. I can't remember the last time someone told me to do something for my benefit." She glanced at him in a way that didn't help the growing need tightening in his chest. "If I've learned anything from our conversations, it's that I like it when you're looking out for me and tell me what to do."

In bed... His heart thudded. That wasn't anywhere near how she meant him to take it, yet that was where his mind went. She held his gaze, almost challenging him—*almost* like she'd thought of that too. Camden should make a joke. A better idea would be to say good night and drag himself to the couch.

She looked away and half laughed. "Life just feels easier when you do the mental heavy lifting and lighten the burdens." She laughed again, but it was deprecating. "*Go to sleep*. God. What's wrong with me? That's not a heavy mental burden. I'm not making sense." Amelia shook her head. "I have no idea what I'm talking about."

He did. He had an unshakeable need to take care of her. He didn't believe in fate, but he couldn't ignore chemistry. That was too damn bad. Their connection wasn't anything they should act on.

"Get some sleep." He couldn't help himself and leaned over and pressed a dangerous kiss to her forehead.

Her sharp intake of breath rocketed through him. His lips remained on her soft skin. The quietest whisper of need rumbled in her throat. Amelia wrapped a hand around his bicep and held him still.

The message was loud and clear. *Stay*. Desire flared in her eyes just as it had before, but the vulnerability was there too. His stomach dropped.

He forced his lips away and touched his forehead to hers and closed his eyes. "I can't."

They lingered in the dark. Neither crossed the line, but much was said without uttering a word. Finally, he wrenched himself away and managed to roughly say, "Night" and kicked himself all the way back to his blanket on the couch.

CHAPTER FIFTEEN

THE POWER HAD returned sometime after Amelia somehow fell asleep the second time. The struggle was real. If insomnia had been hard to deal with at home in her condo, it was damn near impossible to manage with a shirtless Camden sleeping in the same house. She could still feel the kiss he'd placed on her forehead. She'd gone her entire life without sparks exploding in her lungs like glittering fireworks—all that from a chaste good night kiss.

Well, it wasn't that chaste. Had she really asked him to stay? Embarrassed heat rushed up her neck and swallowed her whole.

Daylight would cast an awkward blanket over them. Amelia didn't want to go downstairs and face reality or the dead-sexy man she'd semi-propositioned during a middle-of-the-night conversation. Her cheeks burned. He deserved to be canonized if he didn't breathe a word.

Amelia took a few minutes to procrastinate, snooping through the bathroom and closet, then she readied for the day, dressing and tying her hair into a loose, low bun. After another scrutinizing glance in the mirror—nothing could be done about the dark circles that had taken permanent residence under her eyes—she crept downstairs.

The heavenly scent of coffee met her. She scanned the living room. A pillow and blanket were folded at the end of the leather couch. Amelia inched farther away from the stairs and saw Camden hunched over his phone with a pen in one hand as he jotted notes on a small pad of paper.

"Good morning." She beelined for the coffeemaker and the mug he'd set out for her. She could feel his gaze. The last night replayed in her mind a thousand times for every step she took.

"There's tea bags in the cabinet if that's what you prefer."

"Coffee packs more of a caffeine punch." She poured a cup, still not hazarding a glance at his face. "Pretty sure I won't function today without it." Slowly, she turned around. That intense, soul-searching gaze of his was locked on her. *Good God.* His scrutiny was far more like a smolder. "Did you sleep okay on the couch?"

"I can sleep anywhere."

"I seem to have the opposite problem." She opened the fridge and found it mostly empty. Behind her, Camden walked across the kitchen, opened a cabinet, and held out two plastic bottles: sugar and shelf-stable creamer. She took both. "Thanks."

He remained nearby as she doctored her coffee. "Any more nightmares?"

Nervous heat crawled up her neck. "Nope."

She girded herself for a serious talk. Camden would set ground rules. The biggest one should've been a no-brainer: She shouldn't have asked him to stay with her. *Stay* hadn't been specific. She could have just meant in the room, on the far side of the bed. But with all the energy bouncing between them, what she'd said had been *a lot.*

"That's good." He returned to his place at the breakfast bar, a complete gentleman who didn't mention a peep about anything from the previous night. "There are protein and granola bars in there." He gestured at a pantry door. "Oatmeal and a couple other add-water-and-heat options."

The butterflies in her stomach didn't think that was a great idea. They stormed around like metalheads in a mosh pit. Still, she went through the motions of making apple cinnamon oatmeal. As she moved to the microwave, Camden grabbed the football from the counter. He paced. Her butterflies rioted. The microwave beeped, and Amelia retrieved her breakfast and watched him pace. His forehead was tight. His eyes were downcast. Each toss of the football was executed from muscle memory. She wasn't sure he realized he was even holding the thing.

"What's going on?" she asked.

Camden turned and clapped a hand over the ball. His long fingers flexed into the leather. "There's someone I want you to meet."

Well, hell. Not only did he not want to talk about last night, he wanted her to meet someone, perhaps a shrink. After everything she'd been through, a mental health checkup probably wasn't a bad idea, but she wasn't sure any therapist would believe a single word she said. Maybe *that* was why she'd poured her soul to Camden. She needed an outlet, and he knew the truth.

"Why are you making that face?" He lifted the football to his shoulder and, with a get-ready gesture, waited for her to raise her hands. "Catch."

She caught the soft pass. "Do you want me to see a psychologist?"

His eyebrows rose, but he didn't answer. Instead, Camden clapped his hands together once and held them out. "Back at me." She gingerly threw it in his general direction. He caught the ball and didn't laugh at her awkward toss. "That wasn't what I was thinking of, but it probably isn't a bad idea."

"There's not a therapist on Earth who will believe a word I say. They'll gaslight me. I'll get upset, and a vicious cycle will start."

He laughed. "Well, good thing I wasn't going to suggest a psychologist." He walked to the far side of the counter and tossed the ball again as though playing catch during a breakfast conversation was par for the course. "Good catch." He spun the ball in his hand and gave her an easy throw. "There are plenty of therapists who will believe you. There's probably more spies per square mile around here than anywhere else in the world." He reached out and snagged her very bad throw. "Or you can keep talking to me. Unlicensed. Untrained. But *un*-judgmental."

Maybe he mentioned "un-judgmental" because of their late-night conversation. Right then, she didn't feel judged and wasn't a tenth as mortified as she had been when walking into the kitchen that morning. Maybe the coffee helped. Maybe it was just Camden.

She chewed her lip. "Who should I meet?"

"A woman who worked adjacent to Hailey and Jonathan. They traveled in the same art circles and worked for the same agency."

"Oh…" Her eyebrows rose. She hadn't been in the same vicinity of the person Camden might want her to talk to. Amelia's interest was piqued. "Will she help me find Hailey?"

Camden twirled the ball in his hands. It didn't take someone well-versed in human behavior to see he wasn't sure if Hailey was still alive. "Maybe."

"When do we meet her?"

"I don't know." He frowned. "She's not entirely bought into the idea of meeting you."

"Why not?"

"She hasn't said exactly, but I think she doesn't see the value in it."

"Why do you?"

Camden pursed his lips and tossed the ball to himself. "It might give you some closure."

Amelia chewed the inside of her cheek. "Because Hailey's dead?"

"One of two distinct possibilities."

"What's her name?"

"Beth."

Beth sounded like a reasonable name for a reasonable person. Amelia's thoughts fast-tracked. "I could tell Beth I'm willing to help find Hailey. She could put me to work, maybe track down whatever they're working on. I wouldn't even hold it against them that they tried to ruin my life to cover up their mess."

His grin hitched. "I can run that by her, but I don't think it's her call." He set the football on the counter and eyed her uneaten oatmeal, which looked like gelatinous goo. "Let's walk down to Mount Vernon Avenue for breakfast."

As if on cue, her stomach grumbled. At least it was quiet enough that he wouldn't have heard. Going out for breakfast was one hundred percent better than cold oatmeal and anything else their safe house might have stocked.

Amelia had learned several things about safe houses since her arrival. First, not every safe house was built like the ones in the movies. Theirs didn't have a generator that kicked on, nor did it have a security system of laser beams and motion-activated security cameras. The doors and windows looked industrial-strength but weren't hard to open. Second, the cabinets were packed with shelf-stable food that probably wouldn't be a culinary delight. Third, many weapons and tactical things were shoved into and secured in various hidey-holes, crevices, and drawers. She'd never been inches away from a gun before and had no idea how many varieties of knives were available.

The bathroom mirror cabinet had bathroom-sized weapons just like the bedroom closet had closet-sized weapons. All of that, she learned after quickly snooping before getting ready and finding what was, according to her best guess, some kind of shotgun that could immobilize a rhino. It seemed to her that Camden could have mentioned the firepower casually shelved within arm's reach of probably every room. Then again, maybe it wasn't something he thought much about.

THEY STEPPED OUT the front door, and Camden breathed in the crisp air that carried the scent of sunshine and cold weather. Sunbeams streamed through the bare trees. Wet leaves carpeted the street and sidewalks and were plastered over parked cars.

He placed a hand at the small of Amelia's back as he guided her in the right direction. They meandered toward Mount Vernon Avenue. A light wind picked up as his phone buzzed in his pocket. Camden knew it would be Beth before he saw her name.

> **Beth:** *Who are you and how do you have so much influence over what I do?*

After Amelia spitballed the idea of looking for Hailey, Camden had decided he wasn't above asking for favors. That Boss Man enjoyed pulling rank over people at the CIA was simply a bonus. He held up his phone. "We have our meeting."

Amelia stopped short. Her eyebrows arched. "With Beth?" Her smile made her dark eyes sparkle. "I knew she'd be open to help."

"*Open* might be a stretch, but she's going to meet us." He typed a short response to Beth. "We can get our breakfast to go."

An hour later, Camden pulled into a Fairfax County neighborhood that looked ordinary and boring, and it was except for the CIA property at the end of a cul-de-sac.

"Here we are." He slowed as the GPS announced their destination. Tall pine trees wrapped around the backyard of a small house intentionally made to be forgettable. Nothing about it was interesting nor ignored. The landscaping was generic, the grass trimmed. The drapes hung closed, and the porch light was likely on a timer.

The house would have the lore of suburban gossip. Maybe neighbors recalled an older couple had once lived there. Perhaps the house had been stuck between two parties litigating an unending divorce. No one in the neighborhood would be able to remember names or faces, and more importantly, no one would ask questions because the HOA bills were paid on time and the grass never grew too long.

Camden's black SUV with government plates would likely raise an eyebrow or two if anyone was home to notice. But it was the middle of the workday on a tiny cul-de-sac. Whoever saw his government plates would forget by the end of the day. He parked in the driveway next to Beth's Lexus.

"Is Beth nice?" Amelia asked.

He considered. She presented herself as nice, but Amelia might not know what he meant. Camden decided to answer with a warning. "She's a spook. Trained to manipulate people. So take anything she says and you feel with a grain of salt."

"Do you trust her?"

He scoffed. "Absolutely fuckin' not."

Amelia laughed at his honesty. "All right, then. Good to know. Let's meet Beth the Spook."

From the moment he told Amelia about the meeting with Beth, she'd perked up. Amelia had walked faster, talked faster. Her cheeks had more color, and her voice had a hopeful edge that made him nervous. She wouldn't get from Beth what she imagined she might. The urge to repeat his warning hung on the tip of his tongue, but he stopped short. Amelia would be able to see through Beth's song and dance.

They approached the front door. He didn't bother to knock and walked inside. "We're here."

The house was furnished as generically as the exterior had been maintained. Looks were deceiving though, and he bet bells and whistles were staged throughout the space to ensure its occupants' safety. Beth walked from the living room.

Camden lifted his chin to say hello.

As though her last text message hadn't said to screw off, Beth smiled like a queen welcoming them into her castle and strode with her hand outstretched. "Amelia." She was warm and personable and scarily likeable. "It's really great to meet you."

"Likewise," Amelia replied, though she didn't match Beth's level of bullshitting bluster.

"Would you like coffee?" Beth guided them toward the kitchen. "I brought pastries from one of my favorite little places. The almond croissants are my favorite, but you can't go wrong with the coffee cake muffins." She gestured to a platter awaiting their arrival. "They're made with oranges and are pretty much an excuse to eat cupcakes for breakfast."

Amelia hovered by the counter and barely glanced at the spread on the table. "We just ate."

Beth shrugged happily, playing the part of the happy homemaker putting on a domestic show. "More for me."

Camden eyed Beth and Amelia. He compared the two women. He shouldn't have, but his brain categorized them before he could focus. They were both type-A and driven, successful in their arenas, and they were memorably, distinctively attractive, but that was where the similarities ended. If anything, they were opposites. Beth wore fancy high heels and clothes that cost a small fortune. Amelia wore simple flats and jeans that Camden couldn't steal his eyes from. Beth's hair seemed to laugh in the face of the recent rain and humidity. Amelia had tied her smooth, dark hair into a low bun at the nape of her neck.

"You worked with Hailey and Jonathan?" Amelia asked, not wasting a moment of time.

Beth angled her head. Her eyes cut to him and back to Amelia when he didn't meet her inquisitive gaze. "We traveled the same circles, but no. Our assignments didn't intersect."

"Do you consider yourself friends?"

"Sure. I did. They were great people."

Camden noted how Amelia spoke in the present tense and Beth in the past. That made sense, but the distinction made him uneasy.

Mistrust darkened Amelia's eyes. "I thought I'd met most of their friends. My sister and I are really close."

A model of patience, Beth nodded with a perfectly crafted empathetic smile. "My job is very different from theirs."

"How so?"

"I socialize. I flirt. I meet people and establish myself as someone who knows a thing or two about art and history."

"That's how you know Hailey and Jonathan?"

Beth nodded. "They taught me a great deal and have saved my ass when I was in way over my head." For the first time, her expression didn't look expertly crafted for maximum manipulation. "I'm really sorry for your loss."

Amelia stepped back and bumped against the counter. He wondered how many times she'd heard that phrase and how many times her mind had kept her from screaming that Hailey was only missing and not dead.

"You okay?" Camden asked under his breath.

She nodded, not keeping her voice as low as his. "I haven't been sleeping much lately."

Sympathy registered on Beth's face. That was the second time he believed her expressions since they arrived. "I have problems sleeping too," Beth admitted. "Nightmares."

Amelia's cheeks paled unevenly. He could see her pulse dance in her neck and didn't know if sadness or fury was to blame.

She turned toward him. "Could we talk?" With a nod toward Beth, she added, "Privately."

He shoved his hands into his pockets. Maybe taking Amelia there wasn't his best idea. "Yeah, sure."

"I can step out if you like." Beth pushed her perfectly coiffed hair behind her ear and smiled reassuringly. "Or, if there's anything I can do—"

"There's not." Amelia backed from the kitchen and beckoned him toward the front door.

Beth remained unfazed, keeping pace with Amelia's retreat. "I'll step into the living room and let you two have the kitchen."

"I'd rather go for a walk."

"It's freezing outside." The corners of Beth's eyes tightened. "And I think it's supposed to pour again soon."

He glanced out the living room window and noted the much darker skies. Beth wasn't wrong.

"I'm not going to melt." Amelia's eyes bore into Camden. "Will you?"

He laughed. "Nope."

Beth moved ahead of them and opened a closet door in the foyer. "I'm sure we have an umbrella around here somewhere."

"Stop. I don't want anything from you."

That wasn't entirely true. If Camden hadn't known better, that edge of paranoia in Amelia's words would have caught him off guard, but she was well within her rights to not trust Beth.

"Don't worry about an umbrella. We'll be fine." He took a backward step and bypassed Beth as she had the audacity to look offended. "Let's roll."

Beth laid her hands on her hips. "That's ridiculous."

Amelia made him proud by suppressing what had to be a monumental eye roll, though as she passed, she tacked on, "You'd be shocked to hear all of the ridiculousness I've put up with lately."

Camden had a good idea how done Amelia was with Beth and the CIA. That didn't bode well for her hopes of working together to find Hailey. They walked out the front door as the first fat raindrops fell again. He was exhausted by the weather and wished for Abu Dhabi's warmth. Camden eyed Amelia's shirt and shoes. Neither would do well in the rain. "I'll grab your coat." He headed toward the SUV.

"I don't want it." She trudged over the lawn. "I just want to clear my mind."

"Guess the wind and rain will do that." He jogged to catch up. His arm itched to wrap around her, as though protecting her from raindrops would make everything better. "What's the matter?"

Amelia didn't seem to notice the rain.

"Are you concerned she was wearing a wire? That the house is bugged?"

She stopped abruptly. "No. That never occurred to me. Why would she—" Amelia shook her head. "God, why am I dealing with this insanity?"

The rain rolled over them. "But you won't stay inside or take Beth's umbrella?"

"I just wanted to leave. I didn't want to touch anything from her or *the CIA*. It couldn't be any clearer that she thinks Hailey is dead, and it felt stupid to ask about helping find her. I mean, Jonathan is dead, and I can't process that yet." She balled her hand into a fist and looked like she might scream or cry—either one would work for the situation. "I miss them both so much. All while Beth is buying the perfect pastry, talking about how great they are. I wanted to strangle the smile off her face."

"Beth isn't the enemy." Though he agreed she could have taken her picture-perfect persona down several notches. The CIA's involvement wasn't making Amelia's grief any easier. "She's a tool in your arsenal. You can use her to get what you need."

Then again, maybe he shouldn't have been giving Amelia hope. Camden ran a hand into his wet hair as rain soaked his shoulders and his clothes clung to his back.

"I need to keep walking."

He nodded and kept by her side. The rain poured over them. They reached the top of the cul-de-sac.

Her head dipped back, and she stared at the clouds. "Cam, when will this get easier?"

He'd never lost a loved one. He'd never had to deal with the unknown. "I'm not sure, sweetheart." Not having the answers made him feel helpless. The only thing he could do was help her regain her composure and get her out of the rain. Little droplets ran down her cheeks and caught on her eyelashes.

"Do you want to keep walking or head back?"

Amelia wiped rain from her face and headed down the cul-de-sac toward the main road. "I want to find my sister."

If her sister was still alive. Given the amount of time that had passed, what had happened to Jonathan, and the crazy way Amelia ended up in prison, he didn't think Hailey's survival was possible. "I know."

"No, you don't." She yanked him to face her. "*I* want to find her. As in physically." She released him and gestured blankly toward the rain-slicked street. "I want to search for her. Look at places they think she could have gone."

He pinched the bridge of his nose. Even ignoring the level of danger she was asking for, no evidence existed that Hailey was alive. "I don't think it works like that."

"Tell me what to say to Beth to make it happen."

The more desperation he saw in her eyes, the more he wasn't sure Amelia needed to gallivant around the CIA's backyard, searching for a missing asset. "There's no telling what—"

"Camden, please."

"You need to understand what happened leading up to that night." He didn't have permission to explain, and she didn't have clearance. Yet there he was, about to open his mouth because he couldn't stand her radiating pain. "Are you familiar with the phrase 'NOC list'?"

She shook her head.

"Essentially, it's a list of agents and their covers. It identifies who is undercover and who they are in their everyday real lives." He rubbed the back of his neck. "I'm not privy to its reach or the damage or how much is still unknown, but..." He really needed to shut his mouth.

"But what?"

In for a penny, in for a pound. "A couple of weeks ago, a NOC list hit the black market. An unknown NOC list. No one knew what was on it or who had access. Hell, I don't even know if everyone took it seriously at first."

"It was obviously serious," she said bitterly.

"I'm saying all this because the level of unknowns was—*is*— astronomical. We don't know what Hailey and Jonathan were working on, but it was enough to kill for."

She looked completely unmoved.

"This isn't like an episode of *CSI* or *Without a Trace*. You can't follow a lead and find an answer. It's not that simple."

"Do you think I'm an idiot?" She crossed her arms.

That indifferent expression morphed into one that was somewhere on the scale between indignant and pissed. His stomach bottomed out. "What? No."

"I never suggested it was simple. I just want to discuss it."

Clearly, he'd made a misstep and needed to get better footing in the conversation. "What I'm saying is—" He took a deep breath. "I'm telling you Beth will shoot you down."

"Why?"

"At the most basic level? You're untrained."

"They put me in prison. *Clearly*," she tossed back at him, "they think I can handle some level of danger."

"There were guards, and you were in solitary confinement."

She twisted her lips as the wheels kept turning. Amelia wiped water off her cheeks. "What if you help me too?"

A wild goose chase for a dead female asset that the CIA hadn't turned up? With an untrained woman who was garnering more and more of his attention in *very* unprofessional ways? *No. Absolutely not.* It would be the kind of huge mistake that had earned him the reputation for being impulsive. "Depends."

Her face lit up, and Camden felt that in his soul. She didn't wait for him to backtrack and turned them around, pulling him back toward Beth.

They walked into the house. Fluffy white towels waited for them on a console table by the front door. Beth thought every situation through. It was good to know she was always thinking of the next steps, possible reactions, and their ramifications. She was tenacious. That was probably one of the qualities that made her good at her job. If she wasn't already on her way to being a CIA handler, he bet it would happen soon enough.

He wasn't sure how well Amelia's ask would go, but at least Camden wouldn't be the one shutting it down.

"I started a fresh pot of coffee," Beth called from the kitchen.

"Of course she did," Amelia grumbled.

He snickered. Beth was like some kind of lethal version of a prep school PTA president. Once again, he found himself comparing the two women. Amelia was actually the tenacious one. If Beth was an always-scheming PTA caricature, Amelia was positioning herself as David versus Goliath. But who was Goliath? The CIA? The group who murdered Jonathan and abducted Hailey? *Both, probably.*

Amelia untied her bun, rubbed the towel over her hair and shoulders at lightning speed, and sped off toward Beth while he was still wiping the rain off his face. *Shit.* They should've thought out their request. The wording would matter. It almost had to be Beth's idea. They needed to know all the angles and dangers already and have a plan to overcome them. He needed to channel his inner Liam Brosnan. Camden's team leader did that in his sleep. It was the first time he'd ever wished Liam's cautious forethought was one of his own qualities.

He followed Amelia into the kitchen and saw Beth eyeing her, sensing they were about to drop a burdensome request. Still, true to form and nailing her PTA-president performance, Beth greeted them with a lift of the coffee pot. She poured it into three waiting mugs. "How do you take your coffee?"

"I want to help find my sister," Amelia answered.

Beth set down the pot with unreadable detachment. Her bright smile remained in place as though Amelia had asked about field-trip duty.

"If you tell me what Hailey was working on, I'll jump in. Just hand me a list of everything you know." Amelia squared her shoulders. "I'll tell you everything I find out. I just want to find her."

"Even if I knew what she was doing, her work was classified."

"I'll swear on a Bible or sign my name in blood. Whatever it takes to—"

"It doesn't work like that." Beth *almost* masked her condescension.

Camden picked up on the thinly hidden superiority and was positive that would only fuel Amelia's fire.

"And even if it did," Beth continued, "I don't have time to help you. You can't just go into the field blind, without training, and—"

"Camden said he would help."

Beth's lips flattened before her gaze swiveled, eyes fiercely challenging him. "Did you?"

He grinned, thinking Beth's head might explode. "I can do the heavy lifting, and I'm sure Titan could work out the classified part."

"As if it's that simple."

"Sometimes it is." His flippancy was just enough to balance Beth's condescension. The truth was that he had no idea if Boss Man would sign off on a wild goose chase, but Beth didn't know that. She also seemed to hold Jared in untouchable regard. That would work in Camden's favor. Beth blinked slowly and took her time to calculate a response that said no way.

"We could call Jared now," he offered.

"I bet we could…" Beth let out a deep breath and turned toward the cabinets. "Let see if this place has some peppermint schnapps or something. Because everyone in this room will need it."

CHAPTER SIXTEEN

AFTER BETH TOPPED everyone's mug off with a heavy splash of peppermint schnapps, Amelia was certain their late-morning meeting would leave her shell-shocked. She had prepared to hear details about Hailey and Jonathan that would make her question everything, and that still might happen. The peppermint schnapps hadn't been to soften blows. It had been to manage an insufferable bureaucracy. The only thing she learned that day was that even spies had to do paperwork.

Their meeting took hours, and for most of it, the three of them snacked on pastries while requests were made, questioned, and parried. To Beth's credit, the treats were very tasty and appreciated.

Not until Amelia climbed back into their SUV and the seat warmers kicked on did the gravity of her request become clear. She and Camden were approved to do *something* that no one would explain. She didn't know when or where, just that they had a green light. Both Camden and Beth seemed surprised.

Amelia shivered as something akin to adrenaline pumped in her blood. The windshield wipers and tires on the rain-slicked road were the only sounds for several miles. Camden checked his mirrors and merged onto the interstate. He was so casual. Then again, this was his day job. He didn't need schnapps. The conversations and negotiations were his norm. "What do you want to do when we get back?"

"Take a hot shower and decompress." She glanced at the casual way he drove, alert but at ease. She hated driving in the rain. She hated wondering if the drivers around her were paying attention to the road and conditions—a car accident could easily upend everything. "Your boss—Boss Man—he sounds intense."

"Jared Westin?" Camden snorted. "He is."

"Brock and Parker, not so much?"

"They are in their own ways. Brock's real quiet. Does his job. Disappears. I don't see him much, but Parker is always available. He's a magician with technology and ammunition." He slowed for traffic. "They're mostly based in the US. Though Jared and Parker spent a lot of time setting up our headquarters in Abu Dhabi."

He'd mentioned the Middle East before. "That's where you live?"

Camden nodded. "Yeah."

"Do you like it?"

He gave a pointed glance out the window. "We don't have forty-degree days and rain all the time."

Amelia pulled her coat over her chest. Just thinking about the cold made her shiver again. "Do you like your job?"

His jaw worked back and forth. "It has its moments."

"That's vague." Though she could say the same thing about running Events and Occasions. She liked working with Veronica and enjoyed chasing deadlines with logistical challenges. Despite the fact that she detested the ins and outs of running a business, the sense of accomplishment that came from a completed checklist was always nice, and nobody on Earth would complain about taste-testing samples from potential menus. Events and Occasions used to be lots of fun. *Now?* She didn't know if what happened with Hailey and Jonathan had changed things at work or if that simply changed her perspective on her own life.

"I'm never bored," Camden explained, raising a shoulder. "The pay and benefits are hard to compete with. It works for me. What about you? You like what you do?"

"No," she admitted. Thinking it, much less saying it aloud, was a shock. But it was the truth. How hadn't she noticed that before?

Eyebrows up, Camden glanced her way. "Really?"

She shrugged as though she were indifferent, but really, the revelation still reverberated. "I'm good at it." She could hear the hesitancy in her own voice, as if she were listening to someone else. "Strong repeat business."

"Having your own company, building something out of nothing, that's impressive."

"Maybe…" *Compared to what?* He probably saved people's lives. *Compared to him? Not impressive.* But it did show that she could bust her ass until she got what she wanted. That was how she intended to find Hailey: nonstop, dogged work. Amelia watched the cars pass as they slowed for an exit ramp. "Hailey had an entire adventurous life, and I didn't realize it."

"You knew the important parts of her."

"She loved family and teaching. She loved talking about art." Amelia chewed on her bottom lip. "But there was more than I realized, I guess. She really loved life."

"What do you love?"

"I guess just my sister." Amelia wasn't passionate about anything the way Hailey was. She didn't know why she hadn't noticed that before. She thought about work a lot. It wasn't her world, but it definitely fulfilled a need. "You know what I like about my job?"

"What?"

"I like being in charge and having a surefire way to provide for myself. I started my company when Hailey was getting her master's and doctorate. We flipped roles for a while. It was like I became the big sister. My company offset a lot of costs. Our apartment. Groceries. I'd felt so out of control when our parents died, and when I finally had that taste of control…" The right words wouldn't come. "I could breathe better."

But life was out of control again, and she suddenly remembered asking Camden to just tell her what to do. The idea that he could take over was nearly an aphrodisiac. A blush rose to her cheeks and down her spine. Never in a million years would that have come out of her mouth. But sharing life's responsibilities would be so liberating, even for a moment.

Amelia watched him drive for longer than she should have. After his dark-brown hair dried, it had a mussed, haphazard style that she wanted to touch. It looked soft compared to his harder features. A five-o'clock shadow darkened his chiseled jaw. He was the poster boy for tall, dark, and handsome, and the more she tried to ignore it, the harder it became.

"What?" he asked.

Nothing I would admit to. She quickly stopped staring. "I think I'm hungry."

He laughed. "Well, let me know when you're sure."

She snickered. One second, Camden was smoldering simply by existing. The next, he made goofy jokes. She liked him more and more. His laughter rumbled quietly in his chest and made the corners of his eyes crinkle. Why was she noticing this when she needed to focus on Hailey? "Maybe I just need a nap first."

"You can do both."

That could be true about many things. Amelia chewed on her bottom lip.

They found another tiny parking spot near the safe house. He was able to magically finesse the oversized vehicle into it. The rain had died off again. Grateful for the reprieve, Amelia buttoned her coat and fell into step with Camden. The wind had picked up like it had the night before. She shivered. Wind chimes dinged, and artisan wind spinners danced in yards.

"This neighborhood is adorable." She would love to live somewhere that had so much more personality than her condo complex.

Amelia didn't even want to go back home. Everything she'd found comfortable—the easiness of condo living, the repetitiveness of her day job—had become tedious.

A restlessness overtook her body. Her legs wanted to hurry inside. Her chest ached with a drumbeat that picked up in tempo as they closed in on the safe house. She swallowed away a wave of anxiety. Camden had taken her back there, but he could just as easily have driven her back to her condo.

The idea made her dizzy. She didn't want to go there. "Cam—"

He had inserted the key into his front door and looked over his shoulder.

Panic—dread?—pounded in her ears. Her lungs felt cold, empty, as if she might not be able to catch her breath if she wasn't careful. "I can't go back to my place tonight."

"Then don't." Camden turned back to the door and twisted the key like the conversation had been decided.

She couldn't walk and process the simple solution at the same time.

"Amelia?" He crooked two fingers and pulled her inside as though she were tied to an invisible string.

The house was warm. The lights were off. He reached behind her and shut the door. Her eyes shut for the moment he leaned close. He smelled familiar to her. A wild twenty-four hours had passed. It actually felt like it could have been days, and during that time, she had hugged him, lain by him, even dragged him by his arm. She knew the way he smelled, and it melted away her anxiety. He towered over her, and for a delirious, dreamlike second, she imagined him closing their distance, pressing her against the door, and erasing every trouble. He could kiss her, touch her, do whatever he wanted to her, and she would bask in his attention like a woman starved.

"Doing okay?"

Oh my God. No, she wasn't. Her heart stopped beating. She tucked her chin, embarrassed. Fantasizing about this man would lead to disaster. Beth would never work with Amelia without Camden, and Camden would never work with her if he knew what was continually plaguing her imagination.

He touched her chin. "Eyes on me, sweetheart."

Why did the quiet rasp of his words have to roll over her like that? Amelia steeled herself and raised her face. He looked at her as though trying to read her soul. The intensity made his dark, smoldering eyes shine. "What's bothering you?"

Her lungs weren't getting enough oxygen. "The day's just catching up with me."

He scrutinized her a moment longer then nodded and tossed the house keys to himself. "You sure?"

She nodded.

Camden let out a long breath and hung the keys on the hook by the door. "I gotta take a shower."

He hurried into the dark living room and scooped up the football from the couch.

She couldn't help feeling he had read her thoughts and was unhappy or irritated. Then again, she couldn't blame him for wanting to shower and change into fresh clothes. Theirs had air-dried while meeting with Beth.

Her pants and shirt were stiff and uncomfortable. "I'll do the same." But she didn't head upstairs and noticed Camden didn't turn around, which worried her. "Then maybe we grab food later?"

"Sounds like a plan." But he still didn't turn around. Camden stalked around the kitchen, tossing the football, instead of using the downstairs bathroom to shower.

She bit her lip but returned to her bedroom—well, his bedroom that he was loaning her. His temporary bedroom, where the sheets and pillow didn't smell like him and the walls were bare of personality. What did his real home look like?

Amelia undressed and stepped into the shower. It was high-end and luxurious. Water could spray from any direction she wanted. The floors and towel rack were heated, and the mirrors barely fogged. This house had more tricks up its sleeve than the weapons it hid in the closets. Once her life was untangled and Hailey was home safe, Amelia might invest in a bathroom renovation.

She stayed under the hot water until she was worried none would be left for Camden, then she wrapped her hair and herself in warm towels of thick cotton. She slathered on face cream and opened the bathroom door. Cold air rolled in. Laying her change of clothes on the towel heater would have been a genius move. She decided to warm up under the covers before donning an outfit for dinner. Amelia pulled back the sheets and closed her eyes. She would stay there only long enough to adjust to the bedroom temperature.

CAMDEN CREPT UP the stairs, silently cursing his lack of forethought. "Amelia?" he whispered.

She was asleep, he was sure. He'd heard the water turn off well before he took his own shower downstairs. There hadn't been a peep from her since.

The door was cracked.

"Amelia?"

The November sun had set. The drawn windows were dark. Only a slice of light from the bathroom illuminated the room. She was asleep with a towel wrapped around her hair and the covers pulled up to her chin.

With a towel wrapped around his waist, he crept to the small chest of drawers.

"Cam?"

Shit. "Just grabbing clean clothes. I'll be out in a minute."

A mirror on the dresser reflected the room at his back. Amelia sat up. The hair towel wobbled, and she pulled it down. Her dark hair fell loose around her shoulders. "God, I'm freezing."

He forced his eyes to the drawers, pulled out his needed clothes, and unintentionally saw her reflection again. Amelia wriggled with the covers and removed a second towel. "I fell asleep in a damp towel."

Jesus fucking Christ. That wasn't what he needed to see or hear. He'd all but kissed her when they walked inside and had to walk away from her without looking back. His heart thumped in his chest. Between the two of them, a towel and blanket were all that kept them decent. All of the blood in his body was going to his cock, and he needed to focus on getting the hell out of that room.

She wrapped herself in the comforter and scooted to the edge of the bed. Her eyes met his in the mirror. "Can I wear something comfy of yours?" Her gaze drifted down his back before jerking to the wall, making his pulse pound harder. She added on, explaining, "I didn't bring any lounge-around-the-house clothes."

Her in his clothes? He liked that, too, which wasn't helpful. But a clothed Amelia was much, *much* better than her nearly naked and an arm's reach away. He needed to treat her like a client. No, actually, he needed to treat her like a victim because that was what she was, no matter if they were "working" on her goose chase.

Camden licked his bottom lip, refocused, and nodded. He chose a T-shirt but didn't know what to do for pants. Several clothing options were probably stocked in the closet for people who used the safe house, but again, he thought of her in his clothes and didn't offer to look. He selected his most comfortable gray sweatpants and turned. "You could probably roll these on your waist to make them fit."

The safest option was to throw the shirt and pants at her and haul ass downstairs. The tightness in his chest made it loud and clear that wasn't what he really wanted to do. Camden should've put on the dirty clothes after his shower and stayed downstairs.

"Are you mad at me?" she asked.

His eyebrows arched. "What? No." He racked his mind for ways that he could have made her think he was upset. "Why?"

She lifted a bare shoulder. "When we arrived, I thought... maybe I was overstaying my welcome."

She meant that moment when he damn near ran away instead of taking her against the wall. He was an asshole and needed to get himself in order before he did something he couldn't take back.

"Not at all."

"Oh." She smiled, but it didn't reach her eyes. "Okay."

Uncertainty and tension mixed in the crackling air. He should probably say more, but all he could think about was wanting to get into her bed. He really needed to get the hell out of that room.

"I'm kind of getting that same feeling now." She bit her lip, and a blush rose into her cheeks. "If I did something to make you feel uncomfortable, I'm really sorry."

"You didn't do anything," he said too shortly.

She clearly didn't believe him. Hell, he wouldn't believe himself either. He walked to the edge of the bed and sat, at which point he faced the door that he should've been walking out of. "I promise. I'm not mad. I'm just..." He dropped his head back and stared at the ceiling. "Struggling."

"You don't want to help me with Hailey?"

He snorted. "Work is the last fuckin' thing on my mind." He glanced over his shoulder. "That's my problem."

Her cherry lips rounded as if she suddenly saw his action in an entirely different light.

"I should go downstairs." *Should* was the operative word, but he didn't move a damn muscle.

The comforter rustled behind him, and her hand cupped his shoulder. Her touch heated his skin in a way that he couldn't believe possible. His shoulder muscles tensed. Arousal pounded in his blood with an intoxicating buzz. Camden let out a shaky breath and stared at her hand then into her face again, praying he was misreading everything between them. But that was not what he saw. *Fuck.* "This is a bad idea, Amelia."

She didn't pull her hand away, and he didn't want her to. Of all the women in the world, this one didn't play hard to get. She wasn't the type for games or bullshit, and he'd never been the type to ignore what he wanted, except right then.

Amelia let go. "How come?"

"I don't know how long I'm here for. I could be gone by the morning." Her palm had seared his skin in a way that he would always be able to feel all the way back in Abu Dhabi. He forced himself off the bed and turned. There was a simple answer she wouldn't like to hear. "And you have been through a lot."

"You've helped me survive a lot," she countered with a quickness that made him want to smile.

Instead, he ground his molars until he was certain of what would come out of his mouth. "That's exactly why we shouldn't." He licked his lips. "We're *not* on the same playing field right now."

"I should've gathered you were one for sports metaphors."

He chuckled. She gave him an erection and made him laugh. That was why saying no was nearly impossible. Wasn't that what romance was all about? Though *romance* was more than a quick screw on the job. Camden walked to the edge of the bed. Crawling under the covers would change everything. Then again, who cared? Dynamics were meant to be fluid.

Amelia lay down and rested her head on the pillows. "Do you think I'm attractive?"

"You know I think you're gorgeous."

"I don't know that." She blinked hard. "Cam, you're the only thing I know that's safe. You're the person I trust."

Every. Single. Thing she said pulled him closer. He shook his head. Right then wasn't the time, but there *would be* a time. Of that he was certain. And maybe it didn't have to happen all at once. She wasn't playing games. Neither was he. Her words replayed in his head. *I like it when you tell me what to do*. The possibilities ran through him with volcanic understanding. She wanted—needed—a distraction, and he could do that in a way that would leave both of them loopy as fuck without taking advantage of her.

Camden moved closer. "Close your eyes, Amelia."

They went wider instead.

He eased onto the bed and lay close enough to smell her soft floral scent. "Eyes closed, sweetheart."

Her eyelashes fluttered shut. Her pulse jumped in her neck as her unsteady breathing whispered between her pink lips. Camden touched her cheek. Her lips parted, breath catching. His fingers traced to her jawline and mapped it slowly from one side to the other. The pads of his fingertips drifted down her neck. The quick beat of her pulse played around his skimming touch. "What do you say…" He caressed her collarbone with the back of his hand. His knuckles teased from one side to the other, nearly dipping between the swell of her breasts. "We take it slow?"

She bit her bottom lip, eyes still closed, and nodded.

He would remain in control. He would keep her safe. He would probably be gone before everything got too complicated. "If you say 'stop,' all returns to normal."

She nodded again.

Camden retraced the path to her cheek and threaded his hand into the softest hair he'd ever touched. Her breath hitched. He labored to keep his in check and dipped his mouth to hers. The kiss hit him like a spark dropped into a powder keg. Lust ignited. The immediate sizzle burned hot and fast. Need coursed through his body and cracked through his control like an earthquake.

Her mouth opened to his and stoked a hunger in him that a simple kiss shouldn't have been able to command. Their breaths raced. Her fingers bit into his skin. His hands ached to explore, and his mind tried to renegotiate his promise of taking it slow.

He kissed her until he couldn't be trusted to throw the towel and comforter away, then he ducked his mouth to her neck and breathed her in. His tongue slid to the sensitive spot behind her earlobe and made her squirm. "I am going to kiss every inch of you."

Breathless, she nodded. "Promise?"

"But not tonight."

She froze except for her fingers, which dug into his flesh. His resolve was hanging on by a thread. Camden needed to go downstairs. But his head and his cock were telling him to shut his fucking mouth and crawl into her bed.

"Slow," he reminded both of them.

"Oh God, you're a horrible person, Camden Brooks."

His lips curled, and his chest rumbled. What the fuck was he doing? He could fix this in zero-point-two seconds. Her body would feel so good. Instead, he dragged his mouth to the other side of her neck. "I'm doing this for your own good."

"And you're a liar to boot."

He laughed and lay on the pillow next to her. Her kiss, her swollen lips, and her messy hair went straight to his cock. "I totally am." But he scrubbed a hand over his face and tried to get a hold of himself. "Fucking isn't going to make anything easier."

That might have been the most responsible thing he'd ever said in his entire goddamn life.

He scrutinized her disappointment and the sexy blush of her cheeks and determined the damage. The woman was just as turned on as he was, but maybe she understood what he was trying to do: keeping her safe from him. She was vulnerable. He was temporary. It was that simple.

Amelia let out a long breath. "What now?"

Good question. They still had to eat.

"I'm taking you to dinner." Or he could order delivery for dinner in bed. Would an hour's break meet the condition for taking it slow? Probably not.

He toyed with strands of her hair. Camden forced himself out of bed and readjusted the towel precariously hanging on his torso. He had no way to hide the erection that hung around as though hope was in the air. "What are you hungry for?"

"What's your bedroom look like at home?"

His eyebrows arched, and with a chuckle, he turned for the dresser. She never did what he thought she would. Camden pulled out fresh clothes and shrugged. "I don't actually know. I'm sure it looks nice."

She laughed. "How don't you know?"

"It's an apartment furnished by Titan. I'm sure I had the opportunity to pick options or decor, but I don't think I did." He'd never thought about it before. Stuff was on the walls. Furniture matched. He had pictures of his family, but Camden couldn't recall buying anything for the apartment. "Why?"

"You know so much about me."

"Good thing I'm taking you out to dinner. You get to ask all the questions you want on a date."

She gave him a sideways look. "Date" had caught them both off guard. He liked surprising her. Surprising himself was a bonus.

CHAPTER SEVENTEEN

FOR THE FIRST time in weeks, when Amelia asked herself what on Earth was happening, the possible answers weren't terrifying. No one was trying to kill or arrest her. She wasn't talking to spies or big scary bosses. She was simply going out on a date with a man who could make her hum by just turning his smolder her way.

That wasn't actually fair. He could convince her to do anything with those eyes and that mouth, but *she* had been the one trying to convince him. She should thank him. He was leaving as soon as the grumpy Boss Man said so, and she was probably using Camden to distract herself from reality. She didn't exactly mind him as a distraction, though.

Her clothing options were limited to what she had packed haphazardly from her condo and the gray sweatpants and oversized T-shirt Camden had let her wear.

"We can't go anywhere fancy," she called down the stairs.

"Oh no," he deadpanned. "You're breaking my heart."

She snort-laughed and tugged on jeans and a sweater. Her hair had mostly finished drying while Camden kissed her into a million glittery pieces. She couldn't do much about its chaos other than to wrangle it into what she hoped passed for a messy bun. After a quick swipe of lipstick, she headed downstairs.

He waited on the couch, football in hand, sexier than she remembered him being fifteen minutes prior. How was that possible? His smile crooked, and she knew the football was about to fly her way. Amelia caught his easy loft with more confidence than she could have imagined possible. A lot had changed in a short amount of time.

"Ready?" He grabbed his wallet and the keys off the hook by the door.

It struck her that this was how married couples did date nights. After all, they lived in the same place. No one picked up or dropped off. They didn't say "Good night" or "Give me a call." They just went back into their home and repeated the whole thing whenever they wanted to. On the weekends. On vacations. After work.

A pang of guilt needled her. Amelia had been ignoring work. She'd had plenty of reasons to, but since she was out of prison, she didn't have the same excuse as before. "Can I check in with Veronica before we head out?"

He shrugged. "Of course."

"I don't have my phone or laptop. Can I call her from your phone?" The last time she'd called Veronica, it had been to drop a bomb: She'd needed a lawyer in prison and for Veronica to run the business solo while she was out of touch. They had so much to catch up on, but at the very least, she needed to explain she wasn't in custody anymore.

Camden held out his phone. "I'll be here whenever you're ready."

Veronica picked up on the second ring.

"Hey, it's me."

"Amelia? Oh my God. How are you? Where are you?"

"I—" She caught herself. How could she explain the situation with a special operations babysitter and meeting with the CIA? "Considering everything, I'm fine. What about you?"

"Fine. But who cares how I am? I've been so worried about you."

"Honestly, I'm okay. I'm going to stay offline for a while and wanted to make sure that you're good with that." Veronica could handle the business part of Events and Occasions in her sleep, but dropping everything on her without warning hadn't been fair.

"Of course I am."

"Everything with work is—"

"Amelia. Who cares about work? I'm worried about you."

"I'm in the process of straightening everything out."

"These scary people came and talked to me about you, what you knew, what you and Hailey talked about. I didn't think they'd ever leave me alone."

Amelia's stomach sank. The CIA had been harassing her and probably everyone she knew.

"I'm sorry. They arrested me and then let me go. Big misunderstanding"—*understatement of the century*—"but it's heartbreaking." Her throat cracked. "I just want to find Hailey."

"I know, hon. Anything I can do? Can I drop food off at your place? Run out and get your groceries? Anything at all? I don't even have to knock on the door."

"I appreciate that, but I'm not staying there right now."

"Where are you?"

"Just keeping my head down."

Veronica hummed. "Are you sure I can't do anything for you?"

"No, but call this number if you need me. Okay?" She ended the call and hated how law enforcement was spending more time on Amelia's social circle than on finding Hailey.

She returned to Camden and handed over the phone. "Here. Thanks."

"Everything okay?" His eyes narrowed as though he were trying to read her thoughts.

She didn't want that. Amelia had checked in and was ready to ignore her responsibilities once again. "Work's fine. I'm not needed. Veronica has everything under control."

He didn't look convinced.

"I'm starving, Cam. Can we head out?"

He pocketed his phone and led her into the cool night. At least it wasn't raining. Camden locked the house behind them and scanned the street before leading them on the same path as their breakfast trek had taken.

Her skin prickled as he searched for threats. "Who are you looking for?"

Camden looked down at her with a shrug. "No one. Everyone. Habit, I guess."

She hadn't noticed that before.

The sidewalks were more crowded as they merged onto Mount Vernon Avenue. How many of these people worked everyday jobs only to cover up their real work? How many spied for the United States? For other countries? American spies wouldn't be walking around the US, would they? Well, Jonathan and Hailey had. They'd traveled extensively and lived within an easy drive of three airports, two of which were international.

The more Amelia stared at the surrounding crowds on the sidewalk, the more it felt like someone was staring at her as well. She checked over her shoulder. Had Camden always checked their surroundings before they left the house? She hadn't noticed before.

"Burgers? Barbeque?" he asked.

She inched closer to his side and tried to ignore the lingering feeling that someone was tracking her. "I have an idea." Amelia did a quick mental calculation of their location and thought they were roughly two blocks and a straight shot from a great place she'd used for work. It had limited seating where she could hide and ignore the paranoia that had been creeping up her spine since they stepped outside.

A few minutes later, they were seated on the second floor of a familiar restaurant that touted itself as upscale American. Amelia had always found their catering menu trendy enough to meet the high expectation of bridal parties but reliable enough to earn high praise from corporate head honchos. Right then, she appreciated their low lights and tight spaces where she—or better, Camden—could catalog every person who walked in.

Camden sat with his back to the wall. She almost asked if she could sit next to him so that they could watch their surroundings together. He scanned the room then scrutinized her.

He saw her as vulnerable and fragile.

She painted on an unbothered face. "Brussels sprouts with bacon jam. Yum."

His eyes narrowed. "That's not what you were thinking about."

True, but she knew from experience the entire appetizer section could be devoured without leading him astray and was much better dinner conversation than sharing her new neurosis. He didn't look wowed by her Brussels-sprouts suggestion. She would make a crappy spy. How was Hailey so good at this? Amelia doubled down on her interest in the menu. "Are you more a pork-chop or rib-eye kind of guy?"

"*Amelia.*"

"You said I get to ask all the questions I want."

"Yeah, and I said that before you were jumping at your shadow. What's up?"

First-date jitters? Paranoia? Both? "I don't know," she muttered under her breath knowing she didn't get date jitters and had every reason to be paranoid.

He surveilled the room again then turned his full attention her way. "I'm not going to let anything hurt you. You know that, right?"

What did she know? He *believed* he could protect her. He certainly was trying to keep her heart safe from him in the bedroom. *Out of the bedroom?* There probably hadn't been many times in Camden Brooks's life when he didn't get his way. She also believed she would be dead if anyone else had answered her phone call that terrifying night. Camden had kept her safe from a thousand miles away. No doubt he could do that when they were close enough to touch. "I feel like someone's watching me."

He nodded without taking his eyes from her. "Starting when?"

He was taking her seriously. That alone made her feel safer. "Since we reached the main strip."

Camden glanced over as the waitress returned and smiled at him as though she'd never seen a man before. He didn't seem to notice. If it had been an ordinary first date, that would have been a point in his favor. Since it was their first date after she tried to pull him into her bed, Amelia didn't bother with a tally. She did, however, let a warm flush roll through her as she recalled the way he closed in on her and took her mouth with a mind-melting kiss.

"Ladies first," Camden told the waitress.

Forced to acknowledge Amelia's existence, the other woman asked what they wanted. They quickly ordered the smoked cream cheese with hot honey to start and two rib eyes for dinner. When they were alone again, Camden cut back to their previous conversation. "Tell me if you get that feeling again."

"Do you think I'm crazy?"

The look he gave her might've said yes, but he said, "I know the bullshit you've been through." He turned up a hand as though to say he rested his case. "See something. Say something. Get a weird vibe, read me in on it. Okay?"

She bit her lip and nodded. That was fair. "I've totally screwed up tonight, haven't I?"

He laughed. "You kidding me? I would rather hear what your instincts are screaming than whatever preconceived notion you have on date conversations."

Date made her insides feel gooey. He really was treating it like a date even after clearly pointing out that he was leaving in the near future and rebuffing her embarrassing advances.

He shrugged. "Besides, I owe you answers. The only thing that *needs* to happen is your list of questions."

"Now?"

The corners of his lips quirked. "Shoot."

"Do you have a girlfriend?"

"Ha." He snorted. "Why would I have a girlfriend when I'm here with you?"

"You've gotta be a thousand miles away from home."

"I kissed you," he pointed out.

Kiss was an understatement. Nervously, she twisted her fingers. "What happens on the job stays on the job?"

"Guess I've got more to prove to you than I realized. I'm not an asshole." He tapped his index finger against his water glass. "Is it hard for you to trust me?"

"No, actually. I don't know why I asked you that." She waited as their server returned with their drinks.

Camden thanked her without appearing to notice the ways she batted her eyes at him and ignored Amelia.

Alone again, she asked, "Why don't you have a girlfriend?"

He chuckled as though she'd asked a better question. "The easy answer would be I'm too busy, that work doesn't allow for it. But it's easy to point out that my teammates are all married." He lifted his shoulders. "So that answer doesn't ring true." He took a sip of his Manhattan. "It's simpler.

I'm not the relationship type."

"*Oh.* You're the love-'em-and-leave-'em type."

But that wasn't true. He had clearly warned her against sleeping with him.

"How did I miss that? You don't seem like a player."

He rolled his eyes. "I'm not."

"Emotionally unavailable?"

"Nope."

"Immature?"

"Nah. A little impulsive, maybe, but not immature."

"Hung up on the woman who broke your heart?"

Camden laughed. "Not that one either."

"So what's wrong with you?"

"Guess I'm perfect." He winked. "What about you?"

She rolled her eyes but let out a judgmental sigh. "I'm a workaholic so deep in it that I didn't realize my sister was a spy."

"You're going to have to get over the not knowing."

She tried not to pout. "It's easier said than done." Amelia chewed the inside of her cheek. "I'm a little bit of a control freak." That was why she'd wanted to let go and let Camden take on that burden. *In bed.* Heat rose to her cheeks. She wondered if he knew that. His index finger tapped against the Manhattan again as though he might have an inkling.

Their appetizer arrived. She spooned the cheese onto a toasted baguette—the screech of a fire alarm wailed. Diners gasped. Silverware clattered. False alarm or a kitchen fire? A moment of uncertain surprise hung in the dining room as everyone waited for everyone else to make a move.

"Sorry for the interruption—" the restaurant manager called between wailing cries of the fire alarm. Bright white lights strobed. He directed the room as though flagging a Boeing 747 into a terminal parking spot. "—proceed downstairs—" The alarm wailed again. "—apologize for—"

The diners nearest them stood. Camden caught Amelia's arm. "Hang tight." He scanned the room. For the most part, patrons shoved arms into jackets and gathered belongings. They fell into a single-file line down the stairs. One man was chugging his beer. Another shoveled dinner into his mouth. Most weren't going to wait for the fire marshal to show up and announce they could proceed back to their soon-to-be cold meals.

Camden bucked the trend and ignored the single-file line. He moved to the wall by the front of the building and quickly peeked out the window. A strobe light spun above his head. Amelia crept to his side. "What are you looking at?"

"Trouble."

She glanced at the window closer to her. Her heart seized. "*Cam.*"

Two men were watching the stream of restaurant diners flooding into the cold night. The roar of approaching first-responder vehicles intermixed with the fire alarm. Their lights colored the busy street, announcing their arrival moments before they screeched to a halt.

"Excuse me." The manager hurried over. "You have to leave."

Camden took her hand and hustled down the stairs. He stopped a woman coming from the kitchen as she pulled off a chef's hat and on a coat over a kitchen uniform. "Two hundred bucks for your hat and jacket."

She frowned but immediately took Camden up on the offer when he showed the cash.

"Put it on," he told Amelia. "Quick." He stopped a man wearing the same stained kitchen uniform and made the same offer.

Amelia pulled the white jacket over her clothes. It smelled of grease and food and had stains splashed on the sleeves. He did the same.

"Leave your jacket. Tuck your hair up."

She balled it all under the hat and pulled it as low as it would go. They stayed close to the last group of kitchen workers and followed them into the back alley. For as large and tall as Camden was, he managed to disappear into the small group. Some joked. Others pulled out smokes. He made conversation with a man in Spanish. She ducked her chin. They filtered past two men that stood like sentries searching for a woman on a date.

A fireman poked his head out the door they'd just stepped from. "Farther back. Farther back, people. Remember the drills from kindergarten."

The horde of kitchen staff continued past the dumpsters. Some kept going. Others clumped up. Soon, they would stand out as impostors among the group. She glanced at Camden. Well, maybe not him. He had become one of the guys. How could he morph into another person in front of her eyes? Amelia stood out like a beacon of fear, with her stiff walk and inability to look anywhere but at her feet or Camden.

"Keep walking," he said as though they'd been chitchatting easily the entire time. "Not too fast."

She wanted him to take her hand or to pull her to safety.

"Good. Just like that. Right foot. Left foot." He strolled by her side as they peeled off from the herd. "Don't forget to breathe."

Her boot-camp yogi was always looking out. They made it to the corner. He quickly scanned the street. "All right. Let's ditch the kitchen scrubs."

The scent of grease stayed with her as she handed him the white jacket. He stuffed them into a garbage can as they walked by, arm in arm, on the strangest first date, if it could even be called a date. The night had crashed and burned before it even started to get anywhere good. But she had learned major details on Camden. Most notably, he was a confirmed bachelor.

She didn't know why that mattered. He would return to the Middle East. She would figure out how to kickstart her life again once Hailey was home safe. Whatever happened with Camden would be a fantastic distraction and would never lead anywhere.

She ducked her face into his strong arm and surreptitiously peeked at their surroundings. No one stuck out. Nothing out of the ordinary caught her eye—a sedan with tinted windows crept by.

"Chin down, sweetheart." He'd seen it, too, and pressed his lips to the top of her head as though they were a couple out for a stroll. "Tuck your face close to me."

"They're looking for me."

"Seems like someone is."

The cold weather was their friend. It didn't look strange as Amelia curled into his body. At the corner, they turned off the main street.

Without the bright lights from businesses and headlights, they tried to disappear into the shadows along the residential block. Camden inched apart, pulled his phone out of his pocket, and made a call.

"We've got a situation." Camden explained the fire alarm, the men stationed by the exits, and the cruising vehicle. "You've got my location?" After a long pause, he sighed. "New safe house. New ride." He glanced at her. "I don't think she should either." Camden listened as they walked, and she wished the conversation was on speakerphone. "Got it. Thanks."

He pocketed the phone.

"You don't think I should what?"

"Be at your condominium alone."

Someone was searching for her. Her stomach churned, and Amelia inched closer to Camden as they ambled down the street. "Were those people CIA?"

He shook his head. "If the CIA wanted to speak to you, Beth would set it up. They wouldn't pull a stunt like that to smoke you out of a building."

Amelia stopped cold. "So they were the people who took Hailey?"

"Maybe."

She turned. He caught her arm, reading her mind: she wanted to find them.

"What's your plan?" he asked.

"I don't have one, but—"

"Where's your backup?"

She hadn't thought about that either. "You."

The corners of his lips rose. "I'm supposed to be the impulsive one, sweetheart."

Amelia tugged her arm. The possibility of finding Hailey trumped his reasoning. Camden didn't let her go.

"Well, then come up with a plan," she said.

"They're coming to you. Have any guesses as to why?"

Her first thought had been fear. Her second thought had been to find Hailey. Both were knee-jerk reactions. The why hadn't crossed her mind once. "No."

"You have to have that answer before you go to them." They paused on a corner. Camden searched the intersection as though danger lurked between the parked cars and houses. They crossed the street. "My guess is that you're a witness that needs to be eliminated."

Amelia chewed the inside of her cheek. "I would have said something if I knew anything."

They walked for a long moment, each lost in thought. Finally, he agreed. "You're right. You've been a sitting duck for weeks."

"We should go back and find them."

He shook his head and eyed a car that was slowly creeping down the road. "No, but we do need to get back to a busier street." Camden reached into his pocket and pressed his phone to his ear. "Yeah?" He stopped short and checked his watch. "Sounds good. We'll be waiting."

Her eyebrows arched as he ended the call. "Waiting for who?"

"Colby Winters and a new safe house. We can't go back to where we were." He led them up a driveway as the car with tinted windows crept closer. "Duck down."

They hid between the front of a car and a trash can. She shivered. "Are they looking for you also?"

"My gut says no, which means they're working with an intel deficit."

"How do you know that?"

"I've been with you since I broke you out of prison." He winked like this was just another day on the job and none of this—the fire alarm and creeping cars—was a big deal. "I'm easy to see if they knew who to look for." He thought for a moment. "They did have a spot-on guess that you were inside the restaurant."

"Yeah, how'd they do that?"

He rolled his lips together. "You don't have a phone, right?"

She shook her head. "Not since it was confiscated."

"Maybe they're running some kind of facial recognition. Though how they matched an image of you walking down the street beats the hell out of me." He pulled out his cell phone. Camden's thumbs tapped out a quick message. "We'll worry about that later. First things first: new house. New ride. And I guess I wouldn't mind new dinner plans."

CHAPTER EIGHTEEN

UNANSWERED QUESTIONS PLAGUED Camden. How the hell had anyone spotted her? He had forty-five minutes until Winters would find them. Until then, Camden had to keep moving. He would let Parker sort out how Amelia had been pinpointed.

They couldn't hide in a driveway all night long. He wouldn't find a cab in this neighborhood and didn't trust an Uber. Somehow, some way, Amelia's face had been caught on camera. It didn't make sense. He checked the empty street and took her hand. "Let's roll."

They hurried down toward the businesses and restaurants again. More people meant more places to duck and hide and fewer Ring cameras that could catch them and livestream their locations.

"Where are we going?" she asked. "Hey, you're kind of dragging me, Cam."

If he could've thrown her over his shoulder, he would've. He apologized but didn't entirely mean it. They hit the main drag again. Enough people milled about that they could blend in. They could move with groups. A city bus approached. Its route number and Ride for Free flashed on the digital billboard above the windshield. "There's our ride."

They arrived at the bus stop a moment before it would've rolled by. The doors cracked. Heat enveloped them as they boarded.

"Where are we headed?" he asked.

"King Street in Old Town," the bus driver said.

That didn't mean anything to him, but they sat down toward the back of the bus.

"I know lots of places to eat on King Street," she said.

Good. He liked busy areas and pulled out his phone to update Winters on their changing location.

The ride didn't take long. They stepped off the bus in front of City Hall. Despite the cold, tourists walked through the large open area with ice cream cones. The streets were bustling compared to where they'd just been. It was exactly where they needed to be. A crowd covered the main blocks. Even the side streets had thick foot traffic.

"This way." Amelia led them downhill with signage directing them toward the waterfront. Gaggles of people waited in front of restaurants for seating as heat lamps warmed outdoor patios.

The streets were cordoned off ahead of the river. People milled. Street musicians played. Vehicles could only pass through the intersecting streets that bisected the large space. He almost felt comfortable enough to ask if Amelia wanted to pop in somewhere to restart their dinner. Then another sedan with tinted windows crawled down a side street. A uniformed officer was directing traffic to move. His stomach dropped. That couldn't be the same people searching for Amelia, could it? It wasn't possible, yet his gut said to duck and cover.

They could see Washington, DC, from the bottom of King Street. There had to be any number of politicians and diplomats within a block, not to mention anyone else who required security details rolling by. Hell, even the city might have roving security.

"What's wrong?" Amelia grabbed his arm and searched around.

"I don't know." His pulse pounded. What had he missed? "You don't have your phone on you."

She shook her head. "No."

"Check your pockets."

"For what?"

"I don't know. Check them."

She shoved her hands into her coat. He rushed his hands over her pockets. They could have put a tracker in her jackets and coats, hoping she would wear one when she was released from prison. He came up empty, and anxiety needled him. *Her shoes, maybe? Jeans?* What the hell was he missing? Camden ran his hands over her pants. She wasn't wearing jewelry. She wasn't carrying a tracker.

Time rushed by. He ran a hand into his hair and looked over her shoulder. Uncertainty hammered in his chest. Two men were working their way down from the top of the cordoned-off area. Methodically, they worked side to side, gaining ground.

"Shit."

Amelia spun. "What?"

"We're missing something. They tracked us all the way here. How?"

Her eyes widened. "I don't know."

Camden checked the crowd around them and didn't see anyone else working through the group. They could run toward the river. A large waterfront pavilion on their left had a crowd, or they could go right, where the lighting got significantly darker. Neither would help if they were being tracked. The buses weren't running on the intersecting street closest to the river.

"We're missing something." He was armed and wouldn't let anyone take Amelia, but he didn't want to cause a scene in the middle of downtown Alexandria. Boss Man would have a huge problem with him if that happened. "They started tracking us at dinner. How? Why?"

"I thought I felt someone looking at me when we first walked on to the main drag."

His mind replayed the day: breakfast, CIA meeting, kissing Amelia, heading to dinner—"You made a phone call before dinner."

She nodded. "I called Veronica." Her eyes went wide as she raised her hands. "I didn't tell her where I was."

"You didn't have to." He pulled out his phone. No one should have been able to track him. Camden dropped the phone onto the ground and lifted his foot—but he stopped himself from crushing the device.

"What are you doing?" Amelia demanded.

He grabbed the phone and her hand and ran to the corner where an officer directed traffic to cross through an intersection. He spotted an oversized pickup truck and, before they crossed the street, dropped the cell phone over the edge of its tailgate.

"Camden?"

"They traced you back to my phone." For the first time, he wondered if protecting Amelia was the reason the CIA had detained her. It would have answered any questions from the public and kept Amelia where they could safeguard her. That would be a conversation for Beth.

"You're sure?"

Not one hundred percent. "We're going to find out." He wanted eyes on the men combing through the crowd but needed to keep her out of view. Camden posted against the corner of a building and tucked her under him as though he were making a move. His body pressed against her. He raised an arm over her head and caged her against the wall. "Put an arm over my shoulder." To anyone else, Amelia looked to have his full attention. "Good." He feathered a kiss over her cheek. "I don't want to be the guy that tells a girl to smile, babe, but if you look scared, someone might check on you."

She smiled and tried to relax.

"Good." He scanned the crowd and found the two men. Instead of working through the crowd, they stood together. One man had a phone pressed to his ear. The other scanned their immediate surroundings.

"Do you see them?" she asked.

"Yup."

Amelia's posture tightened.

He was certain the smile was gone. "Just another minute. Relax. We're having a good time."

"The best time," she managed.

"I am," he admitted.

Her tension relaxed against his chest, and he struggled to focus on the problem at hand. Camden narrowed his gaze on the man on the phone. He wasn't a lip reader but was certain the man had just snapped, "Fuck." The other man shook his head, then they both turned and retraced their way up the hill.

He inched back. "We're good for now."

Relief blossomed over her face. Amelia wrapped her other arm around his neck and hugged him. Camden let his eyes sink shut. He breathed her in and let warmth roll through him at the way she fit against him. He was becoming too entangled with this woman. Keeping her safe should feel more like a job responsibility than a requirement.

And what the hell had he been thinking, taking her out on a date? What kind of complication was that? That wasn't taking things slowly. But since she was wrapped around him, he realized he couldn't keep a reasonable space between them. He couldn't stay away and should have realized that from the moment they first spoke. That was why he hadn't let himself even look up her picture. Since he'd gone that far, since he had her in his arms again, he knew they would be in bed sooner rather than later. This sweet hug was to blame.

"What now?" she asked.

Camden moved her to his side and stayed to the edge of the crowd. "We need to find a convenience store and purchase a burner phone. Winters would be nearby soon."

"Then what?"

"New place."

She tipped her face toward him. "And dinner?"

"Dinner and whatever else you want."

Slowly was overrated. They could work off the night's stress in any way she chose.

CHAPTER NINETEEN

COLBY WINTERS'S OVERSIZED four-door truck approached Camden and Amelia on one of the quieter streets in Old Town Alexandria. His truck was almost a mirror image of the one Camden had used to hide his cell phone, and he hoped the men chasing Amelia were as confused as fuck and chasing down a random truck.

They hadn't had anyone follow them since he ditched the phone. How much of Amelia's world had they infiltrated? Parker might be able to back hack the trace and shed light on their identities. But that was doubtful, considering the level of criminal they were dealing with.

Winters slowed next to them, and the window rolled down. He chortled. "Sounds like you two had a hell of a night." He glanced at Amelia, eyes narrowing as though she was a factor he didn't understand, but he unlocked the doors. "Get in."

Camden opened the rear door on the driver's side and helped Amelia in then rounded the truck to join Winters in the front. "Thanks for picking us up."

Winters nodded. "Parker said to tell you if the place doesn't work, he'll find a new one tomorrow, but this is the best he's got on short notice."

"We'll be fine with whatever it is," Amelia said.

Winters chuckled. "I don't think you have any idea some of the shitty places we've had to sleep."

That was true enough, though Camden didn't think Parker would put Amelia anywhere too rough. The GPS on the center dashboard said they were less than twenty minutes out. The directions quickly maneuvered them out of the tight network of Alexandria and onto the highway.

"Any chance we can stop somewhere and grab something to eat?" Amelia asked.

Winters gave Camden a hard look. "You haven't fed her?"

"Been a little busy," he muttered under his breath.

"We almost had dinner," Amelia pointed out. "That rib eye sounded so good too."

"Rib eye, huh? Can't go wrong with a steak." He laughed and smirked at Camden as though he could see the truth about their night out. "You get an appetizer before all hell broke loose?"

"Yeah," she said on a wistful, hungry note. "But we didn't get a chance to eat it."

"A good time was almost had," Winters said, still smirking. "Too bad work got in the middle of it." He checked the rearview mirror and studied her in the backseat, laughing to himself. "At least you had great company. Can't go wrong with my man Cam."

"At least," she agreed, missing the gossipy note in his words.

Camden wanted to smack Winters's attention back onto the road. The man wasn't checking Amelia out, but he was seeing far more than Camden wanted him to. Titan didn't usually have steak dinners with beautiful clients. Hell, Titan didn't usually have beautiful clients, *period*.

"Anyway," he grumbled, "what's going on with you?"

"Nothing nearly as entertaining as this."

All right. His molars clamped. Camden wasn't going to give Winters any fuel and watched the GPS as the miles ticked down instead.

"Let's see what we can do about food." Winters exited the highway and pulled onto a busy road lined with dining options. The GPS recalculated their arrival time and added on five minutes. He named a list of fast-food joints for Amelia. "What are you hungry for?"

She opted for a burger place that was a far cry from a steak dinner. The line moved quickly. The food was as fresh as they could have hoped, and by the time they had cheeseburgers in hand, Camden realized he'd been working on adrenaline and was starving.

They devoured their burgers and fries as Winters filled the truck with details of a job he'd just returned home from. Finally, they arrived at a condominium complex so similar to Amelia's that it might have been owned by the same company: same building styles, same parking lot, same landscaping.

"It never occurred to me how many safe houses could be tucked in perfectly normal neighborhoods." She crumbled the cheeseburger wrapper and stuffed it into the bag. "Do you have places like this everywhere?"

Winters shrugged. "There's a disproportionate number of places near hubs like DC. But yeah, sort of." He parked the truck and tapped on his cell phone. A moment later, Camden's burner phone showed a message. "That should be what you need to get inside. I'll be around if you need anything." He hazarded a quick glance at Amelia and added, "Though I doubt I'll be seeing you any time soon."

Camden gave him a tight shut-the-fuck-up smile. "Thanks for the lift."

"This place looks great." Amelia opened her door. "I wonder why Parker thinks we won't like it."

They walked toward the condominium identified in the text message. The corner unit had an excellent view of the parking lot as well as the street. Camden opened the door with the electronic combination.

"There should be clothes and whatever you need in the closet." He shut the door behind them.

The space was small but nicely appointed. It wasn't the usual type of housing Titan would give him. Perhaps they were low on inventory.

"The pantry should be stocked if you're still hungry."

Her eyebrows rose. "Along with guns and knives, like the last place."

For as much danger as she seemed to be in, Amelia seemed to find that amusing. "Most likely."

"I'll let you know what I find." She took approximately thirty seconds to give herself the grand tour. She came back with a hesitant expression on her face—no telling what weapons she'd found.

"What?"

"There's only one bed." They both eyed the little two-person couch that looked like it was more for decoration purposes than for seating. "And not much else."

CHAPTER TWENTY

ELECTRICITY CRACKLED IN the small space around them. The thumping of Amelia's heart drummed so loudly that she wasn't sure she could carry on a simple conversation. They were grown adults. They'd flirted and kissed and agreed that more would come between them. But they were not anywhere near the level of familiarity at which they could skip off to bed.

That was why people had dates: intimate table arrangements, quiet conversations, touching and teasing that would lead up to a kiss. A kiss would lead to more. And more was what she would definitely want if it didn't feel so awkward. But it did after running out on dinner, riding a bus, and getting a ride home from Camden's coworker.

She laughed nervously. *Was there ever a situation that left him uncomfortable?* His unflappability was sexy and a reminder that this was part of his job. Judging by the stories he and Colby Winters shared on the drive over, their assignments usually involved gunfire, helicopters, and saving the day. Camden could probably do this assignment in his sleep.

His dark eyes tracked her. "I'll sleep on the floor," he offered because they both knew he couldn't pretend to sleep on the couch.

"You're not sleeping on the floor, Cam."

"I know." His lips curled like those of a man who knew exactly how they would spend the evening. "But I thought I'd offer."

The room's electricity crackled again and skipped over her skin, refusing to be ignored. Something about the way he could look at her was as if that sexy smolder and dangerous curl of his lips were promises of things to come.

He closed the distance between them and rested the palms of his hands on her hips. Her heartbeat galloped. Amelia couldn't hide the uneven rise and fall of her chest. Her eyes blinked too fast, nearly keeping time with her breaths.

His fingers squeezed her sides, and her body somersaulted. The swell of her breasts tightened. Amelia tipped her chin up and stared into his dark eyes. The intensity was all-consuming.

His hands left her waist, ran up her neck, and threaded into her hair. He tipped her head back and brought his mouth to hers with a hunger that made her soul leave her body. The kiss was hot and hard and sinfully delicious. She melted to him. Camden backed her until she hit the wall. He trapped her, caged her, held her against him with the heavenly press of his sculpted body with hard cut muscles. She couldn't breathe and didn't want to try. Kissing him was the end all and be all of survival.

"Fuck," he growled against her lips.

His mouth dipped to her neck. Amelia moaned. Desire crashed through her veins like lava. Camden pulled far enough away from her to rip her shirt overhead and let it fall. His large hand cupped her breast, and he nuzzled the spot behind her earlobe. Her legs trembled. She threaded her hand into his silky hair and held his lips exactly where she needed him to stay.

He nipped. She squirmed. Camden massaged her breast, and she would have done anything to make her bra vanish. As if he read her mind, he tugged the bra strap off her shoulder and bared her tight nipple. He palmed the mound as she groaned, and then he smiled against her neck as though his life goal was nothing more than bringing her pleasure.

She reached behind her and unsnapped her bra. Camden pressed his lips to hers again as he stripped it away. He cupped her tits, teasing until Amelia writhed.

She ached for more. Arousal pulsed between her legs. Her body hummed, and she couldn't be trusted to keep herself upright. Camden moved his mouth to her breast, and the wet heat stole the last of her composure. She breathed out a prayer that it would never end.

Camden unfastened the top button of her jeans. "Okay?"

"*Yes.*" Her head swam. He lowered the zipper. Bliss slowed the passage of time. His palm ran over her side, her stomach, but all she could think about was where she so desperately needed his fingers to be. "Please."

He sucked her nipple and slid his hands between her legs. Her arousal coated his fingers, and a stuttering breath caught in his throat. "Sweet fucking woman, you are killing me."

She had no power to speak. Her head knocked back as his fingers worked over her folds, drawing her apart, and centering his attention on the swollen bundle of nerves she'd been hoping he would find soon.

Amelia shifted her stance. Her hips swayed. "Cam, please."

He stole his fingers away and yanked her jeans and underwear over her hips and off her legs. He dropped to his knees and buried his face between her legs so quickly that her mind couldn't keep up.

The wicked hot heat of his tongue nearly shattered her to pieces. She bucked against the wall. His forearm pinned her in place. His tongue circled her clit, driving her higher and higher toward a desperate pinnacle.

"Please," she whispered.

Camden sucked on her clitoris. Two strong fingers parted her flesh and slid into her needy entrance, which was slick with her arousal. She arched, needing exactly what he was giving her. Her lungs galloped. Her body soared. He drove in and out, spiraling the tightening muscles into a building, blinding frenzy. She bucked for more. Her vision clouded. White noise screamed in her ears. The unending onslaught of his tongue, his mouth, his fingers demanded that she fall apart. "Camden, God."

He growled against her pussy, and the orgasm tore her apart like an earthquake. Addictive spasms shook her body, and he milked every reverberation, stretching the bliss until she had nothing left. Amelia was a boneless woman incapable of holding herself upright.

CAMDEN HAD NEVER wanted to be inside a woman the way he needed to be buried in Amelia. He ached, and hard as steel, he couldn't think or breathe or function until his cock was seated deep in her sweet heat.

He swept Amelia into his arms and hurried toward the bedroom. Every nerve ending screamed for more of her. The condo was small, the bedroom tiny, but that large bed was perfect. He laid her in the center and ripped his shirt off.

Amelia bounced up to her knees and ran her hands over his stomach and around his neck. Their lips found each other like magnets. Her tongue touched his and ignited the frenzy again.

"You still have pants on." Her lips tickled against his.

The sensation shot straight to his cock. "Not for long."

She smiled and melted against him. He had never touched a woman that ran so hot and could be so soft at the same time. Hell, he'd never been with a woman who made his brain short-circuit. Bringing her pleasure was like wanting to breathe. Feeling her orgasm like winning the fuckin' lottery. Nothing else was like it.

Camden stripped and crawled over her again. Her hands explored the muscles of his back and slid to his ass. Her fingernails dragged into his flesh, then her fingers kneaded his muscles. The frenzy slowed into something more intense, as if Amelia was memorizing the way he felt over her. He'd never wanted to stay perfectly still and hurry into a woman like he had that moment.

Her eyes found his. The connection nailed him in the chest. "Fuck, you're beautiful."

But it was so much more than that. Her eyelashes fluttered. The corners of her lips curved. Echoes of her orgasm rocketed through his mind. He would make her come again and again and again because he didn't know how else to feed this hungry beast inside him. It demanded more than he knew how to give.

Camden kissed her neck. He caressed her breast. The more he toyed, the louder and more alive she grew. The more she gave, the higher his high climbed.

Amelia stroked his rock-hard erection.

"Fuck, babe." His muscles quaked. If he wasn't inside her soon, his brain would short-circuit.

They needed protection. That wasn't something he planned for on assignments. Camden prayed for a miracle and reached for the nightstand drawer. Inside, he found a snub-nose pistol, eye mask and ear plugs, pepper spray, and box of condoms. Camden said a quick thanks to whoever stocked safe houses.

He tore open the box and quickly covered himself. Amelia pulled him back to her. He'd imagined fucking her since they first connected. Her voice and strength had caught his attention, and then her take-on-the-world attitude and body had dissolved his resolve. That was the order of ways she'd captured him, and he'd loved every moment leading up to her splaying under him in bed.

The blunt head of his erection pressed into the searing warmth of her canal. Her arms wrapped around his neck as he speared into her body. She raised her hips. Her chest heaved.

"Cam."

Hunger demanded he move faster. The way she arched and moaned at the intrusion required him to take his damn time. Going slow was killing him. But it was so fucking good that he wanted to scream.

She stretched around him and erased the rest of the world. Camden flexed and thrust until he'd given her all of himself. His shaky breaths stuttered, and he soaked in every delicious, pulse-pounding tremor of the need that fought for him to fuck. "Good?"

"Very."

His smile tugged. He withdrew himself and thrust again.

Amelia gasped, "So very good."

She squeezed herself around his cock. That was all the go he needed to fly. Camden flexed and thrust. He listened to her begging moans for more. He buried his face against her neck and rode in and out. Her gasping pleas were fuel, and every orgasm he pulled from her tight cunt was like lightning crashing through him.

His bliss built. Her legs and arms wrapped around him until he couldn't keep himself from falling apart.

"Camden. Please."

Her tight voice brought him to the edge. He was so close to shattering. He could hang on. He could give her one more and gave everything she could ever possibly need, faster and deeper until she bucked against him under another tsunami of pleasure. His orgasm slammed against hers and pulsed with pleasure so powerful that he couldn't take another breath without fear of dying.

Camden collapsed. He pressed a sweet kiss to her temple and rolled Amelia onto her side to face him. Their legs tangled, and their breaths raced. Her eyes stayed shut. He couldn't help but think, holy shit, he'd never come like that.

Eyes closed, he lay on the pillow next to hers. His hammering breath finally started to slow. His eyes opened and locked on Amelia. Goddamn, she was beautiful. Funny. Bossy. She had a mind of her own, that was for damn sure. It would get her in trouble, but that was okay because he planned to be around to pull her out whenever it got to be too much.

Amelia tossed her arm over her face. Her breathing was racing just like his. She pulled her arm away and turned so her cheek rested on the pillow. Her lips crooked, and with a smile he felt to his toes, she mouthed, "Wow."

He laughed. *Wow* was the best word for the moment, maybe the best word for this woman.

CHAPTER TWENTY-ONE

T HE MORNING SUN coaxed Amelia awake. Camden was the first thing she noticed before her eyes opened to the new day. Despite the king-size mattress, they had navigated toward each other while sleeping. She was under the possessive grip of his arm and starting to panic.

Going to sleep hadn't been a problem. Her brain had finally shut down under a mix of sheer bliss and exhaustion. That was so very gone, and for the moment, she wasn't sure her brain was cognizant of the human need to fill her lungs with oxygen. Each breath required a litany of mental commands that were normally involuntary. But while she was pinned next to the sexiest man she'd ever touched, managing to inhale was a serious effort. Even when she did, her lungs demanded more oxygen than she'd quietly tried to suck down. Exhaling wasn't much better. Each exhalation somehow sounded like she was a linebacker grunting through the Super Bowl.

If she could escape without waking Camden, Amelia could hide in the bathroom and plan her next move. How had everything seemed so simple before they'd had sex? She'd wanted what she'd wanted and been up front. He'd checked the precursory boxes to make sure she was absolutely, positively ready to fuck and then proceeded to nail her brains out.

Amelia rolled onto her side—he rolled too and pulled her close. Shit. How the hell was she going to escape when she was officially a little spoon? And oh God, was he an amazing Big Spoon or what? Mountains of muscles enveloped her in a sinful warmth. His lips brushed the back of her bare shoulder, and an erratic explosion detonated in her chest. Breathing was overrated.

"Good morning," he murmured.

She almost laughed at how sleep-drenched his voice was, and she would have if not for the intoxicatingly gruff way he sounded. The scratchy timbre worked over her skin as a ripple of goosebumps shivered down her limbs. She should say something pithy and cute, something that would relay how casual everything should still feel, but absolutely zilch came to mind. Nothing but a low-key hum of awareness blanketed her thoughts.

A sexy rumble of quiet laughter shook in his chest. Camden slept sexily. He laughed sexily. Everything about him was sexy. And she didn't even have her own clothes or a hairbrush. He was holding onto the opposite of sexy. Why didn't she see how complicated this would be?

The muffled chirp of his phone rang.

Camden groaned. He reached onto the floor, snagged his pants, and answered the phone with a quick, "Yeah? What?" He grimaced and sat up against the headboard. "Yeah, I was." Whoever had called wasn't Camden's favorite person. Tension ticked in his jaw. "Yeah, we'll be there."

He caught her eye with an apologetic wince, and Amelia understood who was on the phone. "Beth?" she mouthed.

Camden raised his chin.

Well, at least Amelia didn't have to come up with morning-after small talk. She rolled toward the side of the bed. Still on the phone with Beth, he snagged her arm, said goodbye, and tossed the phone aside. Camden scrutinized her face. "You good?"

Her eyebrows arched. Of all the things he might say, that wasn't what she would've guessed. Amelia nodded.

"Gotta tell me, sweetheart. Either way, I want to hear the truth."

"I'm good."

His chin lifted almost imperceptibly, as though he was clocking what she said and whether he believed her. "And we're good?"

"Of course," she said too quickly. But it was the truth. She didn't feel pressured or taken advantage of or anything that should raise red flags. But the truth was also that she felt... *something* that she didn't have a name for. Hell, she couldn't even describe it. It was just a tension that went beyond her forgetting how to breathe.

He'd said "we're" as if they were a *we*, as in a couple—temporarily. She needed to remember they were time-boxed into a peculiar situation. They weren't friends with benefits. They weren't fuck buddies. She'd asked for a distraction, and he'd given her much more than she'd bargained for. *That*... was the indescribable unknown.

His eyes narrowed. "What's going on in that pretty head of yours?"

She had no idea but wouldn't share that little secret. "Last night was a lot of fun." *To put it mildly.* "Glad you came to your senses and decided it was a good idea."

The corners of his eyes twitched. "Glad I did too."

He let her escape, and stealing the top sheet, she covered her body and retreated to the living room, where her clothes still lay on the floor. Instead of grabbing them, she headed to the kitchen in search of caffeine options.

An electric kettle and a Keurig sat on the counter, and she could have dropped to her knees in praise that she didn't have to suffer through instant coffee. The K-cups offered an assortment of options from tea to mocha to dark roast. She chose a medium roast with a pretty label and brewed two mugs of coffee. She would retrieve her clothes after delivering his mug to him.

Camden stepped out of the bathroom with wet hair and a towel wrapped around his lean waist just above the world's most dangerous V-cut of muscles. The coffee mugs shook in her hands for a second before she pulled herself together.

"I have caffeine."

He ignored the mugs and eyed the precariously wrapped sheet tucked into place. "Fuck, you make it hard to focus on work."

Her cheeks heated, and when he stalked forward, she didn't know if the coffees would be tossed aside. But, smart man that he was, he set them on the nightstand and returned to her, tipping her chin up and slanting his mouth over hers. The clean scent of soap and his minty mouth was irresistible—until she remembered that she needed a toothbrush and a quick rinse. "I have to take a shower," she said against his lips.

His phone rang again, and his body tensed. She could almost read the excuses running through his mind so that he didn't have to answer. But for as impulsive as he claimed to be, he let her go, cursing until he answered with the same "Yeah? What?" as before. He raked a hand through his wet hair and said, "I'll text you the address." He hung up, and the hungry glimmer in his eyes had almost dissipated. Camden tossed the phone onto the bed, reached for the coffees, and handed her a mug that she'd doctored with powdered creamer and sugar. "Beth's on her way."

"What?" Amelia had no doubt that Beth would be able to pick up on how they'd spent their night if she didn't jump into the shower. "I don't have my bag."

The problem wasn't just a lack of clean clothes. She didn't have her makeup or hair products or anything that would leave her feeling as on top of the world as she needed to be when facing off with Beth. Then she stopped and turned to Camden. She hadn't even asked the reason for the meeting. How could she have let one night of really great sex erase the reason they were doing this to begin with? Guilt needled under her skin. "Why are we meeting Beth?"

"She says there's some place we need to see."

"Was my sister there?"

He lifted his shoulders. "Guess so. Beth doesn't give straight answers, and I didn't waste my time asking." His finger tapped against his coffee mug. "You ready to go down this path?"

She nodded. "You didn't tell Beth about the people following us last night."

"I didn't say a whole lot of anything."

"How come? I thought the CIA didn't have anything to do with it."

"I don't think they do. Otherwise, they would have just knocked on the door and not gone through that whole shitshow. But…" He shrugged. "Trust but verify."

She sipped her coffee and wondered what news about Hailey the day would bring. Three weeks had passed since that awful night, almost four. Where the hell was Hailey?

"There's different sizes in there." Camden gestured toward the dresser. "I don't know about bras but socks and underwear. I'm not sure if there will be any pants and shirts you want to wear, though. We can swing by your condo later and stock up on whatever you need."

"I'll wear my shirt and jeans from last night." She padded into the bathroom, which was still steamy from his quick shower.

In the corner of her eye, Camden dropped the towel and dressed. This was a terrifying level of intimacy. Or maybe he didn't even think twice. When a person looked like Camden did, maybe modesty didn't matter. But he didn't come off that way. How had she blustered her way into his bedroom? She was so far out of his league that she didn't know which way was up. Until that morning, the idea of getting physical with him had seemed like the best distraction she could imagine. Distractions had consequences.

AN HOUR LATER, Beth had whisked Amelia and Camden from the safe house and wasn't telling them where they were going except that it was someplace Hailey and Jonathan had worked. Camden didn't seem all that concerned. From the back seat of Beth's sleek Lexus, Amelia had come up with ten thousand possibilities and stopped adding to her list only when Beth drove through the front gates of an industrial complex, announcing that they were there.

Amelia scanned the decrepit landscape. Overgrown weeds threaded through a rusted chain-link fence topped with sagging barbed wire. The parking lot looked immaculate compared to the building behind it. The three-story brick monstrosity might have once been a bustling manufacturing depot, but that wasn't the case anymore and probably hadn't been in decades. This place wasn't on her list of ten thousand possibilities.

Camden snorted from the front passenger seat. "Hope everyone's up to date on their tetanus boosters."

"We're not crawling through the windows." Beth parked next to the only other car, a black Mercedes, which stood out like a gothic rose in a sea of dead grass.

Amelia eyed the building. The panes of remaining windows had been grayed out. Iron bars crisscrossed over dilapidated glass. Nobody could see in or get out of that building.

"This wasn't what I pictured when you said we were headed to a place my sister and Jonathan worked." Amelia flicked a glance to Beth. "What is it? A receiving location for black-market art sales? A storage facility?"

"Nope. Nothing like that."

"A dungeon." Camden laughed.

"Getting closer." Beth rested her hand on the door handle. "I will gladly take you back to your *newest* safe house"—she gave Camden the stink eye as though he'd put her in danger and not the missing CIA NOC list that started the whole nightmare—"and forget this whole idea of searching for Hailey."

"No," Amelia said.

Beth's lips flattened. "Amelia, listen. If we get out of the car, everything is going to change."

"Everything in my life has already changed." Why didn't Beth see that?

"No, I mean that everything you know about your sister and your brother-in-law, the memories you have, what you understand about their life and work, it will just…" She made explosions with her hands. "Boom. Be gone."

The warning reminded her of wanting to sleep with Camden. She thought she knew what she was getting into. She practically demanded he kiss her and acted as though she were fully aware of the consequences. But then he took her on a date and treated her like a queen, and what she wanted afterward was so much more intense. Her stomach dropped. Amelia needed to stop thinking about Camden. She forced herself to look out the window. The old building loomed like a dystopian movie set.

"An old scary building won't change my mind."

"It should." Beth clucked.

"You don't get to say that unless it's your sister we're looking for." Beth didn't seem to remember why Amelia was asking for help. She studied the woman behind the steering wheel.

Or maybe Beth did know something of the pain harbored in Amelia's chest. Despite Beth's cashmere sweater, perfect hair and makeup, and keys to a luxury sedan, something marred her socialite appearance, as though Beth had seen far more than she could handle and wanted Amelia to avoid the same fate.

Beth flicked her gaze to Camden as though he had the power to dissuade Amelia from taking the next step. After the previous night, Camden had the power to do a lot of things to Amelia. But none would keep her from searching for Hailey. He didn't give Beth the backup she was seeking.

Beth shrugged and opened her door. "Then let's rip the Band-Aid off and jump down the rabbit hole."

She slammed the door shut. Amelia and Camden sat in the reverberating silence as Beth sauntered toward the dilapidated metal doors. Despite Amelia's cold shower and physical distance from Camden, the atmosphere between them buzzed. Their chemistry burned so brightly that Beth could probably guess what was happening when they were alone.

But right then, that wasn't what Amelia saw in Camden's expression. It was eerily similar to that dark shadow on Beth's face, almost as if he could see what hid behind the warehouse doors.

"Cam, please don't try to talk me out of this."

The tight corners of his dark eyes assessed her. His lips rolled together as if physically restraining an explanation.

"I heard Beth," she whispered. "My understanding of Hailey and Jonathan will shift in some irrevocable, indelible way."

"It's going to mark your soul if you go in there," he said quietly.

He'd already marked her soul. Could she handle another mark? "Understood."

"I don't know if you're going to get the answers you want. It's just as brave to walk away from a fight as it is to stay."

"I'll never learn anything if I don't try."

"You're willing to do that, knowing you might never find Hailey?"

"That's not fair to ask, Cam."

Tension ticked in his chiseled cheeks. Camden ran a hand over his face. "You've got to know what I know: In my line of work and in Beth's, when we say that shit is gonna fuck you up, it's gonna fuck you up, sweetheart, and—"

"Stop trying to talk me out of this. And I *am* fucked up. Okay? My life has already been completely fucked."

Hell, she'd done stupid shit like begging him to take her to bed—that was why he'd first said no. That was the power dynamic he'd tried to explain. Her eyes burned with embarrassment, and she rolled them to hide her humiliation.

"Stop. Wherever your head has gone. Stop." Camden reached into the back seat and clasped his large hand over her knee. "We need to go home."

Home—as if their business with Beth was secondary to the way they'd come together as a couple. Date nights and mornings in bed—as if it were all that simple, as if it were that way and might stay that way as long as they continued to play their game of pretend. She was in so far over her head in more ways than one, yet she didn't want to be far from him.

"I'm going inside with Beth. You should join me."

The corners of his lips quirked up. It wasn't a smile as much as an *"All right. What the hell? Let's do it."*

A moment later, they found Beth shivering in front of a nondescript entrance with peeling paint and an uninviting sense of welcome. Signs pocked the building: Do Not Enter, Private Property, No Trespassing, Enter at Your Own Risk.

Amelia muttered, "This looks like a friendly bunch."

"It's another warning that you're ignoring," Beth pointed out. "Literal signs that say go home."

Ignoring yet another red flag, Amelia grumbled and stared at her feet. "Weird how well kept the parking lot is when everything else around it is falling apart."

Beth didn't even glance at the parking lot.

Amelia had had enough procrastination. "I'm ready to go inside."

"Suit yourself." Beth yanked on the door, which opened wide into a dark hall. "Let's get this party started."

They walked in. Behind them, the heavy door shut as they were hugged by an inky darkness. Her heartbeat quickened. She blinked. Her eyes tried to adjust, but there wasn't any light. Coldness radiated around them. Beth's heels clicked forward, and Amelia followed the sound of her steps. Every step threw off her equilibrium. Not seeing where the floor met the wall was dizzying. The only somewhat calming notion was that

Camden pulled up the rear.

The hallway seemed to narrow, but that was just a guess based on the sound of their footsteps changing. Amelia raised her arms out. Her fingertips brushed a wall. She'd expected cinder block or peeling paint, but the surface was smooth and cool to the touch.

Finally, Beth paused. She cracked open a door. A slice of dim light beckoned them out of the darkness, but she didn't lead them through the threshold. "This is your last opportunity to leave unscathed, Amelia." Beth shifted in front of the door and blocked the light as if protecting them from untold horrors. "We can head out. We'll go have a good meal and too many drinks. You can toast Hailey and celebrate what you knew of her—"

"Open the damn door, Beth. I'm not changing my mind."

Camden snickered.

"To be honest," Beth admitted, "this is what I would have done too."

CHAPTER TWENTY-TWO

T HEY WALKED INTO a softly lit corridor. It was nothing she'd expected of the rusty old warehouse, which had been left abandoned to decay. The air wasn't dank or musty. Surprisingly, it was clean and smelled faintly of sandalwood.

The corridor opened into a large area with ceilings that reached to the top of the three-story building. Gothic chandeliers hung throughout the large space. Well-stocked shelves of liquor were arranged in a striking array. Its row of expensive bottles perched regally in front of mirrors and lorded over an ornately carved bar that could easily seat fifty people along its expanse.

"Whoa," Camden murmured under his breath.

Amelia's sentiments exactly.

Beth flipped two concealed light switches. Running lights illuminated a portion of the bar and the chandeliers. *Whoa again.* The gorgeous room was breathtaking and immense, but despite its size, the space was intimate and protective, as though the deepest of secrets could be shared within its walls. Dark, thick curtains draped the walls and flanked oil paintings hung against the stately wood paneling, fueling its expensive, exclusive—*illicit*—vibe.

Beth waited until they'd soaked up the room then directed them. "We'll go this way."

Their footsteps echoed as they crossed the cavernous space. To fully appreciate their surroundings would've taken hours.

"What is this place?" Amelia tried to take it all in while keeping pace with Beth. "Like a gothic country club?"

"Something like that."

Her mind sifted through the possibilities and landed on black-market art auctions. The Hailey who Amelia knew would never attend illegal sales. But the CIA version of Hailey might. If that was the case, Beth had been wrong. A black-market art sale wouldn't be scandalous enough to wreck her opinion of her sister.

They reached the opposite corner of the empty space and headed into the mouth of another dark hallway. The light faded behind them as Beth surged into the darkness. She moved through the space as though she'd done so a hundred times.

Camden walked by Amelia's side, his hand resting at the small of her back. She inched closer to him and imagined melting against the large barrel of his chest. He was her safe place, not just because of his size or comforting touch—it was the energy that radiated from him, the chemistry that connected them. She felt they were meant to walk through that space together.

They rounded a corner. A rogue strip of light crawled from under a door. Beth strode up and knocked. This was the point everything would change. Amelia sensed the tension and leaned into Camden. The back of his hand brushed the back of hers, a silent reassurance that she would be okay. Nothing would jump out of that office door. She'd survived men chasing her and lived through jail, innocent and trapped. Still, her heart hammered so loudly that she was positive Beth and Camden could hear its drumbeat.

"Yes, come in," a woman called.

Beth opened the door, and the office light momentarily blinded Amelia. She blinked as she followed Beth into the office where everything would change. The woman behind the desk would probably be the person to drop the bomb and destroy what Amelia understood of Hailey and Jonathan. Amelia swallowed over the sharp panic in her throat.

"Thanks for seeing us on such short notice." Beth gestured to Amelia. "This is Hailey's sister. Amelia Stone." Then she gestured to the woman who stood on the other side of the desk. "Amelia, this is Esme Van Alstyn."

Amelia had never met someone that so immediately matched their name. She shook Esme's hand. The woman was older and unconventionally beautiful. Her dark eyes were as black as they were bright. She wore deep mauve lipstick the color of red wine. Heavy gray and silver streaks threaded her dark hair in such a distinctive way that Amelia wondered if they had been precisely placed by an expert stylist. Her handshake was strong like a military man's yet soft, almost sensual, in the way she wrapped her hand around Amelia's. "Lovely to meet you."

Esme's velvet voice was magnetic. Amelia inched closer even as part of her wanted to hide.

Camden didn't seem to notice and shook Esme's hand with his typical gruffness. "Camden Brooks. Titan Group."

Esme's eyebrow arched. "Interesting."

Strange that Camden's employer was interesting. Amelia had learned what Titan did from her conversations with Camden, but Beth and Esme's reactions had imparted what needed to be read between the lines. Titan Group was exclusive and connected.

Amelia realized she was the odd one out. Camden, Beth, and Esme—even Hailey and Jonathan—all had a connection and knew the stakes even if they didn't know the specifics. She, on the other hand, was staring over the edge of a cliff when everyone else had parachutes and was ready to jump. Beth's and Camden's warnings replayed in her mind. Her throat tightened as though someone was slowly tightening her parachute around her neck like a noose. She tried to clear her throat. It didn't help.

"Camden," Beth said. "Why don't we let them—"

Amelia grabbed his arm. "No. Stay? Please." She hated the pathetic note of begging, but the woman in front of her made Amelia's insides shiver.

"Sure." His confident agreement had come before Beth or Esme could shoo him out the door—though Esme didn't seem the type to shoo. She was more the type to say a command and expect it to be completed.

Esme eyed Amelia's hold on his arm then met Amelia's eye as though she were talented enough to read her most guarded thoughts. The corners of her mauve lips quirked, and Esme gestured toward the chairs. "I don't mind if you stay." She elegantly folded herself behind her desk. "This shouldn't take long. Shall I call when we're done?"

Even the way Esme spoke was sophisticated. Amelia heard a hint of an accent but couldn't place it. Or maybe she was just picking up on the primness of proper grammar and perfect posture. She could match her: straight spine, shoulders back, chin up. But that would require Amelia to focus her mental energy on things that didn't matter.

Beth stepped toward the dark hallway. "No need to call. I'll be around when they walk out."

So Beth would probably sit outside the office door. *Why?* Amelia assumed Beth knew what Esme was about to explain. *Plausible deniability? Or an offer of privacy?* Beth seemed like someone who appreciated discretion—a point in her favor.

The door shut with a stomach-churning click after Beth left. Amelia scanned Esme's office. It was a far cry from a corporate office and didn't match the outside of the warehouse. But it absolutely matched the inside. The rich, gothic vibes from the great room complimented her office's wall color, which, she noted, feeling somewhat awestruck, matched the deep wine color of Esme's lipstick. This woman rocked a seriously commanding—though sexy—aesthetic.

Amelia swallowed hard and focused on the computer monitor sitting alone on her dark desk instead of her penetrating gaze.

"Welcome," Esme offered. "Please. Sit."

Amelia realized she was still holding onto Camden's arm. She released her iron grip and forced herself to sit on a plush chair. Their cushions were a deep purple and matched the main room's drapes. Everything about this place was purposeful by design. Why did the exterior look like a decrepit old building?

"My condolences for Hailey and Jonathan."

Amelia hated when people offered sympathies and grievances as though voicing respects was a societal checklist item that had to be acknowledged before further conversation could take place. "Thank you." She couldn't help herself and added, "Though there's no proof that Hailey's dead also."

The corners of Esme's lips rose with uncommitted understanding. "No, I suppose there's not."

Would Esme know otherwise? Or was that just the way prim, proper people responded to Amelia's hope? She waited for the litany of reasons people offered as proof that Hailey had been murdered the same night as Jonathan. Hailey's bank accounts hadn't been touched. Her social media and emails hadn't been accessed. No evidence existed that Hailey had contacted anyone she'd ever met. Not to mention, Amelia had been arrested for murder. That was enough to convince any logical person of Hailey's death.

"This is your…" Amelia tried not to fidget. "Facility?"

Esme's bright eyes danced beneath the feathery cape of her mile-long black lashes. "Beth hasn't told you much?"

"Beth hasn't told me anything except that I shouldn't be here nor talk to you because I will regret it."

"She's not wrong."

Amelia pointed toward the door where Beth was likely hovering and said, "One." She then pointed at Camden. "Two." Finally, she pointed at Esme. "Three. I've heard that three times, but I'm not changing my mind if it helps find Hailey."

"I'd want to know too," Esme admitted. "But I already live in this world."

This world? The world of the CIA? Or Titan Group? Or another world that was uniquely Esme Van Alstyn?

"It called to me," Esme continued, "and I wouldn't change it. But I'm somewhat immune to it now, if I'm being honest."

That sounded more like the CIA than Titan Group. "Immune to what?"

Esme leaned back in her chair and brushed her beautiful dark hair behind her squared shoulders. "That's a complicated question."

Their conversation was a game equally annoying and stomach-churning. Amelia fought the urge to run away or roll her eyes. She offered a different question. "How do you know my sister?"

Esme offered an unguarded smile. Its authenticity pulled Amelia closer before she said, "There are very few people in this world that could hold a candle to her and Jonathan."

The high praise stilled her roiling stomach. Curiosity slowly replaced her annoyance. "You knew them well?"

Esme nodded. "Very."

"Very," Amelia repeated. How had she never heard this woman's name?

Clearly, Esme Van Alstyn was someone worth discussing between sisters who supposedly shared everything.

"*Very*... considering the worlds that we operate in." Esme raised her sharp chin and stared at the ceiling for long enough that Amelia's heart thudded in anticipation. "Let's see. What can I share about your sister?"

Everything.

Esme leveled her long-lashed eyes to Amelia's again. "People trusted Hailey. She helped far, *far* beyond her reach."

"Reach of what?"

Esme continued as though she hadn't heard Amelia. "Hailey was an art collector with uncommonly good sense and an eye that could distinguish between the real deal and a fraud from the highest-caliber counterfeiters. You know all that though, don't you?"

Amelia nodded. "What don't I know?"

"She was..." Esme's eyes glittered. "A ghost." Another unguarded smile curled onto her lips. "Hailey could get into any building, through any security, and do so without leaving a trace of DNA."

Her spine straightened. "Hailey?"

Esme nodded again. "Mm-hmm. Jonathan also."

Amelia tried to picture her boring sister and brother-in-law doing anything sneaky. She couldn't. When she imagined their involvement with the CIA, her thoughts had been more of analyzing information from a computer or attending professional conferences to evaluate works of art for forgeries. Maybe they even authenticated stolen goods that real spies, the kind who sneaked into buildings and kept all their DNA, had found.

"Some people are born with intelligence and cunning. They were." Esme's expression faded to something more nostalgic and perhaps even proud.

Amelia bit her lip. That was a lot to take in, but it hadn't explained how the three of them worked together. "Do you sneak into places too?"

Esme chortled. "Absolutely not."

Amelia's eyebrows arched as she wondered what Esme wasn't saying.

She hummed and gave Amelia another once-over as though still trying to decide how much to share.

"That's not why Beth brought us here," Amelia urged.

"No," Esme answered playfully. She lifted her hands as if to say, *What the hell?* "Hailey and Jonathan had an electric connection. They used that as part of their cover and effortlessly folded into my world. It brought them places their day-to-day lives couldn't."

This was the bomb. Amelia's stomach toed its way to the edge of the cliff and readied to dive over the edge. She swallowed hard. "Your world is not the art history world, is it?"

Esme tipped her head back and laughed. "No."

"Do *you* work for the CIA?" Amelia wondered if she should be picturing Esme as James Bond or Jason Bourne.

Her laughter continued. "Does anyone *just* work for the CIA? Or are we all out there, living the best we know how?"

Amelia glanced at Camden then back at Esme. "Was that a yes?"

Esme sighed. "It's a complicated answer that doesn't have to do with why you're here."

"It sort of does." Hailey and Jonathan outwardly worked with art but were involved with the CIA. Esme was that connection. So Esme was a spy? "What do you do?"

"This place..." She held her arms out and eyed her office as though she could see through walls and was proud of everything in her view. "...is my club."

What kind of club operated out of a broken-down warehouse? Even if the expansive bar was beautiful, it was inconvenient to get to and didn't look like any of the swank establishments where DC movers and shakers milled. Not to mention, Amelia's company threw—objectively—many of the most exclusive parties in the DC metro area. She'd never heard of Esme. The place wasn't on her radar.

"It's one of a few clubs I own across the globe," Esme continued. "I spend the most time here."

This was supposed to have been the big bomb that would ruin Amelia's memory of Hailey and Jonathan. Esme had a club. So what was the catch? Drugs? Did Hailey and Jonathan use their work in art sales to find international drug dealers? Did the CIA deal with those types of crimes?

"Okay." Amelia blinked and looked at Camden for his two cents.

His jaw ticked, and he swallowed hard. But he didn't meet her eye or impart any understanding of what she was missing.

Amelia moistened her lips. "What do you do at your clubs?"

"I help my clients find their true selves. I help them find peace."

"So… you're not a drug dealer?"

Amusement danced in Esme's eyes as she glanced at Camden. Amelia really didn't like how everyone seemed to know everything except for her. She'd never buried her head underground, yet Jonathan and Hailey somehow had secret lives, and Esme and Camden understood each other without speaking.

"No. Not in the way you're thinking."

"Then *what do you do*?"

"I take away responsibilities and teach my clients how to shoulder burdens. It really depends on what they need. Everyone needs a release. I help figure out what kind and facilitate it."

What the hell was all of that? Washington, DC, was home to thousands of corporate consultants who charged thousands of dollars an hour to give opinions, streamline decision making, and optimize solutions. Amelia's job had brought her face-to-face with every variety and type—or so she'd thought. They always name-dropped and offered business cards. None were poetic in describing their occupations. None offered peace and tranquility.

Amelia stood up. "Okay, I'm done." She shook her head. "I came here to get answers, and all you want to do is play games." Amelia should have known that was how dealing with the CIA would be.

"I don't play games. At least, not the kind you're thinking of." Esme stared as though Amelia should have been able to understand.

Camden didn't stand up. He nodded for her to sit down. Amelia wavered but relented and perched on the edge of the thick cushion. The more she tried to understand what they weren't saying, the foggier it became.

"I don't get it."

Camden did.

"What am I missing?"

"Ms. Van Alstyn is a Dominatrix."

CHAPTER TWENTY-THREE

"AM I WRONG?" Camden crossed his arms. He knew he wasn't and wondered why Esme Van Alstyn had talked in circles. His best guesses involved Beth handicapping the conversation, though he didn't know why.

Sex didn't make Camden uncomfortable. Libidos were healthy. Desires were normal. He didn't knock kink or look down on vanilla. He had rules of engagement when it came to sex and had always stuck to them. At least, he had until he met Amelia. Fucking the focus of his assignment should have been a complete no-go. But reality was messy. Their chemistry was fire. Still, he was keenly aware that power imbalances were tricky to navigate. He had the upper hand when it came to them. Could Esme sense that?

"You're not wrong," Esme replied cryptically. Amusement glinted in her eyes, though she held her laughter in with the practiced professional restraint of a woman who was in complete control of her emotions. "There are many words that could be used to describe who I am and what I do. That's one of the best."

Amelia's jaw hung open as the color fled from her cheeks. It took her a century to slap her mouth shut again. Camden couldn't imagine the questions somersaulting through her thoughts and worried she might pass out.

Esme laughed. "I take it, Amelia, that I've caught you off guard."

Her forehead scrunched. Embarrassed confusion clouded her eyes. She blinked as if to force professionalism into her thoughts, in which scandalous questions were taking priority. "So... like... a madam?"

"No. This isn't a whorehouse."

"A *Domme?*"

"It's in the same family, but this is my profession. It's part of how I earn a living. 'Dominatrix' is a better fit."

Amelia's color returned. Camden was no longer worried she would pass out. Since he had jumpstarted the meat of their conversation, he would let the two women drive its direction again. But Amelia managed only to open her mouth and close it again, dumbstruck. It killed him to keep his hands to himself. If he could only squeeze her hand, that would do them both a lot of good.

"I'm—my sister—" Her head tilted. A pink blush blossomed over her cheeks. Given that she'd just been pale as a ghost, bright color splotched across her skin. "I'm not sure what I should say. I—" Her hand abruptly rose with her palm up, like she was trying to halt their conversation physically. "I don't want to offend you, Ms. Van Alstyn."

"Esme."

Her hand dropped into her lap. "I'm just struggling to wrap my head around my sister's"—Amelia gestured toward Esme then about the room—"involvement with you."

"Hailey *and* Jonathan."

Amelia's pink cheeks now leaned toward scarlet. "Right… Okay. *They,* then. I don't know what I'm saying, and I don't think it's my business to ask for clarification. So—"

She faced Camden, eyes begging for assistance. He'd never seen someone want to disappear so badly before. All he could do was lift his chin and silently tell her to soldier on.

Amelia refocused on Esme. "I had no idea the CIA dabbled in…" She gestured vaguely. "This isn't what I thought I was here to find out. And…" She swallowed hard. "I'm not sure how Hailey and Jonathan's, er… *private time* will help me find out where Hailey is now." Amelia squeezed her eyes shut. "God, I don't want her mortified when I bring her home."

"Is that what you're doing? Bringing her home?" Esme cocked her head. "Beth didn't share your end goal."

Of course Beth hadn't. That explained why Esme was talking in circles.

Amelia sobered. "Why do you think I'm here?"

"To find her remains. Proof of death."

Esme's candor landed like a sucker punch on Amelia so hard that it sucked the air out of *his* lungs. He would've done anything to absorb the hit, anything to lessen the emotional roller coaster that Amelia had been thrown onto without benefit of a safety harness. Esme hadn't spoken in an unkind manner, but she could have softened the damn blow.

"I don't think you can help me." Amelia popped up. Her matter-of-fact demeanor was yet another loop of the roller coaster. She was pulling the emergency exit switch and needed to eject. "Cam, you ready?"

Fuck. They had heard all that and hadn't learned any actionable details. Beth had sent them to Esme for a reason. They didn't know why. Leaving would be shortsighted. His jaw flexed, but he didn't stand. They'd already done the hard part. Amelia had to stomach the rest of the conversation to get what she wanted.

"Cam?" she tried again.

"Give it a second."

Amelia shot daggers at him as though he was a traitor.

"Sit." Esme redirected Amelia into her chair with a confident wave of her wrist.

Amelia didn't while silently pleading for him to take her side. Camden didn't want to tell her to stay. He needed her to come to that realization on her own—or walk out on her own. He couldn't be the reason for her regret.

"You need a moment to process your thoughts," Esme tried. "That's fair. Don't make any decisions until your mind has settled."

"Stop telling me what to do," she snapped. "Because I don't know what to do with any of this."

"Then don't make a decision until you do."

Amelia squeezed her eyes tight. Her lips pressed together. She almost looked like she was screaming inwardly and settling her mind simultaneously. Finally, she dropped onto the chair and perched on its cushion. She released a heavy breath. Camden hadn't realized he'd been holding his breath too. She'd made the right decision. All he could do was support her along this hellacious ride.

"I don't know what to do with this," Amelia whispered. "I don't know if I even believe you."

"Understandable." Esme steepled her fingers together. "I can make two promises: First, I'll be up front with you. I won't sugarcoat conversations, but I won't dole out more than you can handle."

Camden bet that meant personally and professionally. He chewed the inside of one cheek to keep his attention on the here and now and not the places he and Amelia could explore in Esme's club.

"Second, I don't have a reason to lie. You want to know about Hailey. I have no reason to hide the truth."

"But if you did have a reason to lie?" Amelia's eyebrows arched. "You would?"

"The important point is that I don't."

The side of Amelia's lip curled with disgust. "Got it. You're unfiltered and won't lie unless it suits you. Okay, then."

Esme moistened her bottom lip and tempered her severe posture. "Amelia, I'm sorry. I didn't realize you still had hope. I didn't mean to offend you."

Again, Esme, the queen of emotionless barbs, didn't sound as though she were trying to hurt Amelia, but her apology lacked even an ounce of compassion.

Amelia pressed fingers to her temples. "So. Many. People. Have lied to me. I've been living in this nightmare, and I don't know who to listen to or believe."

"You believe Camden." Esme gestured at him. "You trust him." Esme's smooth voice could pull the truth from a charlatan without breaking a sweat. "Correct?"

A pause hung in the room. Concern suddenly needled his insides as if a porcupine had taken up residence in his chest. If Amelia didn't agree, that would cut deeply. He didn't know when Amelia's opinion of him had reached that level of importance. Her approval was paramount.

"I do," Amelia said quietly.

The relief was instantaneous. Still, he gave her a quick look with as much humor as he could manage. "Took your time on that, didn't you, sweetheart?"

Her quiet laugh released the tension in her shoulders. *Good girl.* That was a move in the right direction. He gave a quick wink that he hoped she interpreted as a pat on the back, as reinforcement. She could handle the conversation if she grounded herself.

Esme laser focused on him. "Do you think she should stay?"

No dice. Camden wasn't going to convince her one way or the other and almost winked at Esme to keep his footing even with the Queen of the Barbs. "Amelia should do what she's comfortable with."

"*Of course she should.* But now that she's here and we've started down this bumpy road, would she regret leaving?"

That was a slightly different question, but he liked the wording better. It wasn't telling her what to do but rather looking out for Amelia's well-being.

He nodded. "Yeah, I think so."

"Camden," Esme continued. "Neither of you know enough to make an informed decision. I know that. You know that. The not-knowing aside, do you think Amelia can handle whatever she learns?"

Amelia could handle anything. From the first night they spoke, when he hadn't been sure what threats were coming after her, he believed she'd been strong enough to survive. Amelia would've said he was wrong or that she'd been strong enough only because he'd been on the phone with her. That was total horseshit. She could've done it without him.

The same went for right then. Amelia could handle anything they would learn from Esme. Whether or not he was by her side didn't matter—though he absolutely would be.

"Yeah. She can handle anything if it helps find out the truth." Camden pinned Amelia with as earnest a look as he could. His insides hurt that she didn't know that already. "You can do this."

Esme tapped and steepled her fingers together again. "I don't know where she is, but I can start you down the path to find answers."

Amelia pressed her lips together. "Why hasn't anyone else gone down that path? The cops? The CIA?"

"You don't know that they haven't." Esme's eyebrows arched. "I've talked plenty to Beth."

Frustration boiled in Amelia's expression. "Then why did Beth bring me here?"

"There are many ways to solve a problem."

Her blush returned. "*This way* feels like I'm invading a part of them they had kept secret for certain reasons. Not just because they worked for the CIA."

"It was a *job*, Amelia. *That's it*—though it was probably a very fun job."

Amelia's pink cheeks were back to their full color.

Esme shrugged. "My clientele are high-end. Hailey and Jonathan rubbed elbows—amongst other things—with the wealthy one percent."

"I don't think she's ready for jokes yet," Camden pointed out.

Esme's lips quirked. "Between the three of us—and a select group of others—we traded in information. In secrets. This…" She gestured to the walls around them. "Shouldn't be the reason you stay away."

Amelia took a deep breath then let it out very slowly. She mimicked Esme's gesture. "They worked in your sex club, and I don't know how to handle that."

Esme wrinkled her nose. "'Sex club' sounds so seedy. Hailey and Jonathan lived a complicated cover story and absolutely enjoyed themselves while fulfilling their mission objectives." Esme looked between him and Amelia. "But sex is sex, my dear. It brings people closer. It can scratch an itch, uncover new needs, or fix long-buried trauma. It's a wonder drug," she breathed out as though imagining all the carnal possibilities.

Amen. Still, Camden's skin flushed. Esme scrutinized him as though keenly aware of how they'd spent the previous night, as if she knew the way Amelia had asked him to take control and how he'd promised he would take care of her.

All right. They needed to finish the conversation and be on their way. "Now that we know the background information, what did you and Beth think we should do with that?"

Esme's lips curled, and she dragged out her answer into a slow, sensual purr. "Make an appearance, and infiltrate."

"As if it's that simple," he volleyed.

"It is with me on your side."

Anticipation gripped his chest, and viselike tendrils turned the tension up a notch. "Then what's your plan?"

"I'd thought you could be vendors." She hummed. "Maybe even voyeurs. But now that I've seen you two together, there's a much better avenue to consider." She analyzed them as though appraising diamonds on an auction block. "How long have you been partners?"

His pulse picked up the pace. "We've worked together for about—"

Esme flung her wrist. "Give me a little credit, won't you?"

The air crackled. Little sparks of invisible electricity sparked against his skin. The hair follicles at the back of his hair line jerked to attention.

"This is my job, and I'm incredibly good at reading people." Her assessing gaze sliced between them like a razor blade. "You work together *and* fuck. That gives us a lot to work with."

Camden laughed. He couldn't do anything else. But once again, Amelia was ready to pass out. She didn't even bother blushing.

Esme held up a hand to head off Amelia's panic. "Take a breath, young lady. I won't ask you to fuck on an altar. At least, not on day one."

Camden needed all his resolve to keep from laughing. Never in a million years would he have imagined that was his day job. Until that moment, he hadn't made up his mind about the Queen of the Barbs. He didn't trust her. But he liked her. That was enough to handle whatever she threw at them.

"Well, if it's not on day one," Amelia muttered.

"Here." Esme withdrew a black box from a desk drawer and set it on the empty black desk. "I have a gift for you, since you're being such a great sport."

They leaned forward.

Esme opened the box with the flourish of a Vegas showgirl. A black silk mask with long silk ties lay on a dark-purple pillow of velvet. A long black feather rested next to the silk mask. "Easy. Fun."

His pulse punched as if he'd jumped onto a treadmill.

"Think of it like homework." Esme recapped the box and gave it to him while talking to Amelia. "Enjoy yourselves. Get comfortable with the possibilities. Maybe do a little research on your own. That will serve as an excellent introduction for what to expect at my upcoming party."

"Are we supposed to…" Amelia gestured to the box in his hands. "Do that at your party?"

"Not unless you want to—take a breath, Amelia. It's a party. You can't mess it up, and you don't have to take off your clothes."

"Ah," Amelia squeaked. "But some people won't have on clothes?"

"If all goes according to plan." Esme's eyes danced. "If you don't like it, you can leave. You're in control."

"I can handle naked people," she managed hoarsely.

"You will see so much more than skin, my dear." Esme closed her eyes. "Think erotic, artful decadence." Her lips tipped up when her eyelids lifted. "And all of it is built on trust. That's what the three of us need."

"Trust," Amelia repeated, sounding more like she was trying to convince herself than agreeing.

"When it comes to our partnership, *always trust me.*"

Camden preferred to verify before trusting, but that option wasn't on the table. He would trust to a certain extent.

Esme squared her shoulders. "Ask Beth for a dress and suit for the Evening under the Stars event. She'll make sure every detail is covered."

CHAPTER TWENTY-FOUR

THE BLACK HALLWAY gave way to brilliant daylight, and cold air rushed over Amelia's face like a menthol balm. Fresh air had been so desperately needed that she almost pushed past Beth as they exited the warehouse. Amelia's cheeks and neck were hot. Her thoughts were unsteady. Perhaps she was embarrassed, but more than that, she was naïve and suddenly in a world that she'd only read about in sexy books.

A headache lingered at her temples. They traipsed across the well-kept parking lot—which made sense if rich people had their sex parties on site—and slid into the back seat of Beth's Lexus. If only she could hide there. *Please, please don't let anyone talk to me.*

Camden and Beth chatted as though they hadn't been inside Esme's house of sex. Their voices faded away until all she could focus on was the box Esme had given them. Yes, of course she enjoyed her private time with Camden. And, yes, she'd been the one to initiate the conversation, to ask for what she wanted. But Amelia was a vanilla, lights-off kind of girl, except for that time she asked him for what she wanted and that other time he'd pinned her to the wall and dropped between her legs. But all that was in the realm of standard sexiness. Blindfolds and feathers were simple but very much out of her comfort zone.

Did Beth know what was in the box? Amelia couldn't even see it. Camden had tucked it safely out of view in the front passenger seat.

"Do you have a designer you like?" Beth asked.

Amelia jumped. "Uh." She caught Beth glancing at her in the rearview mirror. "Me?" She wore a lot of department-store dresses that blended into the background of events. Her look was professional and unremarkable. No one was supposed to notice her at work. "No."

"What about you?" Beth asked Camden.

He chuckled, seemingly unaffected by the mask and feather they'd been charged with exploring. "I wear whatever is provided for the job and don't care who makes it."

"Oh, come on. You two aren't any fun."

"I think we're plenty of fun," Camden drawled. "This might be the best gig I've ever had." He glanced over his shoulder and winked. "You having fun?"

An instantaneous heat rocketed down her spine and into her cheeks. He must've noticed her blush and took it for an answer.

They were going to attend a party at which clothing was optional. How would this help her find Hailey? Simple: Hailey attended clothing-optional parties. Her sweet, introverted sister and responsible and quiet brother-in-law worked with a dominatrix. They'd partied and played, and now Jonathan was dead. Was this a good idea?

The Lexus accelerated onto a highway. Camden messed with Beth's dashboard until music flowed from the speakers. He was at ease every-where. Every person and conversation was effortless. He would probably take his clothes off at a party if the situation worked for him. Maybe he'd done so for work in the past.

She wanted to take her clothes off with him *alone*. She needed to feel his arms around her again. His touch erased the worries and grounded Amelia in a way she'd never known possible. She felt as if she could breathe in a new, better way.

Going to bed with Camden was more than she could have hoped for. Now, they had a blindfold and feather to play with. Chill bumps rushed down her back. He would know what to do. She could close her eyes and let him work his magic. Even better, they could *both* be active participants. Again, he would know what to do. Warm thoughts rolled deep into her stomach, tightening desire in her core.

"Do you like full-length gowns or short and strappy?" Beth asked.

Amelia blinked hard. Beth checked the rearview mirror expectantly, waiting impatiently for her to answer. Dress discussions were the business at hand. They had an assignment—sort of. And Beth was ready to talk business. Amelia had to be too.

"I usually dress to blend in."

"Doubt that's possible, babe," Camden tossed out as though Beth weren't sitting next to him.

Her eyes flashed to him. "I work in event planning." Fire ignited in her cheeks for the hundredth time. "I probably have a dress that would work if you can share details."

Beth laughed. "*Nothing* will work if you try to blend in." She glanced at her again in the mirror. "Do you like your hair better in updos or down?"

"Up and out of the way."

Beth bobbed her head back and forth, contemplating options as she hummed. "Up and sexy. I have ideas."

Amelia's nerves skyrocketed and stayed stratospheric as Beth and Camden chatted calmly on the way back to their new safe house. He pointed at a highway exit advertising every store under the sun. "We need to make a pit stop."

Amelia spotted the sporting goods store and understood where they were going. Knowing what had caught his eye made her smile. Twenty minutes later, he returned to their idling car with a football under his arm and a plastic bag in hand.

"Hungry?" He offered Beth a drink and a granola bar then handed Amelia the bag, which was filled with snack options. "Take this."

Hunger wasn't anywhere on her mind, but they hadn't eaten in a while. She peeked at the options. He'd raided the shelves by the checkout area and, by the looks of it, bought one of everything.

"You need to eat, Amelia."

He liked taking care of her. That made her insides feel gooey. She decided on a chocolate peanut butter protein bar and bottled lemonade. The first bite was unappetizing, or so she thought. The truth was she was famished. By the time Beth dropped them off at their one-bedroom condo, Amelia had uttered a grand total of no more than ten words, but her blood sugar and sanity were within normal ranges.

Camden set Esme's gift box on the coffee table. Just as in the car, no matter where in the small condo she walked, the box had her attention.

"You doing okay?" He tossed the football to himself and dropped onto the couch. "You've been pretty quiet."

She side-eyed the box and tilted her head toward it. "You don't feel like that thing is sucking the oxygen out of the room?"

His smile reached his eyes. Camden lofted the ball.

She caught it and tossed it back with far less amusement. "How did she know we slept together?"

"You're gorgeous. How could I resist?"

God, could she stop blushing? His dark eyes burned as hot as she felt. Camden rolled the football between his hands then tossed it aside. "Amelia, come here."

His voice rolled over her skin like the silk ties hidden in the box might. She shivered and moved to his side. Camden took her hand and tugged her gently onto his lap. "If you don't want to, all you have to say is no."

"I know."

Camden brushed her hair off her shoulder and, with the tips of two fingers, gently touched her chin and directed her toward his face. His eyes warmed her insides. "You're in control of everything. Dealing with Beth. Searching for your sister. Sleeping with me."

Her heartbeat rushed. "I know—"

His finger caressed her bottom lip. "You're in complete control."

But she didn't control the erratic drive of her heart, nor the way her insides came to life when he barely touched her. Existing in the same space as him was an aphrodisiac. Amelia let her eyes slip shut. His fingers drifted down. Breathing became a chore. Her lips parted with a gasping exhalation, and pinpricks of shivers cascaded across her neck as he caressed her sensitive skin with fingertips down, down, down her neck—and pulling away.

"Anytime you want to stop, sweetheart, you tell me. It's that simple. Do you understand?"

Yeah, she understood. Would he get back to business? She didn't want to think about anything other than the way he made her come alive.

"Tell me with your words."

"I understand," she whispered. "I promise." Could he please touch her again?

Camden inched back. The space between them grew as quickly as her desperation. But he melted her with that trademark smoldering gaze, reached for her, and pulled her down until they lay on the couch, face-to-face.

Amelia was a perfect fit against his body, as though they'd been sculpted to cradle one another. His hand rested on her hip. Her leg rested on top of his. His palm explored from her hip to her thigh, massaging and stroking the back of her leg. His lips took hers and nipped the bottom one. Shooting stars of need blazed a path through her insides. She wanted his teasing kiss all over her body just like the night before. She pressed herself closer. He kissed along her jaw and nuzzled against her neck.

"If you could do this," she whispered, "until I forget everything, that would be amazing."

His smile curved against her skin. Camden skirted his hand under the hem of her shirt. Goose bumps jumped, and a moan caught in her throat.

"Cam, the way you touch me…" *So good. So right.* He was so everything without trying to be.

Only in that moment did she realize that in the past, she'd cued up a mental list of to-dos while in bed that went something like "First kiss. Then touch. Neck kiss. Throat kiss. Chest touch. Remove clothes. Get to the good stuff. Be done with it all." That wasn't the case anymore. His hypnotic ability slowed her mind to everything except them.

His touch feathered over her breast. Heat followed in its wake, a tingling awareness blooming under his fingertips. Her nipple beaded and pressed against his hand. A soft gasp escaped her lips, her back arching instinctively, seeking more. She squirmed. Her skin prickled, hyperaware of every nerve ending as need coiled low in her belly. Her pulse quickened, racing faster as he sinfully played.

"Lift up," he said.

He pulled her shirt over her head and dropped it off the couch. Goose bumps erupted along her arms, the sudden rush of cool air contrasting sharply with the heat pooling inside her. He unfastened the button at her waist and eased the zipper down. Each slow, deliberate movement sent little shocks of anticipation skittering along her spine. He removed her pants as easily as the shirt. The thick length of his erection was pressed between them. Amelia reached for the button of his jeans.

"Not yet." He picked up the box on the coffee table.

The ache of denial throbbed between her thighs, frustration twisting in her stomach. Anticipation stole her breath. Amelia watched him open the box and remove the mask. Her throat tightened, a delicious tension coiling in her chest. Her pulse raced. A mix of excitement and hesitation warred within her, making her fingers twitch where they lay against the couch.

Camden laid the mask just above her head. Out of sight but not out of mind. The weight of the silky mask with its ties, the meaning of complete vulnerability, sent a tremble down her arms and legs. Her muscles shivered. Shyness begged her to retreat, but the molten need coursing through her veins secured Amelia next to Camden.

Awareness pounded in her pulse points and ignited an arousal so deep that it clouded her mind. Yet it also sharpened her responsiveness—every breath, every brush of his skin against hers, every unspoken promise popped in the space between them. She anticipated Camden's next move. As if the oxygen was slowly siphoned from the room, her chest rose and fell in shallow, rapid breaths, edging to the precipice of whatever came next.

Camden's hand froze on her stomach. "On second thought, we should go upstairs."

No, no, no. She didn't want to move. "Or we can stay right here."

The corners of his lips twitched. "I need more room to play."

Her stomach leaped into her throat. He boxed the mask and swept her into his arms.

"Cam—" Amelia laughed.

He liked carrying her.

"You're going to give me whiplash."

"I'm going to give you something. That's for damn sure." He bounded toward the bedroom. The cool air rushed over her skin. Camden laid her in the center of the bed. "Better."

Better... They had more room to play. Excitement sparkled over her skin again.

He removed the feather and mask. The bed dipped as his large body moved to her side. He reached over her bare stomach and placed their gift from Esme next to her hip.

She grinned. "Maybe *I* am supposed to blindfold *you*."

His chest rumbled. "The world is full of endless and unlikely possibilities."

"I don't know that anything is completely unlikely these days."

"We'll see." Camden took her hand in his and placed a chaste kiss on the inside of her wrist. The heaven-sent softness of his lips trailed up her forearm, eliciting an army of tremors. "But for now, the mask goes on you."

The full pout of his perfect lips made her stomach clench. She wanted to hide her uneven breaths. The dizzying way he turned her on was addictive, but it was disconcerting too. He just had a way with women. The man had probably gone his entire adult life making women wet and moving on to the next one. How had she not thought about this before? He was a perpetual bachelor, a man who proclaimed that he never settled down. What did that say about her? She was just one of a laundry list of people he could arouse that easily.

"What's the matter?" He traced his fingers along her jaw and down to her collarbone.

Oh God. How had she not seen it? That was what he'd warned her against. Camden probably didn't even know the difference. It had felt special. She'd trusted him incredibly easily. And it was easy for him because it wasn't new or different. She wasn't special. Her cheeks flamed. Embarrassment doused the arousal because that was exactly what she'd asked for, not thinking that she would start to fall for this man, that she would want him to want her, that she would want to be different from other women before her.

Camden's scrutiny increased when she didn't share. "This won't be as good as it can be if you're not one hundred percent with me."

She didn't know how to share how embarrassing it was that he could snap his finger and turn her on. "I don't know how to explain." *Because this was what she wanted!*

"Do you want to stop?"

"*No.*"

That heart-stopping smile curved over his face again. "Then try to tell me."

She pinched her eyes shut. Even the words were mortifying. She hadn't had long enough to figure out her thoughts. Was he attracted to her? Obviously, they'd had amazing sex. But would he have been interested if she hadn't all but begged him to kiss her?

"Amelia."

"Okay. All right." She stared at the ceiling. "I want you to want..." Her eyes pinched shut. "I'm not saying this right."

He inched back. The growing space between them killed her.

"I want you to want me." Shame sliced her throat with razor blades as she tried to swallow. "Not just do what you think would comfort me."

He blinked as though her words were gibberish. "I have been thinking about the possibilities—about what I want to do to you, with you—every second since we woke up."

Amelia's pussy clenched.

One side of his smile hitched. The corners of Camden's eyes crinkled. "And then Esme hands us a box of fun?" Heat flamed in his gaze. "If I had driven us there, if Beth hadn't been around, there's a damn good chance I would have thrown you over my shoulder and found the closest hotel room. If not the back seat of the car."

Throbbing need pulsed far below her stomach.

He licked his bottom lip. "This—you and me—it's a hell of a good time."

"If you're sure," she managed.

Camden tipped his head back and laughed. "I had you nearly naked on the couch within three seconds of walking through the door."

Well, that was true.

"Remember?" he pressed.

She nodded. "I just..."

Camden pulled in a deep breath and let it out slowly. "Give me all the apprehension you're hanging onto. Hand it over, and I'm going to throw it out the fucking window."

"I don't know why I got in my head all of a sudden."

His smile quirked. "You met a dominatrix who saw us clearly."

Maybe that was it. What had Esme seen? Camden was a walking, talking stud, and she was much simpler, plainer, the woman who disappeared at work and was an introvert. The bigger problem was their unevenness. Her stomach dropped. That was what Camden had warned her about: their power dynamic.

"I can see the wheels spinning." He took Esme's box and placed it on the nightstand, almost out of reach. Then Camden pulled the comforter over her semi-naked body. "Whatever you're scared of, whatever you need, Amelia, I'm going to give it to you. And I'm going to enjoy every fuckin' second of it. Understood?"

Power dynamics existed in everything. That didn't make them unhealthy. He was laying everything out for her. He wasn't toxic. He wasn't dangerous. She might have been falling for someone who was unavailable. That was their inequity. At least she could see the problem and gird herself for fallout.

Amelia reached for the box on the nightstand and pressed it into Camden's hand. She tossed the covers off. "I understand, and I don't want to stop."

"You sure?"

"Positive. What about you?"

Camden licked his bottom lip and removed the mask from the box. A fever rushed over her exposed skin again. Their brief pause hadn't diminished her body's reaction, but the way he asked her questions had smothered her freak-out. Nerves still danced in her chest, but they were the good kind. He studied her face as though trying to decide if she was ready for more. He was careful with her. Her heart swelled.

"Sit up, sweetheart."

She propped up for him and shut her eyes.

He tied the silk mask over her eyes. "How's that feel?"

She nodded. "Good. I can't see anything."

Camden eased her back to the bed. "You worried?"

Laughing, she cataloged her feelings. *Worried? No. Anticipating? Absolutely.* But her laughter fell away when he took the other wrist and kissed her palm. No one had ever kissed her like that. No one ever took the time to explore and check on her.

"Not worried," she whispered.

His tongue traced the lines on her hand. "Then what are you?"

Her eyes pinched shut despite the blindfold. "Vulnerable."

The soft kisses paused. Camden squeezed her wrist possessively before his tongue rolled over her palm again. Her long sigh was a mix of hunger and faith. Her need roared louder than her uncertainties. Trust was a drug.

He set her hand by her side. She tried to guess what would come next. He might remove her bra and underwear. He might kiss her. The possibilities were endless.

The bed shifted under his weight. Camden cupped his hands over her biceps, slid up to her shoulders and behind her back, and unfastened her bra. The fabric loosened. Her nipples perked with the chill of being exposed. The wetness between her legs intensified. She wanted his touch, his tongue. She wanted to search his chiseled face for what he needed but could only lie at his mercy.

Camden palmed her breasts. The symmetrical massage cleared her mind. Intense sensations ricocheted through her. Amelia arched for more.

"So fucking beautiful." The rough pads of his thumbs teased her nipples. "Perked and swollen, reaching for me."

Her breath skittered. His attention moved to her left breast, using one hand to play as the other slid south. A rush of need trailed his touch. Her hips wriggled. Camden hooked one side of her underwear and pulled it down her legs. The soft fabric scratched her thighs and caught on her knees. He snaked them away, then she was naked, blindfolded, and exposed.

Her toes pointed and flexed. Amelia rocked her hips. She could sense everything and still not have a clue what would happen next.

"Want to know what I see?" he asked.

She wasn't sure of the answer, but she nodded. "Please."

"Blush-pinked cheeks and rosy lips the same color as your nipples."

She sucked a sharp breath. Her cheeks heated, surely making them a hundred times pinker. Arousal tickled her sex. She squirmed under his scrutiny. Camden was so literal, so descriptive, so much more than she could have ever imagined.

"Relax, Amelia."

"Easier said than done."

The rumble of his quiet laughter made her smile. His fingers ran down her sternum, down her stomach, as his hand turned over and trailed his knuckles over her belly button. "I see a woman who has always controlled everything." His knuckles grazed her flesh until he teased over her pubic hair. "Giving herself to me."

Her lips parted. Tears pricked her eyes. She nodded.

"Inch your legs apart." She did. His caress skimmed over her sex, focusing on one side of her folds and then the other, working his way closer and closer to her slit. "You're squirming."

Amelia nodded. "You're making me."

He chuckled. "Sit still."

"That's not easy to do."

"You can do hard things, babe."

"There's one hard thing I'd like to do…"

Camden laughed and covered her mouth with a kiss. *God.* She needed him. He was perfect. They weren't following any rules. She could freak out and make stupid jokes, and he didn't leave her side.

He touched her again. She wanted to keep his lips on her, but when his hand fanned over her belly, barely grazing her skin, she was more than content to let him call the shots. His hand ran up her stomach, up her sternum, up until he reached her neck. Her pulse strummed against his hold. It wasn't tight. He didn't squeeze, just moved it to under her jaw— and a softness touched her lips.

The feather.

Her lips parted. Its tip traced the outline of her mouth. It almost tickled. He brushed her lips. Her pulse punched against his fingers.

The feather traced her jawline. The barely-there touch was like a kiss of air. It trailed between her breasts. Camden pulled the feather away.

Warmth teased her nipple before he gently sucked the perked tip in his mouth. She moaned. Camden released her. The feather outlined her breast and spiraled until his mouth took the other nipple. Her mind raced to keep track of his movements. A deep growl rumbled from his chest. The vibrations rocked her clenching body.

"Relax." He nuzzled in the valley between the swell of her breasts.

"Can't when you're making me want to scream."

He snickered, returned the feather to her stomach, and drew lines from the base of her breasts to the top of her thighs. She squirmed. Camden teased one side then the other. The touches drew closer together. A blissful eternity heightened her senses as each line crept closer and closer to her sex.

Camden moved on the bed again. His hand touched the underside of one knee and lifted it, walking her heel back and leaving her exposed. Then he repeated the movement. Amelia wanted to slide her legs down again. Then she tried to rationalize her level of unease. Camden had been as up close as a person could get with her body, and she'd loved it. But right then, he was at her side. The feather outlined the sensitive flesh near the top of her legs. She breathed deep.

"You doing okay, beautiful?" he asked.

"Yes."

"Tell me what you need."

So many things. Your fingers. Your lips. Your kiss. But when it came down to it, all she could say was, "You." Amelia reached out for him and found his hand. "Please."

Camden set her hand by her side. His weight moved away from her as he stood. She heard the metal rasp of his zipper sliding down. Shivers ran down her arms. Her heart hammered. Camden moved to the nightstand. The drawer opened and closed, and the condom wrapper was torn.

"Can I take the blindfold off yet?"

"Nope."

Her smile reached ear to ear, and she couldn't explain why. Seeing him was part of the fun. Her head fell to one side as though she could see through the mask. "That's not fair."

"But it's entertaining." He shoved a pillow under her ass, lifting her hips.

He hadn't worked her open with his fingers or tongue, and she didn't want him to. Amelia wanted his thick cock to part her flesh. She wanted him to thrust into her body and fill her completely.

He came closer. She could feel his warmth as his body caged over her. Her arms moved, hands reaching for his back.

"Stay still. Not yet."

Amelia froze.

He rubbed the hot length of his shaft over her slick folds. "God, woman."

She writhed. The man had no idea.

"Stay still, Amelia." Camden positioned the thick, blunt head of his cock against her tight opening.

The stretching heat was too much and not nearly enough. She raised her hips, needing him to fill her.

"Easy, baby."

Patience had never been her virtue, but, God, he was right. She didn't move. Every part of her needed to, but she simply experienced him taking her.

Camden inched inside her nice and slowly, drawing in and out with stilted breaths and groaning need until he seated himself completely inside her and held still.

"*Cam.*"

His lips pressed to hers, and he pulled the blindfold free. Amelia kept her eyes closed as he kissed her. Their lips broke apart.

Her eyes opened.

His dark ones locked on her. "Don't ever question if I want you."

"I won't."

His hips flexed. "Good, baby."

She gasped. He shifted and eased out of her. Amelia wrapped her arms around his neck. "I didn't know this could be so..." *Good? Creative? Intense?* "Fun."

His eyebrows lifted. Camden dropped his mouth to her ear. "More than I thought was possible. I can't get enough of you."

Well, damn. Didn't he go and make her fall even harder. He rocked into her again and again and again. Her legs climbed his, wrapping to his strength. Camden flexed and fucked. He drove her sky-high, to the brink of ecstasy. Their need mixed with kisses. Their gasps galloped. His forehead touched hers, eyes holding hers as she came apart.

Amelia cried his name as the orgasm hit. Every muscle in her body clenched, and hanging onto him, she felt his release as he strained into her body. He collapsed, catching himself before he crushed Amelia on the bed. Their breaths seesawed. His chest hammered against her.

Finally, he carefully disentangled himself from her. "Don't move, sweetheart."

Camden disposed of their protection and crawled back to her side. He pulled her close, his big spoon to her little one, and folded the comforter over them. She picked up the blindfold by the silk tie and dangled it in front of them. This little bad boy had driven her to the edge of insanity.

"Where's the feather?"

"In the nightstand."

She let the blindfold drop on the bed. "You're going to look very handsome in a suit."

He laughed against her neck. "Glad you think so." Camden turned her to face him. "What happens between me and you has nothing to do with whatever Esme has in mind. Okay?"

She nodded.

"But when it comes to that, trust me, and I won't let you down."

CHAPTER TWENTY-FIVE

AMELIA DIDN'T THINK it was possible to share a bed and have breakfast with Camden and remain immune to his charms. She woke in the warm embrace of his thick muscles. His sleepy grin made her stomach flutter right before he gave her a morning kiss that could melt diamonds. Her belly flips were on maximum volume all day long, even when she and Camden visited her condo for new clothes.

They couldn't simply show up at her condo. If people were tracking her, they likely had her condo under some kind of surveillance. She checked over her shoulder. They had parked in a neighboring parking lot and sneaked to her unit through the strip of grass that backed the building.

"Why didn't they show up when we were here last?" she asked.

"Don't know."

Camden never sounded worried. Even when he armed himself before leaving for her condo, he was still relaxed. Amelia unlocked her front door and let him inside first. Everything looked just as it had when they left before—not exactly up to its pre–search-warrant glory but headed in the right direction.

He flipped a light switch and checked his wristwatch. "All right. In and out in five minutes or less, right?"

She shuffled past him. "I'll be as quick as I can."

His heavy footsteps followed her into the bedroom. Amelia grabbed an overnight bag.

"Wait." He poked his head in the small walk-in closet. "You have to have something bigger than that." He pulled a large suitcase off a shelf. "Fill this bad boy up with everything you can."

That was her huge suitcase, the one she took on long vacations or shared with Hailey on a girls' weekend getaway. "I don't know if I need all that space."

"Beth is going to show up with designer dresses and crap for Esme's party. You probably want your own"—he raised a shoulder—"girl things."

Amelia wanted killer lingerie and thigh-high stockings. What she had was Spanx. Those would be needed, though. She took a quick mental inventory of her closet. It wasn't all boring and practical. She had jeans that made her butt look cute, especially if she wore her new black boots. And there was that V-neck shirt that dipped farther down than she realized when she purchased it. She hadn't worn that anywhere, but she suddenly had a reason.

Camden checked his watch again. "Just shove everything in, and let's roll."

Amelia swept her sweaters and shirts off their hangers then cleared out her jeans and pants, packing haphazardly. She took more time with her underwear and bras because she would die before bringing the bra that should have been thrown away a year before or the droopy cotton undies. She packed a small selection of hair and makeup products but none that she would be heartbroken over if they had to abandon it like the bag left at the last safe house.

"One minute," Camden announced.

She tugged the zipper shut on the mishmash of belongings. Camden took the suitcase as though it were empty, and she followed out the front door, which she relocked quickly.

They retraced their steps behind her condominium and to the neighboring complex's parking lot. They had gotten in and out in less than ten minutes. "I'm curious if anyone would actually show up."

He eased them out of the parking lot. Humming, he arched his eyebrows, seeming to play out the possibilities. "Let's find out."

They pulled into her complex and backed into a parking spot diagonal to her unit. She could barely see the front door, but that didn't matter. Two black sedans with tinted windows screeched into the parking lot. They didn't bother to park in a space and blocked several cars in. Men jumped out and rushed toward her front door.

"That answers that." Camden used his phone to snap a few pictures. "Duck down." He cruised out of the parking lot without attracting notice.

Amelia stayed down but turned and watched through the back window. Four men opened her door—they had a key?—and hurried inside her home. She couldn't imagine what she would have done if she'd been home—nothing, if she was being honest. *Her against four of them?* They didn't have search warrants. They had their own set of keys to her house. Her stomach roiled.

Not until they reached the highway did she finally felt the nausea disappear. "Those weren't cops."

"Nope." His jaw worked from side to side. "You know what we never considered?"

She'd thought of hundreds of things and wondered what she had missed. "I don't know."

"We assumed law enforcement left your place like we found it. That they tore it up while serving their search warrant."

Amelia bit her lips. "But it could have been those people."

"They're looking for you, but…" He checked his rearview mirror for the hundredth time. Maybe he'd seen something that raised his hackles. "Why? Because you know something? Witnessed something?"

She nodded.

"But maybe they're looking for something you have."

"Like what?" Amelia bit her lip.

Camden drummed his fingers on the steering wheel. "Do you have keys to Hailey's?"

"Not anymore. I have all my keys on one ring, and when they impounded my car—" She shrugged. "I haven't seen it since then."

"We need to get your car back," he pointed out.

"We need to get my life back." She wrapped her arms over her chest.

The downside would be losing Camden. Once everything was safe and normal again, he would move on. Knowing that and *understanding* that were two different animals entirely. She would have a crater in her chest when he left.

The highway road noise thundered around them. She wondered if he was thinking about the same thing. This was his real life—swoop in, save the day, be on his way.

Amelia hadn't thought about work or—"Oh crap." Her stomach bottomed out. "What day is it?"

"Tuesday. What's the matter?"

She tried to think back to her calendar, to the last update she'd had on Jonathan. She'd been playing pretend this entire time when real life should have been calling. She didn't want to do everything alone. Honestly, she didn't think she could go on without Camden's help. "I need to ask you a favor that's not easy to say no to."

He glanced over then checked his mirrors again. "I'm pretty good at saying what I need to."

"Jonathan's funeral is tomorrow. Would you go with me?"

"Yeah, of course. Why wouldn't I go with you?"

She didn't want to bury her brother-in-law. Emotion clogged her throat. "People think I murdered him. Not to mention that I'll be a crying, snotty mess."

"Forget the fact that it's my job to be with you. Of course I'll go. And fuck what people think."

THE PICTURES CAMDEN had taken at Amelia's condo didn't yield answers. He'd sent the shots to Parker and Shah. Neither had been able to identify the men. The vehicles had been rentals. The rental applications had been secured with cash and fake identification. The two men who had picked up the rental cars from Dulles International Airport had spent a fraction of their time on security footage. Their faces had been obscured, and they had left no record of how they'd arrived. They were good. Professionals of a caliber that made Camden's skin crawl.

His phone chimed. Liam's name was illuminated on the screen. Part of Camden missed being home with his teammates. Part of him was scared Liam would pull him off the job. After all, they weren't being paid. He honestly wasn't sure why Jared continued to allow the situation to go on except for some kind of commitment to a greater good.

He answered the call. "Hey, brother. What's up?"

"How's it rolling?"

"Same as always."

Liam laughed to himself. "I don't think anything about your gig is ordinary."

"Yeah, well…" He couldn't disagree. "You pulling me back to Abu Dhabi?"

"Hell no. Boss Man has some kind of ax to grind with the CIA, and it sounds like shit hasn't wrapped up yet. Has it?"

"Nope. I couldn't tell you who's causing Amelia a problem. But it's not going away."

"Yeah. I spitballed with Shah and Amanda."

"What'd you come up with?"

"A whole lot of nothing." Liam let out a long breath. "What's on the agenda?"

"The brother-in-law's funeral tomorrow." He bit his tongue.

No way would Camden discuss their meeting with Esme and the world Hailey and Jonathan had been associated with. Liam had spent too many years convincing him life wasn't always a party. The last thing his team leader needed to worry about was Camden at a sex party on the clock.

"Playing it by ear after that, I suppose."

"Maybe you should talk to Chelsea. Amelia might be a good candidate for witness protection."

Liam's wife, Chelsea, had been a federal marshal and was very familiar with the witness protection program. The truth landed like a bomb in his chest. They didn't know who was after Amelia. They didn't know why she was in danger. The CIA had caused this shitshow, so the least the federal government could do was give her a new identity. Poof—she would be gone. She would be safe but a memory. *Fuck.* That killed him.

CHAPTER TWENTY-SIX

T HE NEXT DAY, Camden tugged at the tight collar of his dress shirt. He didn't mind wearing suits or dressing to the nines if the job called for it. Apparently, the exception was funerals. He hadn't worked a funeral before. More than that, he was uncomfortable that Amelia would be in a church full of people. Whoever was looking for her had to know Jonathan Dumont's funeral would be a good bet to find her.

"Are you sure there are investigators here?" Amelia asked as they walked into the large church.

"Without a doubt."

If he had to guess, multiple agencies would have a presence: the CIA and FBI, not to mention the local police department. All were investigating wildly different angles of the same crime.

They clocked Amelia and Camden the moment they walked into the services. The various agents stationed around the church seemed to find him more interesting than her. *Good.* He wasn't in the mood to unceremoniously explain to anyone how law enforcement had been barking up the wrong tree when they arrested her and that they were missing a huge part of the problem: Amelia was still in danger.

The funeral was held at a DC church large enough to hold a crowd. Whatever Jonathan Dumont had done in life, he'd left behind many people who wanted to offer condolences and say goodbye. Surreptitiously, Camden opened the camera on his cell phone and scanned a video of faces. He would send that to Parker and Shah. Maybe they would be able to cross-reference it against the video footage from the airport or Amelia's condo. If they could get a name, that would go a long way toward keeping her safe.

"Amelia Stone?"

They turned to face an older man with a gentle demeanor.

"You have reserved seating." The man smiled at Camden with a nod. "There will be room for both of you."

They were seated in the row behind Jonathan's parents. Camden didn't like a room full of people at his back. The minister's words were short but familiarly heartfelt. He prayed for answers and that Jonathan would be able to rest. Camden surmised that was a reference to the length of time needed before investigators would release his body—no one had a clue how many federal agencies had claimed jurisdiction—and waited for international family to arrive. Amelia whispered that she was certain Jonathan had never met the minister before, but they didn't know for sure. Esme's world catered to everyone.

The eulogies made Amelia cry. He squeezed her leg and left his hand on her thigh. She entwined their fingers, and he wished like hell he could make everything easier for her.

Finally, a sweeping refrain played on the organ as the services ended. Without a graveside burial service, he could do nothing more than extract Amelia safely and let her recuperate at home—or, rather, their safe house.

Jonathan's parents turned in their pew and saw Amelia. Camden's chest tightened. He was aware they'd talked but wasn't sure how Mr. and Mrs. Dumont would act when faced with the woman who had been not just accused of but arrested for the murder of their child.

"Amelia," Mrs. Dumont said with a quiet French accent, reaching for her hand. Her face was void of tears, but her eyes were sad. "Thank you for coming."

Mr. Dumont nodded stoically to Camden then greeted Amelia with a friendlier nod. "We're hosting a small reception at the private residence of a family friend. Would you join us?"

"Sure." Amelia's watery voice killed him. Her tear-stained cheeks turned toward him. "This is my friend, Camden Brooks."

Mr. Dumont extended his hand. "You've been taking care of Amelia?"

"Yes." Camden then offered his hand to Mrs. Dumont. "I'm sorry for your loss."

"Thank you." Mrs. Dumont let her husband take her elbow. "I'll have someone send you the address." She glanced toward the man who had seated them and raised her chin. "We will see you there."

The Dumonts turned to speak with others. Condolences were shared. Someone even mentioned how long the funeral had taken to arrange. Camden wouldn't have had the manners of the Dumonts. Amelia made a disgusted face and whispered, "I really want to leave."

The aisles were packed with slow-moving mourners. Short of knocking people out of their way, they had no choice but to process out slowly with everyone else. The usher who had been signaled by Mrs. Dumont offered Camden the address of the private reception. He sent the address to Shah.

Amelia clung to his side. "There are so many people here."

"Funerals do that sometimes."

"There are so many parts of Jonathan that I didn't know."

Camden rubbed her shoulder. "Isn't that the case with most people?"

"I wouldn't have thought it about him and Hailey. It's unfair to learn about them like this."

His phone vibrated with a message from Shah.

American residence of a French diplomat. Former chief executive of the European Defence Agency.

That was interesting and maybe a little too close to home for Camden to be comfortable with. He typed quickly.

Camden: *What do you know about Jonathan Dumont's parents?*

Shah: *Give me five, and I'll let you know*

"Everything okay?" Amelia asked as they finally passed the law enforcement stationed at the door and stepped into the cold sunlight.

"Just getting a lay of the land before we walk in someplace." He slipped on sunglasses and glanced at Shah's message.

Philippe Dumont: retired from the French government's Ministry of Foreign Affairs.

Brigitte Dumont: fundraiser for art museums and board member for a dozen European charitable boards.

How about them apples? Jonathan Dumont's parents were French spies. He scanned the crowd and wondered what else they might learn from who had been in the church. Camden sent the videos to Shah and asked him to see if any names or faces were worth noting.

"What's going on?" Amelia eyed his phone. He'd been texting more in the past five minutes than he usually did in a day.

"I don't know yet. Could be nothing."

She rolled her eyes. "Are you really trying to protect me from something?"

Would it be so bad if he were? It was his job, after all.

"Jonathan's parents were diplomats."

She hummed. "I bet the French throw amazing diplomatic receptions. The food and wine alone might be enough to make me daydream about work."

Amelia didn't get the significance of diplomatic jobs. She saw it through her lens as a professional party planner: food, wine, locations, guest lists. Camden's point of view was decidedly more intel and analysis. He didn't want to change her perspective on the Dumonts unless he had to.

After searching around and finding no threats, he guided her to the car. If someone wanted to abduct or kill Amelia, right then was as good a time as ever. Where were the threats? The better question was why they weren't there.

Camden pushed that to the back of his brain to let it marinate. He plugged in the address.

Amelia glanced at their destination. "Georgetown. Fancy."

Her train of thought was yet another reminder that Amelia was strong as hell but unprepared for the danger she'd been forced into. He maneuvered the stop-and-go traffic across town and fifteen minutes later arrived at the address, a three-story federal-style brick house. Black shutters framed the large windows. A wrought-iron railing curled around dual staircases to the front door, flanked by manicured ivy.

He cruised by.

"Is that it?" she asked.

"Yup."

Valets waited for arrivals as chauffeured sedans dropped off. Camden wanted to circle the block first and give Titan as much time as possible to analyze the videos he'd sent. By the time they'd returned to the front door, he didn't have an update. This wasn't exactly like going into a dangerous assignment.

How risky could a funeral reception be? "Ready?"

Amelia nodded. He parked and offered their names to security, who stepped ahead of the valet. They were approved with a nod, and Camden left the car running as the valet approached, rounding the hood to get Amelia. He scanned the brick sidewalk and opened her door.

Camden waited for the needle pricks of unknown eyes on his back. He searched mentally for the anticipation of danger. It didn't come. Tracking them from the church would've been hard. Where were the attack dogs that had followed them across Alexandria?

Maybe the men searching for her were using her guaranteed location to search some other place she might've been. Perhaps their safe house was being compromised again. *What the hell were they looking for?*

The front door swept open ahead of them, and they were greeted and directed into a parlor room of stately-looking people dressed in black. Amelia stayed by his side. They bypassed the small clumps of guests talking intimately and ambled into the formal living room. Mr. and Mrs. Dumont held court by a gas fireplace. Waitstaff worked through the space with trays of champagne and bite-size appetizers. It was a sad little party for people with lots of money and connections. Amelia didn't fit into the mix.

From what he knew of Amelia and Jonathan, they didn't either. Then again, that was their cover. He understood Amelia's confusion.

Jonathan's parents joined them with a less formal greeting than at the church. Mr. Dumont asked, "Camden, who did you say you worked for again?"

Interesting. He hadn't said, and the man had remembered his name. "Titan Group."

Mrs. Dumont's head tilted slightly. "Security?"

They were familiar with Titan—another interesting facet about the

Dumonts. "I'm a friend," Camden offered.

Of course Mrs. Dumont was aware of Amelia's arrest and release. Given their diplomatic connections, she had been informed of much more. How did she know about Titan? Was she worried that Amelia needed protection after the arrest? Before…?

"I never met Jonathan," Camden volunteered, "but I've heard so much about him. He was a son to be proud of."

"We were." Mrs. Dumont laid a hand on Amelia's shoulder. "How are you holding up? Any news on Hailey?"

"No." Her jaw clenched. "No one will tell me anything—even though they don't believe I have anything to do with it anymore."

The Dumonts nodded, Mr. Dumont adding, "Such nonsense."

"They wasted too much time on that ridiculousness," his wife concurred.

"I don't think they'll find out who did this," Mr. Dumont admitted. "As much as I would hope for justice."

Camden studied the man. They were a well-heeled family with connections, given everything he'd learned. Why wouldn't they pull some strings and demand more manpower? Why weren't they involved in Amelia's release from prison? No evidence could've shown she was guilty. His intuition rang warning alarms in his head. If they knew Titan Group, then maybe Titan knew the Dumonts. Maybe Jared Westin did. That could've been the reason Camden had been sent on what essentially started as babysitting duty. He shoved his hands into his pockets, fidgeting.

Another couple approached the Dumonts.

Amelia stepped back. "We'll let you go."

"Amelia." Mr. Dumont rested his hands on her shoulders. "They were good people who wanted what was right in the world. Don't let the loss change you. They wouldn't want it."

He stepped back to allow his wife to give Amelia a polite squeeze. Tears welled in Amelia's eyes. Camden wasn't too hampered by emotions to see holes in the conversation. Why did it feel like they knew more than he or Amelia did? Camden thanked them again and whisked Amelia to the corner.

"They think Hailey's dead." Amelia sniffled. "And I want to hate them for it."

At that point in time, most logical people would hold the same sentiment. He wasn't holding his breath to find Hailey alive and kicking somewhere. Tears slipped down Amelia's cheeks. He shielded her from prying eyes, kissed the top of her head, and prayed she didn't ask if he thought Hailey was still alive.

CHAPTER TWENTY-SEVEN

T WENTY-FOUR HOURS LATER, Amelia had gone from standing in one gorgeous home to standing in another. Everything in Beth Tourne's condo apartment was either white, luxurious, or a work of art. In most cases, it was all three. Amelia was scared to breathe the wrong way and accidentally shatter some thirteenth-century vase on loan from the Smithsonian or the Met.

Despite all that, she figured Beth was about as laid back as Beth could be.

She hovered between the makeup artist and the stylist charged with readying Amelia for the night.

"Damn, Amelia, you are hot to trot, lady." Her lips pursed as though something was missing. "We need wine."

"Good idea."

Wine might've been about the only thing that could get Amelia to Beth's level of chill as she readied for Esme's party. *Esme's party.* Her stomach bottomed out for the hundredth time. Any time she thought of the looming night, crash went her stomach.

The stylist turned Amelia around to face the mirror. "And you worried that I would buckle you into latex, paint your lips black, and scoot you out the door like a vamped-up Elvira on her way to a ball."

"I didn't say that—oh..." Amelia stared in the mirror. "I look like a different person."

Black lace was painted over her arms and shoulders and down a deep V-cut between her breasts with a base material that perfectly matched her skin tone. It was completely sheer and melted over her body like a black shimmering glow that cupped her curves. Still, the dress somehow covered her modestly as the lace became a black sheath dress that reached to midcalf. The unusual hemline would've been discreet except for two slits that ran up her thighs.

"I didn't know dresses like this existed in real life."

The stylist hooted and tossed her head back, making her braids click. She reached around and patted herself on the back. "I knocked it out of the park."

"Yeah, you did. I don't even recognize myself." Then Amelia eyed the makeup artist, who had painted her eyelids with champagne shimmer and added feathered eyelashes. She used a lipstick that glimmered every way that Amelia turned her head. "Even my face glitters." Amelia turned to the two women, who were now packing up their bags. "You two are magicians."

"Va va va voom." The makeup artist studied the stylist's work, pleased, and said with a laugh, "You should see what we can pull off when we're tasked with turning you into the Hunchback of Notre Dame."

Beth returned with two glasses of white wine in hand. "Wow, Amelia."

"That's what I said." She took one of the wineglasses offered.

She waited for Amelia to take a sip. "Do you like the wine?"

It was fresh and citrusy. Beyond that, the intricacies of its flavor and taste were lost on her.

"I usually enjoy a nice glass of wine, but maybe a shot of something that burns would be a better choice for tonight. You know, a little liquid courage." She suddenly realized how ungrateful she sounded. "Honestly, you don't have to waste your wine on me."

"Pfsh." Beth waved a hand. "You'll do fine, and I'll waste what I want on you. You deserve it."

"You're only saying that because your colleagues had me thrown in prison."

Beth snorted. "Good point. I should break out the really good stuff." But then she shrugged and held the wineglass up to the light. "But kidding aside, I have to know this for work. It's research."

"Here's to research." Amelia took another sip. "I would say I wish my job was dresses and drinking, too, but it sort of was. *Is*," she corrected. "I taste-test menus for events. Why do you have to know about this?"

Beth hummed. "I have to know about the Clos de Vougeot, a French commune in the Burgandy region that produces world-renowned wines." She lifted her wineglass to the two other women, who had just about finished packing. "Would either of you like a glass of work research?"

Laughing, they declined, citing other assignments they were headed to shortly.

"Doing hair and makeup for spies. Oh, the lives you all must live." Amelia fidgeted with her wine glass. "I'm a little jealous."

With a wave goodbye, they each pulled wheeled bags out of Beth's enormous bedroom.

The stylist called, "Don't forget to have fun."

Amelia took another sip and thought of the night ahead. Fun wasn't what she'd thought about having. Maybe she would start with not having a panic attack. *Fun...*

Beth set her wineglass down, clasped Amelia on her shoulders, and turned her to face the framed floor-to-ceiling mirror. "You look fantastic."

"I look like someone else."

"That's all part of the game." Beth picked at an invisible lint piece and smoothed her hand over the fabric. "Do you remember what to do if you're uncomfortable?"

Her heartbeat jumped. She was uncomfortable *now*. Before Camden set eyes on her, before they'd walked into Esme's crazy party, her nervous system was shouting: danger ahead. Still, she wouldn't get answers if she stayed home and buried her head. Amelia nodded. "Defer to Camden."

"Exactly. Someone asks a question you don't like? Look at Cam. See something you don't understand? Look at Camden. Don't have a damn thing to say? Camden is your golden ticket."

Her throat ached. She nodded and must've looked unconvinced or ready to throw up.

Beth continued, "No one will know your dynamic or lack thereof. This will be the kind of party where subs defer to their doms, partners need permission, et cetera, et cetera. Okay? Just stay calm and quiet, and Camden will handle any rough patches."

Amelia could do that.

Beth stepped back and assessed Amelia from head to toe. She flushed. She tried to clear her head, but all the uncertainties and unknowns bubbled into her glitter-and-lace-covered chest.

"I know what Esme explained, but I don't entirely understand what we're doing tonight." She bit her bottom lip. "These might be people Hailey and Jonathan worked with. They might be a lead. But how will I even know if it is?"

"Don't eat your lipstick," Beth chided. "Have you ever gone to a party where you don't know anyone—" Beth caught her expression. "Right, professional event planner. Of course you have, which means you know that situation where you have to go in and make a friend. You make small talk with people you might never see again. Do that until Esme tells you otherwise. She'll know who Hailey and Jonathan circulated with."

"But how will I know if someone says something important?"

"You won't. You take information and debrief it with analysts."

That actually made sense. She bit her lip again but stopped at Beth's chiding voice in her head. "Do you think the people who took Hailey will be in the room?"

Beth laughed. "Absolutely not. These won't be the people who get their hands dirty, but the employers of the people who took her? Yeah, maybe."

The possibility jackknifed her heart. "Maybe…?"

"It's a safe bet that several party guests have their own goon squads on their private payrolls."

That didn't settle Amelia's nerves. "I don't understand how no one at the CIA knows who Hailey and Jonathan were focused on. I don't get it."

"There *was* someone who knew," Beth reminded Amelia. "But that person is dead." The brightness in her expression faded to somberness. Her shoulders dropped as though that was simply the price they paid for an office mishap.

Wasn't that all the more reason the CIA should be storming Esme's party? The murders and abduction were obviously connected. Why weren't federal agents attending tonight? Or maybe they were, but no one had told

Amelia. She recalled what Esme had said: There were many ways to find a solution to a problem.

The doorbell rang.

Beth shook off her grimness. "That would be your handsome partner in crime." She leaned in close like she was about to share a secret. "His stylist sent me a couple pics. Dark suit. Dark shirt. Matches his dark eyes and hair. He looks like one of those movie stars who plays schmexy Italian mobsters."

Amelia looked away and laughed, certain that Beth and her CIA skills could sense her stuttering pulse and rising internal temperature. Camden was already a fantasy. Throw him in a well-fitted suit, and Amelia might pass out.

"Wait here," Beth directed, "and I'll grab him."

Amelia took another long sip of her wine as Beth disappeared. She never drank before a work event. That night was different. She had many reasons to be nervous.

Beth squealed at her front door. Amelia's stomach base jumped into the abyss. Their chatter mingled with Camden's approaching footsteps. Her insides vibrated with anticipation, then Camden entered the bedroom. She nearly melted into a puddle of sheer lace and feathery eyelashes. Hollywood actors had nothing on Camden. He was leading-man material: tall, dark, and handsome with a lethal dose of danger.

Camden stopped short, like he'd run into an invisible wall, and pulled in a sharp quick breath. "Damn, Amelia." His eyes ran from her head to her heels and back to her face. "You're about to steal the show."

"Isn't she?" Beth squeaked. "I thought the dress was gorgeous, but when I saw it on Amelia, I died..."

She continued, but the words went fuzzy when Camden stared at Amelia like that. His gaze wrapped around her like his large warm hands had before. He covered her, caressed her, floated her to the highest possible place before her body would combust.

Camden held out a hand. Amelia placed hers in his palm and let him pull her close. Dark heat simmered in his eyes. Desire ticked in his jaw, and the corners of his luscious lips curved.

His mouth dipped to her ear. "You take my breath away."

"Mine is already gone," she whispered.

Beth prattled on, oblivious to their sizzling chemistry, which was making Amelia's knees weak.

He side-glanced toward Beth and cleared his throat. "Maybe I should have stopped for flowers or something. This is like we're headed to an adults-only prom."

Beth stopped as though he'd sprouted two heads. "What? No. Flowers would detract from the dress."

He grinned. "Nothing would detract from this woman."

"Honestly, Amelia," Beth chided, "if he wasn't so handsome, I'd shake him."

Handsome indeed. The man made the suit. That was true. *And this man… larger than life. Broad and towering and absolutely irresistible.* Amelia rested her hands on his lapels. "If I freak out and don't know what to say, I'm supposed to look at you." She stepped back as his eyes dropped to the slice of her leg now showing. "Okay?"

Camden did a double take on the slits at her thighs. "I've been read in and will handle it," his voice rumbled. "No sweat."

"If I freeze up—"

"I'll handle it, Amelia."

She nodded, nervous but trusting him with her life—and her sister's. "We might meet someone tonight who knows where Hailey is."

"And if you think that's the case," he said quietly, "keep it to yourself. We'll debrief later."

She nodded again. Her nerves were getting worse. "That's what Beth explained."

"You ready to go, beautiful?"

Sweetheart. Beautiful. The way he said those words made her feel important. A quake of tenderness skipped over her senses.

She would go anywhere with him. "Absolutely."

The sound of her confidence was surprising, but by his side, she supposed she could believe anything was possible. Camden slipped his hand around the small of her back and turned them toward Beth. "We're heading out."

"Let me know how it goes."

"Will do." Calm and collected, Camden led the way out Beth's apartment door. They were alone, and in a heartbeat, this unflappable man had spun Amelia to the wall. "Jesus fucking Christ, Amelia. We are not getting out of this building until my—"

The elevator dinged, and voices entered their floor. They both held their breaths, not knowing if people would come their way. The voices grew louder. Camden growled, and the intoxicated flutter in her chest flittered. He inched back, and out of the corner of her eye, she saw Beth's hoity-toity neighbors approaching with a fluffy white dog.

"You don't want to mess up my lipstick anyway," she said.

"The hell I don't." But Camden took her hand with a deep, tested breath.

They passed the neighbors. Even the fluffy dog gave Camden and Amelia the once-over, as though they didn't approve of the way he had her pushed against the wall and how, with her head tipped back and lips parted, she'd been ready for anything he'd wanted.

He didn't release her hand on the elevator ride to the lobby until they reached the CIA-chauffeured car service that waited in the horseshoe driveway of Beth's fancy building.

"Ma'am." The driver opened the door for Amelia to slide in.

Camden joined her from the opposite side. Between them was the night's invitation. It was midnight blue with engraved lettering on thick card stock. Delicate silver constellations were etched around the intricate silver words.

The Sapphire Accord cordially invites you to
A Night under the Stars

Share a Celestial and Sensual Evening
on the Third Saturday in November

Black Tie Attire with a Touch of Stardust
No Weapons, Cell Phones, or Recording Devices

No weapons? That wasn't something she'd ever added to an invitation before. "Are you unarmed?"

"I don't need a gun to keep you safe."

She understood that and hadn't thought he carried a knife or a gun on his person regularly. But maybe that was a foolish assumption. Their safe houses were practically decorated with weapons. Maybe Amelia was oblivious. She certainly had been with Hailey and Jonathan.

She picked up the invitation. Its beveled edges were gilded in silver. "These were handcrafted."

"I think the Sapphire Accord has a hefty discretionary fund."

Amelia tried to imagine Esme's clientele or her guest list.

He took the invitation and stowed it in his inner suit pocket and took her hand again. "It will all work out tonight. Try to have fun."

She snorted. "You and this dress are about the only fun that will come of tonight."

"Don't say that when the party hasn't even started. Look at it this way: It's gonna be a once-in-a-lifetime experience." He shrugged when she didn't appear to buy into the excitement. "Or you can pick up party tips for events. This'll be like corporate reconnaissance."

She side-eyed him but couldn't keep her worried scowl when he looked at her as though they were going to an amusement park. "All right. I'll try. What type of work do you usually do?"

"Not this."

"I know. But..." She squeezed his hand. "What was your last assignment?"

He glanced out the window as they pulled onto the interstate. His thumb caressed her knuckles. "An arms dealer in Syria was playing both sides of the fence. Someone found out and took his children. We brought them home."

She bit her lip but remembered Beth's order to leave her lipstick alone. "It doesn't sound like he's a good guy."

"Not at all," Camden agreed. "But his kids don't have a say in their father's work. And they were young. One wasn't even talking much." His lips flattened into a thin line. "Actually, none had much to say. They were terrified. But now, they're home." He gave her a long look. "I can see the wheels turning, Amelia. What are you thinking?"

"You were probably paid with money earned in…" She paused to think over what she said next, not wanting to offend him. "Really questionable ways."

"Yeah," he agreed. "Does that mean his kids should be left to suffer?"

"No…"

"Did the guy learn a lesson?" Camden shrugged. "No idea. Not my place to play judge and jury."

She drank in a deep breath. The world wasn't black and white. Hers had been until recently.

"You did a good thing, then."

"I did my job. We extracted kids that were in a bad place. Not my job to raise them or instill a moral compass. Their father's an arms dealer. The odds aren't great they'll end up as UN peacekeepers—then again, they might *because* their dad's facilitating death for profit."

"Do you remember every assignment?"

"Some, I try hard to forget." He turned her hand over in his and traced the lines and creases of her palm as though mapping out a puzzle. "What about you? Any nightmare events that you want to forget?"

She tried to remember standout headaches. Then she tried to recall her favorite events. Everything seemed so pointless: the stress over guest lists, menu choices, motifs, and color palettes. She used to enjoy that part of work, even if she hated the business side of things. Whether she liked it or not didn't change the truth—she'd simply been good at it.

"I don't remember when work changed from something I had to do to pay bills to… thoughtless monotony." She chewed the inside of her cheek instead of her lip. "Maybe Hailey knew that and never told me about her other job so I wouldn't feel as completely uninterested in my company as I do now." She shrugged, unimpressed with herself.

The driver exited the highway and said over his shoulder, "We're five minutes out."

Knowing she needed reassurance, Camden squeezed her hand. "You ready?"

She made a face.

"I'll take that as a yes."

She might throw up. "You're such an optimistic guy."

"Baby, I am the king of optimism with you on my arm. Anything can happen tonight."

His calmness didn't help hers. The sheer lace was suddenly too tight. The feathery eyelashes obscured her vision too much. She might've been teetering on the edge of a panic attack.

"I don't know if I can do this."

The driver pulled into the warehouse lot, lined with expensive valet-parked cars and a row of idling hired vehicles. So many people were at Esme's warehouse. Her shallow breaths quickened as a sheen of sweat surfaced at the back of her neck.

"Look at me, Amelia."

But she couldn't. Instead, she stared at the ugly, dilapidated industrial building. It had been transformed into a showy work of art. Blue-and-purple lights beamed artfully over the imposing imperfections of rusted and barred windows.

Her breath caught. "It's so..." She couldn't explain how the transformation changed everything into a sultry fairy-tale ball. Finally, she turned to Camden. "Magical."

Their sedan paused before pulling into the line of vehicles snaking to the front entrance. The driver asked over his shoulder, "Are you ready, ma'am?"

If she were to freeze, if she forgot what to say, she was supposed to turn to Camden. Their eyes met. Tonight was her first step to finding Hailey. Amelia would be that much closer to answers if she walked into Esme's party. The queasy storm in her stomach continued to protest, but she nodded to the driver. "Yes, I am. Thank you."

They rolled into the queue, and with the driver's quick reminder of their exit instructions, they stepped into the chilly night.

Nothing seemed out of place as they were dropped off. Their invitation was checked as though it was any other tony Washington, DC, gala. The dark entryway that Beth had led them through days before was lit with long silver tapered candles in sconces and alive with laughter and voices.

She walked in on Camden's arm. Just like when Amelia had first met him in person at the prison and when he melted into the kitchen crew in a back alley, Camden breezed into the party with enough chill to get them both through the evening.

The candlelit hallway opened into the main hall. Guests wore breathtaking dresses and titillating costumes. Many were naked or wore only collars and nipple clamps. They socialized as though it were any other party, unaffected by the various levels of undress that surrounded them. Waitstaff passed flutes of champagne and hors d'oeuvres. It could have been any charity gala that Amelia had organized if not for the various levels of undress and signature touches that Esme had to have overseen. Black silks hung like erotic ropes amongst the chandeliers. Aerial performers dangled from them, wearing masquerade masks and not much else. Their glittering bodies twisted and twirled high overhead.

Camden snagged two drinks from a server and handed her a flute. "Want to make a lap around the room?"

She sipped the bubbly champagne. "You're asking me like I have any idea what we should do."

"Mix and mingle and see who we meet."

What if Esme introduced them to someone who was essentially naked? She would blush and stammer and not remember anything of importance. Thank God for Camden, patron saint of chill.

They eased along the outskirts of the room. The guests were a mixed lot: old and young; vanilla and dressed to the nines; kinky and barely dressed. Enough black leather and latex were in the room that Amelia was right to worry that Beth might've dressed her like a BDSM princess. But those who donned the leather and latex looked as though it was a choice that defined them. Amelia would have looked like a plastic-wrapped copycat and was happy to let the sheer black lace and double slits announce to the room exactly who she was.

Maybe the dress *was* her—or at least who she wanted to be. Nothing in her closet had ever been that thrilling.

They eased by two women having a lively conversation. One of them haphazardly petted a third woman, naked and on her knees, as if she were a submissive pet.

They reached the far wall. What Amelia had thought were provocative performers posing against the wall were women and men covered in paint with their hands tied overhead by ropes and wide satin sashes. They didn't look uncomfortable and were mesmerizing.

Next to each person on display stood an immaculately and fully clothed partner. Some partners ignored the people tied at their sides. Others spoke with onlookers, discussing their subjects as one might at an art gallery. Still others interacted. They touched and teased. They played. Amelia's blood raced. She couldn't look away but didn't know where to let her gaze land.

"Doing okay?" Camden asked.

She swallowed and wanted to make sure of her answer first. Her body was reacting to what she saw. It wasn't fear or aversion but curiosity. Bondage was being presented as living art.

He stopped them. "Amelia?"

"I'm fine." And she meant it.

Amelia glanced behind Camden's shoulder. He turned toward the couple that had captured her attention. The woman wore a blindfold just like Amelia's. Other than the sashes binding her hands overhead, shoulders to the wall, and legs apart, she was naked and squirming under the soft torture of a feather.

Camden dipped his mouth against her ear. "Guess their box came with ropes."

Breathy laughter was her only answer. The idea of Camden tying her in place and touching her made arousal twirl in her stomach. She would be completely at his mercy—no decisions to make, nothing to think about except the pleasure he would pull from her. She shivered.

"We should keep walking." His palm smoothed down the sheer lace. A trail of sensitive goose bumps thrilled at his touch. "Where to next?"

She glanced at his face. Camden scanned the room. His eyes never stopped moving as though cataloging every person around them. Yet he did it in a way that no one would notice his roaming search. Looking at their surroundings was perfectly expected. She should try to take it all in the way he did.

"Toward the bar?" she suggested.

He lifted his chin in agreement. Amelia took his elbow as the crowd became denser. She focused on the costumes and dresses. Diamond necklaces were as plentiful as bejeweled collars. Eyes fell on her too. Her dress was appreciated. Her body was as well. The attention didn't feel good. She clung closer to Camden. "I like the shadows better."

"Got it." Camden maneuvered them toward the outskirts again.

They approached the other way, which was lined with living sculptures on pillars. Her breath caught. Camden slowly ran a hand down her spine and pulled her closer.

His chin dipped to her ear. "Still doing fine?"

The way the man kept checking in on her would keep her grounded.

She swallowed hard and nodded. "Yes, thank you."

With the cadence of her breath under control, Amelia was able to face the pedestals again. Each one held a person posed and immobilized by intricately tied knots. Artfully arranged spotlights lit the displays, casting them in silvers, purples, and blues.

Some were blindfolded.

Others were gagged.

All were utterly motionless.

The time and talent necessary to tie each knot… the surrender and submission to be tied… Amelia couldn't fathom but couldn't look away.

Esme appeared at her side. "Welcome."

Amelia shouldn't have been surprised at how easily Camden greeted Esme. Their easy conversation flowed before she managed to say hello. Esme's attire reminded Amelia of her usual event clothes, though they weren't the same. With diamonds and a black bodice dress, Esme dripped sensuality. But she was also not on display like her guests. "Esme, thank you for inviting us."

"In this setting, you'll call me Mistress Esme."

"Of course." There was so much to absorb. Camden had said Mistress. Amelia would have to do better on picking up details for tonight to go smoothly.

"Gorgeous, isn't it?" Esme asked her of the pedestalled display.

"More than I could have imagined," Amelia breathed.

"Shibari. A form of Japanese rope bondage. It takes a very intimate, trusting partnership to create such beauty. Some subs will pose for a few minutes. Others much, much longer. The ones joining us tonight have been chosen for their experience and abilities." Esme gestured to the people standing to the side of each pillar, just out of the spotlights' focus. "Those are the riggers responsible for their care and well-being. They watch for distress and have tools ready to release them if there's a problem."

"They're artists."

"With ropes and knots in place of plaster and paint." Esme grinned devilishly. "You two should try it sometime. There are lessons."

Camden's eyebrow arched with interest.

Amelia balked. "I'm not the sit-naked-on-a-pillar type."

Esme laughed. "No one jumps into calculus without first learning how to add." She pointed a finger at Camden. "Don't let her say no without learning all the possibilities."

Amelia opened her mouth to protest but didn't have a reason other than fear of the unknown. She turned toward Camden and let him handle Esme. Before he could, another woman joined their conversation.

"Mistress, what a wonderful gathering," the other woman said. A naked man followed on her heels.

Esme's face lit up and warmly greeted only the woman. No one acknowledged the naked man. Er—*almost* naked. Something leather and metal was wrapped around his cock, and Amelia wasn't sure where to look.

"Mistress Marissa," Esme said, "let me introduce you to Michael and Briana, who I've recently become acquainted with."

"Lovely to meet you." Marissa didn't mention the man with his chin tucked by her side.

Amelia wondered if Marissa was her real name. Briana didn't seem to fit Amelia. The name Michael didn't work for Camden, either, but she supposed that wasn't the point. Why hadn't anyone told her they'd have secret code names?

"Marissa is an art importer."

Amelia's focus fell entirely on Marissa. Elephants could've been dancing around a naked orgy, and she wouldn't have noticed. "An art importer?" Her voice might have sounded too eager. "Do you have a specialty?" Hailey had once told Amelia that was the easiest question to rely on when socializing with her professor friends. That probably worked for her bondage-party friends too. *Why not?*

The other woman beamed. "Yes. Venetian glass. I helped Esme source her chandeliers." Marissa caught Amelia's gaze drifting toward the ceilings. "No, not these. Too southern Gothic for my taste."

"Every room can't be adorned in crystal flowers and gold leaves."

Amelia laughed because Esme did. Camden cracked a smile. *Oh, the small talk of the rich and powerful.* Amelia wished the conversation would shift to anything that would help find Hailey.

Esme gestured to Camden. "Michael recently purchased the rights to the Vidalario collection, making him the very lucky owner of a Bouvant that I would very much like access to."

"Oh, a Bouvant." Marissa pressed her jewel-encrusted hand over her heart. "I wasn't even aware there was one out the wild."

Again, someone could've told Amelia what stories Esme would use ahead of time. If she'd had time to memorize the details, she would be less likely to screw up. But Camden fell into the back-and-forth schmoozing with little effort, as if he brokered Vidalarios and Bouvants in his sleep.

Esme pivoted the conversation. "Briana orchestrates events that make my little shows look like shindigs at the county fair."

Somehow, the schmoozing came to Amelia almost as well as it did to Camden. Listening to herself was almost an out-of-body experience.

"I wonder if I've ever been to one of your productions." Marissa raised her brows at Esme.

"If you haven't, you—and your buyers—would..."

Esme's words turned into static. Amelia laser focused on a man fixated on her. She was sure she knew that man. But she couldn't see him anymore. He'd disappeared into the party. Where had she seen him before? The funeral? No. Maybe at the reception hosted by the Dumonts? Her heart raced. Her skin prickled with a warning. Someone was watching her.

Camden needed to know. They needed to—

"Briana?" Camden asked.

Her long, feathery eyelashes batted. "I'm sorry—"

Another man—a scarier man—was speaking with the man she'd just seen. They both turned toward her. Amelia jumped back and ducked behind Camden.

"It's so nice to meet you," Camden offered Marissa. "I think we need to get some air."

Amelia glanced over his shoulder. Had that been the man who chased her that first night when life had turned upside down? But she didn't see either man anymore.

"There's a lovely rooftop garden," Esme added. "Fresh air under the stars if you haven't been upstairs yet."

That was all the excuse Camden needed as Esme guided Marissa away with expert finesse.

"Cam, I—"

"Not here."

She took his hand and threaded past the human sculptures and under the aerial acrobats. She didn't look over her shoulder but could feel the men watching her. Or maybe she'd made it up in her head. *Why would they be here?* Beth had said the people who did the dirty work wouldn't be at Esme's party, only the people who employed them.

She tried to remember what they'd been wearing. Perhaps she could describe the men to Camden. But she couldn't recall details. Maybe the problem was all in her head. The stress of the night, the made-up cover stories, and bondage art had tricked her mind into danger. Amelia's stomach bottomed out. *God.* She'd screwed up a potential lead. Maybe Marissa was Hailey's contact.

"Maybe I didn't see what I thought I saw."

"Don't say anything yet." Camden pressed her closer to his side. "Wait until we're alone."

A glass elevator with a uniformed operator carted them to the top of the three-story warehouse. They walked out into the cool air. Many guests had had the same idea as they did. Camden pushed them through a throng of people. His hand was at the base of her spine. Camden took her partially drained champagne flute and handed his and hers off to passing waitstaff with such elegant coolness that she could imagine him as James Bond.

She pushed onto her tiptoes and pressed her lips to his ear. "We need to leave."

Worried, Camden dropped his gaze to her. "What did you see?"

"Beth was wrong." Her gaze bounced over the large space.

The cold weather hadn't kept most people inside. They gathered around the outside heaters surrounding a bar. Others were using the more secluded space to enjoy their private activities out in the open.

"I can't be here."

Camden checked their surroundings. His eyes skimmed over laughter and fornication, searching for what spooked Amelia. "Amelia, honey." He caught her cheeks in his hands and forced her to focus on him. "What did you see?"

"The man who chased me."

CHAPTER TWENTY-EIGHT

C AMDEN TUCKED AMELIA behind a trellis draped with fairy lights, silk, and ropes. He didn't like his angle, but it was the best he could do to keep the elevator and the crowd in his line of sight. He could manage without a weapon. But his biggest problem was a lack of information. They hadn't planned to visit the roof. Hell, he hadn't known it was an option. Esme hadn't provided them with the exterior schematic. No one had counted on Amelia blanching and all but falling out of her cover story mid-conversation. They'd stupidly convinced themselves she could simply defer to him in the event of a problem. Everyone had been wrong to let her do it, including him.

Her gaze swiveled from side to side.

"No big deal. We'll head home." He didn't have his phone to signal the driver. Their extraction instructions relied on the valet and staff at the building's entrance. Calling up their car wouldn't take long, but Camden wanted her surer on her feet before they bailed.

Panic drained the color from her face. He followed her gaze to the elevator. A single man, tall and wiry, fitting the description Amelia had given that first night, scanned the opposite way they had maneuvered. "Okay. We have sight of him. We'll avoid—"

"Oh God."

His gaze shot back to the elevator as another man entered the fray. Camden couldn't place him. "Who's that?"

"I think he was at the Dumonts' reception."

Camden had a way with faces and couldn't recall that one. "I don't remember him." But that didn't matter.

"Or maybe when we went out to dinner. I don't know."

"All right. Take a deep breath. They don't see us." Possibilities rolled through his mind. The best-case scenario was that the second man was a federal agent, and he was tracking her pursuer. Worst-case scenarios were a much longer list. "We'll leave and figure this out later."

Shah and Parker would be able to do wonders with Esme's guest list. No way had someone simply sneaked in.

She shook her head. "What if they have Hailey?"

"They don't have her here." He took her hand and snaked through the crowd. They stayed along the perimeter. Why the hell had he gone to the roof? "You keep an eye on the second guy. Let me know if he heads our way." With his focus trained on the first man, they skirted around conversations. He pulled up short.

She clung to his arm. "What?"

The first man had pulled a hairpin turn and retraced his footsteps. He was moving quickly as if he'd gleaned information about their position.

"Cam—" She pointed the opposite way. "Guy two is angling our way."

Fuck. "No problem."

There couldn't possibly be only one way on and off the roof. He assumed that, much like the dark hallways Beth had led them through, the exits and emergency doors weren't lit. They existed. He just had to find them.

Both men were coming at them from different angles. He didn't know what they intended to do when they got to Amelia, and he wasn't about to find out. Camden beelined toward a table of men smoking cigars. "Anyone got a light?"

"Sure—"

He swiped a Zippo. Curses trailed as he pulled Amelia toward the bar. "Sorry, man."

"*Cam?* What are you doing?"

"Keep moving with me, babe." He strode by the bartender and searched the bar's liquor shelf.

"What the hell?" the bartender demanded.

Camden ignored him, eyed the labels, and swiped two of the highest-proof bottles he could spot.

"You can't—"

With one bottle in hand and the other tucked under his arm, Camden dragged Amelia again, with another trail of curses.

Both of the men who'd been tracking Amelia now spotted him. They rushed forward, knocking over people and tables. Smart party guests hurried away from the spectacle. Curious ones leaned into the drama and got in the way. But no one was in the danger zone when Camden pulled the pour spout from the first bottle. He handed it to Amelia. "Dump this behind us."

Wide-eyed and terrified, she didn't question him. Amelia turned the bottle upside down. He pulled out the second pour spout and did the same. They rushed between tables.

"Empty," she announced.

Camden grabbed it and smashed both bottles on the cement tiles. "Run for the elevator." He double-checked that their trail of liquor had avoided the partygoers, lit the Zippo, and threw it onto the shattered glass. It ignited with a whoosh. Fire licked over their liquor trail and danced. But it was only enough to create a distraction.

Camden ran toward her. Amelia had called the elevator. Its glass doors opened as he arrived. The operator jerked back as they jumped in. He caught the chaos behind them. Camden hit the button to close the door.

Amelia pressed against the glass wall as they closed in on the first floor. "That was him."

"The guy from the first night?" he asked, knowing the answer already.

"Yeah." Her chin bobbed up and down as her long eyelashes fluttered.

For a moment, he thought she would fall apart completely. But then he saw she was the same woman from the first night and their date night. Amelia's backbone was made of steel.

"Esme isn't going to like that," she said.

The elevator dinged as they passed the second floor. Camden laughed. "Neither is Beth, but I don't care." Getting Amelia out safely was his top priority.

The elevator opened. The lack of security blocking the way gave Camden another round of questions about the party they'd walked into with the CIA's backing. Esme had sent them into a dead end. *On purpose? And what the hell had those men intended to do?* If they wanted to eliminate Amelia, there were easier ways to do that. They'd had a clear shot. The only possible answer was they'd wanted to grab her. Beth and Esme were the ones who'd given them the opportunity.

CHAPTER TWENTY-NINE

"THIS IS NOT how tonight was supposed to go," Beth announced when she walked into Camden's safe house. She stopped short, staring at Amelia. "God, that dress and makeup is enough to make me stop what I'm doing." She tilted her head. "Are you sure the two men who looked at you weren't *looking* at you? Given where you were and all..." She gestured from Amelia's head to toe and back again. "You're fresh on a scene that probably doesn't get many new faces. And you're gorgeous."

"Give me a break, Beth," Camden growled. "You sent us there. How much do you think I trust you at the moment?"

"If I was the problem, those men would have been *here* and not crashing a private party."

"Private with a very exclusive guest list. So Esme is the problem. *Your* Esme."

"No." Beth shook her head. "Look. I'm just spitballing ideas, my friend. I don't know if Amelia was spooked or too new to the scene. It could have been the dress."

"Like I said"—his irritation rumbled like thunder—"give me a fucking break, Beth. That's the biggest load of bullshit."

Amelia didn't like the pseudo-compliment or the way Beth downplayed the evening. Camden had literally set a fire. That wasn't hysteria. She glanced his way. His scowl had deepened.

She rolled her lips together. "Why would the men who killed Jonathan and took Hailey be at Esme's party? I mean, they're looking for me. But why? They could've pointed a gun at me from a hundred yards away and killed me. They could've done that at the restaurant too."

"That's what I've been wondering," Camden muttered.

"I don't know," Beth admitted. "I bet Esme would like to know as much as we do."

"No, I'm pretty sure we care more." He stopped and held out his hands. "Everything touching this situation has been a clusterfuck. It was before Titan was brought into this, and it hasn't stopped yet. What the hell is going on with you people?"

Beth wasn't fazed as Camden bore down on her. "If I had any idea—"

"No, Beth. You're supposed to show up here with ideas. Things a little deeper than spitballed bullshit on Amelia catching everyone's eye."

Her phone rang. "It's Esme. Can you cool your jets for a hot second, or do I have to go outside and freeze while I take the call?"

"Take the damn call." He spiraled the football into the couch and stomped into the kitchen.

Camden rummaged through cabinets and drawers as if the answers to his questions were organized in Tupperware. He strode around the kitchen like a caged panther in a zoo.

"Cam." Amelia waved him over. "Sit with me."

At the very least, they could eavesdrop on Beth's phone call together. Thus far, all Beth had said was "uh-huh" and "perhaps."

He perched on the edge of the couch.

"Easy, cowboy." Amelia laid a hand on his back, slowing running it up and down. It would be performative to remind him he was the reason she was safe. "Thanks for fighting the good fight against the CIA."

His shoulder muscles tensed, and he glanced over his shoulder. "That's not something you have to thank me for." Irritation flexed in his jaw. The tendons on his neck seemed more pronounced. Camden glared at Beth as if he wanted to say more, but he shook his head, pinching the bridge of his nose.

Beth ended the call and didn't look more informed than when she'd answered. "Don't shoot the messenger."

Camden growled and leaned back on the couch. He crossed his arms. "Productive conversations don't start that way."

"Well, then, we're on the same page before I even start." Beth smiled. "Esme's just as surprised as we are, and even more surprisingly, she's not furious you tried to burn her building down."

"The fire burned itself out before we even reached the first floor," Camden grumbled.

Beth rolled her eyes. "Don't try to impress me with your savvy skills, Camden Brooks. You brought a lot of attention to yourself."

"Actually, no." Amelia hated the way Beth turned every part of this into their fault. "It was the two men knocking tables over to reach us who were the problem."

"The two men *on her guest list,*" Camden added.

Beth stared at the ceiling and searched for answers. She found none and gave up. "Fine."

Camden jumped up and squared off with Beth. "Fine, only if you agree that you or Esme fucked up."

"You're looking at this all wrong." Beth ignored him and paced the living room. "This could be a great thing. You want the people who took Hailey, right? Well, now we know they don't want to eliminate a witness. They want access to you. They're trying to find you."

"Tell me something we haven't figured out on our own."

"This could be very advantageous." Beth crossed her arms. "Your perspective is off on this."

Camden glowered. "Yeah, if we put on rose-tinted glasses. Just because they didn't take her out with a sniper round doesn't mean they're not trying to get rid of a witness."

"Maybe it's sort of like how the CIA managed to have me thrown in prison," Amelia pointed out. "To keep me quiet."

Camden ran a hand over his face. "That would be a hell of a thing if they are one and the same. What are they scared you'll say?"

Beth scoffed. "What? Like the CIA offed Jonathan? One of our own? Then we took Hailey? Where? Why?" Her lips sneered. "Now we want to grab Amelia? Forget that I've been with you and know where you are." Restless, she paced again. "That's a hell of an accusation."

"Well, I've had a hell of a night."

"Maybe you ought to run your theories by Jared Westin before you run your mouth and sink a partnership that is tenuous at best right now."

"My conversations with him didn't work out well for you last time. You sure you want me to—"

"How about this for my brilliant idea?" Beth narrowed her eyes on Camden. "You could go back to Abu Dhabi. We'll put Amelia in witness protection. That would make my life easier. Probably hers too."

"*What?*" A lightheaded panic rolled through Amelia.

Camden couldn't leave yet, and she had no intention of walking away from her life—at least, not with some secretive relocation program.

"Enough." She stood up. "This isn't helping."

Her stomach turned. Amelia already knew this, but hearing it out loud made it real. Camden would be called back to his office on the opposite side of the world. It might not be that day or the next, but it would happen. She wasn't in the real world. They were playing pretend.

She swallowed hard. "Let's regroup in the morning with cooler heads."

Neither agreed.

"I'm the one they're chasing, so my vote trumps both of yours." She turned around with a lump in her throat. The best-case scenario would be rescuing Hailey. Camden would still leave. She'd always known that their temporary fling was just that. But apparently, she'd forgotten, or worse, she'd fallen for him. Amelia called good night and didn't look back.

CHAPTER THIRTY

CAMDEN WOULD BREAK Amelia's heart if she let him. That couldn't happen. She'd started their whole *dynamic*, as he liked to call it, and she'd presented herself as mature enough to manage her emotions. Theirs was a workplace fling. It couldn't go anywhere.

Amelia peeled off her eyelashes and stepped into the hot shower, determined to wash away the night's shimmer and glimmer. But the shower didn't erase her stress. The certainty of future heartache weighed down her arms and legs. If only she could separate the here and now from the future. She should—*would*—enjoy her time with Camden. *End of story.*

They would find Hailey. Life would return to normal. Honestly, Amelia was lucky to have met Camden. He opened her eyes to how humdrum and monotonous her life had been. Everyone around her loved their jobs, their lives. Amelia had been coasting.

A hollowness carved deep into her chest. She was too tired to luxuriate under the hot water. She gave up on the shower, toweled off, and climbed into bed. Her arm reached for the opposite side of the bed, his side. Not for the first time, she wondered what his home was like, what it would be like to lie in his bed and smell his scent on the sheets. The dull hollowness expanded. Amelia pulled the blankets under her chin.

Camden knocked on the door and cracked it open. The hall light flooded their room. "Can I come in?"

"It's your bedroom too."

He waited a long moment then moved to the side of the bed. "What's going on?"

She didn't know what to say and shrugged.

Carefully, he eased onto the edge of the mattress. Tears burned the back of her throat. Too much had happened that day. Too much had happened over the last month. Jonathan was dead. Hailey was gone. People wanted to get her—whatever that meant. And Camden would leave. She wasn't sure when he would be gone, but that was the truth of the matter. Their worlds didn't intersect.

He stroked her wet hair and trailed his fingers along her jaw. "Amelia?"

"I miss Hailey." The tears slipped free. She didn't know why that had come out of her mouth. She was missing *him*, and they hadn't even gone their separate ways yet. It was his touch and the way he said her name. All of it was too much, too nice. And it would eventually be a memory. She'd attached herself to him after he'd warned them they shouldn't get physical, and she'd promised she wouldn't.

Camden stood up. Her heart sank—all the more proof she really should be alone. Wanting what she couldn't have wasn't healthy. But he didn't leave. Amelia glanced over. He unbuttoned his dress shirt and stripped to his boxers. Camden pulled back the covers, slipped behind her, and pulled her against his chest.

He curled around her body and pressed his lips behind her ear. "Do you want to talk about Hailey?"

She shook her head.

"You want to talk about Beth? The party?"

Amelia shook her head again.

His chest expanded with a soul-squeezing breath. Camden rested his chin against her temple and brought her impossibly closer to the broad slope of his chest. "Do you want to talk about us?"

A pathetic explosion of hopefulness splintered in her heart. But reality was reality. The splinters sliced like glass. There was nothing to talk about. They had both been clear when they first slept together. She couldn't change the situation, and telling him anything different would end what they had sooner than when she had to let him go back to Abu Dhabi.

"I'm just exhausted." *Exhausted and tired and scared and feeling too many things at once.* It wasn't healthy.

Camden shifted away from her. Cool air prickled over her still-damp skin. He was leaving, and she couldn't handle it.

Her arm reached back. "Stay?"

"I'm just taking off my watch." He unstrapped it, laid it on the nightstand, and returned to wrap her against his hard body. "I'm not going anywhere tonight. I promise."

That was what she needed to hear—yet it also hurt. How was he able to be with her so effortlessly? Amelia twisted in his arms until she faced him. Her eyes had adjusted to the dark enough to see his intense eyes. As they locked together, everything inside her hurt again. "Why are you doing this?"

The corners of his eyes tightened. "Holding you?"

She shook her head. That was too basic. She wanted to be able to look into his soul and read him like a book, but the only questions she could think of were surface level. She didn't know how to dig deeper without exposing herself. "Why are you helping me?"

He shrugged, knowing she already knew the answer. "Titan Group has a vested interest in their partnership with the CIA. The CIA doesn't work on US soil. So here I am."

She swallowed hard. "That partnership is the reason why no one has tried to ship me off to witness protection? Because Titan and the CIA—"

"No, Amelia. Just—no." He ran a hand into his hair. "Before I met you, this assignment was more to prove to my boss I could handle additional responsibility. Dealing with bureaucracies. Something other than using a weapon and jumping out of helicopters." He scoffed at himself in a self-deprecating way. "I thought Boss Man was firing me before he assigned me to man the phones the night you called." He pulled in a long breath. "You and I talked. We clicked. I"—he brushed hair off her cheek—"needed to help you."

"I'm not going to find Hailey, am I?"

His lips rolled together. "I don't know, baby." He touched her cheek and eased an arm around her side. "But I'm going to help you do everything you can."

"While you're here," she amended for him.

Tension ticked in his expression. He licked his bottom lip then gave the smallest, most heartbreaking nod. Her eyes pinched closed.

"Amelia?"

She didn't want to look at him. In the best-case scenario, Camden would use this as the perfect example of why they shouldn't have even shared a kiss. In the worst-case scenario, she would cry on his shoulder.

"I'm really tired." The tears were coming. She couldn't fight them and turned in his arms. They spilled quietly onto the pillow. "Good night."

Still perched on his side, he stroked the back of her hair, hovering as though he had more to say. An eternity ticked by until he finally kissed the back of her head and whispered, "Night, baby."

CHAPTER THIRTY-ONE

THE MORNING HAD fortunately given Amelia a new perspective—or at least time to wrangle her feelings so that they would stay out of sight. She'd awakened in Camden's arms, memorized the feeling, then started her day as though she hadn't had a stray heartbroken thought.

Perched on the couch with a large coffee in her hands, she eyed Camden's cell phone in the center of the coffee table. He'd warned her that his boss was going to be grouchy. Jared Westin went far beyond any level of grouchiness she'd ever encountered.

"Goddamn the CIA," Jared barked. "Damn them all. Fuckin' headache. Every one of them."

That hadn't been her first Jared phone call. Not to mention, Camden's warnings had been plenty. But she still couldn't wrap her head around a workplace where people actually growled and freely cursed. If Jared hadn't been scary, the entertainment value would have been pretty high. Camden lay on his back, tossing the football overhead as the torrent continued.

Another man jumped into the conversation when Jared took a breath. "This is what we know—"

That was Parker. She was beginning to recognize voices, which gave her an odd level of reassurance.

"Why didn't you say something already?" Jared snapped.

Parker snorted. "Just thought you needed to talk your feelings out, Boss Man."

She leaned over the phone to double-check they were still on mute. "Your office is a zoo."

Camden laughed. "Parker's a literal genius and top-notch ballbuster."

Good. They could use all the brainpower they could muster, and Jared probably needed someone to knock him down occasionally.

"The Sapphire Accord says they don't have security footage," Parker said. "Did you see cameras?"

Camden unmuted off the call. "None."

"Fine. I pulled the highway cams and tracked exit-bound traffic within two miles of Esme's. Cross-referenced that with dates of similar gathering and eliminated any vehicles with plates tied to hired car services."

"That seems like something the CIA should have done," Amelia whispered.

"They might have thought of it, but I don't know anyone who can work as fast as Parker."

"We can hear you," Jared grumbled. "Parker doesn't need to hear how fuckin' smart he is."

"*Parker*," Parker said, "knows it already but doesn't mind anything that drives Boss Man up the wall. So have at it."

"They're like an old married couple," Amelia pointed out, "the kind that could use therapy."

"Enough already," Jared grumbled but without the bite that he used on Parker and Camden.

Amelia grinned.

Camden snorted. "All right, Parker, what do we get with that list?"

"About fifty-three vehicle registrations tied to individuals, twenty-seven to corporations."

"That's a lot of possibilities," Amelia mused. "Did anyone search highway cameras the night my sister went missing?"

"I don't know," Parker admitted.

"We could ask Beth or check with the feds." Camden shrugged as though he already knew that would be an unproductive fight. "Or we could just let Parker get what he needs."

What did that mean? She pursed her lips and watched Camden.

"Jared?" Parker asked. "Want me to see what I can find on my own?"

Seconds ticked by. Was "on his own" like hacking it?

"Fuck it. Yeah. Go for it—Cam, we'll call you back once we get into the file."

The line disconnected.

"Get into the file as in…?" she asked.

"I don't ask how Parker gets the job done." Camden shrugged again and tossed her the football. "We should stay in and keep a low profile until we know more information. They're not showing up here, so Beth's not our leak."

"I'd rather do something more proactive." She tossed the ball to herself like he did. Concentrating on it was enough of a distraction that she didn't toss it back.

"We don't have anything to do yet. Going out in public does nothing but put a bull's-eye on you—you know what we could do?"

Jumping back into bed was her first immediate thought. Her cheeks blazed. "What?"

"Figure out why the hell they're following you."

His cell phone buzzed, and he glanced at the screen. "Esme Van Alstyn."

Amelia's stomach dropped. She didn't want to face the upset dominatrix, but they probably owed her an apology for starting a fire.

Camden stood to take the call. He paced and listened and ignored Amelia's request for speakerphone. Finally, he tossed the phone onto the couch, held up his hands for the football, and easily caught her bad toss. "She wants us to come back."

"Is she mad?"

"At us? No. Actually, pretty sure she was embarrassed." He spun the ball between his hands. "No one could identify the two men or, for that matter, us."

"Really?"

He shook his head. "Doubtful. But probably, no one wants to be involved in any part of an investigation that would require them to be on the record." He dropped onto the couch. "The only thing she's certain of is no one got into her party without one of her invitations."

"So she knows them."

"They could each have been a plus-one, which isn't vetted as carefully. Apparently, the Sapphire Accord's rules on guests allow them to anonymize their dates so long as they take responsibility for their actions."

"Bet no one did that." She pouted. "So, Esme isn't helpful. Why would we visit her?"

"She and Beth spoke. There's another party. A Night in Paris. Actually *in Paris*—"

A knock sounded at the front door.

Amelia turned toward the door. "Who's that?"

Camden dropped the football and quickly opened an end-table drawer. He pulled out a handgun and ammunition. "Sit on the couch."

Her heart slammed into her chest.

He crept to the window and peeked out the shade then quickly moved to the door. He flattened himself to the wall and checked the peephole. Nobody seemed to be out there, but he pressed his fingers to his lips and urged her to duck. He checked the peephole again then glanced between the blinds of the closest window. Finally, he cracked the door.

A loud noise exploded. Smoke and chaos filled the entryway. Camden slammed the door and deadbolted it before she could scream. "Amelia. Here. Now."

The balcony door at the back of the condo exploded open as if a SWAT team had bashed it in. Smoke bombs clattered toward them. Her eyes and throat burned. "Camden!"

Amelia couldn't see anything. She tripped over the coffee table. Heavy boot steps thundered toward them.

"Amelia."

She crawled toward his voice. His arm wrapped her to his chest. Gunfire exploded. Bodies fell by their feet. She screamed.

Camden grabbed her around the waist. "We've got to get out of here."

She couldn't see anything. The smoke burned. Snot and tears covered her face. The front door flung open, and a wave of fresh air smacked her. The relief vanished with instantaneous pain, as though she'd run into a lightning bolt. Shock. Pain. The jolt froze her muscles and killed her scream. Everything went black.

CHAPTER THIRTY-TWO

"**Y**OU'RE NOT GOING to die on me today, asshole." Beth's familiar voice grated over Camden's senses. He wanted to get away from it but needed to wake up. "Open your eyes."

Damn. He was trying. An angry brunette came into focus, along with everything else. Camden jerked away from her. His head spun. His arms reached for Amelia. He was on the floor. His hands reached to find her.

"Stay awake. But take it easy." Beth squatted next to him then spoke into her phone. "Just him. Two tangoes down. We're going to need a cleanup team and medical transport."

Nausea swam over him. He fought to sit up. "Amelia?" His throat hurt, and her name fell short on his lips as though his lungs didn't have enough oxygen.

Beth grabbed his arm as he tried to stand. "Try the couch first."

He didn't agree so much as he stumbled onto it. "Where is she?" His brain rattled behind his eyes. He couldn't think for the pounding. Even sitting up was too hard. His equilibrium couldn't find its center. Camden propped himself up on the arm of the couch so that he wouldn't give in to the pain and lie down with his eyes closed again.

Beth took his hand. "Water. See if you can drink." She wrapped his hand around a cold bottle. "Try."

He squinted at her. "Amelia?"

"Drink first."

God, this lady. He gagged on a sip. His stomach convulsed. Pain made the small amount of water he'd drunk want to come back up. "Where's she?" Stringing words together was killing him. *What the hell happened?* He hadn't been shot. *What had happened?*

Beth sat on the edge of the coffee table in front of him. "I can't believe you're alive."

That didn't calm his panic. "Where is Amelia?"

"I don't know."

Fuck. His eyes pinched shut. *Damn.* His chest hurt. His chin dropped, and his gaze partially focused. Charred fabric hung in ribbons down his torso. Burned flesh marred with blisters and singed skin made his stomach turn again.

"Who is this? Brock?" Beth snapped into her cell phone. "I don't know. Gone." She shook her head. "Don't know how, but he's still alive." Beth stepped gingerly over a body on the floor. "I'll get it to Parker ASAP." She ended the call and snapped pictures of the dead men's faces then turned toward Camden. "Drink more."

He rubbed a hand over his face. "What happened?"

"Looks like someone rammed a cattle prod into your chest."

Why couldn't he remember anything? The effort to raise his arm made nausea roll over him again. Sweat tickled his brow. His stomach dropped. Amelia was gone—just like Hailey.

Beth's frown indicated that she shared his same thought. She gripped his shoulder as he struggled onto his feet. "No. Wait. You need to see a doctor before you go outside and drop dead."

AMELIA HAD WASHED her face half a dozen times and couldn't remove the scents of chemicals, smoke, and Camden's burned flesh from her nose. Her cries and demands went unanswered for hours. No one released her from the windowless bathroom she'd woken up in. Hours had passed since her eyes opened—no telling how long she'd been unconscious.

What happened? For the hundredth time, she tried to remember and came up with nothing except the certainty that the haunting smell of burned flesh was Camden—that and the excruciating memory of an electric shock.

What if he was dead? She dropped to her knees in front of the toilet. *Think.* She'd been screaming. Her throat felt like it was bleeding. There had been gunfire. Her ears still roared from the loud explosions.

The doorknob twisted. The man she'd seen at Hailey's and then Esme's glowered. "You are a fucking pain in my ass."

He left the bathroom door open and stepped back. "Walk out here"—he gestured to a rundown motel room—"or I'll drag you out."

Behind him was the way to escape. All she had to do was get out. Camden's words from the phone call on the first night rushed back to her. *If he finds you, fight back. Don't freeze. Don't try to reason. Don't waste your energy screaming. Bite. Use your elbow. Use your fingernails. Knee him in the nuts. Fight dirty. Do you hear me?*

Amelia lunged. Her fists slammed into the man's chest. She needed to get around him and fought for the door. He was stronger than he looked, but he wasn't fighting for his life. She smashed her head from under his chin, snapping his head back. He groaned but didn't let go. Amelia had to fight. She smashed her knee into his groin.

"Shit," he wheezed and doubled over.

Amelia raced for the door. He snaked an arm around her neck and dropped both of them onto the floor. Pain exploded at the back of her head. Black-and-white stars detonated as he flipped her around like a rag doll and locked her neck in a choke hold. Amelia clawed his face. She wasn't getting enough oxygen. She couldn't take another breath. Her hands were so heavy. Her muscles ached. Spots pocked her vision.

"I'm going to break your neck like your sister," he growled.

Broken neck. Like my sister. Amelia gave up. It was that easy, knowing Hailey was gone, and the darkness rolled over Amelia again like a suffocating blanket.

CHAPTER THIRTY-THREE

AMELIA AWOKE IN the center of a bed in the cheap motel room. Half drowsy, mostly terrified, she jerked upright. Her stomach churned. Nausea rolled over her as though she'd had too much to drink. Her head throbbed, and her throat ached. She blinked as the nightmare she hadn't been able to escape flooded her thoughts.

That man had killed Hailey.

Hailey was dead.

As soon as Amelia's head stopped spinning, she opened her eyes again. Tears fell as she stared at the stained popcorn ceiling. She wasn't sure how long she lay silently crying and mourning her sister. There was no one to rescue. Not Hailey, and she didn't care if anyone found her anymore.

Amelia rolled onto her side. Bottles of water, juice, and ibuprofen sat beside a lamp with a broken shade on the bare nightstand. No phone was there, but a blinking alarm clock was. The headache medicine called to her, but Amelia didn't trust anything in the room.

Was Camden looking for her?

Was he even alive?

Why the hell was this happening? She couldn't think. A headache pounded at her temples. The ibuprofen would be helpful. The bottles of juice and water seemed to have their seals intact. She inspected the medicine. It still had the safety wrapping, which she tore free. The foil seal remained in place. After a mistrustful moment, she decided they could have killed her already with far less work than it took to poison headache medicine. She cracked the water bottle open and swallowed two pills.

Stuck with her heartache, Amelia settled against the flat pillow and pulled the thread-worn comforter over herself. If she didn't die an awful, poisoned death from the medicine she'd just swallowed, her head would feel much better, and she could come up with a plan.

Or she could at least survive until Camden found her—unless, she reminded herself again, he was dead too.

Her life was unrecognizable. Less than three months before, Amelia had been at a golf course, sitting in an office off the pro shop, watching the weather radar and hoping the MacAlister-Richmond wedding would finish before the first fat raindrops fell on the ceremony. That had been the peak level of stress in her life, virtually nonexistent.

Now… Hailey and Jonathan were dead. *Camden? Maybe.* And Amelia was here, trying to make heads or tails of living in hell.

She drifted into a fitful nap. Eventually, her headache and nausea lessened, and with the help of the water and juice, she felt somewhat more like a human who had the strength to investigate her surroundings.

Quietly, she crawled out of bed and inspected the room. A bag of gas-station junk food and magazines sat next to a remote on a vanity that had probably once held a television. They'd left her without a phone or television. If they'd taken the time to remove those, they'd probably come up with a way to keep her from walking out the door.

Still, she crept carefully across the old carpet and tried the door. The handle turned easily. Her heart jumped with hope. Cautiously, she peeked out to the outside world and saw that she was located on the second floor of a crappy motel. An open-air walkway guarded only by a rusted railing overlooked a deserted parking lot. Emboldened by the late-afternoon sunlight and chilly temperature, she inched out.

"Going somewhere?" a gruff voice asked.

She jerked back, slammed the door, and quickly secured the dead bolt and slid the safety lock into place. Her head spun, and with her heart stuck in her throat, Amelia rushed back toward the bed.

He didn't come in after her. He hadn't been the same man from the bathroom. Had it been the man from the Esme's party? She couldn't think straight.

Amelia dove back under the covers. She hid for what felt like hours until her stomach growled, reminding her of the gas-station food waiting for her. She crawled out of bed, eyeing the door as if it had the magical ability to unlock itself, and beelined for the bag of food. She wasn't a Twinkies-and-Ding-Dongs kind of girl, but nothing had ever looked so tasty.

In a matter of minutes, she devoured a fluffy pink mini-cake and polished off a bag of salted cashews. The sugar and salt overdose threatened to bring back her headache, but she downed a bottle of water and decided it was as good a meal as she could hope for.

Someone knocked on the door.

Amelia's arms wrapped protectively over her stomach. Fear rushed back. She didn't move. Even if she'd wanted to run, she couldn't move a single muscle. Camden's voice came back to her, ordering her to breathe. She tried to inhale and hold it. Her insides jittered.

The knock came again. It was polite and so totally unnerving that she inched toward the door. Each step strained her body. Her mind revolted at the idea that she might open the door to danger. Sweat dampened the back of her neck as the roar of blood rushing in her ears warned of incoming threats. Still, she peeked out the peephole.

Black hair with perfect silver highlights. Deep mauve lipstick. Esme Van Alstyn waited on the other side. Shaking, Amelia unlocked the door but kept the sliding latch in place and drew a deep breath as she peered out the peephole again.

Esme stepped closer. She didn't smile, but her blank face shifted to something expectant. "Hungry, Amelia?" She held up a paper sack that promised food and shook it in front of the peephole. The bag dropped out of sight. Esme inched closer to the flimsy door. "Open up."

"What the hell is going on?" she muttered loud enough to be heard outside.

"That's a long story." Esme offered the bag again. "I have fruit. Want a banana? A grilled chicken Caesar salad, a grain bowl, and a chicken-and-bean burrito." Her dark lips quirked. "I wasn't sure what you might like. So I ordered several things."

Amelia placed both hands on the door and tried to see around Esme. The fishbowl lens blurred everything around her. "I want to leave."

"Not hungry, then? Suit yourself. Can I come in? We have a lot to talk about."

"Go to hell."

Esme beckoned to the man guarding the door and stepped back. "Why do you have to do everything the hard way?"

CHAPTER THIRTY-FOUR

CAMDEN REFUSED ANY painkillers that weren't topical and was making everyone's life miserable. Beth could go to hell. The doctors weren't signing off on his release. Camden wasn't getting answers. The hospital administration was apparently scared of releasing him until Titan Group's designated physician signed off on his treatment plan, and that asshole hadn't shown up yet.

The private hospital room closed in on him. The monitoring equipment beeped and reported that he needed to settle down and relax. That wasn't going to happen. Not for the first time, Camden removed the monitors and paced the room, ready to walk out the door as soon as he knew leaving wouldn't get him fired. He probably needed street clothes too. Someone had confiscated them under the guise of having medical staff check him out, and they wouldn't give them back. Flapping around in his hospital gown wouldn't help him if he escaped.

A nurse inched into his room and eyed the monitoring equipment that he'd removed. Nothing was wrong with his heart, and the beeping was pushing him to the point of madness.

She didn't let go of the door but held out a cell phone. "You have a phone call."

Camden snatched the device. "Hello?"

"I hear you are causing the staff a lot of heartburn," Jared groused. "Would you sit your ass down so they can do what they're supposed to do?"

"I'm fine."

"Yeah. Sure you are. That's how people blasted with that much voltage are after a half a day. Look, man." Jared let out a deep breath. "If there was something to tell you, I'd have told you. If anyone had a lead, you'd know about it. We're doing our best. But if you don't take care of yourself *now*, you won't be worth a shit when I need you." He cleared his throat. "When *she* needs you. Do you get me?"

Camden's molars gnashed. "There has to be—"

"I'm tell you there's not and that I'm wasting my time making sure you listen to doctor's orders when I could be doing more important things—things you want me doing, brother. You hear me?"

Camden grumbled.

"That nurse still standing in the room?"

"Yeah."

"Don't fuck with her."

"I'm not—"

"Jesus shit, do you think I would be on the phone with you right fuckin' now if multiple folks with medical degrees think you need to sit down and take your medicine or whatever?"

He glanced at the nurse, who probably could hear every word Boss Man was bellowing. "All right. I read you."

"Loud and clear, asshole?"

"That's affirmative. Loud and clear." Camden handed the cell phone to the nurse. "I'm going to sit down." He hooked a thumb over his shoulder. "On the bed. You do whatever you have to do."

She pocketed the phone. "I wasn't the one who tattled on you." She gingerly pulled the gown apart and, careful of his bandages, put the stethoscope in her ears then to his chest.

He tried not to grumble. "My boss has eyes and ears everywhere."

She moved the cold metal over his skin. "That's what I hear."

"Drop the gown back." She pressed the stethoscope below his shoulder blades and listened to his lungs. She pulled the fabric back into place. "You're not dying."

"That's what I keep saying. Can I get out of here?"

"Any reaction from the antibiotics?"

"You mean that big, fat needle someone drilled into me? No."

She checked his chart. "It'll go a lot faster if you're hooked back up."

She nudged her head to the monitoring equipment. "At least until a doctor says you're good to go."

He frowned at it. The idea of tiny wires keeping him in place made his skin crawl. "Anyone have a ball around here that I can borrow?"

The nurse paused what she was doing. "Like a stress ball?"

"Like a football. Baseball. Hell, I'd take a basketball. I can't sit still and think with empty hands."

"I don't know how much you have to think, but I'll call over to peds and see what they have."

"I could walk there myself if you point me the right way."

She laughed. "Well, you'd have to get by the armed guards at your door to do that."

Camden really didn't like being in this room. "Wire me up again."

The nurse quickly attached the blood pressure cuffs and wires to his chest and left with a promise to find him a ball.

As soon as the door shut, it opened again. Beth wasn't who Camden wanted to see.

His never-ending headache throbbed again. "What do you want?"

"I don't know why I always get hospital duty. My bedside manner isn't great." Her high heels clicked toward him. "Esme and I have been over everything a dozen times. The names on Titan's list weren't in Hailey or Jonathan's orbit."

"Someone's working with bad information."

"Or not enough intel," she countered. "They crossed a lot of names off the list based on car registrations." She sat primly on the lone visitor chair. "Anyone give you an update on the mercenaries you dropped?"

He shook his head.

"Probably because there was none. We didn't get anything off them."

"Nothing?"

She shook her head. "No IDs. No matches to databases. Nothing."

"Great."

"But I *do* have good news, though."

Amelia was gone, and they didn't have any leads. The only thing that would help was if Beth helped him escape. "You know who my doctor is, and I'm leaving any minute?"

Beth rolled her eyes. "Why are you tough guys such pains in the ass? No."

"Then what?"

"I know what Hailey's handler was working on."

That had his full attention. Information like that would help find Amelia.

"That's almost better than discharge paperwork. Spit it out."

"Russia has been placing mistresses on the arms of some of the most influential men you can think of."

"Like honeypot sleeper agents?"

She nodded. "Yup. We don't know if any are active and trying to influence or just waiting for their marching orders."

Despite his headache, possibilities ran through his mind. "The Russians got the NOC list and learned about Hailey and Jonathan's involvement with Esme."

"That's a working theory."

"Who knows about this?" he asked.

"Titan and my section chief. Beyond that?" She shrugged. "No idea."

"Esme?" he asked, even though Beth would have mentioned if Esme had been told. *What if Esme was one of the sleeper agents? What if she'd known her tight-knit network had been infiltrated by the CIA?* Hailey and Jonathan would have been easy enough to take care of. Camden's thoughts returned to Amelia. *Why did they take her? What did they want?* "Do they think the CIA has other agents embedded in Esme's network?"

"No idea."

The blood pressure machine beeped, and a mechanical voice spoke. "Relax your arm for a reading." It beeped twice more and repeated the message.

"This is fucking ridiculous," Camden said. "You've got to get me out of here."

The cuff contracted on his arm. "Reading in progress. Remain still."

He huffed. "What are we waiting on?"

"Jared has a doctor he wants you to see."

Beth's phone vibrated, and she answered and turned away to listen before ending the call. She didn't act as though new information had been shared. "Stay put. I'll see what I can do."

Her high heels clacked on the floor. The heavy door shut with a resounding click.

His blood pressure reading announced itself as abnormal and asked him to sit still next time. Camden was going to lose his mind.

CHAPTER THIRTY-FIVE

"BACK UP, AMELIA," Esme called as though she were warning a friend about a low ceiling, not a bruiser about to kick in a door.

The man who had been guarding Amelia appeared in front of the door. He reared up a leg, and Amelia jumped back. The door splintered from the lock and swung open with such force that the door smacked the wall and shut again. The broken door latch still swung back and forth.

Esme opened the door. She looked utterly out of place with her dark suit and bag of food.

Amelia staggered back until she hit the bed. She had nowhere to go. Nothing made sense.

"What the hell are you doing?"

Esme walked in and casually shut the door.

"You killed my sister."

"No." Esme shook her head. "Absolutely not."

She gestured to the broken door. "Those guys did."

The same people just broke down the door and let Esme in. One of those men had been at the Callaghans' house and Esme's party. They had to be who took her from Camden—from a safe house.

Amelia skirted around the bed. "How could you? You worked with them."

Esme was unmoved by her accusations. "Hailey's death was tragic."

If only Amelia had done things better. She'd wasted so much time that night. She could have kept her questions to herself when Jonathan and Hailey demanded she get help. Amelia could have run faster. She could have stayed out of the window. Guilt rolled over her like a tidal wave.

"Screw you, Esme."

They were dead. Jonathan and Hailey had been doing good things in the world. Amelia didn't know what those things were, but they were good enough that people wanted to stop them.

Esme used the broken dead bolt to secure the door as best as she could and closed the distance. "Are you sure you're not hungry? Banana? Chicken?" She glanced about the room. "This place is disgusting. Anyone with half a heart would know even a light bulb would take care of the place."

"Go away."

Esme set the food on the nightstand. "Listen to me—"

"No."

She laughed. "How do you think this will play out? I'll just walk you to the parking lot? Find you an Uber?" She opened the bag and offered a Styrofoam container. After an awkward moment, she set the food down and crossed her arms and tapped the toe of her high heel as if reprimanding a toddler. "I need to know what Jonathan and Hailey told you that night."

Amelia moved to the far side of the bed. She was cornered. "Even if they did tell me something, I wouldn't tell you."

"They"—Esme thumbed over her shoulder—"will kill you if you don't help. You understand that?"

Fear percolated in her guts.

"It will hurt," Esme continued coolly. "And I'm supposed to be the one who makes it excruciating. Do you get that?"

"I don't know anything."

"They're willing to do whatever it takes to get what they need. Tell me what Jonathan and Hailey told you that night."

"Nothing."

Esme scowled. "I really don't want this to happen. Is there a light bulb that can go off in that brain of yours? Or are you just a half-hearted excuse for your sister?"

Something in Esme's expression was different from the two other times they'd met. She couldn't place it but couldn't let it go either. That wasn't even the way she spoke. Maybe the cadence was wrong. Something was off.

"Please let me leave. You don't want to do this."

"You're right." She placed her hands on her hips. "But that doesn't change anything."

CHAPTER THIRTY-SIX

THE HOSPITAL RELEASED Camden the next day. The CIA had offered another safe house. Camden declined with a string of indignant obscenities that made his counterpart smirk. Beth had even offered him another vehicle, but he wanted nothing that came from outside Titan.

Shah arranged for a vehicle and a cell phone. Camden found the car in a designated location and pulled himself into the front seat. His body ached like someone had used his sternum to stir up hot coals.

He didn't know where he was going and didn't have a plan. Shah and Amanda suggested Titan's US headquarters, but Parker hadn't come up with new information to work on. At least, that was the line everyone continued to feed him.

After running a series of red lights and making U-turns, Camden decided no tail was following him. He pulled onto the highway. His first order of business was to visit Esme. He pulled up to the vacant-looking warehouse and parked next to her Mercedes.

The entrance was locked. He scoured the building for doors. Each was locked. Some were chained. How couldn't this place have security cameras? He returned to the main entrance, pulled out his wallet, and withdrew a set of lockpick keys. The tumblers were complicated, but alone with the sun shining, he had nothing but time.

The last tumbler fell, and he let himself inside. The hall was cold and dark.

"Esme?" Camden wove through the familiar corridor. "We need to talk." He found her office with the slip of light showing under the door and banged on it. "Esme, open up."

The door opened, and unfazed, she looked at him as though he were a petulant child. "I do business by appointment."

"I want to know who the men were on your guest list."

"I don't—"

"Tell me."

"Or what? You'll yell at me? Hit me? Kill me?" She smiled sweetly. "I'm not easy to take down."

"Who are they?"

"I've told Beth everything I know."

"That's first-class bullshit."

Esme returned behind her desk. "I understand your girlfriend is gone."

Girlfriend caught him off guard. "You know where she is?"

"If I did, wouldn't that be something I would have shared?" She steepled her fingers together. "Let me ask you a question." She gestured for him to take a seat, though he ignored her. "Camden, if you want to talk shop, sit down or leave. There's no situation where you will lord over me like that."

His nostrils flared, but he sat down. "What?"

"Tell me how you met."

"No."

"Titan was helping the CIA cover their ass, wasn't it?" Her long fingernails tipped together under her chin as she hummed. "The night when everything went down, Hailey didn't call you. She didn't talk to you, did she? Only Amelia?"

His molars ground together.

"What did she tell you that night?"

"Why?"

Esme shrugged. "Maybe if I knew more, I could help."

"She didn't tell me anything."

Her steepled fingers tapped together before she dropped them into her lap. "I guess I can't help."

His phone rang.

"Feel free to answer," Esme said.

He held the phone to his ear. "Yeah?"

"Where are you?"

Beth wasn't who he expected to be on the other line. "What do you want?"

"We have a problem."

"We've had a lot of those lately."

"There's an issue with Esme."

"You don't say." He held the phone against his ear and hoped the volume was low enough that Beth's words didn't travel. "I can't find that right now. Give me ten, and I'll look."

"Damn it, Camden," Beth snapped. "Are you with her?"

"Sure, yeah. I said I can look."

"Call me when you leave."

He hung up. Camden shoved his phone into his pocket. He didn't like that Beth had his phone number. Every time the CIA crossed paths with him, shit went down.

"Are you going now?" Esme arched an eyebrow. "Or would you like to continue this unproductive back-and-forth?"

"If you know where Amelia is and don't tell me, I'm going to find out and make your life miserable."

Esme held his gaze. "If I could tell you, I would."

He wasn't sure what he wanted from Esme. Had he really thought he might find Amelia there? "Somehow I doubt that."

"Relock the door on your way out."

Camden's chest ached. It was more than the blisters and burns on his chest. He couldn't find Amelia, and an ever-increasing panic had shredded his heart. He retraced his steps and was momentarily blinded when he returned from Esme's dungeon and into the sun.

Why did Esme want to know about the first night he'd spoken to Amelia? Camden put the car in drive and tried to strangle the steering wheel. He didn't know where he was driving. Camden could only think about the most blaring problem: His woman was missing. He had no choice but to find her. But then what after that?

His temples throbbed. He would make sure she was safe, then the job would be over. He would be heartsick, but one way or another, Amelia would have answers. That was what mattered.

The main phone number from the Abu Dhabi headquarters appeared on the center dashboard as his phone rang.

He jabbed the screen. "Yeah?"

"Are you driving?" Amanda's voice flooded the car through the speakerphone.

"Yeah. Pulling onto the Beltway."

She paused as though waiting for Camden to offer more details, but he didn't have much of a plan.

"Where are you headed?"

"Don't know yet," he admitted.

"Do you know Beth Tourne is trying to find you?"

"Yeah."

"Do you want to know what she wants?" Amanda pressed.

"I already have the gist. There's an issue with a local contact."

"Camden, are you okay?"

"No. Everything's fucked. Amelia is missing, and we've got nothing but problems." He checked traffic as he merged.

His phone buzzed.

"I sent you GPS coordinates."

"To what?" The only answer he needed to hear was Amelia.

"I don't know."

Camden's grip tightened.

"But that's where you need to go," Amanda said.

The call ended. Her message was displayed on the screen. With one touch, the directions loaded. He recognized the street name from the night he'd called in the emergency help request in Arlington, Virginia.

Twenty minutes later, Camden pulled onto the street. Unmarked vehicles were parked in a driveway and on both sides of the road. He parked behind one and spotted Beth's Lexus. What the hell was she doing here?

A man in a suit was guarding the front door and stopped Camden.

"I need to talk to Beth Tourne."

He spoke into his shirtsleeve and waved him to one side. "Stay here."

A minute later, the door opened, and Beth gestured for him to step inside. "It's fine. He's with me."

Camden sidestepped the guard and, without saying hello, said, "We have an Esme problem."

She gave him an annoyed look over her shoulder. "You shouldn't have gone to see her."

"Why?" He stepped around agents holding imaging devices over the floor and against the baseboards.

A woman was standing on a step stool and imaging the ceiling.

"She's on our payroll," Beth explained.

"That wasn't hard to figure out when you arranged for an introduction."

"The problem is Esme might be on someone else's payroll also."

That stopped him cold. "Whose?"

"I don't know. Whoever killed Jonathan, Hailey, and their handler?"

They walked by the Dumonts' home office. No fewer than five agents were crammed into the space and tearing the desk and walls apart.

"But logic says if there were Russian sleeper agents working in her house of fun, then she might have something to do with that."

They reached the kitchen. A man was inspecting the inside of the oven. All the kitchen drawers had been pulled out and stacked on the dining table as a young agent sat, tediously bagging what had to be dozens of items.

Camden gestured to the house. "Why's this happening now?"

"Jonathan's dead."

"As a doornail," Camden confirmed. "I went to his funeral."

"Hailey's missing. No body has surfaced. Amelia's missing. Again, no body."

Pinpricks of cold fear skipped over his shoulders. "Why are you talking to me like this is news?"

"Forget whatever your situation with Amelia has become and think: Hailey and Amelia could have been sleeper agents, and the men 'chasing' her"—Beth put air quotes around "chasing"—"were her extraction team."

His mouth fell open. It snapped back into place. "Are you out of your fucking mind?"

"Event planning in DC? That puts her in contact with highly targeted assets. It's an angle we hadn't considered."

"So you're telling me that you're not looking for Amelia... but treating her like a target? *A spy?*"

"Yes."

"Goddamn, you people are so stupid."

"If you and Jared Westin hadn't interfered, she would still be in US custody."

He smacked his hand against his forehead. His heart raced at the absurdity. "You're insane. This is ludicrous."

"Actually, it makes a lot of sense, but you're too close to the situation." Beth put her hands on her hips. "She seduced you, Camden. She used you. And now, she and her sister are gone. Frankly, you're lucky to be alive."

Camden pressed his fingers to his temples. He believed no part of Beth's explanation. "And that's why you're tearing apart this house? To find proof?" He shook his head. "Why you destroyed Amelia's house? Absolutely unbelievable."

"Amelia's condominium?" Beth pursed her lips but then shook her head. "The Stone sisters are sleeper agents. They could have been radicalized in their teens and put to work during college. Their cover was blown. They killed Hailey's handler and husband and disappeared with everything needed to prove the work Jonathan died for."

CHAPTER THIRTY-SEVEN

ESME REAPPEARED WITH two men that had been tending to Amelia. She wasn't sure how many days had passed since Esme left—definitely one, possibly two. Her captors had kept the motel room in a timeless, dayless state. She couldn't tell whether they brought food in that morning or at night. But since Esme was there, she had questions.

"In the mood to chat?" Esme laid a long bag on the vanity where Amelia's food was always set.

"Maybe."

"Have you given any thought to what I had to say before?"

She had—more than she would admit to. Amelia's mind was starting to play tricks as though her brain had mapped out a conspiracy theory with red strings tied to random thoughts and random words. It didn't exactly make sense. She was grasping at straws or maybe decoding secret meanings. More likely, she was losing her grip on reality.

"And what do you think?" Esme extracted a long, slender rod from the bag.

She thought about food. Who paired a banana and chicken? And the non sequitur about the lighting? And was she a half-hearted fool? The words weren't in the same order. They weren't even the correct words, not exactly.

"You told me to trust you."

Esme cackled and asked the men, "Has she told you anything?"

They shook their heads.

"Amelia, this is your last chance before this gets ugly. What did Jonathan and Hailey tell you?"

Nothing other than stupid words that would bring help. Banana. Light bulb. Chicken. Heart. "Nothing."

Esme sighed. "Tie her hands behind her back."

Amelia jerked away. "No—"

They manhandled her arms and twisted her wrists.

"Easy," Esme snapped. "The only one who gets to make her cry is me."

The men snorted and laughed and zip-tied her wrists behind a chair. Esme strode straight over and tipped Amelia's head back. "Eyes on me."

Tears leaked down Amelia's cheeks. Esme wouldn't look away. "Think, you stupid girl. What did Jonathan and Hailey tell you?"

Government secrets and covert instructions? None of that. They'd only given her four words that were supposed to save her. Amelia mouthed *banana*.

Esme gave an imperceptible acknowledgment that she'd seen her lips move and maybe understood. She pinched her face. Esme's nails pricked against her skin. "Did you say something?" Her lips curled with sinister anticipation. "Try that again."

"Light bulb, chicken, heart." Her whisper wasn't audible. She was essentially saying gibberish.

Esme smacked her face away in disgust. "I'll have the room now."

The men snickered as they left. Then they were alone, and Amelia whispered hoarsely, "Why didn't you tell me?"

"I couldn't talk to you until you figured me out. Otherwise, you might go screaming your head off." Esme laid the rod on the bed and returned to her bag. "There's a lot happening, and we'll both be dead if either of us messes up."

"My sister?"

Esme paused and turned her full attention to Amelia. "She didn't mess up." She blinked back tears. "I'm sorry."

"She really is dead."

Esme nodded. "I'm sorry I couldn't tell you before."

"Why?"

"A list of Russian sleeper agents disappeared. They had a good idea they'd fallen into American hands but hadn't been able to pinpoint who."

"How do you know that?" Amelia asked.

"I work for them too."

She jerked back. Esme was a double agent?

"The only person in the CIA who knew that is dead. So I'm fucked." Esme lips flattened. "Absolutely fucked unless I get myself out of this."

Triple agent? So Esme was one of the good guys? Amelia tried to understand. "Beth doesn't know?"

Esme shook her head but pointed at the implements from her bag. "Which is why we're going to get to all this."

Amelia didn't understand. Tears burned the back of her eyes and throat. Hailey was dead. She couldn't be rescued and brought back. "Do you know where Hailey is?"

"I have guesses. Later, once we're out of this mess, I'll help bring her home."

Amelia nodded. So many tears had been shed since the first night, and it still hurt to think. "Why do you trust me now? Because of those words?"

Esme tilted her head to the side as though thinking through what she might say. "Hailey gave them to you. That's one reason, and the second is Titan Group. In theory, I trust them. In reality, there's Camden. He believes in you."

That caught Amelia off guard.

"He might even love you," Esme offered. "If I'm going to put my life on the line, I might as well do it with his woman."

Amelia's heartbeat jumped. "I don't... It's not like that."

"It is." Esme's lips quirked. "I thought I could see it on the first day. He thinks you can handle anything. But then I saw him today." She studied Amelia. "That man will find you, and I'm tying my horse to that wagon. Between the two of you, it will clear my name."

How could Esme possibly think Camden had fallen in love with her? Then again, if one ignored their circumstances and the fact he was leaving and just looked at them as a couple—she loved him. That was why her heart had hurt at the thought of witness protection while he went home to Abu Dhabi.

"We're running short on time," Esme said. "This is going to have to be believable."

"What is?"

She'd returned to the bag she'd brought in. "I'll do what I can to make it look the part. But you're going to have to handle a lot."

"I don't know what you're talking about."

Esme gave her a look that kicked her stomach to the floor. "What do you think I'm supposed to be doing here?"

Her heartbeat picked up with nervous worry. "Um… getting me to talk."

"Yes. How do you think that normally happens?" She removed a small case from her bag and held two small dark-red pills. "Crush these between your molars. It will taste horrible. You'll want to gag. That's what we need, a bloody mouth leaking. Have you ever acted in a play?"

Amelia shook her head.

"You're gonna start tonight. Just pretend you're going for an Oscar and an Emmy." Esme popped the pills into Amelia's mouth. "Bite."

Amelia crushed the gel tabs and gagged. They were just as foul as Esme had warned.

"A little bit louder for the cheap seats."

Amelia tried not to retch.

Esme petted the side of her head. "This is going to get worse before it gets better, but you can do it. I will be with you the entire time."

Amelia choked. She had too much saliva in her mouth. She wouldn't swallow the rancid taste. "Free my—" She gagged. "Hands?"

"I can't." Esme frowned. "We need welts on your wrists." She tugged Amelia's hair lightly. "Tip your head back."

"No." Panicked, she shook her head. She would drown with that crap in her mouth. "Can't." She tipped her head forward instead, and blood red drool dripped onto her legs. Her breathing hitched. She choked and gagged again.

"Okay. Spit it on the floor." Esme stepped back and waited for her to finish nearly dry heaving. "Now head back." She held a small bottle the size of her pinky filled with a clear liquid and uncapped it.

Fear gripped Amelia. "Why?"

"It will swell your eyes up." Esme cupped her cheek. "It'll burn. But it's nothing permanent."

"*No.*"

"The other option is to give you black eyes the old-fashioned way."

"No." She bucked against the chair. The zip ties cut into her wrists. "I don't like this. I don't want to—"

"I'm doing it one way or another." Esme lips flattened. "We have to stay alive, kid. Think of everything you love. Think of your man."

The drops went in. Amelia cried out.

"Little louder for the boys outside the door."

God, she hated this lady.

"You're doing a good job, Amelia." Esme stroked the back of her head. "Just like that. Make sure they hear you."

Amelia didn't have to pretend. Her face burned. She couldn't see through the stream of tears as her eyelids swelled.

Esme stepped away and returned. She cut off Amelia's sleeves and rubbed a lotion over her arms. "This will make your skin look horrible after impact."

"Impact?" Amelia blinked through the burning tears at the rod in her hand. It was skinny, like a chopstick, but as long as her arm.

"We need bruises," Esme warned. "This one will sting, but lean into the pain. On three: one, two, three." The skinny rod smacked Amelia's arm. Esme frowned. "I can make it hurt more if you need the incentive to cry out."

"Fuck you."

"That's the spirit. On three again. Here we go. One, two, three…"

Hours seemed to pass, though it could have been minutes. Esme worked Amelia over, yet she didn't. Amelia was in pain, but it was nothing compared to how bad it could have been.

"Last indignity." Esme took out a small digital camera and snapped photos of her face, neck, and arms. "All done, my dear."

"Can I see what I look like?"

Esme pursed her lips then decided, holding up the camera for Amelia to see. She looked beaten to within an inch of her life.

"I have to leave. The men from earlier will untie you and leave you food. Don't get out of bed for at least an hour. Don't eat all the food at once. Remember how you look, and act that injured." She cupped Amelia's face. "You are just as strong as your sister."

Tears fell down Amelia's cheeks. "Did she suffer?"

"I wasn't there, but from what I've been told, no. It was quick, and her spirit remained until the end."

Amelia dropped her chin and let the tears fall. Hailey was gone. Amelia hadn't been able to find or save her, but she'd died protecting what she believed in.

CHAPTER THIRTY-EIGHT

A BOOMING KNOCK pounded on the door. Camden jerked up on the couch and checked the time: five in the morning. He quickly gathered his wits and threw off the blanket. He might not trust a CIA safe house, but this was Titan's. He would stake his life on their resources as long as he didn't have contact with Beth or Esme.

Camden checked the peephole and groaned. Nothing good was about to happen. Then he let his boss inside. "Morning, Boss Man."

Jared strode into the room. His eyes were tired. Dark circles promised he hadn't had a lot of sleep. Camden checked outside for anyone else then shut the door.

"Sit down," Boss Man ordered.

Dread curled in the pit of his stomach. *Fuck. Why would Boss Man be here?* They'd found Amelia. Amelia was dead—no other reason for Jared motherfuckin' Westin to make a house call. Everything about his world crashed.

"You're going to keep it together," Jared demanded.

"Not making that promise, Boss Man."

Jared's nostrils flared, but he lifted his chin in understanding. "I have to show you something bad, but it comes with good news." He didn't waste time and held up his phone.

"Fuck." His stomach roiled. "*Fuck.*" Camden snatched the phone and paced, staring at his beautiful woman, beaten and swollen and drooling blood. His nausea turned into a blood-boiling rage. His teeth gnashed. "Where is she?"

"That's the good news." Jared watched him, maybe deciding how much to share.

"*Where is she?*"

"Somewhere in Maryland. Techs are still working their magic for a precise location."

What were they still doing here? They could at least start driving. "Let's go."

"Cool your jets. The damage has been done. It's proof of life. She's still alive—"

"Doesn't fuckin' look like she's doing all that well." Camden ran his hands into his hair and pulled. "The CIA think she's a sleeper agent. We need to get there before them."

"They're the ones who intercepted it, and yeah, they're hunting her."

"*Fuck.*" He couldn't think. They had to get to Amelia first.

"Asshole, listen up." Jared waited for Camden to look. "They're also asking if you want in on this." He smirked. "You can probably thank Beth Tourne for that."

"That woman is not on our team."

"That woman is giving you a shot to figure this out and maybe talk to Amelia before they take her to some black site and you never see her again."

He pulled his hair until it hurt then turned back to Jared. "How'd they intercept the picture?"

His scowl tightened. "That's the same question Parker asked, but it doesn't matter. We'll deal with that after the job's done."

Jared's phone buzzed. He answered it with a grunt. The lines on his forehead deepened, then he hung up. "Ready to suit up with their extraction team?"

A flare of hope slightly cooled his raging panic. "They found her?"

"Think so." Boss Man nodded. "You wanna keep talking or roll out?"

Camden dressed in record speed. They hit the road in a souped-up Suburban. *Government plates. Damn it.* The idea of using another CIA-proffered vehicle made his skin crawl until Jared messed with the dash-board. Lights spun as their tires flew. Morning traffic pulled out of their way. Though they were flying down the left lanes at top speeds, time passed painfully.

Finally, they pulled into a run-down shopping center that was still bustling with cars. Jared parked near the gathering of unmarked government vehicles. The stores could have used fresh paint and new signs like every other business he'd seen within the last few miles—the kind of place where people kept their heads down and never saw anything. Camden reached for the door.

"Hang tight."

He turned toward his boss, itching to get into the fray.

"This is their show," Jared cautioned.

"Got it. I know the drill."

"They say hold, you hold."

"I got it—"

"I know you got it and you know the drill and all that crap, but you've never had a stake in the game like this before."

Tension ticked in his jaw. "I'm not the young gun who jumps first and asks questions later anymore."

He had to get in there because Amelia was trapped and in pain. Jared could question him later.

"You've more than proven yourself on this job." Jared snorted. "Didn't expect you to find a woman along the way. But that seems par for the course lately."

His teammates all had wives. They'd been single when Titan hired Camden. The Abu Dhabi headquarters had remained just as much fun but now with families in the mix. He'd never thought about that until recently. Hell, he'd never noticed the transition. One teammate then the next had settled down. He'd been the holdout, the guy who everyone thought wasn't serious. He hadn't been. Apparently, that had changed.

"All right." Jared nodded. "Go."

Camden jumped out and quickly found himself in the center of a gaggle of team members gearing up.

"You Titan?" a man asked and pointed at the back of a van. "Suit up, and check your comms."

He strapped the Kevlar over his chest and placed his mic. The earpiece crackled as he fit it on. "Test, test."

"This is Zulu team reading you crystal clear, Ace."

Their team leader walked over and shook Camden's hand. "Clint MacIntyre. Everyone calls me Tyre. You good to go?"

"One hundred percent."

"I understand your girl's in there."

Possessiveness gripped his chest. He was grateful to be there and anxious to get a move on. What exactly had Beth said when orchestrating this operation on US soil? It wasn't exactly unheard of for CIA case managers to sidestep the complication of laws when their own people were in a tight spot. But Amelia wasn't CIA, and for that matter, she and her sister weren't on their good side either.

No matter—Camden confirmed that Amelia was his. "Yeah. She is."

"You saw the picture?" Tyre asked.

His molars clenched. He would never be able to erase the picture from his memory. It would haunt him. "Affirmative."

"We have strict instructions to transport her to a private medical facility. They'll get her checked out and patched up. So long as you don't do anything stupid, this will be a simple in and out. Are we on the same page?"

Camden agreed.

Tyre gestured over Camden's shoulder. Another person handed him an H&K MP7. Small and made to defeat body armor, the little submachine gun was exactly what he wanted with a new team working in an urban setting. Camden inspected his weapon. With the safety in place, he dropped the bolt release and checked the magazine. It was good to go. He slammed the magazine up and into the grip. His hand ran up and thumbed back the bolt release.

"Load up." Tyre gestured a circle over his head. "You're with me."

They split into two groups. One piled into the gear van. Camden's was an armored SUV. The heavy door shut with a thud, and they rolled out of the parking lot.

Tyre turned from the front passenger seat. "Two-story motel and two points of access to a metal walkway. We've had eyes in place since oh six hundred. Tangos have a standard rotation with two men stationed at her door. Zulu-One"—he pointed out the windshield at the van driving ahead—"will neutralize and close in on the farthest access point. We will take roof access and drop in." He gestured to the three of them shoved in the back seat. "Mikey and Rogers, broadside. You and me right down the center. Engage and neutralize. Mikey and Rogers will take our six. You post left side. I'm right of the door and will breach. You getting all this, Ace?"

"Affirmative."

Tyre checked their whereabouts as they rumbled into a pocked parking lot. "All right, boys. GTG?"

Camden had never been so good to go in his life. They moved out.

A voice crackled in Camden's earpiece, "Zulu One in position."

They skirted the back of the motel. A rickety metal ladder clung to the backside of the building. They climbed the rusted rungs. Their weight strained the ladder. At the top, they kept low and spread out at Tyre's direction. With hand signals, he positioned them. The roof ledge overlooked an overhanging balcony walkway with about three feet of clearance. They couldn't see their marks.

"Zulu Two in position."

Static crackled. Amelia was underneath them. His heart raced to pull her out of hell.

"Zulu One. You're a go," Zulu base command ordered.

An eternity crawled by before Camden saw the men push from the back of the van. Their action was obscured by a sign and cars in the parking lot. From their rooftop vantage point, they saw Zulu One spread out and attack. He lost a line of sight on each, but the updates poured through the earpiece.

He finally heard, "Tangoes section A and B neutralized."

"Good work, Zulu One. Zulu Two, in place and ready?"

"Ready for a green light," Tyre said.

Time ticked by. Camden's pulse jumped with each second, but his attention had never been so hyper-focused.

"Zulu Two. You're a go."

Tyre held up his hand for their countdown. Camden's pulse kept count of the seconds until his team leader said, "Go."

Down they dropped. The booming sound of four men on the walkway was like thunder. Zulu Two operated as if they'd practiced together a hundred times. Mikey and Rogers flanked him and Tyre. They converged on two tangos and quickly disabled the threats.

Tyre moved into place. "Ready?"

Fuck yes. He raised his chin and his weapon, ready to take down anyone in their way. Tyre didn't use much force to knock the door in. "Hands up. Hands up."

They pushed in. The room was empty. *God damn it.* Then two hands rose from the other side of the bed. *Amelia.* Camden hustled across the small space and lowered his gun. "You're okay." He flicked the safety and pulled a terrified Amelia into his arms. Camden breathed her in and never wanted to let go. "It's okay. Everything will be okay."

Her arms wrapped around his neck. "I knew you'd come."

"Opening up the gates of hell wouldn't have stopped me, sweetheart."

"Target located," Tyre's voice crackled in the earpiece. "Send medical."

CHAPTER THIRTY-NINE

AMELIA WOULDN'T LET go of Camden. The urgency to talk to him, to explain what had happened and who Esme was, was making her mind rush. "Cam—"

"Ma'am." The man behind Camden gestured for her to step toward him. "Can you walk okay?"

"Yes." Amelia didn't know what to say. She had to stay with Camden but couldn't tell everyone what had happened. Esme had said to trust no one, and at that point, Camden was the only person on Earth who could get her to recount the last few days.

"Careful," Camden said.

"It looks worse than it is—I have to talk to you," she whispered.

He touched her cheek. Emotion clouded his eyes. She needed him to know the truth, but he offered her toward the other man. "Go with Tyre. They'll get you checked out—"

"I *have* to talk to you."

Camden tucked her hair behind her ears. His fury was evident. Tricking him wasn't fair. Amelia had to tell him what was going on.

"Please," she whispered against his ear, begging. "Before they take me. You need to know what happened—"

"Ace," the other man barked. "It's time."

Camden took her hand and stepped back. "It's all right. I'll find you."

No. This wasn't going well. What would happen when their doctor checked her injuries? Could they tell how her eyes had swollen? Would they know she felt a third as bad as she should? Or would they ignore it all and toss her back into jail? She didn't trust anyone except for Camden. "Where's Esme?"

"Maybe in fucking prison where she belongs."

This wasn't good.

Two EMTs entered the small motel room. Camden urged her toward them. "I'll find you. I promise."

"Ma'am, you need to let these two take you in." The man behind Camden reached for her.

Amelia stepped toward them but quickly backtracked and hugged Camden again. "None of this is real—" And in case they threw her back in prison again, or worse, if they were people Esme had been trying to hide her from, she added, "I love you."

Uncertainty or confusion narrowed his dark eyes. She wasn't sure if he heard the first thing she'd said, but he definitely heard the second. Camden didn't look thrilled, but at this point, she didn't care. She was too tired and mentally exhausted. Secrets were what had gotten her into such a mess. She wouldn't have them if she could help it.

The other man pulled her from Camden and handed her to the EMTs. She glanced over her shoulder and couldn't read his face. It might have been confusion or shock.

The EMT moved into her line of sight and flashed lights in her eyes. "Can you walk?"

She nodded but needed to focus on Camden. A man had him by the shoulders. "Let's go."

"I'll find you," Camden called, then he was gone, taking with him all the light from the room.

Amelia shook. Lonely and unsure when she would see Camden again, she was scared about what would happen next. She'd never fallen in love before and wasn't sure exactly when the switch had flipped. It had sneaked up on her amidst the heartache and fear October and November had given her. Now they were dragging her away from the only thing that made sense.

A SLEW OF favors had been called in again, and Camden would owe Jared for the rest of his life. But he had located Amelia—most importantly, she was not at a black site. They'd taken her to a hospital north of Baltimore and stuck an armed guard outside her door.

The guard had Camden's name on an approved list and let him walk in. Everything was working out so easily that his anticipation ratcheted up another hundred levels. She'd told him, "I love you." That pretty much was the be-all and end-all of conversations.

"Hey, beautiful."

Amelia sat up on the bed. "Camden."

He closed the distance and wrapped her in his arms, breathing her in. Far too much time had passed since he held her and even more since they were alone, and he relished the way she molded to his body.

Amelia inched back. Her fingers pushed to her lips, and she mouthed, "Don't say anything."

The bruises on her cheeks and the hollows by her nose and eyes had yellowed. Her lips weren't swollen any more. But the darkness in her eyes worried him. He needed to get her out of there. "I'm not going to say anything I shouldn't."

She cupped her hand around his ear. "I want to leave. You have to get me out of here."

"When did they say you could—"

She clamped a hand over his mouth. Unease tightened in his chest.

Quietly, she whispered with her hand against his ear, "I need to leave. It's not safe here."

"There's a guard making sure no one comes in—"

"Shhh!" She clamped her hand to his ear again and whispered, "That guy isn't keeping people out. He's keeping me in."

She looked terrified and terrible, like she needed to stay where her doctor's supervision wasn't far away.

"This isn't reality," she whispered again. "And I'm scared they're going to find out." Her bloodshot eyes pleaded with him. "You don't believe me."

What wasn't reality? His mouth went dry. Worry thickened in his chest. The beating had done something more than physical. "I believe you." He inched back. Didn't Titan have special doctors that could handle this? Brain trauma? PTSD? Camden ran a hand into his hair.

"You need to get me out of here." She looked furtively over his shoulder. "I can't stay here. Do you believe me?"

He believed she was scared. "All right. I do." Camden let out a shaky breath. He could get her out and to another doctor if need be. "Let's go for a walk."

"I promise. They won't let me out of this room."

Camden held out his hand. "Trust me. Okay?"

She looked at his outstretched hand then into his eyes. "It won't work."

"Come on." He guided her off the bed. They paused at the threshold. "It'll be fine." Camden opened the door. "Hey, man. We're going to walk through the halls. She needs to stretch her legs."

"I can't let you do that." His hand moved to rest on the Glock at his side.

Well, fuck. "Why?"

The guard took a step closer and blocked the door like a human barrier. "Orders. She can't leave."

Amelia wasn't wrong.

"Medical orders?" He shifted and gave her an understanding once-over but tucked her behind his back. "I think it looks worse than it—"

"*No.*"

"Has she been arrested?" Camden took a large step back and kept Amelia behind him.

The guard stepped into the room. "They've authorized restraints if she doesn't stay put."

This wasn't how he planned things to go. He stepped back again. "I mean…" He snorted. "It's not like she's dangerous. We could just"—he took another step back—"walk around with you. A fun little threesome."

The guard hadn't seemed like the joking type. He growled and lorded over them, stepping inside the room just enough that the door swung shut behind him.

"Sorry, I have to do this." Camden coldcocked him then landed an undercut to the guard's jaw just in case. He grabbed the guard before he hit the floor, snagged his radio, and took Amelia's hand. "Let's go."

They stepped over the man and shut the door.

"Keep calm." Camden turned off the radio and dumped it into a linens basket and rethreaded his fingers with hers. "Don't make eye contact with anyone." He tried to keep their gait relaxed. "Just like that. Easy does it. A stroll around the hospital." He spotted an exit sign that promised to lead them to sanctuary as long as they minimized attention and kept moving.

"Cam—"

"Head down." He pushed on a heavy door that led to a stairwell, certain cameras were mounted on the corner behind them. "Can you move faster?"

"I can run."

He glanced at her socks and gown. "Sure about that?"

She cinched the waist of her hospital gown and offered a smile that reminded him that not much could keep his woman down. "Positive."

They ran. With two floors left to go, the door below them burst open with hurried voices. Camden bailed onto the floor labeled Rehab and Patient Care and forced it to close quietly. He hoped not many nurses and doctors would be roaming the corridors.

"Doing okay still?" he asked.

"I'm fine."

Camden wasn't sure she'd seen her reflection in a mirror lately. But that would be for a different conversation. They hurried down a hall and followed signs for hospitality and a food court. Another stairwell offered another way out. They hustled down the stairs, not bothering to slow down as they sprinted through the lobby, passed security's orders to stop, and burst out into the cold day with the sun blazing overhead.

They didn't stop until they jumped into his car. The tires screeched around each bend in the parking garage. Camden didn't wait for the electronic arm to let them out. The broken piece rolled over the top of their vehicle, and he merged into traffic.

"Put your seat belt on—"

"Esme did this to me."

He swerved when his head snapped. "What?" He checked the road again then his rearview mirrors. Since no one was following, Camden dropped to the speed limit. It wouldn't look good to be pulled over with a hospital escapee in the passenger seat.

"It's fake. Sort of."

He gave another glance. "They think Hailey is a double agent."

"I think Esme *was* a double agent."

"And...? She beat you up?"

"It's fake, Camden. Like some kind of CIA medicine that messed me up. I don't know. But she saved me, and if anyone finds out..." She shook her head. "I don't know what will happen. I don't know who knows."

Camden worked the new information over in his head. It didn't make sense. "They're tearing Hailey's place apart. Looking in the walls and imaging the floorboards."

"Why?"

"I was hoping you would know that." He let out a deep breath. "They think she might've been a double agent. The both of you."

Amelia's mouth fell open. Then her eyes closed. She seemed to grow smaller by the second. "Hailey's dead."

Shit. He'd been sure Hailey wasn't alive, but Amelia sounded as though she'd learned news that had erased all of her hope. "You're certain?"

"The man from the party. The one from that night, who chased me. He killed her." Her lips trembled. "Esme knows more. She will help me find Hailey—" Her voice broke. "To bury."

Camden checked his mirrors and pulled onto a side street. The houses were quiet. No one was even walking a dog or strolling down the sidewalk. He parked and pulled Amelia to his chest. "I'm so sorry."

She sniffled. "I mean, it's been so long. It didn't make sense that she was hiding or someone took her without asking for ransom or something. I just had hoped."

That was one of the things he loved about her. Camden stroked the back of her head.

"I kept thinking back to that night," she sniffed. "If only I'd run faster, if I'd done what they said to do quicker—" She stiffened in his arms. "Oh my God."

A shiver shot up his spine. "What?"

"*Oh my God.*" Amelia pulled back and pressed her fingers to her temples. She scrunched her eyes shut and doubled over, almost as if she was in pain. Maybe she was.

"Amelia? What?"

"They were chasing me. Not killing me. Then Esme kept asking me what Hailey and Jonathan told me." She shook her head. "They didn't say anything." Amelia leaned back in her chair and stared out the windshield as if concentrating on a detail a thousand miles away. Her head cocked. "They're searching Hailey's house?"

He nodded.

"They're not going to find it."

His stomach bottomed out. "Find what?"

"Jonathan gave me something that night. I—" She shook her head. "I forgot. It was so trivial. I was concentrating so hard on the code words. Finding the right house. Not dropping the damn key."

"What did they give you?"

"An old book."

That didn't make sense. "How big was it?"

"I don't know. Just an old book. Like the antique-looking ones that people buy as props. You know? Where all the spines look the same. To show off. Not to read."

"What happened to it?"

She pressed her fingers to her temples. "Jonathan tucked it under my arm. I didn't drop it. God, I can't remember everything from that night. I was so scared—" Her eyes widened. "I left in the kitchen."

"You're sure?"

"I don't know." She bit her lip. "No. It was so stupid. So random. I forgot I was even holding it." She grabbed his arm. "You heard me that night. I wasn't my best."

Actually, she was. That might have been the first night they talked, but he'd never known anyone forced into a situation like that, unarmed and untrained, who came out the other side.

"We've got a new safe house." He caught her mistrustful stare. "Titan set it up. No connections or contact with the CIA."

"You trust that?"

"As much as I trust you."

Her weak smile flickered. "That's a little or a lot?"

"Babe, that's with my whole damn heart." He loved her too.

That was something he needed to say, but right then wasn't the right time. But she needed to know soon.

Her flickering smile brightened and steadied. "We'll go there and then figure out how to get the book?"

Camden snorted. "You don't shy from adventure." He laughed and pulled away from the curb. "I gotta call my boss. He's going to flip out about that security guard."

She chuckled. "Have you talked to Beth?"

"No."

"Do you trust her?"

"No. But Jared does—and she's the reason I was able to help on the extraction team."

"If you hadn't been there…" Amelia shook her head. "I said—"

He held up a hand. "Hang tight on revisiting that conversation. I don't want to have it right now."

"Are you upset with me?" she asked in a small nervous voice that killed him.

"Amelia."

"I promised I wouldn't get attached, and—"

"*Amelia.*"

"I'm just trying to make sure we're okay."

He tipped his head back and hooted. "Sweetheart, I just knocked a guy out and stole you out of the CIA's custody. We're good, and I don't plan on telling you anything else while I'm driving down the road, trying to figure out where the hell we're at."

"Why?"

"Fuck, Amelia." He scrubbed a hand over his face and laughed. "Because telling you I love you while my hands aren't on you isn't my plan.

Are you hearing me?"

The corners of her lips quirked. "Later, then?"

"Woman, you are killing me." He grabbed her hand and brought her knuckles to his lips. "Yeah. You'll hear all about it. Later. Promise."

CHAPTER FORTY

THE CAR CRUNCHED on the stone driveway in front of a secluded cabin somewhere in Virginia where Interstate 66 turned from a commuter headache into rolling hills.

"Home sweet home." Camden parked and glanced at Amelia in her hospital gown. "You don't have shoes… Don't move." He jumped out and rounded the hood, grabbing her door before she could protest and pretend that hobbling across the stones and mulch wouldn't bother her feet.

Gingerly, she stepped out. He swept her into his arms.

"Camden, my butt is hanging in the wind."

"Good thing there's no one around to see it." He set her on the small porch and unlocked the doors.

She pointed toward the roofline. "*This* safe house has cameras."

"Very observant."

"Someone might've seen my butt."

He snorted but made a mental note to check the security feeds.

Amelia walked in and picked up the football. "How do you always have one of these?"

"You'd be surprised how many Wal-Marts and Targets stock sporting gear."

She rolled her eyes and nailed him with the ball.

"Your aim's getting better." He tossed the ball to himself and caught it. "You sure you don't want an ice pack or medicine?"

"It looks really bad, and it's real. I can't wash it away. But it doesn't hurt the same as if someone punched me in the face. Not like the bruises on my arms. Those I feel every time I brush against something."

He wanted to knock a hole in the wall. She was bruised and hurt, and he hadn't been able to stop it.

"Oh God, I didn't ask—" She extended her hand toward his chest. "You were hurt."

"That was the least of our problems."

Amelia approached him with her eyes locked on his shirt. "That's not true. I know what it did to me, and I was just holding on to you. What did they do to you?" She lifted the hem of his shirt and saw the bandages. "Camden..."

"It'll leave a scar. Nothing that won't heal."

Her head tipped back. "I'm sorry."

"You didn't do it. Come on. Let's find you some clothes." He led her to the bedroom. The closet and drawers held an assortment of sizes. "Sweats. Jeans. Whatever you want."

"Do you care if I use the shower first?"

"Of course not." He returned to the living room and decided that was as good a time as any to call Jared.

The phone rang once. "Are you a goddamn idiot?" Jared shouted. "I thought you were over your impulsive shithead era."

"Eh." Camden dropped onto the couch and kicked his feet onto the coffee table. "We had to get out of there."

"Knocking out a security guard and mowing down the parking gate was the best way?"

"When you put it like that—"

"*That's what you did, Camden.* Fuck, you're a headache."

"I think Esme's a triple agent."

Boss Man paused. "Why's that?"

"How'd we get Amelia's picture?" he asked again. "Parker figure that out yet?"

"No."

"Does the CIA think Esme worked Amelia over?"

"No idea. Did she? Because rumor has it Amelia wouldn't say shit to anyone—which was *why* they were holding her."

"Or getting ready to arrest her for espionage." Camden couldn't fathom the mental gymnastics they were doing to pull that logic together.

"Esme might've made her look like that, but it wasn't done the way we think." He jumped up and paced. "You know what everyone keeps asking Amelia?"

"What?"

"They want to know what Hailey and Jonathan told her before she ran to get help."

"What was it?"

Camden pursed his lips. He trusted Jared Westin with his life. "It wasn't what they said. They gave her something to leave at the other house. Something stupid. So trivial that she forgot."

"Huh…"

"Yeah. I kinda want to get my hands on it and know what it was."

"Camden—"

"Don't you?"

"Curiosity killed the cat. Ever heard of that one, genius?"

"Fortune favors the bold, Boss Man."

Jared didn't answer for a long moment. Then he asked, "What are you going to do about it?"

Good question. Camden hadn't had time to game out the situation. Amelia would never get any peace if that book wasn't located and turned over. He wasn't sure who needed it, and considering he trusted no one outside Titan, he wasn't sure how to handle it without seeing what it was. "Nothing right now. Lie low and wait until her shiners disappear."

Jared let out a long breath. "What do you need from me?"

"Can you patch things over with Beth and her people?"

"Like hell." Jared snorted. "Clean up your own mess."

Camden grinned. "Worth a shot."

"She doing okay?" Jared asked, his tone less prickly.

"I don't know. She might be putting up a brave front. She heard details about her sister and knows she's not coming back."

"Shit, man. I'm sorry."

"Yeah. Think we all knew it. She just had to get there."

"This whole thing was needlessly avoidable," Jared muttered. "All right. Well, you're not fired. You're not even on my shit list, if you can believe that. Make up with the spooks, and keep your mouth shut about what Amelia remembered. Let's touch base in twenty-four to forty-eight hours."

It was a plan. He tossed the phone aside and scooped up the football. They would play house for a few days and figure out what the Dumonts had Amelia stash at the other house. *Then what?* He spun the ball in his hands. He would follow her anywhere in the world. Or they could stay there. Camden might be able to sweet-talk his way into a job with the feds if they forgot about the guard he'd knocked out. But government assignments weren't all that interesting. He would be miserable. But he would be with Amelia.

A better idea was Titan. Their US headquarters wasn't far from this safe house. He could run that by Jared. But leaving his teammates would be hard. Still, he had options that worked with his single priority: Amelia Stone.

He turned toward her approaching footsteps.

"What's wrong?" She wore an oversized sweatshirt and leggings and had blow-dried her hair.

"You look comfortable."

"Don't change the subject." She crossed the room and tipped her head back. "You have a thousand questions running through your mind."

"I called Jared and let him chew my ear off."

"Oh… Is he going to make you return me to the hospital?"

Camden laughed. "No, but I have to make sure Beth doesn't hate me. The security guard too. Though that guy's never going to forgive that sucker punch."

"It was for a good cause."

He placed his hands on her hips. "You have no idea what went through my mind when you were gone." His grip tightened. "Fuck, I was scared, and I don't think I've been scared a day in my life." Camden leaned over and rested his forehead to hers. "Losing you like that." His eyes shut. He let out a long breath and met her eyes again. "It could have gone wrong in a hundred different ways. I don't want to let you go again."

"I'm right here, and I'm not going anywhere."

Camden led her to the couch, sank down, and pulled her onto his lap. He kissed her temple and rested his lips against her hair. "I've never met anyone strong enough to handle what you've been through and smart enough to stay alive."

"I'm not. It's been blind luck."

"Yeah, you are, babe. Starting on that first night." He kissed her forehead and thought of everything she'd become to him. "And when you called back, I was done for. I didn't know it yet. But damn, Amelia. You became my favorite person, and I hadn't even met you."

A blush rose to her cheeks.

"I don't know what next week or next month looks like, but it'll kill me if you're not in it somehow." He touched her chin and directed her face up. "Eyes on me, sweetheart." Their eyes locked. His heart squeezed. "I love you."

CHAPTER FORTY-ONE

A MELIA WOKE UP with a grand idea that Camden wasn't going to like. She rolled onto her side and rested her cheek on his bare chest. The sun had risen, but their little safe house in the woods was surrounded by trees and kept their bedroom quiet and shaded. "Are you awake?"

"Sort of." Camden folded his arm over his face. "What's up?"

"I came up with a plan."

He sleepily grumbled, "For breakfast?"

"To get the book."

Camden raised his arm off his face. His eyebrows arched over wide-awake eyes. "What kind of plan?"

"A KISS plan." Maybe she should have started the coffee before throwing her idea out there. "Ya know: Keep it simple, stupid."

He pinched the bridge of his nose in a valiant effort to rid himself of any brain fog, which she appreciated. "Simple sounds good. Does your simple plan have specifics?"

"We just knock on the door and ask to retrieve the book." Amelia smiled her best, most confident, reassuring grin and could tell it had little effect on Camden. "Before you say no—"

"I didn't."

"We both know you weren't about to say yes. So listen, because I've spent all morning thinking about this."

"How long have you been awake?"

"Long enough to know my plan will work."

He scrubbed a hand over his face. "We need coffee."

She *had* known better. Coffee should've been her first move. Fifteen minutes later, they had hot mugs of heavenly scented caffeine and were seated at the small kitchen table.

"Hailey and Jonathan had keys to the Callaghans' house. They were on friendly terms."

"The house you snuck into," Camden pointed out. "Where law enforcement descended when they were out of town."

"Well, yes. But it shows they had a good relationship, and while I was inside, I got a sense of who they were. Family focused. Neighborly. That kind of vibe. I think they might let me get the book."

He took a quick sip. "And if that doesn't work?"

"I don't know. What was your plan? Break in? We can just do that later."

His lips tugged. "You crack me up."

"I'm serious. That's what you would do, right?"

"Let me get this straight. You just want to get dressed and head over."

"Now?" She thought about it. *Why not?* "Yeah. Now."

"Amelia—"

"Come on, Camden. What more could go wrong?"

He snorted.

"This is the least dangerous thing we have done in weeks," she pressed. "And I'm going to, whether you like it or not. So you might as well come with me."

He could've pointed out she was carless, clothes-less, and likely the subject of a federal manhunt. But Camden sighed and stood. "Did you see any to-go mugs?"

She jumped to her feet and scurried back to the bedroom to search for clothes that might fit her.

By the time she found suitable clothing, Camden had found to-go cups for their coffees. Amelia took the coffee and paced.

"Cold feet?" he asked.

A little bit. But more than that, adrenaline flowed in her veins. She would have answers soon. "Eager."

The drive to Hailey's neighborhood took almost an hour. Not until they turned onto the familiar street did the circumstances come to mind again. It wasn't a game. It wasn't an adventure. They were visiting the neighbor of her dead sister and brother-in-law. Raw memories cut through the adrenaline.

"You doing okay, babe?"

She bit her lip. "Yeah." But she couldn't hide the lack of pep that had been in her voice all morning.

"We don't have to do this right now." He paused at a four-way stop and checked the mirrors. No other cars were around. Camden waited for her answer.

She had to do it. Finding the book was the final step to ending the whole headache. It was what Jonathan and Hailey had tasked her with protecting, even if she'd blanked on it until recently. "Let's go. I want to do this."

They parked in front of the Callaghans'. Her stomach dropped. "They're not going to let me look for a book I left, are they?"

"If they don't, we go to plan B."

"Break in?"

He shrugged. "I'll pick their locks. You grab the book. No one would know the difference."

That would be easier. But she felt sneaking into their home would be another violation. "I'll come up with something to say." She rested her hand on the door. "Come with me?"

He chuckled. "Yeah, of course. There wasn't a chance I was letting you do this alone."

She'd known that already, but it still made her feel safe and protected. They made their way to the front door. Adrenaline punched in her blood.

When Amelia rang the doorbell, an older woman answered. "Can I help you?"

What had I planned to say? Something had been there. But it was all gone.

The woman looked at Camden. "Is everything okay?"

"I—" Amelia swallowed hard and stared at the staircase behind the woman. She glanced into the living room that she'd run through in the dark. A purr caught her attention. Their cat slinked through Mrs. Callaghan's legs and looked up at Amelia as if it recalled their fateful night together. Abrupt tears rimmed her eyes. Her breath caught. "Your cat saved my life." A tear fell down her cheek. "She…"

Camden laid his hand on her shoulder. "I'm sorry we disturbed you." He gently tugged Amelia. "Come on, babe."

Another tear fell. Amelia stepped back. "I'm sorry I broke into your house."

Mrs. Callaghan stopped with the door partially shut. Her head tilted. "You're Hailey's sister?"

She nodded and had never thought about what the police might have told the Callaghans. Amelia had had so much on her mind. "I was trying to help." She wiped her cheeks. "They gave me your key. I'm sorry."

Mr. Callaghan came to the door and rested his hand on Mrs. Callaghan's shoulder. "Can I help you?"

"This is Hailey Dumont's sister," Mrs. Callaghan said quietly. "I didn't get your name."

"Amelia," she whispered.

"Would you like to come in, Amelia and…?" Mrs. Callaghan glanced at Camden.

Camden extended his hand and introduced himself.

Amelia nodded. She didn't know why they were offering hospitality when she'd violated their home. The Callaghans showed them into the living room. Amelia went to the window. "I looked out this window and saw the man chasing me." The cat threaded herself between Amelia's legs.

"I don't think we ever got a good answer on what happened," Mr. Callaghan explained. "We just knew about Jonathan and Hailey."

"I'm sorry for your loss," Mrs. Callaghan said.

Amelia's chin dipped, nodding as she managed to say, "Thank you."

This was the first time someone had said that without Amelia explaining that Hailey wasn't necessarily dead. It was almost comforting that Hailey's trusted neighbors were the ones to say it. "They said they watered plants for you."

Mrs. Callaghan nodded. "They were fantastic neighbors."

"What did our cat have to do with this?" Mr. Callaghan scooped up the cat and petted her softly.

The corners of Amelia's mouth pulled down. "Do you want me to tell you what happened?"

They nodded. She left out the part about calling Camden, instead saying she called 911, and explained where she froze, where she hid, and how their cat kept her sane.

"That's..." Mrs. Callaghan pressed her hand to her chest. "You must have been so scared."

Mr. Callaghan held the cat toward Amelia. "Do you want to hold her?"

She nodded. Her eyes burned, and fresh tears came again. Amelia cradled the cat to her chest and buried her chin against its silky fur. It purred, and her heart squeezed.

"Why did you stop by?" Mrs. Callaghan asked.

Amelia focused on the cat. "I brought a book with me. They gave it to me, and I left it in your kitchen." She looked up. "I was hoping I could get it back."

"Of course, honey," Mrs. Callaghan said. "I didn't even notice it."

"You don't mind?" Amelia asked.

"Not at all."

Amelia retraced the steps she'd taken weeks ago and found herself at the little desk in the kitchen. The book was easy enough to find. She set the cat down and selected the tome from the books and magazines. "This is it."

"That's not ours," confirmed Mr. Callaghan.

"So we can take it?" Amelia asked.

They both shrugged.

"Thank you," Camden offered. He put his hand on her shoulder. "We appreciate your time."

Amelia turned it over in her hand as Camden guided her out. The old worn fabric cover and faded spine didn't offer much hope of exciting news. She didn't know why they'd wanted her to have it. When they got inside the car, she flipped the hardcover open and thumbed through the well-worn pages. Only the first and last sections of pages turned. The middle pages were stuck together.

Amelia flipped to the last page that turned and sucked in a breath. "Camden." Two small microchips had been hidden in a section of the pages that had been hollowed out. They were kept in place with pieces of clear tape. "What are they?"

He leaned closer. "The answer to what everyone has been killing for."

She slapped the book shut and closed her eyes. "Jonathan had two cell phones in his hand before he gave me the book."

Camden drove out of Hailey's neighborhood. "Those could definitely be SIM cards. Maybe microchips."

Amelia stared at the faded book cover and wondered if it was really worth their lives. "What do we do with it?"

"My first thought is to give it to Parker." Camden slowed for a red light. "What are you thinking?"

"Not Beth."

He snort-laughed. "*Not* Beth."

She traced her finger along the spine. "What about Esme?"

"Eh, I don't know about that. We have no idea what you're holding."

"She saved my life." Amelia opened the book again and stared at the innocuous chips. "It might just be her client list."

"If that's the case, she already has it."

"Is it crazy that I want to see her again?" Amelia chewed on her bottom lip. "Maybe to just say thanks. We don't have to mention what we found."

"Every time we've come in contact with Beth and Esme, we've had problems."

"True."

"Then again," Camden grumbled. "Like you said, she saved your life. All right—" He changed lanes. "We'll make a pit stop at the warehouse. But if we see any cars other than hers, we bail. Deal?"

NO CARS WERE at Esme's warehouse. Camden parked in front of the entrance. Something was different, but he couldn't place it. "No one's here," he said. "We'll head to Titan HQ."

"Wait." Amelia opened her door.

Camden should've known it wouldn't have been that easy. She'd left the book on the center console. "Amelia?"

But she didn't hear him. She was tugging on the main doors. He let out a breath, shoved the book into the glove box, and made sure to lock the doors. They'd gone through hell because of that thing. He wouldn't let someone just scoop it out of his vehicle—not that a car alarm would stop anyone.

"What are you doing?"

"Use your special lockpicking kit and open this up." She slapped her hand on the metal door. "Esme, open up!"

"I don't think she's in there."

"Can we check?" Amelia asked.

Camden looked around. Something was off. He couldn't figure it out. No cameras watched them. No one was in view.

"Please?"

He scanned the perimeter. "Quick in and out, okay? Because I don't think she's in there." Opening the door didn't take much work. He loudly called, "Anyone around?"

Silence.

Amelia strode into the dark.

"Give me a second." He pressed the car fob again to triple-check the doors were locked then used his phone as a flashlight. "In and out. Agreed?"

"Yes."

They retraced the semi-familiar path in the shadows until they reached the great room. The bar shelves were empty. The decorations were gone. Their footsteps echoed as they crossed the large space. Anticipation needled the back of his neck. He unsheathed the compact snub-nosed gun from the holster at the small of his back. Amelia didn't notice.

They walked into the far hall toward Esme's office. Time passed slowly. His heartbeat drummed with a warning. Something was off. They arrived at her office. An overhead light illuminated the space with a harsh brightness that he hadn't seen before.

"Esme?" Amelia called through the open door.

They stepped in. Gone were the black desk and purple cushioned chairs. Gone was everything—except a small envelope on the floor labeled "Amelia."

She snatched it.

"Wait." He reholstered his weapon, but Amelia was already pulling out the card inside. "What is it?"

She held up a thick piece of card stock. "Numbers?"

His heart sank. With sudden clarity, he understood what Esme had left Amelia. "Coordinates."

Her head cocked, not understanding.

Camden swallowed against the painful rusty knot that tied in his throat. "It's Hailey."

Amelia's lips parted. Instant tears filled her eyes and fell. "That's where she is?"

He folded her into his arms. Whatever was on the microchips didn't matter. He would ensure they ended up with the right person. Amelia's involvement in everything was done. She had what she set out to find: her sister. Now Hailey could be buried, and both women would have peace.

CHAPTER FORTY-TWO

ONE WEEK LATER

THE EARLY DECEMBER afternoon sun was dipping westward. The cemetery staff had removed all the chairs except for the row where Amelia remained. She wasn't ready to leave Hailey and Jonathan's grave site yet and hadn't wanted company. She'd even asked Camden to leave.

Time crept by. Long shadows reached to her with heartache, clinging to her in the steady chilly wind as it cut into her soul. Nothing would be the same again, yet Amelia's heart didn't ache with the unknown.

"I wonder if you learned how to sneak in and out of buildings from those nights we were sneaking out as kids." The memories stuck, familiar yet so long in the past. She dug the heel of one shoe into the grass. "I wish you would have told me what you did."

Maybe Amelia could have helped Hailey and Jonathan. Surely, they could have used Events and Occasions for sneaky situations. Hell, as Amelia thought about it, she figured she'd probably organized events with spies milling about. The thought sent hollow laughter rattling in her chest. Covert assignments at glitzy galas might be the only thing that held her interest in her business since she'd had a taste of the adventurous lives others around her had lived.

The wind picked up. She ducked her chin to her chest. The drying tear streaks on her cheeks burned as though grief had left painful marks on her skin—but she had to laugh.

Covert assignments? "I'm glad you kept your kinky secrets to yourself." It would've made movie nights weird if she'd thought Jonathan was waiting to tie Hailey up. Amelia tilted her head toward his grave. "No offense."

That levity was enough for her to take a deep breath. Laughing made her less alone. She had Camden, after all—even if he would be all the way on the other side of the world. What was she going to do without him? "I fell in love, Hails." Her throat ached. That time, the razor-sharp pinpricks were for him and their upcoming separation. "I wish you could have known him."

"Amelia?" Veronica called, approaching from several graves away. "Can I join you?"

She wiped her cheeks and pushed her hair behind her ears. "Hey. I didn't know you were still here."

"I left after the services but thought I might find you here still." Veronica sat next to Amelia. They faced the grave site for a long moment before Veronica wrapped an arm over her shoulder. "I missed you."

"I missed you too." Amelia rested her cheek on her business partner's shoulder. "Though you killed it without me." That was something to think about. Veronica seemed to love the corporate side of owning a business. She didn't dread things like running payroll and understanding profit-and-loss statements.

Veronica squeezed Amelia. "Actually, that's what I wanted to talk to you about."

The real world was calling. She wasn't ready to answer, but always responsible, she did. "Do you want to go somewhere and talk?"

"No. I just wanted to give this to you." She untucked a manila envelope from her large purse. "I wanted to let you think about it, and then we can touch base later."

Amelia's stomach dropped. Surely, Veronica wouldn't quit on her, especially not at Hailey's grave. She eyed the legal-size manila envelope in Veronica's hand. "Please, please, please don't quit."

Veronica snorted. "Quit? Of course not." She lifted the envelope. "I brought this here because I thought it might be a family decision." Her gaze shifted to the graves. "I know you started your company to support Hailey."

Her eyebrows arched, and Amelia took the proffered envelope. Her fingers hesitated at the flap, not ready for what lay inside.

"Go on," Veronica pressed. "It's not going to bite."

She held Veronica's gaze for another moment before opening the envelope. Papers inside were official looking and somewhat densely worded. "What is this?"

"An offer." She raised her shoulders shyly. "I want to buy you out."

Her mouth fell open. The world tilted on its axis like an amusement park ride. "What?" Her gaze moved to the top of what was now clearly a legal document. The header read: Agreement of Purchase and Sale of Business Assets. "Are you kidding me?"

Veronica rolled her lips together. "No."

"Why?"

"Well, now that I know my phone was tapped and people were chasing you, and *that* was the reason you couldn't reach out to me." She fidgeted. "But even before that, I thought you wanted to... I don't know. Have another life."

She had wanted another life at one time. She could have figured that out after Hailey found her professional footing and settled down with Jonathan, but Amelia had been terrified of giving up the stability her business offered. Everything she'd done since their parents died was to make life as predictable as possible. Now, she couldn't look away from the legal jargon. The script blurred, and all she could imagine was that she was holding onto an escape hatch that led to a life she couldn't have dreamt of fleeing into. What would another life even look like? *Could it involve Camden?* Her pulse picked up.

"It's a good offer," Veronica said. "I appreciate everything you've built and—"

Her eyes dropped to the offer amount. *Oh my God.* "That's a big, not-fooling-around number."

"I applied for a loan and was approved." She blushed. "It's not exactly fuck-you money, but it's pretty good."

"It's more than pretty good, Veronica."

"It's definitely enough to let you have space and time to figure out what your future looks like."

A different kind of tears burned in her eyes, a hopeful kind. In the past few months, Amelia had cried in fear and frustration. She'd sobbed in grief. Her tear ducts were overworked and exhausted. But these were shocked, grateful tears. "Veronica, I can't—"

"If you're not ready to leave, then that's one thing. If you're unsure about what to do, then take your time. There's no expiration date on the offer." Veronica gripped her hand with both of hers. The warmth in her hold matched that in her voice. "But if you're saying no in an automatic, unthinking reaction, then *stop*. Give it some time. Let it marinate before you make a decision."

Amelia clutched the sales agreement. Her fingers pressed into the thick paper as though the bite of pain could give her clarity. "This is…" She tried to reread the offer, but tears blurred her eyesight. "A lot."

"That's what your business is worth. It's a fair offer. One that you deserve."

Amelia thought about the insurance company that had recently contacted her. She apparently had been the beneficiary of Hailey and Jonathan's life insurance. She was also going to receive proceeds from their home, which would be put on the real estate market. The money had felt icky, as though she had unknowingly entered a cruel lottery and was winning prizes for their deaths.

But Veronica's perspective was a new one. Even if Amelia hadn't wanted it, loss could also offer possibility, opportunities, the ability to invent a new life—one that wasn't tied to where she lived.

CHAPTER FORTY-THREE

HEAVY SNOW CLUMPS landed on the windshield. Camden flipped the wipers on. He hadn't lived through a snowy December in years. He drove Amelia's car up the winding mountain road toward the rental cabin. Since she was out of danger, Camden didn't have to be by her side morning, noon, and night. He'd missed being around her as they tried to live their normal day-to-day lives. Work left her distracted, and Camden was more or less on vacation, occasionally checking in with Liam and running odd jobs for Titan's US headquarters. This was the weekend they would figure everything out.

Not knowing how it would fall out made him twitchy. He loved her. That was a simple fact. Their lives were on separate continents. Unfortunately, that was another simple fact. He didn't know what to do about things he couldn't change. Uncertainty cranked the tension in his chest, and his grip tightened on the steering wheel as though holding tightly to something would hold everything else together.

"There it is." Amelia pointed at the driveway. "Home sweet home for the next three days."

Home could be anywhere. It could exist even if they weren't together. But that really didn't feel right. The thought of life without her—a life filled with middle-of-the-night phone calls like the ones that had brought them together, separate time zones, untold days apart—made the most fundamental part of him long for Amelia even as she sat inches away.

He'd never committed himself to a woman before. He didn't avoid commitment, but there simply had not been a woman or a reason that made him want to. He finally had one. Amelia was his everything. The thought of time apart was terrifying.

Camden parked in front of the small cabin. It was so far from life in Abu Dhabi that he couldn't think straight. Fat snowflakes fell in the cloudy afternoon light. Forecasters were calling for three to four inches of snow, just enough to turn the woods into a winter wonderland.

"We'll go in first, have a look around," he said. "Then I'll get our bags."

Energy radiated from Amelia. She was excited. Snow had turned her a little bit giddy. *Very cute.*

"I love the snow." She opened the door and stepped into the fresh powder. "It's one of my favorite things."

That was another thing she would lose in the Middle East. What did he have to offer this woman? No snow. Remote work—and that was if she would be interested in running the business side of Events and Occasions while Veronica handled the in-person responsibilities.

Or he could move. Titan US was always a possibility. Jared had made it clear that Camden would have a job no matter where he wanted to report. Leaving his teammates wasn't ideal, but they would understand. The decision was all Amelia's. He would do whatever it took to stay together.

She ducked her head back inside the car. "Are you getting out?"

"Yeah."

Snow crunched under his boots. He met her in front of the car, and Camden used the electronic code to open the front door. The interior of the cabin matched the pictures online. "This is nice."

"It is," she breathed.

The cabin was warm. The host had left a few lights on. The space wasn't big, but they didn't need much. Firewood was stacked next to the fireplace. A giant welcome basket perched on a table, containing gourmet snacks, wine, apple cider, and a bag of roasted coffee beans.

Amelia slipped her coat off and hung it on a wall peg. Camden inspected the cabin for problems.

"Any boogeymen?" she asked.

"Nope." But a large bed and a steam shower grabbed his attention. He reached for her hand. "The bags can wait."

"Actually…" She pushed onto her tiptoes then rolled back onto her heels. "I want to show you something."

"Does it involve you getting undressed?"

Amelia rolled her eyes but couldn't hide her smile. "No."

"Then maybe it can wait."

Still wearing all her clothes, she pulled folded papers out of her purse and walked toward the large couch facing the fireplace. "Will you make us a fire?"

His interest was piqued. Camden shucked his jacket and tossed it on the back of a chair. "What's that?" He eyed her hands but moved past and kneeled in front of the fireplace.

Logs were already positioned inside, and he opened the flue. The host had even packed fire starter at the base of the logs in a way that passed his quick inspection. All Camden had to do was strike one of the long matches. He ignited the fire starter, watched the kindling catch, and, when he was sure the logs would light, repositioned the fireplace doors.

Amelia still had that same beaming energy from the car, but as he studied her, he saw more bubbling under the surface. A hint of nerves showed themselves as her fingers danced around the edges of the papers. What he'd thought was simple excitement for a weekend away in the snow was showing itself to be something more.

"What's up?" he asked.

She unfolded the papers and smoothed them over the coffee table. Camden sat next to her. It was a legal document. Large bold print read: Agreement of Purchase and Sale of Business Assets.

Anticipation paused his heartbeat. Camden scanned the document. He turned to look at her. "Veronica wants to buy your company?"

Eyes wide and cheeks flushed, Amelia bit her bottom lip. She reshuffled the papers so the last page was on top. "Veronica *did* buy my company."

The signatures were there, the notarized stamp, yesterday's date. His heart crawled into his throat. He hadn't known that was a possibility. He never imagined she could just sell.

"I wanted to talk to you about this, but I needed to make the decision for myself." She licked her bottom lip and looked at him, totally aware that she'd made a leap into the unknown and was still waiting to see if she would crash or fly. "Without you feeling like you had to say something one way or another."

"You sold your business?"

Surprise—shock, really—rocked him. Her business had been a safety net. It had been a foundation for her and Hailey to fall back on, no matter what life had in store for them. Life had given them so much—too much. That was why Amelia had built that company from the ground up. For her to walk away from it—it wasn't just a decision. It was a declaration, a rebirth.

Amelia nodded. "I sold my business."

"We're celebrating?"

He wanted to confirm. She could sell her business, be relieved, and still be unhappy—but she was beaming. God, she was glowing. This wasn't loss. This was freedom.

Amelia nodded again and wrapped her arms around his neck. "Yes." Her lips brushed his. "Right here on the couch, with the fire roaring. Lots of celebrating."

This woman. His lips found hers. Everything he'd wanted to talk to her about—the future, the options—they all disappeared. He pulled away from her long enough to strip her shirt overhead. Camden buried his face between her breasts as he unfastened her bra. Amelia arched into his kisses. She moaned as his tongue slid up her neck.

The heat from the fireplace reached them. It was just warm enough that they didn't shiver as their clothes piled next to the couch. Amelia straddled him and rubbed against his thick length. This could be—*would be*—the rest of his life. He loved her—no questions there.

And what they had wasn't just passion. It was a promise. Every touch, every kiss, every breath they shared was a vow, silent but unshakable. He'd spent years running into the unknown, but for the first time in his life, he wasn't searching for something. He had already found it. *Her.*

This was a whole new understanding of the way the world worked. They didn't have to date and see if things would work out. Without question, he understood that they would. Amelia was it for him. He would spend the rest of his life making sure she believed he was it for her.

She raised her hips and angled over his cock. Camden gripped her waist and flexed his fingers into her waist as she sank onto him. His thickness pressed deep. She surrounded him with an intensity he couldn't fathom.

Her hair fell over her shoulders. Her eyelids pressed closed. Amelia's chin tipped up with his full length seated inside her.

His molars ground. Remaining still took all his strength. Her eyes opened. Camden's hands roamed up her back and down to her ass and squeezed. He lifted her up and pulled her back again. Amelia's lips parted and gave him a panting, gasping, needy breath that removed the last of his control. He flexed and thrusted. Her tits bounced. Her eyes shut. The spiraling clench of her body and her greedy moan of need were intoxicating.

"Cam—"

He rolled into her until she collapsed against his chest. Amelia gasped in his arms. Camden held her in place and carefully turned them until he was on top.

The fire crackled. Amelia was loose and languid in his arms. Their mouths connected. His tongue swept against hers. He could stay there for hours, gently moving in and out of her, pulling the last of her pulsing tremors.

He kissed her temple and brushed his lips against her cheek. "I love you."

Amelia tightened her arms around him. "Forever and ever."

"Without a doubt."

She kissed him, intensifying the fire between them. He could see their future and saw she could too. Her hips rose, urging him again.

Camden flexed into her. "Fuck, baby."

She moaned for more.

He slid in and out. Amelia arched. She writhed. Once again, her core gripped him, tightening around his cock. He gave her hard thrusts, deeper and faster until her begging cries drove him to the brink.

Amelia came apart. The waves of her orgasm rolled through him like a honeyed hurricane. Camden came with her, spasming as she rocked against him, thrusting until he lost the world around himself.

Their galloping breaths slowed. Lying with her by the fire like this was everything he'd always needed. Every impulsive leap into the unknown had simply been him looking for her. Now that he'd found her, everything inside him settled.

"I want you to come home with me."

Amelia touched his cheek and lazily ran her fingers into his hair.

He wanted to offer her all the stability she could ever dream of. "Be with me. Stay with me forever."

The words came out rough and raw, as though they'd been buried deep inside a part of him he didn't know existed. He hadn't said marriage. He didn't have a ring—yet. But he was asking so much more than that: to be his always and forever.

Her dreamy smile touched his soul, and without a doubt, Camden could see their life together. It would be unscripted and unbelievable, a wild ride that would continue on the roller coaster course that had started with a single phone call. The future was unpredictably, extraordinarily theirs, and he wouldn't want it any other way.

EPILOGUE

THE LARGE SCREENS showed security footage from the gala partying several floors below Titan's Abu Dhabi operations center. Camden spiraled a football toward Shah, grateful he wasn't assigned to cover the event. That night, none of his teammates were. He tried to catch a glimpse of his wife working from the sidelines, but Amelia was nowhere to be seen. That was her favorite way to run the show: from the shadows. Little did she know how the tables would turn.

The secure doors swooshed open as the football shot across the room. Camden snapped the ball to his chest.

"Caught red-handed," Amelia announced as she walked in with Amanda.

"One day, the two of you are going to miss." Amanda put her hands on her hips.

"Never." Camden tossed the ball to himself but then made a show of carefully stowing it in a filing cabinet.

Amanda gave a subtle nod to Shah. Camden strode to Amelia and wrapped an arm around her waist, pulling her close. They'd been married for six months, and every day since she slipped his ring on her finger, he'd fallen harder and harder for her. He didn't know how it was possible to wake up and need Amelia more than when he'd fallen asleep, but he wasn't complaining. "How's it going down there?"

"Easy, breezy." She tilted her head to give his mouth access to her neck. "We're just taking a small break before the live band transitions to the deejay. When do you leave for Cairo?"

"The project's been postponed."

"Oh—problem?"

"Nope." He glanced over as Shah and Amanda left the operations center. Camden hadn't worked there since his return, but his wife's office, where she organized parties and had absolutely nothing to do with the business side of things, was on the same floor. *My wife.* He liked the way that sounded. "I ordered a sandwich and was going to pick it up. Want to split it with me before you go back?"

"Sure."

They took the elevator downstairs and entered one of the restaurants that was far more popular with the team's wives than with any of the men he worked with. It was the kind of place that served social-media–worthy cocktails and meals that were as pretty to look at as they were to eat. They said a quick hello to the hostess and beelined for the bar.

"Hey, man," the familiar bartender greeted them. "Food's not ready yet. Go back there, and I'll bring it to you." He pointed toward a private room. "Two minutes. Tops."

"I didn't realize how hungry I was until we walked in here." Amelia threaded her fingers into his.

Camden opened the door to the private room.

"Happy birthday!"

Amelia stopped cold. Her hand squeezed his as she took in the packed space. "Oh my—" Jaw dropping, eyes wide, she looked up at him. "Are you kidding me?"

Amanda and Angela, the women who worked in the office with Amelia, wrapped her in their arms and tugged her away from him.

"You're not the only one who can plan a party." Amanda grinned.

Angela handed Amelia one of those drinks that people liked to take pictures of.

"But I have to go…" Amelia gestured toward the floor where the event she had just left was still partying.

Jared crossed his arms. "It's covered."

Amelia turned to Camden. "You threw me a birthday party. I can't believe it."

"You said your family always did."

She rapidly blinked her dark eyes and said, "Thank you" before Chelsea and Jane linked arms and pulled her away.

The night passed in a blur of friends and fun. Laughter and camaraderie flowed like the food and drinks. Camden watched the people in the room. His teammates—the men he trusted with his life—and his boss had believed in him. Their wives and the operation center staff had accepted him and Amelia. They were part of his family even before he realized it. Now, they were Amelia's also. If he hadn't been sure of that before, partying the night away to celebrate Amelia confirmed it.

It was getting late, but Liam handed him a fresh beer. "She was surprised."

"I don't think she had any idea."

"What about the—" Liam cut himself off as Amelia and Chelsea joined them. He checked the time. "You ready to head out?"

Chelsea folded against Liam's side. "I think we're all about partied out."

One by one, everyone hugged, slapped hands, and chin-lifted their way out until Camden and Amelia were the last ones left.

"There's one more surprise. Come on." He pulled her from the party room and out of the restaurant. "We have to go upstairs."

The elevator sped them to the hotel floor that housed most of the Titan suites. As they approached their apartment, he recalled the anxious expression on her face when they first walked in together. He'd promised she could do whatever she wanted to turn it from a bachelor pad into their home. More than a year later, he was certain it was exactly what she wanted—except for one thing.

Camden opened the door. Shah waited in their living room.

"Shah's my big surprise—" Amelia's eyes locked on the black kitten curled in Shah's arms, and she sucked in a gasp. "Are you serious?"

Shah offered her the kitten and raised his chin. "Just taking care of this fluffball until you arrived."

"Oh…" Amelia wrapped it against her chest.

The kitten purred as if it recognized its human mama.

"Cam," she whispered as Shah saw himself out. "I was hoping for a cat one day." Amelia settled onto the couch with the purring kitten. She cradled the tiny ball of fur against her chest, pressing a soft kiss to its head. "*Now* you've made me the happiest person alive. Every time I think I'm there, you make me so happy I want to scream."

The kitten purred and flexed its little feet on her lap.

Never in a million years did he think this was the turn his life would take. Camden settled next to her and draped his arm over her shoulder. He tucked her closer, and his lips brushed against her temple. "Happy birthday, baby. I promise to always make your dreams come true."

WHAT TO READ NEXT

Follow Colby Winters (Winters Heat), Jared Westin (Westin's Chase), and Beth Tourne (Hart Attack) into the Titan series!

Already a Titan reader? Pre-order A Very Titan Christmas, the newest book coming out on October 7, 2025.

WINTERS HEAT, TITAN BOOK 1

After putting her life on the line to protect classified intelligence, military psychologist Mia Kensington is on a cross-country road trip from hell with an intrusive save-the-day hero. Uninterested in his white knight act, she'd rather take her chances without the ruggedly handsome, cold-blooded operative who boasts an alpha complex and too many guns.

Colby Winters, former Navy SEAL and an elite member of The Titan Group, has a single objective on his black ops mission: recover a document important to national security. It was supposed to be an easy in-and-out operation. But now, by any means necessary becomes a survival mantra when he faces off with a stunning woman he can't leave behind.

When Titan's safe houses are compromised, Colby stashes Mia at his home, exposing his secret—he's the adoptive father of an orphaned baby girl. Too soon, danger arrives and Mia lands in the hands of a sadistic cartel king with a taste for torture. As hours bleed into fear-drenched days, Colby races across the globe and through a firestorm of bullets to save the woman he can't live without.

A VERY TITAN CHRISTMAS

When a snowstorm traps Bryce Richardson in a secluded Vermont cabin with the one woman he never stopped loving, he's supposed to be focused on security—not second chances. But Rachel Porter, daughter of Senator Porter and the only woman who ever really knew him, is back in his life with a desperate ask: pretend to be her boyfriend for the holiday... and keep her alive.

Silverberry Ridge might look like a picture-perfect winter postcard, but beneath the twinkling lights and pine-scented air, political power plays and security threats swirl. As Titan Group protects the senator's hush-hush summit, danger creeps closer. For Bryce, duty comes first. For Rachel, survival means trusting the man who once broke her heart.

In a cabin filled with holiday tension, buried feelings reignite and the lines between fake and forever blur. But when enemies close in, the question isn't whether love gets a second chance—it's whether it survives at all.

ABOUT THE AUTHOR

New York Times bestselling author Cristin Harber packs her military romance, romantic suspense, and new adult romance novels with steam, sizzle, and action of all types. Whether you want fireworks in the bedroom or a hunky ex-military team that saves the day, her bestselling romance novels will make you swoon and smile.

The ACES Series:
Book 1: The Savior
Book 2: The Protector
Book 3: The Survivor
Book 4: The Guardian
Book 5: The Defender
Book 6: The Bodyguard
Book 7: The Saint

The Titan Series:
Book 1: Winters Heat
Book 1.5 (prequel to book 2): Sweet Girl
Book 2: Garrison's Creed
Book 3: Westin's Chase
Book 4: Gambled and Chased
Book 5: Savage Secrets
Book 6: Hart Attack
Book 7: Sweet One
Book 8: Black Dawn
Book 9: Live Wire
Book 10: Bishop's Queen
Book 11: Locke and Key
Book 12: Jax
Book 13: Deja Vu
Book 14: A Very Titan Christmas

The Delta Series:
Book 1: Delta: Retribution
Book 2: Delta: Rescue*
Book 3: Delta: Revenge
Book 4: Delta: Redemption
Book 5: Delta: Ricochet
*The Delta Novella in Liliana Hart's MacKenzie Family Collection

The Only Series:
Book 1: Only for Him
Book 2: Only for Her
Book 3: Only for Us
Book 4: Only Forever

7 Brides for 7 Soldiers:
Ryder (#1) – Barbara Freethy
Adam (#2) – Roxanne St. Claire
Zane (#3) – Christie Ridgway
Wyatt (#4) – Lynn Raye Harris
Jack (#5) – Julia London
Noah (#6) – Cristin Harber
Ford (#7) – Samantha Chase

7 Brides for 7 Blackthornes:
Devlin (#1) – Barbara Freethy
Jason (#2) – Julia London
Ross (#3) – Lynn Raye Harris
Phillip (#4) – Cristin Harber
Brock (#5) – Roxanne St. Claire
Logan (#6) – Samantha Chase
Trey (#7) – Christie Ridgway

Each Aces, Titan, Delta, and 7 Brides book can be read as a standalone (except for Sweet Girl), but readers will likely best enjoy the series in order. The Only series must be read in order.

ACKNOWLEDGEMENTS

So much goes into telling a story: the daydreaming, the second-guessing, and the hours spent typing the manuscript. I am grateful to my family and loved ones who do their best to help make that possible. Thanks especially to my husband, who faithfully ensured I had something to eat (mostly a chef-quality meal) while I was at my desk.

Thank you to Kim Killion for all my gorgeous covers; Lynn McNamee, Kelly, and Virge for polishing this manuscript; and Samantha Cole for her insight on Mistress Esme and the Sapphire Accord.

The biggest thanks go to Team Titan! You've been patient with me while I ramp up my writing schedule. I am always grateful to you and everyone who has read my books.

www.ingramcontent.com/pod-product-compliance
Lightning Source LLC
Chambersburg PA
CBHW020404260626
47156CB00007B/2228